Written by: Konn Lavery

Second Edition Edited by: Will Gabriel

First Edition Edited by: Robin Schroffel

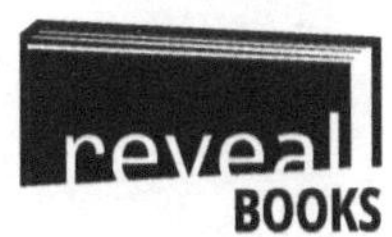

ISBN-13: 978-0-9958938-4-9

Published in Canada by Reveal Books.

Book artwork and design by Konn Lavery of Reveal Design.

Photo credit: Nastassja Brinker.

Printed in the United States of America.

Second Edition 2018. First Edition 2014.

Find out more at:

konnlavery.com

THANK YOU

A big thanks to everyone who has followed and supported me in pursuing the re-releases of the Mental Damnation series. The novel that you have is the third book. It was originally titled Fusion and released in the fall of 2014. However due to the massive overhaul of the series it has been renamed to Purity.

I was initially quite nervous to re-release the series back in the spring of 2017, thinking it would make fans upset. However it was the complete opposite, everyone was very interested in the new direction the series has taken. So thank you all.

I'd also like to thank my mother, Brenda Lavery for supporting my creative outlets even before I could walk. Thanks to Meghan Cooper for encouraging me to follow my dreams and spark my writing career. Thanks to my brother, Kyle Lavery who always eager to read the new work. A thank you to Will Gabriel and Robin Schroffel for working on each edition of this book.

Also thanks to my father, Terry Lavery and my sister, Kirra Lavery. Lindsey Molyneaux, Nastassja Brinker, Suzie Hess and all of my friends and fans who continue to show interest in my writing. It would have been a much more difficult journey without all of you!

MENTAL DAMNATION
PURITY

Just under a week has passed since Krista has been diagnosed with the nightmare-enhancing brain disease Mental Damnation; the symptoms are more self-evident than ever to Dr. Alsroc who continues to pursue a cure.

Krista is now burdened with protecting her friend Marilyn's dark secret and Paladin's pressing offer. He promises her safekeeping at the price of exposing her people's history to him – what will he use that knowledge for?

In the underworld, Darkwing's quest to find Krista grows more complex. His morals are challenged, threatening any hope of seeing her again.

Malpherities, Krista's ghostly companion, urges her to keep her mind focused on Dreadweave Pass and ignore her issues at the High Barracks of Zingalg. The two are forced to partner with an immoral paladin who has a personal interest in helping Krista escape from hell. Meanwhile the corrupt god, the Weaver, strains his army to find the young girl. They send a fallen angel who is determined to bring her to the Weaver so he can use her blood in his necromantic ritual that will set him free!

VII
VI
V
IV
III
I
II
I
II
III

TABLE OF CONTENTS

CHAPTER I

Paradise

Endless light leaving no shadow,
no darker half.
Each side mirrored, and applied to all.
Only the good and the worthy is what we see.
Because we chose to deny thee.
Even as they hiss and plea, we do not break to their sorrow.
For we are an endless light leaving no shadow.

Up high we are defined as pure.
Down below they are nowhere near.
This is the gift that has been given,
when both halves are one.
Where darkness is none.
Praise be to thy Father who watches over all.
The Creator,
Our merciful lord granting us the will.

That in hopes good is what they fulfill.

One day your children will return to you,

Father.

men," came the voice of a male who kept his head low, his broad jawline pressed against his bare chest, his eyes closed as the soft wind blew past his long eyelashes. He brushed his blond hair from his face and opened his piercing sky-blue eyes, staring out into the endless sky of white above him. It was an empty white where the light did not project from any given focal point, leaving no sharp shadows over the scene. The space below blended into rich blues, oranges, and yellows forming stars, gases, and clouds. Hundreds of spiralling, glowing objects could be seen in the distance. The elements directly below were larger spheres filled with bright colours, orbiting a large, bright yellow star.

"The Creator's work is infinite," the male remarked while releasing his hands from their prayer formation. He stood straight from his leaned pose against a marble railing that looked out onto the contrasting scene of white and colour. "Perhaps that is what causes such confusion to mortals who stray from the light and walk the path of sin. Up here in the clear space, we are not confused by so much distraction."

It was not a concept he fully understood. How could one not follow the obvious path defined by the Creator, even in the darkest of times? But that is what made him differ from the countless mortals down below: he was created by the gods—with purity.

"Crasoe," came a soft womanly voice that echoed faintly.

The male, identified as Crasoe, turned back to face the long, narrow, winding marble path whence the sound originated. The path had ribbed marble columns on each side, supporting the ceiling above.

Railings were constructed between the columns with nothing but empty space under the path. At the end of the hall was an ascending staircase where a thin, pale-skinned female stood straight. Her stiff posture made her body's toned form clearly visible; every ounce of flesh was hardened muscle. A rugged scar ran from the top of her neck down to her hip.

"Yes, Rahiie?" replied Crasoe, who began to walk down the path leading to the female. His long, white, silky kilt brushed his legs as his sandals quietly slapped the ground with each step.

"Why do you gaze down upon the mortal realm? Their imperfect world is nothing like up here, in the Heavenly Kingdoms."

"Because, sister, I was praying to the Creator, strengthening my faith that he will continue to bless us with endless light. That is what these prayer pods and the Temple of Solitude are for."

Rahiie looked down to the ground with her electric blue eyes and pressed her black lips together. "That, I do understand."

Crasoe reached the end of the hall, stopping mere inches away from the female. "How are you?" he asked.

She raised her head so they were at eye level and shook her head. "I came down here to pray."

Crasoe placed his hand on her bare shoulder, carefully avoiding the black, bony spikes that pierced out of the end of her clavicles. "We may be angels, but we aren't free of temptation."

Rahiie placed her right hand on his own while raising her other, mutated hand. It was enlarged, bumpy, and consisted of a thumb and two fingers. "No, we're not."

Crasoe held his gaze on his sister's face. Her cheekbones had small black spikes projected outward and two large, twisted black horns erected from her forehead. He wasn't interested in those details; no, he was focused on her eyes.

"You never seem to judge me for what I have become, my dear brother," Rahiie said.

"Our physical forms are mere temporary vessels." He continued to stare into her pupils, not blinking. "The eyes are the window to the soul. I see you for who you are."

Rahiie smiled. "I wish the gods could see me as you do." She turned, stepped closer to the railing, and looked to the cosmos below. "We were created with smokeless flame—purer than the mortals below, who are made of mere mud."

"Yes. I am familiar with our history."

"Then why are you and I so different? Or any of us who fought in the War in Heaven, for that matter?"

"Because the gods designed us to execute our given tasks; we're harbingers of justice and followers of their word. Now that the war is over, we struggle for a purpose."

"We shouldn't be designed with flaws. That should be left for the mortals." Rahiie clutched her mutated fist.

"We're remnants of a time that has come and gone, my dear sister. The time for soldiers to fight the demons of Dega'Mostikas's Triangle is over. Our function lacks a niche in this new era."

"I almost envy the thousands we lost in those years."

"Don't. Envy is one of the Seven Deadly Sins. You know what will happen if you start to envy." Crasoe leaned against the railing, his bare shoulder pressing against his sister's. "I do have difficulty accepting the gods' decision to sign the Truce of Passing, but we must remain faithful. The Creator wills it so."

She slammed her left hand on the railing. "Blasphemy, and you know it, Crasoe! The gods made our kind to cleanse evil." Her lips trembled while she took a deep breath. "Do they even care what this Truce of Passing has done to us? We're voided. Our allies who perished at least will experience eternal bliss in Death's Vortex."

"You're quick to desire a place we know nothing about."

"The ghouls describe it as a resting bed for all souls."

"Those are the words of ghouls—creatures who spawn there. We know nothing of the nature of that place." Crasoe gently placed his hands on his sister's arms, turning her to face him. "This isn't you talking: this is Dega'Mostikas's scar."

Rahiie's eyes moved back and forth, scanning her brother. She breathed heavily through her slim nostrils. Crasoe knew that his sister was only suffering from the infectious wound she sustained from bullheadedly assaulting the Devil himself.

Crasoe stroked her black hair so it rested behind her horns. "This is why veterans like you and I come to the prayer pods to reconnect with the Creator: to cleanse ourselves from all the bloodshed we have caused."

"Unlike you, brother, I am haunted by Dega'Mostikas daily. This mutation . . ." Rahiie turned to look back into the open space below. "You're also the finest soldier the Heavenly Kingdoms have to offer. I cannot help but feel envy. I am not aiming to buff your ego; it is just a fact."

Crasoe nodded. He knew she was right: he had slain thousands of demons before the Truce of Passing. His combat skills were matched by none.

"The gods value your battle tactics. That's why they still use you to hunt rogue demons and angels. Me? I offer nothing."

"Untrue. They've made you a key member of the Ring of Judgment. You've been to hell and back."

"It's a political position. I am a warrior."

Crasoe ran his hand along the polished marble railing. "It's temporary until we can purge the infection."

Rahiie frowned. "I don't know how you do it, brother—how you hunt down our former comrades from the War in Heaven."

"Their lust for blood has strayed them far from the light, making them vampyric in nature. They are obsessed with the sin of wrath. A fallen angel is not of our kind. We do not need to commit a sin to sustain our life force."

Rahiie shook her head. "Is that what you have to tell yourself to complete a bounty?"

"I didn't ask to be assigned to hunt down vampyres, but it is my function in this new era. As yours is within the Ring of Judgment, deciding among the gods which of the three hells a soul will be sent to."

"I guess our roles are reliant on each other: you bring fallen angels for us to judge, and I judge them."

"Remember sister, this is only temporary. It is why we must pray to the Creator so we are brought closer to the light." He paused. "I've come to terms with my wrathful craving of bloodshed."

"Brother?" Rahiie said. "But denial of evil is one of the foundational practices."

Crasoe swallowed heavily. "I haven't confessed this to anyone but the Creator in my prayers. Desire is a mortal emotion; it can lead to temptation, and temptation leads to evil and ultimately a dependency on sin."

"Then why do you confess to me? I am not a god and cannot forgive your sin."

"I know you struggle with the sin of envy. As you said, we are flawed by design—created to cleanse evil in a former era. We are unique among angel kind."

Rahiie leaned her head against Crasoe's shoulder. "Brother, I don't know what I would do without you."

"Pray to the Creator, Rahiie." Crasoe nodded toward the staircase. "I must go. My praying session is complete and I must meet with God Ha about some dogmatic issues with Dega'Mostikas's Triangle."

"Oh? Anything I should be aware of?"

"I do not know yet. For now, focus on your prayers." Crasoe leaned forward and kissed his sister on the forehead. "Be well."

"You too." Rahiie displayed a weak smile as Crasoe stepped away.

It pained him to leave his sister while she was experiencing such grief, but he had his duty to attend to. She was at the safest place she could be, praying to the Creator.

The angel reached the staircase and gradually made his way up to the main floor of the Temple of Solitude where dozens of similar staircases descended to the prayer pods below.

If the gods or the other angels knew of our struggles, they would not take kindly to us. I must hide it from them and pray for guidance. It is why the Creator is here: to help us. I only fear my sister's willpower is not strong enough. He knew his sister suffered the greatest from the War in Heaven. Her mutation and the scar Dega'Mostikas left her was a constant reminder of the violence during that time.

After the war, Rahiie and Crasoe had to forcefully adapt to their new roles. Crasoe was assigned missions to ensure the Truce of Passing was kept intact. On this day, he was to meet with God Ha—one of the younger gods—who was responsible for security of the Heavenly Kingdoms. He often consulted with Crasoe on tactical ideas for how to handle the demons, angels, or other beings that could prove to be a threat to the heavens or the Truce of Passing.

Their meetings often burdened Crasoe with tracking another rebellious being—angel or demon—who refused to heed the truce.

Crasoe reached the top of the stairway where the marble flooring was almost as reflective as a mirror. The room was large and circular with a domed ceiling and numerous balconies overlooking the main floor. Similar balconies extended from the upper levels. Crasoe had made countless visits to the temple before and always admired the architecture. This temple was where he preferred to connect with the Creator through prayer.

If I continue to focus on my prayers, the Creator will bring me to the light. I mustn't forget that.

At the gold-trimmed wide-open entrance of the temple, Crasoe sprung from the ground and into the air, away from the white staircase leading to the main road. He extended his broad grey-and-white wings to their full length, gliding over the circular-bricked streets of the Heavenly Kingdoms. Beyond each edge of the road was the same colourful cosmos below: the mortal realm.

The main street branched off into various side roads leading into other marble buildings, mostly meditation temples or study chambers. Just because one made it to the heavens didn't mean their journey had come to an end. The Heavenly Kingdoms—for mortals—only brought them to the realm of the godly where they were closer to reconnecting with the Creator.

There are too many distractions in the mortal realm for them to think clearly. Their thoughts are too influenced by the physical world around them and they struggle to see beyond it. Here, there is less noise and more like-minded beings who too seek unification with the Creator. This gives us an advantage in becoming closer to him.

Crasoe flapped his wings several times, soaring lower to the ground. He was in the second tier, the Tier of Diligence in the Heavenly Kingdoms. God Ha's chamber was kept in the first tier, closer to the heavenly gates.

Each of the seven tiers found within the Heavenly Kingdoms was dedicated to one of the Seven Heavenly Virtues. God Ha's chamber, being in the Tier of Temperance, was focused on justice.

Crasoe soared down past the road, toward the vast coloured space and the Tier of Temperance. At first the tier couldn't be seen, but the further he flew, the more it became visible. This level was made of marble and an impenetrable metal only found within the

Heavenly Kingdoms. He was directly above God Ha's round chamber in the centre of the tier, with roads spiralling outward around it and branching into smaller dome-shaped buildings.

Other angels could be seen flying in the distance—some in pairs and others alone—carrying on with their daily tasks. Heaven was a busy place, highly involved with the affairs of the mortal realm. All prayers were answered by the gods and the Creator, then tasked to the angels.

Crasoe tilted his wings back as he got closer to God Ha's chamber. His arched wings made it easier to slow down for a gentle landing. He guided himself toward the wide, curved balcony located at the top of the smooth metal building. The balcony had a direct path into the top floor, and waterfalls poured into pools on both sides of the white metal walkway. At the far end of the room was another circular extension; this one had a throne in the centre made of solid gold. God Ha was always known for his lavish taste.

Crasoe landed on one knee, hands extended to the ground as his wings folded inward against his back.

He stood up and his ears picked up on an enchanting melody echoing from within the chamber—the most soothing voice he had ever heard. The gods often used angelic music to strengthen the spirit of the Heavenly Kingdoms, as they had found a direct correlation between one's spiritual strength and their exposure to music. The vocalization was often nondescript rather than discernable language; this left the sounds more open to one's interpretation.

Indeed, they were right. Crasoe could not place the singer of the melody he heard within the chamber, but the sound made all the hairs on his back stand on end. It was something that sounds had never done to him before. He listened more intently, feeling his muscles unwind from his flight while the singer's pitch gently meandered. No voice had given him such an experience of sudden harmony. Normally, he would block the singers out and focus on his discussion with God Ha. Today was different. Why was a voice causing him such a stir? He had to know who the voice belonged to.

It is possible my sister's suffering is affecting my psyche.

Crasoe kept his calm, alert, and dominating presence as he marched into the chamber, observing God Ha sitting in his golden throne at the far end. The god was cross-legged and barefoot, exposing his coal-black legs against his gold-trimmed, cream-coloured kilt. From the waist up, his skin was ivory. His broad torso was exposed and his wide, muscular arms rested against his knees, palms facing upward.

It was always difficult to tell if the god was staring at you or in meditation due to the deep orange and black wooden mask of a smiling human face he wore over his own.

The closer Crasoe approached the god, the louder the melodic singing grew, flooding his eardrums and numbing his mind, drowning any thoughts he had of his wrathful nature or his sister's sorrow. His eyes scanned the chambers, the waterfalls, the pools, and God Ha's throne; where was it coming from?

There. Crasoe's eyes swept to the far right of God Ha's throne. Beyond the circular platform was another angel, who balanced herself on a thin pole that rose from the pool of water. Her one bare foot kept her upright from the pole, with her second leg perched on her thigh. Her pale skin seemed to bloom from the light reflecting off the water. Her light-blue, semi-transparent dress draped over her one shoulder leaving her back exposed; the fabric rode down just above her knee.

Crasoe was awestruck momentarily, watching the angel. Her eyes were closed while she hummed the wonderful melodies with ease. Her hands and head moved up and down in motion with the pitch of her voice, her wavy blonde hair moving with her.

"Entrancing," he murmured to himself. *Keep your gaze on Ha. He might be watching.*

Crasoe brought his eyes back to the god and straightened his posture, realizing he had briefly slouched at the sight of the singer. *Not even the deepest battle wound has caused me to slouch over, but the sound of singing does?* Unlike Crasoe and Rahiie, some angels' functions were not to engage in battle, but to express creativity like the angel who sung before him.

Crasoe exhaled heavily through his nose, trying to regain his mental focus. He continued onward to the end of the walkway that joined the circular extension where God Ha was seated on his throne.

"God Ha." Crasoe kneeled, putting both of his hands on his raised knee.

The god's head swayed steadily. "Crasoe. What an honor it is to see you," came his excessively deep voice. The god raised a hand at the singing angel. "Thank you, Glamorous."

The female angel acknowledged Ha and softened her singing, adjusting the speed of her melody to fade into ambience.

Crasoe regarded God Ha. "I would not miss our meetings; we are key to maintaining the Truce of Passing."

"Indeed." The god extended his legs and stood from his throne, standing at least a third taller than Crasoe. "I rely on your skills."

Crasoe rose. Without turning, he glanced over to the singing angel whose eyes were now open. She stared directly at him with her bright green eyes.

He felt a surge of fire rush through his face and down his body. Quickly he returned his gaze to God Ha, who was looking off to the opposite direction at the window, viewing the horizon of white sky and the colourful space below.

Focus.

God Ha kept his back turned. "It is what we were assigned, and it is what we will do. I believe we've made quite a partnership, with your expertise in the field and my divine knowledge of justice."

Crasoe moved to the god's side and joined him in gazing out the window. He felt his back tingle now that he had turned away from the angel. *She must still be staring at me.*

"What is it that you wish to discuss, God Ha?"

"Dega'Mostikas's Triangle." The god turned to look down at Crasoe. The emptiness of his mask always brought a cold feeling to Crasoe's being. "Specifically, I wanted your input on Dreadweave Pass. Your sister was one of the angels who took part in the Ring of Judgment's banishment of the Weaver, correct?"

"Yes. That is correct."

God Ha returned to his throne and sat, resting his elbow on his thigh and his head in his hand. "Rahiie must have seen the Weaver then—known the look in his eye just before he descended to his prison in hell."

"I suppose she would have. Why?" Crasoe brought his hands behind his back, slowly turning to face the god. He didn't want to turn around, knowing that the singing angel would be in his line of sight again; she sent an unfamiliar feeling throughout his body and mind that held the disorienting power of a poison but the wonderful sensation of enjoyment. *It is like being stunned by a brutal blow, but it isn't pain I feel: it is ecstasy.*

"I just wanted to confirm that she was there during his banishment. I'll speak with Rahiie separately." The god stood upright and placed both hands on the throne's arms. "What I find disturbing is what we've learned of the Weaver."

"What might that be?"

"The Weaver has learned to funnel his will beyond his prison, within Dreadweave Pass."

Crasoe raised an eyebrow. "How is that possible?"

"I do not know. There must have been an immoral angel among those who banished him. The prison would be impure from the beginning and would allow him to channel his will through it."

Crasoe exhaled through his nose, knowing that God Ha was suggesting his sister. "Could it not have been a god who was immoral?"

Ha chuckled. "You of all should know that the gods are infallible—incapable of corruption."

"So why was the Weaver sent to hell?"

"Temporary punishment for straying from the truth."

That's not exactly convincing, Crasoe thought.

God Ha continued. "We all know his dark arts were found within the Book of Consulo and he refuses to share this book with us. If we had it, we could truly be rid of Dega'Mostikas with one ritual."

"Indeed we would, except that the Weaver refuses to tell anyone how he found it. Before that, everyone assumed it was a myth."

"Perhaps with another few thousand years of imprisonment, he will give up his pride and tell us." God Ha leaned forward. "But this is why we've met. We want the Weaver to stay in his prison and repent, but he is now able to use his necromantic arts once more. He is experimenting with the mortals of Dreadweave Pass, building his own personal army."

Crasoe shook his head. "Are you sure?"

"Yes. We know because the Weaver has sent a squad of his army—deformed mortals—into the lower tiers of the Heavenly Kingdoms as a message. We slaughtered them immediately."

"What's the message?"

"He is coming for us."

"Why can't we intervene with his rituals? It is clearly a deliberate disobedience to the sacred law of mortals having free will. Dreadweave Pass is supposed to allow mortals to repent for their sins, not be tortured and mutated into minions of a fallen god."

God Ha shrugged. "We must abide by the Truce of Passing. If we do not honor it, nor will Dega'Mostikas and we will return to all-out war."

"Is that not what you and I want?"

God Ha let out a low laugh. "I appreciate your desire for a forceful approach to handling Dega'Mostikas, but it is not about what you want; it is about the betterment of the Heavenly Kingdoms and the safe passing of mortals into the afterlife."

Crasoe bit his lip and took a quick glance over to the angel, who was still looking directly at him. She continued singing but smiled slightly, causing Crasoe to swallow heavily.

Stay on track. "What is it you require of me?"

"I would like you to investigate. If we can build a stronger case against the Weaver's practices, we might be able to bring it to the Ring of Judgment and Dega'Mostikas himself. Then we can explain to them that the Weaver is breaking the Truce of Passing."

Crasoe exhaled heavily. He hated politics and finding evidence of the obvious. "What troubles me is that we are bound by the Truce of Passing, yet the Weaver can send his minions to attack the heavens."

"He denies these minions as recent creations—claims they were failed experiments prior to his banishment. He tells us he cannot perform his arts within his prison. An unlikely story, but neither the Ring of Judgment nor Dega'Mostikas have investigated further. I, for one, know he is practicing his necromantic arts again."

Crasoe smirked. "True instinct never lies."

"So please, Crasoe, go now and see what you can discover for us to use against the Weaver. If you need to bend the law, do it sparingly— and inform me if you do so I can protect you from doubt."

"Of course." Crasoe bowed and turned to exit the chamber, taking one last look at the singing angel. His eyes ran up her thin legs, curved hips, and lean torso to her large eyes—which were once again closed as she chanted. He felt another rush of fire run through his body, this one coming from his chest. Whatever the sensation was, it was new to him.

CHAPTER II

Play Nice

Cold winds blow in a clear field.
The ground reflects the emptiness of skies.
By a rock there was a hand on a shield.
I see.

The corpses of those who were not meant to be.
The blade extended my reach, seeping the life of my foe.
Expressing my desire to end.
Their souls fly and their exposed innards flow.
I see.

A life I chose to no longer be.
Now the other is gone. There is only I.
Dominance in my perception.
All others are forced to comply.
I see.

Those above will not favour me.
Here I am,
In the land of the damned.

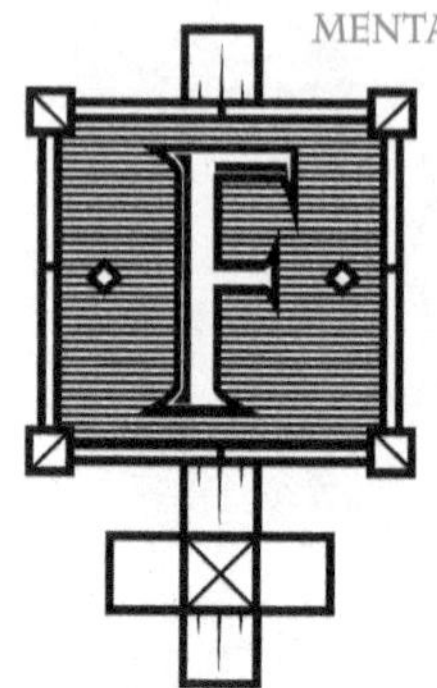

rom the moment of self-awareness, we observe, interpreting what we perceive around us based on the limitations of our physical being. Physical traits affect the thoughts that run through our minds while we navigate through life.

Thoughts are in direct relation to how you are represented in the world. If you think with anger, it is what you will project onto others. If you think with hatred and have no resolution, the entirety of your life will incubate an inner turmoil that will only be exposed when confronted with the afterlife—when you are judged in the Heavenly Kingdoms.

The Heavenly Kingdoms' gates are a sight all souls are bound to see. Few will see beyond the gates. Souls struggle through their mortal life to live without sin. Most do sin; most hate, and the gods deem them unworthy, sending them into one of the three hells of Dega'Mostikas's Triangle. One of these hells is Dreadweave Pass.

The thoughts written above are memories—musings of a being who went through life and was brought to the holy gates of the Heavenly Kingdoms only to be denied and tossed into Dreadweave Pass, where he would have a chance at redeeming himself.

His name was Dievourse, and he was angered to be denied into the heavens. He had suffered in the mortal realm and dedicated himself to war and bloodshed. He became a tactical strategist and expert swordsman, using his skills for his own personal gain, and killing anyone who stood in his way. Now, because of this, he was forced to live a second life of agony.

It surprises me that they did not banish me to one of the deeper levels of hell, where I would be unable to repent my sins, Dievourse thought. His solid white eyeballs stared out into the deep red sky and its swirling black clouds. *Instead they put me here, in Dreadweave Pass. The one hellish realm designed to be a place of repentance, allowing the souls who descend here to live a second life to earn their place in the Heavenly Kingdoms.*

The memory of descending into Dreadweave Pass after being rejected at the Heavenly Kingdoms' doors was still quite clear in Dievourse's mind. *The outer-body feeling of emptiness was dominant, while the visuals were blinded by light. I only saw silhouettes of several feather-winged angels; one in the middle had horns. They pointed to a burning triangle below, denying me entrance to the heavens. Whether I was floating or standing at the golden gates, it didn't matter because either way, I began to fall.*

Dievourse recalled clearly seeing the warm light and the angels above gradually become small specks in sky, eventually fading from sight. *When I descended, my master—the Weaver—found me. Even though he is trapped inside the prison the gods built for him, a crack in his prison lets him project his necromantic powers onto the plane of Dreadweave Pass.*

At that time, the Weaver had yet to build his powerful army of 'puppets'. *I was his first creation, and I am his greatest.* The Weaver had led Dievourse to the fallen god's prison by transmitting clear directions into Dievourse's mind. *I had thought they were visions or a distant memory that I had forgotten. In reality, it was my new master leading me to him.*

Dievourse—pale, naked and covered in mud from awakening in the damp Blood Swamp of Dreadweave Pass—followed the vision that was transcribed into his mind. The visuals led him directly to the Weaver's prison. The prison was kept at the bottom of a spiral staircase in an underground chamber.

I had pushed the heavy stone doors aside and entered the dark, foggy space. It was difficult for me to see with my human eyes; all I could see was the Weaver's massive double-thumbed hands extending out of the darkness. He claimed he knew my history and offered to give me great power if I kneeled before him as my saviour, denying the gods and the Creator. At the time, I was enraged at being rejected by the heavens and I acted on the opportunity. Now I question if that was in my best interest.

Dievourse had been seized by the Weaver's large hands and dragged along the cold stone ground onto a marble table. Beside him was a much larger, barbaric man who screamed in a language Dievourse could not identify. The Weaver used a hand to grab hold of the man, his thumbs clamping on each side of his head. With the other hand, he began to paint glyphs over the man's chest, written in blood.

I did not know where the blood came from, but a moment later the man bellowed an unforgettable scream of agony, just before his head was torn free from his body with a single twist of the Weaver's hand. It was the first successful puppet assimilation the Weaver had performed. He wanted to merge the brawny body of the barbarian and the intelligence Dievourse held into one being.

The Weaver's hands moved onto Dievourse's head, clamping down in a similar fashion. His hands performed the same glyph pattern on his chest. *I felt a seeping sensation that drained all senses I had in my body. In that moment, he tugged on my head, ripping it free from my figure. I cried out in pain, feeling my skin and bone tear at the neck. I was certain I would pass out from the shock, but the Weaver was able to keep me fully conscious during the procedure with his unholy power.*

The amount of blood was immeasurable as Dievourse watched himself be torn free from his small body and brought onto the barbarian's. *The moment the dangling remains of my neck touched the decapitated body of the man, I could feel my flesh begin to wrap around and fuse with the body. Instantly I began sensing what the body was experiencing, even though it was not my own. It took me weeks to become familiar with the body as my mind was accustomed to the small, dangly shape I was before.*

The Weaver had performed one of many necromantic rituals he had learned from the Book of Consulo: a book thought to be a myth—a fool's dream. It was believed the book held knowledge to alter time and space. It was said to have been created by God, the Creator of all, as a fallback in case the world he designed was uncontrollable. With the book, anything created within the heavens could be undone.

The Book of Consulo was the reason why the Heavenly Kingdoms had banished the Weaver in the first place. He had experimented with this process prior to his banishment—failed experiments. The process of tearing mortals apart and mixing them together did not give them a fair chance at repenting for their sins. When the Weaver creates a puppet through this process, they are compelled to obey him, breaking any free will they had.

Thankfully, the Weaver kept my consciousness and will intact. He needed someone to dictate the army he wanted to create, unable to leave his prison himself. Dievourse snorted and looked down to the dirt road beneath him. He sat on the saddle of a large four-legged puppet that was designed to function as cavalry down a wide red-dirt path. The puppet was compiled from two torsos—which made the saddle—and eight legs fused in pairs, making it as high as a horse. Its neck was short and meaty, holding up the abnormally large, pointed head.

"It angers me, lieutenant." General Dievourse spoke suddenly, breaking free from his memories. He turned his gaze to his comrade, another puppet who was covered from head to toe in leather armour and rode on his own monstrous steed. He wore a range of belts and buckles wrapped around his chest and waist with sheaths holding a vast range of blades, all designed for unique forms of torture and murder.

The puppet acknowledged his words and nodded, keeping his hands on the rope that wrapped around the mount's sharp-toothed mouth. "Sorry?"

"I was the Weaver's most prized creation for centuries."

"Yes, as you've mentioned, before El Aguro."

General Dievourse had been closely involved with the creation of the lieutenant, directing what pieces would be grafted onto him to make him an effective killing machine loyal only to Dievourse. It was a gift from the Weaver, after Dievourse had expressed his distaste for El Aguro.

The Lieutenant wore a leather skullcap with a line of spikes from front to back. The cover on the cap draped down, keeping the back of his neck protected. He wore shaded goggles to cover his eyes, which made his mouth the only visible portion of his face. But it didn't matter where he was looking; all that mattered was the loyalty he showed to Dievourse.

The general sighed. "Before the gatekeepers. The Weaver had me commanding his drone puppets—the small ones and the monstrous ones. But he is paranoid; he would always ramble on about whether the puppets would behave as he wished."

"The life of a prisoner has eaten away at his mind."

"He just did not trust me, because I think for myself, so he experimented with his knowledge of the Book of Consulo until he had created a new type of puppet: the gatekeepers."

"Hence El Aguro."

"And those before him. The Weaver claims they are designed to guard the portals he created. 'Beings of unmatchable power.' It baffles me how the Weaver can still believe this after Hazuel's death while I remain alive. Clearly I am superior to his gatekeepers."

"Indeed. I fail to understand why we must comply with the gatekeepers."

"I do not know what possessed my master to take this route and divide my responsibilities with El Aguro. Perhaps the Weaver did not think I could handle the army on my own, or perhaps he truly did not trust me anymore."

"These are theories, sir. It is the way the Weaver wishes for us to operate. He is our master—for now." the lieutenant added.

"You are correct, lieutenant. For now. We must discuss with El Aguro how we plan to prepare for the Weaver's freedom. Do not forget about what we discussed when we met with Ast'Bala and Danil, though. This meeting is a decoy. We must delay the Weaver's freedom." General Dievourse and the lieutenant were traveling to the City of Blood, the largest, most occupied city in all Dreadweave Pass. It was a place where mortals had learned to establish some form of civilization in this blood-raining hell. El Aguro's gate resided in the core of the city. Most of the cities in Dreadweave Pass were governed by one of the Weaver's puppets.

I would prefer if my master didn't bother trying to govern the mortals of this realm and would just convert them into puppets. However, I know he uses them as camouflage for when the Heavenly Kingdoms occasionally turn their attentions to Dreadweave Pass. If the gods saw nothing but mindless mutated servants and no mortals, they would know that the mortals were unable to repent for their worldly sins. Instead, the Weaver kept mortals around to avert suspicion. Still, it wouldn't do for the mortals to control Dreadweave pass—hence, the puppet-run government.

The two rode past a stone statue of a blood droplet with the Weaver's iconic eye in the centre, the same eye that was engraved on the blood-red breastplate Dievourse wore. Beneath the stone eye were the words 'City of Blood.' They were getting close.

"When do you think the puppet squad will return with the new child the gatekeepers reaped?" the lieutenant asked.

"It is hard to say. Gatekeeper Danil has informed me he gave the young girl the mark, and like all marked ones, it takes time for it to affect their souls and break them free from the physical boundaries of the mortal world."

"If only the marked ones crossed realms to Dreadweave Pass in a predictable location, we could develop a system for gathering them the moment they entered this realm."

"Ideally, yes—and the Weaver has tried. Unfortunately, the process is not perfected because mortals have free will, even in the subconscious."

"The reaping process remains a mystery to me."

"The mark opens the mind and acts as a tunnel into Dreadweave Pass, but it doesn't dictate the mortal's choices. Because of this, where a marked one first arrives is highly manipulated by their thoughts at that time. In the end, their realm-crossing abilities are still controlled by the mortal."

"It makes the whole reaping process risky. In theory, a marked one could enter and leave Dreadweave Pass as they please."

"Yes, but to comprehend this is beyond most beings' understanding. Especially with a child; they barely know how to function in the mortal world, let alone when crossing into hell. They'd need a mentor willing to teach them. It is to our advantage that the Weaver only needs children's blood to perform the ritual that will set him free."

"Do we know roughly where the child will spawn?"

"Yes. The Weaver is highly tuned to each marked one's thoughts. When they are marked by a gatekeeper, he begins building a mental link with them to understand how they behave and predict where they will spawn. The Weaver can detect the disturbance in mental energy when a marked one arrives in his realm. The pulse of the latest child originated from the Blood Swamp, so I have ordered a squad to search there and obtain her."

"Excellent. What then?"

"Thankfully we now have Ast'Bala and Danil's cooperation. With the child, we will finally be able to begin."

"And to think the betrayer thought we were fools."

"That is Cursman's loss. For now, we must keep this among ourselves and continue with the Weaver's plans. We are to meet with El Aguro to determine the Weaver's next step toward freedom."

"Does El Aguro know of our agenda?"

"No—and we will keep it that way."

Dievourse longed for the days of war, and the time was finally coming when he would be able to take part in the greatest war of all. *I ensure this will be a war that will end the reign of the gods, the mortal realm, and Dega'Mostikas's Triangle. No being will be able to dictate my life ever again.*

General Dievourse and the lieutenant crossed over a large circular-bricked bridge and continued through the forest, staying clear of the ditches on both sides of the wide road, which led into a forest covered in low fog. Up ahead were two black stone towers with a gate between them: the entrance to the City of Blood.

At the open gate, there was a pale-skinned human in a chainmail shirt and black pants who was wide-eyed with fear. He stepped to the side as General Dievourse and the lieutenant approached. The man stood stiffly and avoided eye contact.

He is a smart man. He knows who I am and knows I think too little of his life to get in my way.

The lieutenant moved in behind Dievourse, since the gate was only large enough for one to pass through at a time. Beyond the gate was the busy hustle of the City of Blood. Civilians moved through the narrow streets away from Dievourse and the lieutenant. The city's black and red buildings were a minimum of three storeys tall; most the buildings were taller and connected wall-to-wall or through pedways over the streets. The alleys were crooked, dark, and littered with the poor and infirm.

Dievourse couldn't bother himself with the design of the city; it was made by the mortals who lived there and the final details of the city were dictated by the Weaver's puppets. The tabards that hung from the buildings were paintings of the Weaver's signature eye, among other iconic shape-based glyphs found within the Book of Consulo.

The general hated visiting the city; he wanted to burn it and watch the horror in the eyes of the mortals. Even though they feared him, it wasn't enough. His constant desire to force others to embrace his dominance was everlasting and never satisfied.

It was my gift in the mortal world and my curse here, where I must restrain myself to do only my master's bidding. I crave to exercise my superiority over these fools. In due time.

Dievourse led the lieutenant down the central road of the City of Blood to a large black tower, known as the Talon, in the middle of the city. It was at least three times taller than any other building around. The Talon housed El Aguro's gate at the top of the structure, his chamber directly below it.

El Aguro prefers high locations. His ability to fly makes it convenient.

Dievourse's mount let out a snarl and jerked to a halt as a young male wearing a green cloak tripped onto the brick road in front of him. The mortal scurried to his feet, brushing his brown hair from his face and behind his long, pointed ears.

"Who dares block my path? A nymph?" Dievourse shouted, his nostrils flaring, stretching the pale skin on his skeleton-thin face.

"I'm sorry, my lord," the mortal stuttered, his long eyebrows slanted outward, and backed away from Dievourse. His yellow eyes were wide open with fear.

"Sorry?" Dievourse shook his head, his straight white hair brushing against his neck. "You be so bold or stupid to obstruct my path, then say you're sorry? Are you not aware of who you are disturbing?"

"I am, General Dievourse, sir. I apologize." The nymph backed away and took a bow.

Dievourse whipped his mount with the leather handle and marched closer to the nymph. "If you knew who I was and had the proper respect for that, you would not have even stepped in my way to begin with." He extended a hand that wore a blood-red steel gauntlet, grabbing the man by his hair.

The nymph let out a yelp as he tried to run away.

Dievourse tugged on the nymph's hair, lifting him free from the ground until he was at eye level. "Then you have the nerve run? Who do you think you are, boy?"

"N-n-no one, sir. Please put me down." The nymph's eyes began to water from the constant jerking on his hair.

Dievourse held the nymph higher and glanced out into the street where the civilians watched in awe. "See what happens to you when you don't take control of your actions? When you make a mistake?"

The nymph cried out in pain, his legs dangling wildly in the air. "Stop! Please!"

General Dievourse brought the nymph back to eye level. "Stop? You really are a special kind of ignorant, aren't you?" Dievourse plunged his free hand into the nymph's mouth, stretching his lips.

The nymph gargled, placing both hands on Dievourse's wrist in a weak attempt to pull away. The general grasped the nymph's squirmy tongue and tore his hand out of the nymph's mouth, taking the tongue with him, his sharp gauntlet ripping the lips. The tongue peeled from the nymph's oral cavity, stretching the flesh until it snapped from his throat.

General Dievourse dropped the nymph to the ground and threw the tongue in front of his steed. The beast kneeled and chomped on the bloody tongue, devouring the flesh in seconds.

The nymph remained on his knees, hands in the air while trying to scream through the gushes of blood that oozed from his mouth and down his neck. But no screams were heard—only gargling noises erupted from his throat.

"*Never* get in my way!" Dievourse whipped his mount with the leather handle and marched forward down the street.

The lieutenant followed behind, unsheathing the dagger under his armpit and slitting the nymph's throat as he passed. He gave one kick to the nymph's face, throwing him to the ground.

The civilians watched motionless, pressed tightly against the edges of the street to stay clear of General Dievourse and his lieutenant.

Soon after, the pair arrived at the base of the Talon and dismounted. A puppet guard with four arms, wearing a black kilt, took the leather handles of both mounts and tied them to a post off to the side of the main entrance.

General Dievourse pushed open the narrow blood-matted door leading into the black tower. Inside the Talon it was quite dark, and under normal conditions a man would not be able to see. Incidentally, Dievourse's and the lieutenant's eyes were engineered to see in low-light conditions.

The main corridor of the Talon was open and circular, and the walls were built by the stacking of branches and twigs. In the centre was a spiral staircase leading upward around the thick black stone pillar wrapped in dead vines. It was a long climb to the top floor, but Dievourse had done it countless times in the past.

Yet another discussion with El Aguro. It seems more and more frequent that I must consult with him before making a choice. I swear the Weaver favours the feathered monstrosity.

The lieutenant followed close behind the general as the two marched up the wooden staircase. The steps were crooked and planks were missing here and there. Some steps creaked when pressure was put on them.

El Aguro has always been a being of peculiar taste.

Loud cawing echoed through the tower as several crows soared by Dievourse. He swatted them aside as he marched up the stairs. *The crows take refuge in this tower until El Aguro gives them orders. How I'd love to crush one in the palm of my hand.* But Dievourse knew it would be imprudent. It would only anger El Aguro, making him even more difficult to work with.

After over a hundred steps, the two reached the top. The floor was a thick weave of branches supported by large stone joists from the centre column, extending to the edges of the tower. The pillars against the walls curved inward, forming a dome with dozens of windows spread aimlessly throughout the chamber. The dome was constructed from more branches, with several stone columns, ending in a pointed tip. It was as if Dievourse was in a massive bird's nest.

Corpses littered the bed of the nest with crows picking the last remaining pieces of flesh from the bodies. More of the mangy birds were perched on branches that poked out from the wall, cleaning their feathers.

"General Dievourse," came a deep, reverberating voice. A gust of wind picked up, funneling to a large flock of crows perched high above. The wind sucked in all the crows in the chamber, forming them into a large cluster of feathers. They cawed repeatedly as they clumped together, making it impossible to tell where one bird began and another ended. Each bird's wings tore open; their jaws stretched to form an armoured breastplate and pointed helmet, and split-open beaks formed a mask concealing the face inside. The ripped wings interlocked, creating a long kilt draping above two feet with long, sharp talons. The wind died down and the twisted birds formed a humanoid figure clamping onto the branches.

Dievourse folded his arms. "Get down from there and converse with us." He hated El Aguro's dramatic entry and informal behavior. *Why is it so hard for him just to function like a civilized being?*

El Aguro leaped from the branches, and the twisted crows beneath his waist morphed into dozens of flapping wings, allowing him to glide gracefully to the ground.

"Dievourse, Dievourse . . ." The wings below El Aguro's waist connected back into the long kilt and talon-toed feet. "What a pleasure it is to see you."

"You knew I was coming and you know why."

"I did, but can I not be pleased to see you? Since the Weaver has ordered me to watch over the City of Blood, I do not get out often."

"No, but you send your crows to do most of the work, and they convey your personality quite well. Isn't that how you found Danil and Ast'Bala?"

"Yes, they are my eyes and ears, as I am to our master. That worked quite well, don't you think?" El Aguro extended his arm and his black hand shifted into the head of a crow, beak opening and closing. "A little bird told me that those two have found a suitable child for our master."

"So it would appear. Gatekeeper Danil reaped the child."

"Well, he is off to a promising start."

Dievourse remained stony in contrast to El Aguro's haughty manner. "Apparently. I have sent a squad to find the child in the Blood Swamp; it is where the Weaver senses her first crossing took place."

"Exciting, is it not?"

"Indeed. The Weaver will be free before we know it. He will be able to see firsthand how large his army has grown. It is great enough to make the Heavenly Kingdoms crumble. We should begin rallying our troops and gather them to the Weaver's chamber to acknowledge his freedom and prepare for war."

El Aguro folded his arms. "Has the Weaver confirmed that he desires this immediate course of action?"

"No, he has not, but we must—"

"Then there is no need to gather the army!" El Aguro spread his arms wide. "You are acting on assumption, General Dievourse. The Weaver's word is our action. If he has not wished it so, we do not perform."

General Dievourse clenched his jaws. *This is the precise reason I long for the day I can destroy this feathered pest. He refuses to think and mindlessly obeys our master. I will plan my own destiny.* "Use your brain for once and put your drone behaviour aside." He pointed to one of the windows. "Our master has been rotting away in his prison for so long that the path of vengeance has been lost. You and I are outside his prison and are responsible for keeping his plan intact. The army must be gathered so we can formulate an attack against the Heavenly Kingdoms."

"Are you proposing that our master has grown senile in his imprisonment? Dievourse, this makes me question your loyalty."

"I propose that you think. Our master is tired. You know he desires the freedom that we embrace. I guarantee once he is free, his mind will be renewed."

"Your behaviour is questionable, general. You do not have faith in our master's choices. However, you do have the honor of speaking with him on a more regular basis than I, since I have been assigned to guard my gate and govern this city."

"That is precisely why you must listen to me when I say we need to prepare for our master's freedom."

El Aguro nodded. "Your tactics are overtly forceful, general. Let me consult with the Weaver directly."

Exactly as I hoped he would behave. Dievourse knew that El Aguro was shrugging him off. He resisted the urge to grin at his successful manipulation. *El Aguro's ego blinds him. I knew he'd so easily do the opposite as I requested out of spite toward me.* "As you wish."

"Apologies, Dievourse. We work together, even if we must deny the other's intentions." El Aguro bowed. "Is there anything else you wish to discuss?"

"That appears to be all." General Dievourse nodded.

"I'm glad we could move this along quickly. You must excuse me, as I have other duties to attend to. Please see yourself out. I appreciate the time you took to consult with me, General Dievourse. Safe travels back to our master."

General Dievourse marched back to the stairwell with the lieutenant close behind. It sickened Dievourse that he had to remain civil with El Aguro. Their master held him in high regard and if Dievourse did anything unfavourable toward El Aguro, the Weaver would punish him severely. *Just because I am his first creation does not mean I get privileged treatment. As much as it inconveniences me, I must work my own agenda around this fool.*

The pair reached the bottom of the long stairway and exited the Talon, returning to their mounts.

"Why do you tolerate El Aguro, sir?" the lieutenant asked, mounting his puppet.

"Because in the Weaver's eyes we are considered equals and are supposed to work together to serve him. Besides, El Aguro is one of the Weaver's finest creations from the Book of Consulo. Unlike his other creations—or gatekeepers for that matter—which are bound by a physical essence, El Aguro exists in the form of a spirit, able to possess any creature's body."

"Like Dega'Mostikas's demons."

"Exactly right. The Weaver formed El Aguro from the blood of a demon that was banished to Dreadweave Pass and the extracted spirit of a crow."

"The sort of ritual he plans for Sporathun."

"Yes. Occasionally, demons and angels are banished here where the Weaver can make use of them."

"Being a gatekeeper made of a demon makes El Aguro deadly, and a thorn in our sides. If you need me to execute him, I will."

Dievourse smirked and mounted his steed. "Your willingness is noted. However, one of his ability can only be matched by a being of equal level."

"Sporathun?"

"Yes, he could potentially become the sixth member aiding in our freedom. For now, though, we must cooperate with El Aguro because he is favoured by the Weaver." He whipped his mount with the leather rope, urging him back toward the City of Blood's entrance. "Now, we wait. The Weaver will surely summon a meeting about my reckless proposal once El Aguro speaks with him."

"El Aguro seemed to question us. The tactic of rallying the troops is a bit forward, even for you—even though you were lying."

"That was the intent. I knew El Aguro would not agree and the Weaver will not agree either. He knows I am not that aggressive and it will cause him to hesitate. We need him to be defensive. With any luck, he will order the gatekeepers to slow down their reaping so he does not attract the attention of the gods."

"Of course. What of the child in the Blood Swamp?"

"When my puppet squad finds the child, we'll take her."

"Then we inform the other three?"

"Yes. Then we will enforce our supremacy upon all who defy us. The Heavenly Kingdoms, Dega'Mostikas, and the Weaver will crumble before me."

42

CHAPTER III

Heart of Fire

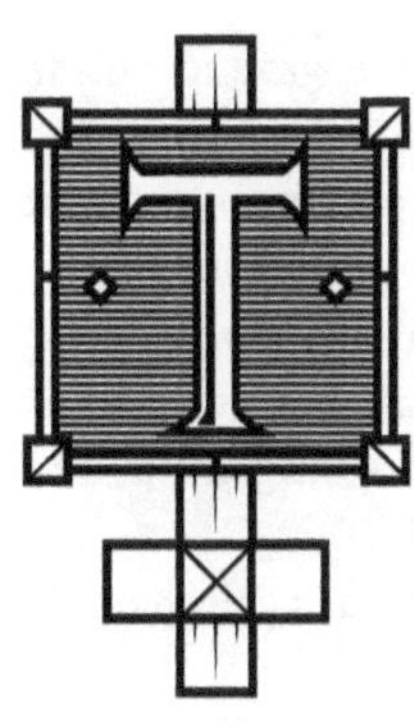

he remnants of decapitated, burnt bodies littered the moist soil. There were more arms than there were bodies, and disfigured torsos with stapled scars poking out. It wasn't a typical worldly battle scene. Strips of a red sky peeked through swirling black clouds behind the dense branches of the forest. The bark of the forest's trees expanded and contracted. Those closer to the corpses moved inward and outward faster than those further away. Each tree's bark formed crude faces with mouths open and eyes wide as if they were watching the climax of the battle that had just taken place. A vazelead girl lay in the dirt, her scaly tail perked high, and a human female dressed in bronze and leather armour held a curved sword to a ghostly figure's throat.

"No, please!" Krista cried, the flame that surrounded her eyes flickering intensely while she scurried to her feet. She dashed forward to tackle the human, identified as a paladin by the pendant around her neck. However, Krista's foot slipped in the damp dirt and her body slammed into the paladin's hip, bouncing off her metal-plated skirt, and Krista tumbled back onto the ground.

"I beg you!" she continued to cry, wiping her wet black and blue scalp-feathers from her face.

The paladin glared down at Krista, covered in dirt and blood from the swamp's pools. She kept her stance spread wide and her arm arched back, prepared to execute the ghostly figure—a ghoul, Krista's friend Malpherities, who kept motionless knowing he was helpless.

Krista tried hitting the paladin's legs with her fists but only hurt herself. She had forgotten that her hands were still badly bruised from the night before in the real world. She yelped after the third punch, but continued to attack.

"Stop . . ." Krista groaned, lowering her head.

The paladin frowned and threw the ghoul to the ground beside Krista, his body splattering the mud from the harsh impact. She slowly placed her sword back in the sheath strapped onto her back and looked down at the two, her long ponytail waving side to side.

Krista got up on her knees and did her best to take Malpherities into her arms, but he was bigger and heavier than her despite his translucent appearance. "Thank you," she said, looking up at the paladin.

The human nodded and kneeled beside Krista. "What's your name?"

"Krista Scalebane."

"What are you, Krista? I can't say I've seen your kind before."

"Vazelead."

The paladin raised an eyebrow. "Not quite how I remember your sort."

"Wait, were you at Mount Kuzuchi?"

The paladin shook her head. "Listen, what happened in the mortal realm doesn't really matter while we're in the Dega'Mostikas's Triangle. We are in hell." She rubbed her cheek while eyeing Krista. "How old are you?"

"Three hundred."

"You don't look a day older than fifteen. I must have forgotten how slowly vazeleads age compared to humans." She pointed at the ghoul.

"What is a young girl such as yourself doing here with that thing?"

"He's my friend," Krista said and held him tighter.

Malpherities jerked from Krista's grasp.

The paladin grabbed hold of the ghoul's wrist. "Don't go anywhere."

Krista lifted her bandaged hands. "He's been helping me since I got a mark on my hand. It looks like this one." She brushed her scalp-feathers aside, revealing Ast'Bala's mark on her neck, her first from Mental Damnation that behaved as a beacon for Danil to find her. "This is all very confusing to me—maybe you know something about it? Please don't kill us; we mean no harm."

The paladin stared at the mark on Krista's neck and shook her head. "I don't trust ghouls," she said and closed her eyes, clutching Malpherities's wrist in one hand and her pendant in the other. "Fear not, for I now watch over you; be not dismayed, for I am your master; I will watch you, I will redeem you, I will uphold you with my righteous right hand."

Malpherities attempted to yank free from the paladin's grasp but her grip was too tight. The paladin's necklace lit up with a white flame that channeled visibly through her bloodstream, through her arm, and onto Malpherities. The holy flames swirled around both of his arms, exiting the human's body and encircling the ghoul's wrists. The flame began to cool and gradually faded, leaving behind a gold and bronze bracelet on each arm. The image of a cross was in the centre of the bracelets, carved from a white gem.

The paladin let the ghoul go and smiled. "Amen."

Malpherities projected a high scream, loud enough to numb Krista's ears for a second, while he struggled to slip the bracelets off.

Krista's mouth dropped. "What did you do?" she asked. "Are you okay, Mal?"

"That bitch shackled me!" Malpherities shouted. "She made me her slave!" His eyes widened in shock.

"That's not fair, let him go!"

The paladin shook her head. "A little girl shouldn't make friends with unholy beings unless they're under supervision. Ghouls spit nothing but lies."

"He has a name: it's Malpherities. Is he in pain?"

"No," the paladin replied.

"But my soul is bound to her," Malpherities said.

"Mal, I'm so sorry." Krista took hold of his hand.

The ghoul broke free. "Nothing to apologize for, it's this self-righteous pale-skin that shackled me."

"Why, though?" Krista questioned.

"I already told you." The paladin smiled and sat on the ground, crossing her legs. "Ghouls aren't to be trusted."

"Neither are paladins," Malpherities sneered, grinding his sharp teeth. "You've interfered with much greater concerns, human!"

The paladin raised an eyebrow and turned to face Krista. "You do realize what I did for you, little girl?"

Krista shook her head.

"I'm doing you a favour by enslaving the ghoul. If he tries to do anything tricky, I've got him under my watch. Don't forget, I saved you from those puppets."

Krista glanced around the swamp. She was so overwhelmed, she'd forgotten about the monsters that were chasing her. "Oh, puppets. Thank you," she mumbled. *Why did the paladin do this to Mal?* She didn't quite understand how a soul could be bound to someone, or what it meant. Then again, she barely could grasp that she was now in hell.

"I'm Fierel." The paladin offered her hand.

Krista shook it politely. "Hi."

"How long have you been here?"

"I just got here, and I want to go home—badly."

"No one goes home," Fierel said with a frown.

"But I was in my room, and then it turned into this awful place." Krista waved her hands to demonstrate her room falling apart. "Malpherities told me I could return home when I am relaxed."

Fierel looked at her hands. "Were your hands wounded when you were marked?"

"No, I guess I was hitting things in my sleep. But the two marks I have look the same, except the one on my neck is dull."

Fierel extended her hand, moving Krista's head aside without asking to see the mark on her neck. "They found a new gatekeeper," she murmured. "So you haven't died yet?"

Krista squinted. "No." *Malpherities asked me the same thing when I met him.*

Fierel leaned back with a relieved smile. "That's great news," she said, then paused. Her expression became serious again. "Then I take it you know nothing of those puppets."

"No."

"They were here to deliver you to their master—the Weaver."

Krista felt her stomach twist from the name of the Weaver. "How did he know I was going to be here?"

"He always knows when and where, which is why I had never found one before. Today appears to be my lucky day," said Fierel.

"What do you mean by found *one* before?"

"You're the first youth I've seen in Dreadweave Pass. Normally the puppets snag them before I have a chance to find them."

"Why do you want to find someone young?"

"Krista . . . Almost everyone here is dead, but it's common knowledge in Dreadweave Pass that children are being brought here while they are still alive in the mortal realm. Mortals being in the living world and the afterlife at the same time isn't something the Heavenly Kingdoms does or supports—which makes you, Krista, very unique."

"I'm unique because I'm in Dreadweave Pass?"

"Yes. You're here not by the will of the gods, but because of the Weaver and his gatekeepers."

Krista widened her eyes. "You know about gatekeepers . . . So you know about Mental Damnation?" She felt a slight surge of excitement, recalling that the half-breed Abesun had mentioned that the key to her freedom was in the heart of the gatekeeper who brought her here.

"Mental Damnation? If that's what you call being in both the mortal world and the afterlife, then yes, I know a little bit about it. Everyone here knows to a degree . . . Except for the Heavenly Kingdoms."

"Can you tell them so they can get me out of here?"

"They aren't the easiest to get in contact with while we're in hell. Dega'Mostikas's Triangle is filled with mortals screaming in agony, being punished for their sins and claiming they're innocent. The Heavenly Kingdoms doesn't keep an ear out for the actual innocent ones like you. It's not worth their time."

Malpherities snorted, his white eyes glaring at Fierel. "Getting the attention of the Heavenly Kingdoms is unlikely; you would have to do something extreme. Anything the Weaver has done up to now has been overlooked by the gods. What could you possibly do that would be more impressive than what the Weaver has managed to pull off?"

Fierel looked to the sky. "I've been asking myself the same thing since I've been condemned here."

Krista exchanged glances with Malpherities. The ghoul clenched his teeth and tightened his three-fingered hands.

I don't think Mal is too happy with any of this.

A groan was heard in the distance from where Krista first arrived in Dreadweave Pass.

Fierel stood up. "Come; we shouldn't stay here. More of the Weaver's puppets might be roaming about."

Krista got to her feet and brushed some dirt from her clothes.

"Come on, Mal." Krista offered a hand to Malpherities.

The ghoul shook his head and helped himself up, floating beside her.

Fierel began marching down the path that Malpherities had started on before the puppets attacked. Krista followed close behind the paladin. It was hard to tell if she was friend or foe. Krista had no idea who she was and Malpherities insisted that she was not to be trusted.

She's kind of like Paladin in the High Barracks of Zingalg. They both have black-and-white views and never see choices in any other shade. They're impossible to argue with.

"Tell me, ghoul." Fierel looked back. "Why would you help a girl? What can she offer you?" The paladin made a pulling motion with her hands in the air. A couple of bright white chains flashed from Fierel's palm and channeled down to Malpherities's cuffs. The chain then tugged on the ghoul's bracelets and disappeared, drawing him closer toward her.

Unreal.

"I have no desire to help the Weaver. I assist a hidden group who oppose his will."

Fierel shook her head. "Never heard of such an assembly."

Krista watched as the paladin walked. She noticed that the colour of Fierel's eyes matched her bright fire-orange hair—almost like Krista's eyes. She was dressed in scraps of leather and metal armour and was tall, slim, and looked fit—unlike most of the humans Krista had seen while at the barracks.

Malpherities chuckled. "If you had, then they wouldn't be hidden, would they?"

"Where were you going before I arrived, Krista?"

Krista pointed forward. "Malpherities was taking me to a town where we'd be safe."

"Not to this secret resistance force?"

Malpherities let out a deep, rumbling growl and ground his teeth.

"Where is this town?" Fierel asked.

The three pushed through some short, leafless shrubs and reached a gravel road covered in flat rocks, mud, and small pools of blood. On the other side of the road was more swampland. Fog surrounded the area and made it difficult to see beyond twenty paces.

"Evergut." Malpherities nodded, indicating the road.

Fierel smiled. "That, I've heard of."

Krista stepped onto the muddy road and brushed her drenched scalp-feathers aside. They were flat and heavy from the blood. "Does Evergut have anywhere I can bathe?"

Malpherities shook his head. "No."

"Can we find somewhere?" Krista asked.

"Most likely not." Fierel started walking up the path Malpherities pointed to. "There is only one river that has water in the Weaver's realm." She pointed up. "The skies don't even rain water; they only spray more blood."

"Is the river far? Can we visit it?" Krista said.

"No. We're going to Evergut. The river is dangerous." Fierel said.

"Why?" Krista asked.

"It's the only source of water. Everyone and everything wants it. If the Weaver is after you, it may bring unwanted attention."

"Going to Evergut won't?"

"Evergut is a small town built by mortals who were sent here by the gods. They are beings who grouped together to survive the landscape. They are no different than you. There are many towns like it in the Weaver's realm."

The further the three moved up the road, the less swampy the scenery became. The breathing trees were still scattered across the landscape but there were no more blood pools. The fog was not as thick here, and there were a range of rocks the size of humans spread over the terrain.

"So the sky rains blood—is that why everything is stained red?" Krista asked.

"Quick learner." Fierel smiled, but it wasn't clear if she was sarcastic or sincere.

The trio remained silent during their travel. Krista kept a close watch on the paladin. *I don't know if we can trust her; it feels like we're her prisoners, not her friends.*

Krista looked off into the forest to see the trees were still animated. The bark appeared to stare right at her.

Creepy.

Malpherities sighed. "Why would a paladin be here, in the Weaver's realm?"

Fierel remained quiet.

"It seems odd to me that such a noble being, blessed by the gods, would be here—in the land of the damned." Malpherities grinned caustically. "I didn't think it was possible for the gods to place an unrighteous judgment on a sacred mortal like a paladin. What could have you done that was so unholy that they would banish you here?"

Fierel reached her hand out and tugged on the invisible chain to pull the ghoul toward her. She kept pulling until she had him by the neck. The ghoul gasped for air as the paladin clenched her other hand into a fist and slammed it into his face at lightning speed.

"Stop!" Krista shouted.

Fierel threw several more punches at the ghoul and dropped him to the ground.

"My banishment is none of your concern." She pressed onto his face with her boot.

"Stop!" Krista rushed to Malpherities and tried to pull his head from under the paladin's foot.

The ghoul hissed. "You dishonour the gods to use your blessed powers in a land filled with mortals repenting."

"Perhaps that is the problem with the gods," Fierel said. "The Truce of Passing was imprudent." She let the ghoul's head go and turned to march up the path.

Krista had no idea what they were talking about; nothing made sense here. *She seems so angry—I'd better not ask.* Like always, Krista was better off worrying about her immediate issue: survival.

She helped the ghoul back up and they continued to follow Fierel.

The blood refused to dry on Krista's body. The atmosphere was so humid, it seemed like she'd always be covered in this damp, gooey mess.

Being drenched in blood made Krista miss the High Barracks more; she knew even the underworld was more bearable than this awful place. She wanted to be back in her warm bed and be rid of Dreadweave Pass for good, or even in the cave in the High District she'd sometimes used for shelter in the underworld. Even though the underworld was where she'd been infected with Mental Damnation, it was where Darkwing was.

That boy . . . how would he handle all of this if he were in my shoes? Darkwing is always so strong when faced with danger. It was a characteristic she admired dearly about him. *He made me feel safe. I wonder what he's doing in the underworld? Probably lots more without me to take care of.* Krista always knew she held him back. There was no telling what he could accomplish without her to restrain him. She only hoped that he was happy. *I'm on my own now, on the surface and in hell. Darkwing really wouldn't believe me if I could share all of my adventures with him.*

Krista looked up at the paladin. "Fierel, I want to go home."

"I bet you do."

"I knew someone who managed to. He killed the previous gatekeeper."

"Lucky mortal."

"I'd like to do the same."

Fierel laughed. "You want to kill a gatekeeper?"

"Abesun did it, so why can't I?" She bit her lip. "Can you help me?"

"Do you even know where to start looking for a gatekeeper?" Fierel asked.

"No. But Abesun, who killed the old gatekeeper, told me to keep a strong will and I'll return home."

Fierel remained silent.

"Will you help me?"

Silence.

"Why did you rescue us then?" Krista shouted.

"You needed my assistance. Otherwise the Weaver would have gotten you."

"I need it now, too! What's the point of rescuing me from the Weaver if you're not going to help me?" She was aggravated with the paladin, who was just like Malpherities—never giving any informative answers.

Fierel sighed. "You think you can kill a gatekeeper?"

Krista was unsure what to say. "I don't know."

"So you need me to kill it for you?"

"Yes," she confessed.

Fierel smiled. "You're honest. Honesty is something not found in a ghoul. I'm honest as well. You can trust me."

Malpherities laughed.

"Can I trust you?" Fierel continued.

Krista glanced at Malpherities, who stared back at her. She nodded. "Yes."

"All right, I'll assist you in finding this newly risen gatekeeper."

"What would a fallen paladin have to gain from this?" Malpherities asked. "You want to reclaim your former glory and return to the earthly realm? Or perhaps you aim even higher, for the Heavenly Kingdoms?"

Fierel clenched her fists. "The Heavenly Kingdoms are a lie. They tell you they are moral, but they only follow laws. I follow true moral justice set by the Father."

"Aren't moral beliefs and laws the same? It's all from the point of view of he who created them," Malpherities replied.

Fierel glared at Krista, pointing at the ghoul. "This is why I locked him up: so he cannot be free to spread his twisted words."

I really don't know who to trust anymore. She'd previously shaken hands with Malpherities—a sign of trust. But Fierel had a point: he did indeed twist words, and spoke as little as he could.

The road took the three up a steep hill. The air here was not as humid as at the swamp, and the gravel on the road was dry and dusty. Krista slipped once and it raised red dust in the air. She was careful not to breathe in—the dust had a metallic odour to it from the blood.

It took several minutes to reach the top, where a cluster of wooden buildings stood in the distance at the bottom of the hill. It was a small town. On this side of the hill the scenery was even more barren; it looked more like a rugged wasteland covered in sharp rocks and boulders. Trees could still be seen but they were few and far between. The fog had cleared for the most part, but what remained still made it difficult to see further than the town. The details of the buildings were clearly visible. The town was linear in design, following the straight road leading into the distance. There were a couple of two-storey buildings, but the rest were single-storey and flat-roofed, made from logs. Lights could be seen through the window frames, creating silhouettes of humanoids moving inside.

"Are there any of those 'puppets' in this town?" Krista asked.

Malpherities shook his head. "No, just damned souls."

Like me, I suppose.

"So why were you taking Krista here, ghoul? Is that where this hidden group is?" Fierel asked.

"It's not worth our time with you here now, paladin." Malpherities sneered.

Fierel pulled on the ghoul's chain again, throwing him to the ground. "You will take us to where you were going. Your secret little plan isn't going to stay hidden from me. I'll burn you slowly inch by inch to get it out of you."

Krista clutched her scalp-feathers with both hands. "Mal, please, let's just do what she says."

Malpherities eyed Krista then Fierel and he exhaled heavily, blowing dust in the air. "In the tavern is where we'll meet the resistance," Malpherities said.

Walking down the hill was harder than climbing up; it was steep and the gravel was loose, so they skidded with each step they took downward.

It took twice as long as the ascent, but soon they reached flatter ground and reached the town in less than a hundred steps. The logs that framed the buildings were roughly hewn, almost as poor as the skill of the builders themselves. Wide cracks were left between the crooked lumber, allowing outsiders to peek inside. Some of the cracks had been filled with red mud, but most of them were left open. The window frames were splintered and most of them were covered by curtains made of animal hide. The exteriors of the buildings were tinted red from the bloody rain. Most of the buildings were crooked and rotting. The streets were empty and had no benches or street art; the only light was cast from the interior of the buildings.

Malpherities led them to the right of the road toward one of the two-level buildings. It had a porch leading up to swinging saloon-style doors.

Fierel looked up at the sign above the doors and scowled. "'Gut Fillers'? Sounds like a classy place."

Must be a tavern with a name like that. Krista smiled.

Fierel followed behind Malpherities and took Krista's arm, forcing her to follow close beside her while they walked up the porch. The wood creaked with each step.

"Stay close," Fierel whispered, pushing the two doors open.

The tavern was filled with many beings; most appeared to be human but it was difficult to tell through the crowded room and poor lighting. Some of them were paler, others almost red and hunched over; still others had brutish, caveman-like figures, and more had sharp ears and were very thin. Krista found it difficult not to stare at all of them. One thing was consistent among the different beings: they had matted hair. Some wore it in dreadlocks or tied in a bun to keep the dirty hair clear of their face. They wore linen clothes that were covered in holes and red stains. Chances were they didn't eat much, either; their frames were bony and their skin, wrinkly.

Above the crowd of people there was a chandelier hanging in the middle of the room, holding three large candles dripping with wax.

The bar was to the left and there were plenty of round tables packed with beings pounding back drinks from their tin mugs.

It doesn't look like they're trying very hard to live. I never even had time to drink in the underworld, and this place is much scarier.

There were two paintings hung on the left side of the bar. They were depictions of bright green hills, a forest in the distance and a castle in the centre complete with red shingles and several towers. On the back wall of the bar there was a head of a beast mounted on a polished, red wooden board. The beast's head was purple, bald, and had a single eye, with an extended muzzle and two sharp fangs. A stench caught Krista's nose, rather strong and familiar. She recognized it as some sort of alcohol.

I swear I've smelled it in the High District before.

Malpherities slipped by a blonde human, who held a tray crowded with drinks against the apron around her waist, and moved to the back of the tavern where it was less crowded. The ghoul approached a man who sat alone at a round table, his hooded head lowered as he stared into his empty cup.

Krista swallowed heavily, nervous at the sight of several belts around his waist holding an arsenal of daggers. His attire made her a bit uneasy, too: it consisted of leather gloves and boots with black slacks tucked in, a grey cloak, a black leather vest, and a deep-red shirt underneath which covered his unusually brawny chest. Lastly, he had a scarf covering his upper chest and neck, just underneath his whiskered jawline.

He seems shady.

Malpherities's presence caught the man's attention and he raised his head, showing the long scar running across his right eyebrow down to his cheekbone. His black hair dangled in front of his face down to his scruffy chin. "I thought I told you never to return here," he spoke in a hoarse voice. His ivory irises, barely discernable from the whites, glared with rage at the ghoul.

"So where's this resistance force you were talking about?" Fierel demanded.

"Resistance force?" The man snorted.

Malpherities pointed at the man.

The paladin pushed the ghoul against the wall beside the man, causing the painting above to shake. "Where is it? Did you lie to us?"

The man chuckled. "Would that surprise you? Resistance force? Come on." He crossed his legs and leaned back in his chair, arm resting over the back.

Fierel exchanged looks with the man.

His eyes moved up and down the paladin salaciously. "Honestly, sweetheart, did you think Malpherities would tell you the truth?"

She shook her head and pressed the ghoul harder against the wall. "Where did you think lying would get you other than your grave?"

Krista tried to pull Fierel away from the ghoul with both of her hands on the paladin's arm. "What is wrong with you? I asked you to leave him!"

The words surprised Krista as soon as they left her mouth. She wasn't often so demanding. *I have to stand up for myself. Darkwing can't protect me anymore. I am on my own.*

The man leaned over to look at Krista. "Were the Weaver's men supposed to take you?"

Fierel loosened her grip on the ghoul. "Yes, they were."

The man sighed and looked at Fierel's torso. "What's your name, darling?" he asked the paladin, his eyes moving to the pendant on her neck.

"Fierel." She put her hands on her hips. "Yours?"

The man's eyes scanned the room as he rose from his seat. "Cursman. Judging by this crowd, we should probably talk in private." He glanced around the tavern. "I've got a room in the inn upstairs." He moved past the three, and motioned for them to follow.

His cloak swayed from side to side as he weaved through the crowd, leading Krista, Malpherities, and Fierel to the opposite side of the tavern beside the bar. There was a staircase in the corner leading up to the second level.

The three followed Cursman up the narrow stairs. Paintings of the hellish landscape of Dreadweave Pass adorned both sides of the walls, making the stairwell feel cramped. The wood creaked with each step they climbed.

This level was quieter and lined with over a dozen closed doors. The flooring was made of the same crooked wood as the rest of the building. Krista noticed cracks between the planks that allowed her to see into the tavern below.

Cursman led them to a door numbered 4 with black paint. He brought a key ring from his pocket and used a large rusty key to unlock the door. With a click from the lock, he looked back at the group and nodded. "Come in."

The three walked inside the small room, furnished with a cot with red sheets and a rectangular nightstand with a lit lantern on top.

Krista kept between Fierel and Malpherities; she felt the safest between the two of them.

Cursman locked the door behind them then rushed over to the

window and drew the curtains.

Fierel folded her arms.

Cursman took his hood off, revealing long, sweaty black hair that reached his shoulders. "Malpherities, what are you planning?"

"I managed to save a child this time." Malpherities gestured to Krista.

"You know that children aren't seen in these lands—so you bring one right into town and then throw a paladin in the mix? Do you have a death wish? I said I don't want to be a part of this."

"I don't have a choice," Malpherities said and raised his arms, showing Cursman the bracelets.

Cursman scowled. "No choice? Everything I've ever seen you do is your idea, no matter the extent you have to go."

Malpherities brought his hands behind his back, flaring his nostrils.

Fierel sighed impatiently. "Why'd you take us here, ghoul? If there's no resistance force, what's the idea?"

Malpherities pointed at Cursman. "He can assist us."

"What can he do? He's only a man."

"Yes, a man," Cursman said defiantly. "More than you can say." He smirked at Fierel.

Fierel stood tall. "With words like that, it only makes sense the gods banished your soul here. Sexist swine. "It also explains why you would befriend a ghoul."

Cursman laughed hoarsely, then broke into a coughing fit.

Fierel sighed. "We're getting out of here; the ghoul is playing games with us." She snatched Krista's hand.

"All right!" Cursman rubbed his neck. "It's not every day you find a child and a paladin in Dreadweave Pass. This could get out of control quickly, so I'll lend a hand."

"How?" Fierel ground her teeth.

Cursman glanced around, ensuring he had everyone's attention. "I was once an assassin in the Weaver's army."

CHAPTER IV

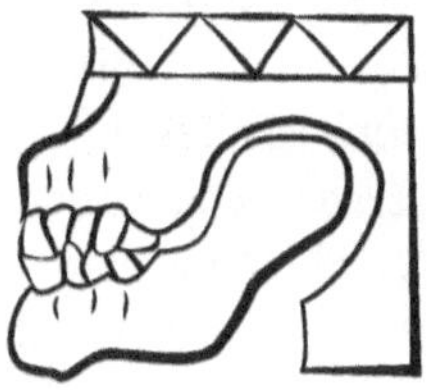

Locked Memories

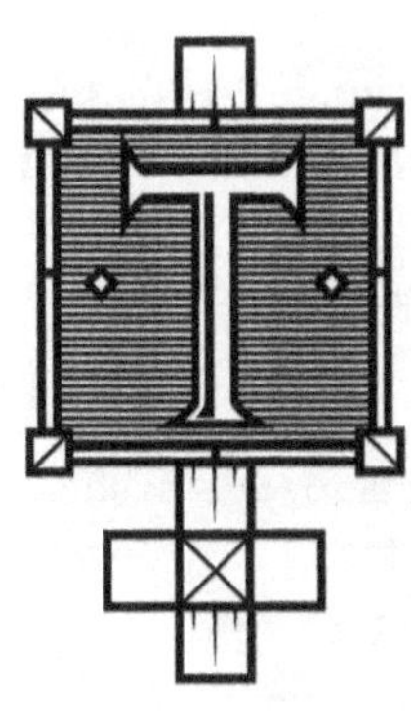he red-tinted room was deathly silent except for the muffled laughter from the tavern below. Light flickered from the half-melted candles, casting a soft light in the small space. Krista, Fierel, and Malpherities remained still, standing together near the door. They were slowly absorbing the shocking news just delivered by Cursman, a man known to Malpherities but a stranger to the others.

Finally, Fierel smirked. "I'm supposed to believe this? Only puppets serve the Weaver and you clearly bear no resemblance to those fiends."

Cursman untied his scarf and undid the top three buttons of his shirt, showing that the thick scar trailing down his face also wrapped around his neck, which was held together by staples. The pale skin of his torso had been reinforced with exterior bone, making his chest broad and seemingly impenetrable.

Krista felt her heart skip a beat in terror. Was Cursman a threat? It looked like he really was a puppet. *It's just like one of those creatures from the swamp. I'd never seen anything like it before,* Krista thought with a shudder.

Fierel's smirk faded and she crossed her arms tightly.

"I was an assassin," Cursman said as he began to rebutton his shirt. "The Weaver took extra care in assembling me. He wanted to keep my face lifelike so I would blend in with the other humans. He used me to prevent the development of a rebellion. I followed him for years but decided I could not serve him anymore, so I left."

"Just like that?" Fierel raised her eyebrow.

"Yes. This is why I am keeping a low profile in Evergut. So what was it you wanted? It better be worth my time."

"We need to find the gatekeepers."

Cursman let out a hollow laugh.

Fierel and Krista exchanged glances. "What's so amusing about that?" the paladin asked.

Malpherities pointed at the paladin. "You should know that finding a gatekeeper is difficult; they cross between here and the mortal realm constantly."

Fierel shrugged. "So we will wait for them at their realm gate, since that is where they enter and leave. Can you show us where the gates are?"

"They have other tasks; you can't just wait around for one to show up." Cursman took a deep breath and relaxed his face. "Why do you need to find a gatekeeper? They're powerful beings, beyond any of your strengths. They match the strength of the angels from the Heavenly Kingdoms."

Krista looked to the ground. "I want to go home."

Cursman raised an eyebrow. "Sweetheart, the gatekeeper will only take you to the Weaver. Trying to find them is foolish."

Fierel sighed. "Tell us, Cursman: if we want to kill a gatekeeper, what can you do for us? We want to find the gatekeeper to her realm." Fierel gently lowered Krista's jacket collar and pointed at her mark on her neck.

Cursman stroked his bristly jawline. "I still don't get how a child and a paladin show up in Dreadweave Pass one day, together at that."

Fierel shook her head. "It's none of your concern."

"It is if I am going to help you. I'd like to know what helping the girl gets you, lady. She may be fresh meat, but I wasn't banished yesterday—Dreadweave Pass ain't exactly full of charitable types."

Fierel eyed Malpherities, then Cursman. "All you need to know right now is that I've rescued her from the Blood Swamp and we're going to help her get out of this realm, okay?"

Cursman shrugged. He bent and examined the mark. "Okay, what I can tell you then is that this mark's design is slightly different from those I've seen before." He paused and looked at Fierel. "The Weaver found a new gatekeeper, I take it?"

"Yes. And as we know, with every new gatekeeper, the Weaver creates a new gate. An experienced eye can tell the difference between each gatekeeper's mark.

Krista raised an eyebrow. "So it's like their signature?"

"Indeed, sweetie." Cursman nodded at Krista. "The Weaver believes in starting a new gate with a new gatekeeper. I do know where the previous gatekeeper's portal is, but this new one? Couldn't tell you. I've been out of the Weaver's army for quite some time."

"It's a start," Fierel said. "Can you take us there? We may find clues leading to the new portal if we visit the old gate."

"You won't find clues. Everyone knows when a gatekeeper is killed, the portal is abandoned—it's nothing but old ruins now. If necessary, I could take you to the one active gatekeeper portal I know of. Gatekeeper El Aguro is still alive and well. It will be dangerous, though—because it is still being used. They're often guarded by puppets."

"Understood. I've never seen a gate before and want to get a sense of what we're up against. The more we understand these gatekeepers, the better. When can we see the abandoned gate?"

Cursman grinned and folded his arms. "Hold on there. I said I *could*. Why would I *want* to help you?"

Fierel casually bent down then suddenly sprang up, drawing a hidden dagger from her ankle bracelet and charging at the man. She pressed him against the window with her forearm and brought the knife to his throat. "How about I offer you your life?"

Malpherities chuckled. "Where would threatening him get us?"

Fierel didn't blink, staring at Cursman. "We can find others who will help us."

"Go ahead. Slay me!" Cursman encouraged, tilting his head back. "It'll end this living hell."

Please, no. Krista looked away, afraid that the man's throat would be sliced open any moment. She didn't want to see another death. There had already been so much blood. It frightened her.

Malpherities moved down to Krista's eye level. "Fierel won't kill him; we need his help."

Krista nodded, still feeling her heart race.

"Now might be a good time to calm your mind and practice controlling your perception."

"Try to go home? Now?" Krista's eyes widened.

Malpherities nodded. "Close your eyes and relax."

"If I kill you, it won't be a release from hell. You know you'll end up in a far worse place," Fierel said.

Krista followed the ghoul's instructions. She decided to focus on steady breathing to block out Fierel and Cursman's argument.

Breathe in and out.

"I'm willing to take my chances," Cursman replied.

Fierel whispered back but Krista didn't catch what she said.

In . . . and out.

Fierel and Cursman's words began to fade, but she couldn't tell whether they were whispering even lower or if she was starting to cross realms.

This isn't real. I'm in my bed. Krista bit her lip. She felt herself breathe in and out evenly, filling her lungs with air and then releasing it. The muscles on her back tingled, her fingertips were cool, and her hands were sticky from the blood. Her mind fell silent for just a moment, hearing nothing from what surrounded her physical presence; no thoughts buzzed through her mind.

A rumble broke the silence. "Fine!" Cursman shouted, slamming his fist against the wall beside him.

Krista's eyes sprung open and she saw Fierel back away from Cursman. "Shit," she mumbled.

Malpherities patted her back. "It's okay. We'll try again."

"I felt silence for a moment."

"That's good. Very few manage to master realm-crossing in their first attempt, or even the second. Perhaps it is too early for you still."

I can't focus here . . . She shook her head. "Who else can cross realms?"

Cursman folded his arms. "Perhaps you're right, lady."

The ghoul leaned into Krista's ear. "We'll talk about this later."

Fierel put her dagger back into the sheath of her ankle bracelet. "Good. Take us now."

"All right. So you want to visit this abandoned gate first?"

I really would rather just rest. I feel so exhausted, Krista thought while eyeing Cursman and Fierel, their postures more relaxed. She leaned closer to Malpherities. "What did they agree upon?"

"Cursman has a mutual interest: our distaste of the Weaver."

Fierel stepped back to Krista, lightly placing her hand on her shoulder. "Yes."

"You're in luck; it's the nearest. Trust me, though, you'll find nothing there. Not even puppets to guard it."

"Take us there," Fierel ordered. "I must learn about these portals. I've never studied one up close. Besides, Krista claims her friend was the one who killed its gatekeeper, and I'd like to learn more about how he died. It may help us."

"All right, fine. Let me get my things and we'll head out." Cursman scurried around the room to grab a few items from the floor and the nightstand. He stashed some clothes and a couple of books in a leather bag.

"Now we'll learn a bit about who these gatekeepers are," Fierel said, patting Krista's back.

Cusrman rummaged about the room for a few moments then swung a bag over his shoulder and nodded at the group. "Let's get moving."

The four left the room and walked back down to the bar, where there were still large crowds of people drinking in huddled groups. Fierel, Malpherities, and Krista waited by the entrance while Cursman dropped his key off with the bartender. He waved goodbye and nodded at his new companions as he walked past them through the swinging tavern doors.

The three followed Cursman off the porch and down the dirt road leading out of Evergut.

Krista counted the buildings on each side of the street, but only reached twelve before the town's edge. *Compared to the City of*

Renascence, there really isn't much to Evergut.

Fierel kept her hand on Krista's shoulder as they walked. Despite Krista's attempts to discreetly break free, the paladin kept her grip tight. Krista was uncomfortable with Fierel's hand on her; it felt intimidating and demoralizing.

"It still doesn't make sense to me," Cursman said as they passed the last building in Evergut. "Why would a fallen paladin want to help a girl damned in hell?"

Fierel didn't answer and kept her upright posture as they walked. She whispered to Krista, "Stay close to me," and let her hand drop to her side.

Krista did as Fierel asked. *Even if Malpherities doesn't like her, I should keep on her good side. She is pretty scary when she's mad.*

"She thinks she's better than everyone in the Heavenly Kingdoms," Malpherities answered.

Cursman snickered. "Interesting."

The man led them to a fork in the road about a hundred paces from Evergut. They were faced with two paths: the left path was wide, like the path they'd been walking on, while the right path was smaller, just large enough for two to walk side by side. It was rockier and less worn. Cursman turned onto the smaller path.

"This track doesn't get used much. Everyone knows it leads close to the gatekeeper portal," Cursman said, pointing ahead.

There were fewer trees in the distance, and far ahead, three large mountains were compacted close together. They hadn't been visible at Evergut due to the fog, but now that the group was further away from the town, the mist had begun to thin. Most of the rocks here looked identical: flat surfaces with sharp edges layered on top of one another, pointing at different angles. There was a slight wind that picked up as they travelled, blowing dust into their faces.

"The portal is near the base of the mountain, just before the steep portions." Cursman pointed up the road. "Chances are it's deactivated, you know. The Weaver has no use for a portal without a gatekeeper."

"I still want to see it," Fierel replied. "I want to understand the size of these gatekeepers and their portals."

"Trust me, beautiful—physical size means nothing with the gatekeepers."

Krista didn't pay much attention to the rest of their conversation; the scenery kept her distracted. The endless plain of rocks, crevices, and hills spreading for miles around was too mesmerizing to ignore. The road extended upward toward the mountains, leaving steep ditches on both sides of the path, deep enough that a fall would break a bone. She looked up to the open sky, staring at the range of reds from deep blood to a vibrant rose shade like the tunic Paladin wore. The black clouds were different here than on the surface world; they were thinner, sharper, and shaped like spirals.

This land seems surreal.

A loud grunt came from the side of the road and Krista spun her head toward the noise. She spotted a naked man with torn skin and exposed muscle tissue wandering the ditch. He limped as he walked and seemed to be stuck in the lowest portion of the drop, unable to climb the steep path.

"There's a man down there," Krista whispered. "Is he an abomination?"

"Ignore it." Fierel spoke softly. "It is only a Lifeless One."

"What's a Lifeless One?" Krista squinted.

Fierel looked down at the naked man. "They're like puppets but without a soul—empty bodies. They're rejects of the puppets the Weaver creates. From what I've heard, the Weaver occasionally makes mistakes when making them and the soul breaks free from the body. He needs their soul intact to command them. Otherwise, they're useless."

"What happens to the soul?"

"It stays here, in Dreadweave Pass. A lost spirit. Don't worry about the Lifeless Ones. They only attack the weak; remain strong and you won't be pestered."

"Why do they attack the weak?" asked Krista.

"They're nothing but empty shells, and they're angry at the beauty of those filled with a soul—the fullness and warmth of having a spirit. They think it's unfair they've lost their own when others still have theirs," Fierel replied.

"I've never felt full or warm with a spirit. Do I have one?"

"You have always had one. You wouldn't know how it feels to be empty unless you lost it," said Fierel.

Krista stared down at the man in the ditch as they walked past him, watching until his soulless form disappeared into the distance. It was hard for her to grasp the concept of a soul and the difference between having one and not. However, she found Dreadweave Pass entirely difficult to understand.

The road began to flatten out and the ditches on the sides were no longer as deep and not nearly as intimidating. There were a few trees growing just after the ditch, but they were small and bare. In the distance, more trees were grouped together, interspersed with large, sharp, flat boulders.

"The mountain may look near, but the portal is far," Cursman said, stopping in his tracks. "We might be best setting up camp."

"We press forward," Fierel ordered.

"I'm tired," Krista whined. She had many more complaints—the dried blood on her body, her fear of the land—but she figured it'd be better not to mention them. The group she was with didn't seem to be the most caring type. *Even though everyone tells me they are on my side, it's hard to believe considering how they're acting.*

"The girl needs rest." Malpherities pointed off the road. "There's plenty of shelter under the rocks, away from the wind."

Fierel bit her lip. "Fine."

Krista collapsed on the path. "Finally."

The paladin kneeled behind her and slipped a dagger into her hand. "I'm off to get some firewood. Stay with the group and don't hesitate to kill if you must," she whispered, then stood.

Krista felt the rough and rusty handle of the dagger, then tucked it in her belt under her jacket.

"Where's she going?" Cursman asked, watching Fierel carefully move down the ditch.

"To get some firewood," Krista replied.

The man nodded, eyeing Krista's hand as she poorly tried to conceal the dagger. "So she gave you a knife?" He chuckled. "Believe me, girl, if I was going to do anything, I would have done it by now."

"So the paladin would burn you to ashes?" Malpherities asked.

"I'm not a puppet," Cursman replied. "I am a man."

Malpherities folded his arms. "Right."

Cursman looked around for a few moments then pointed in the

direction Fierel went. "Let's set up camp just off the road here."

The group helped one another move down the steep ditch, finding the easiest spots to make their next steps. The task was slow and required patience, but eventually, all three made it down into the desolate terrain.

Cursman led them to a large rock where one of the higher flat layers extended outward, providing cover from the wind.

He sat himself down beside Krista and Malpherities.

"Well," he began, pointing at the dagger under Krista's belt. "Do you even know how to use one of those?"

Krista kept her head low. *I shouldn't talk to him.* "No." *Why did I answer?* She found it tough to not reply to someone when they spoke to her; it was an impulsive behavior.

Cursman nodded as he looked her over. "So you didn't die?"

"No." She lifted her head. "Why does everyone think I died? Mal asked me and so did Fierel."

Cursman shrugged. "People usually come here after death—that, or if they're an angel or a god, they've done wrong in the Heavenly Kingdoms."

"Why do people come here when they're dead?"

"Well, we didn't please the Heavenly Kingdoms in life, yet no one up there is really angered by us. So they send us here to make up for all the sinning we did while alive." The man brushed his hair from his face and stared off into the sky. "Although times are changing. The Kingdoms are overflowing with too many souls to live comfortably, so the gods sometimes send us here even if we were good."

"They send you here even if you should be in the Heavenly Kingdoms? That's not fair. And what if the gods don't want to give you a second chance?"

"If they see you unworthy of redemption, they send you to one of the deeper levels of hell in Dega'Mostikas's Triangle until the end of days. Dreadweave Pass is only the first level." Cursman spat on the ground. "But if the Heavenly Kingdoms are actually angered by you . . . they will go beyond all hell and send your soul into Death's Vortex—and there's no coming back from there."

The words sent a chill down Krista's spine. She had never really heard any religious lore or mythology except while with the Eyes of

Eternal Life. But there, they didn't talk so much about consequences—it was all about waking the Risen One.

"This all sounds like a bad fairy tale." *The Heavenly Kingdoms can't be that spiteful, can they? I'm so confused. It was easier at home in the underworld—we kept our faith in the Five Guardians.* Krista felt homesick. Back in the underworld it was simple: if you didn't trust the Five Guardians, the Renascence Guard would kill you and you would be gone.

"What is Death's Vortex?" Krista began to play with her scalp-feathers like she often did in stressful situations, winding the feathers around her index finger.

Cursman raised his eyebrow. "You don't know about Death's Vortex?"

"No, or about the Heavenly Kingdoms, either." She took the dagger from her belt and scratched lines in the ground. "My society taught us a different faith. This is all new to me"

"This isn't faith, sweetie. This is reality. Death's Vortex is another realm."

"Like this one?"

The man shrugged. "I suppose. It's a one-way ticket for mortals; when they go to Death's Vortex, they don't come back. Only the immortals can pass through to explain to us what it looks like."

"Like Mal?"

Malpherities nodded. "I was born in Death's Vortex."

"What did it look like?" She stopped fidgeting with the knife.

"It's a cold blue plain of connected souls, forever spiralling into a black core."

"What's in the core?"

Cursman shook his head. "That's all he's ever told me, too. I suppose if fate brings me there, I'll understand." He squinted and stared at Krista. "What about you? Are you good? Or have you sinned?"

Krista brushed her scalp-feathers from her eyes, feeling the dried blood peel from her skin. "I don't know." She sighed. "I had to steal a lot, and my friend Marilyn told me that is a sin. But my parents died when I was little. I don't know if that makes it okay."

The man nodded. "Better than I did."

"What did you do?"

"Perhaps another time." He rubbed his eyes. "How old are you?"

"Nearing three hundred."

"An ancient race. Your maturity takes longer to develop, I assume?"

"Than a human's? I think so. I've just been me throughout my life, learning new things every now and then." She scratched her head. "Why didn't the gods let you go to the Heavenly Kingdoms?"

"Like I said, perhaps another time."

"How long have you been here?"

The man paused, furrowing his brow. "Too long. I don't remember."

Krista ran her tongue along her sharp upper teeth. *Everyone here seems to understand this place, except for me.* She felt out of place among the group. All three of her comrades had been in Dreadweave Pass for some time. *It's a good thing I met them all; I can learn from them.*

The three sat in silence, staring off into different directions. Cursman kept his gaze to the sky, Malpherities scowled at his bracelets, and Krista stared at her dagger. *I've got to learn to fight, especially if I have to find Danil and kill him to get out of here.*

"So we're visiting an empty gate first. If every gatekeeper has one, then Ast'Bala and Danil have one—why are there so many?"

Cursman rested his hand on his chin. "The mark on your neck is the symbol of your world. Only one of the gates goes there."

"Are there other worlds like mine?"

"I would think so, if gatekeepers are entering them, but I haven't been to any."

"Are you from my world?"

"Yeah. I belonged there."

Krista nodded. "So you know about the Kingdom of Zingalg?"

"Sure do."

The three sat in silence staring into space. She picked some dried blood off her skin, then fiddled with the dagger again to pass time, hoping that Fierel would arrive soon so she could get some sleep. She didn't trust Cursman yet; despite his friendly personality, she found his scruffy appearance, long hair, scar, and grim expression creepy.

It doesn't help knowing he is one of those puppets.

"I assume you don't want to be taken to the Weaver?" Cursman looked over at Krista.

She smirked, finding the question amusing. "No, I don't want to see him. I want to go home."

"And finding a gatekeeper will help?" Cursman folded his arms.

"We have to kill the gatekeeper that gave me the mark on my hand," she said.

"Mark on your hand? What about your neck?"

"It's a weird story. I actually have two marks. The first one on my neck was to tell another gatekeeper about me."

"You've seen two gatekeepers in your world?"

"Yeah, they are both former leaders my people—vazeleads. But Ast'Bala, the first one, said he couldn't bring me to Dreadweave Pass. He said his job was to pick a gatekeeper for my world." Krista dropped the knife in the dirt. "Kind of confusing. Then he picked Danil, the gatekeeper who brought me here."

Cursman nodded, staring at the dagger. "Your people must be strong if the Weaver made this Ast'Bala find another gatekeeper of the same race. So you plan to kill Danil, the gatekeeper? Why?"

"Because my friend who escaped from here said the key to freedom is getting the pendant that is in the place of their heart."

"Let me get this straight: you're going to carve open the ribcage of a being who was once a leader of your kind, infused with the Weaver's strength, yet you don't even know how to use a dagger?"

Krista felt her blood boil from frustration. "I know how." She snatched the dagger and held it upright, tightening her grip, ignoring the pain from her hands.

Cursman rose to his feet and brushed the dirt off his pants. "All right, prove it."

Krista remained seated, loosening the grip on the dagger. "Now? I don't want to hurt you."

Malpherities broke into laughter. "I'd like to see you try."

Stupid males. She hissed and stood up with the dagger poised and ready to strike.

Cursman remained motionless, unsmiling, watching her.

Krista swallowed, hesitating. *Do I strike now? Why is he doing this? Both him and Mal are acting like this is a joke—like I can't do it.*

She took one deep breath. "Here goes nothing," she muttered and dashed forward, raising the dagger. Keeping her head low, she charged Cursman.

Krista was only a footstep away when Cursman grabbed her wrist with one hand and her head with the other. With a shove, he pushed her to the ground while stepping to the side, avoiding her clumsy fall.

She lost control of her balance and fell face-first into the dirt, dropping the dagger. Her nose hit the ground when she landed, tail up in the air.

Malpherities laughed. "I warned you."

Krista used both hands to push herself up. She wobbled a couple of times before she got to her feet, brushing the dirt off her face, feeling a bit of blood run down her nose. *This is humiliating.*

She scratched the back of her head, keeping it low. *I feel so useless. Why didn't I learn anything from watching Darkwing?*

Cursman smiled as he leaned over and picked up the dagger, wiping the rusty blade on his shirt.

"I guess you're right," Krista said, shrugging.

The man approached her and offered her the dagger's handle. "You won't survive long here unless you learn how to fight."

Krista took the blade and slipped it in her belt. "Can you teach me?" she asked, wiping the blood from her nose.

The man brushed his hair back. "I could."

She felt afraid—afraid that Cursman would say no, afraid that she would not be able to defend herself, afraid that the puppets would overtake her and she would be forced to meet the Weaver. Krista clutched her hands together. "I'd be forever grateful. Please."

Cursman walked a short distance away to where a lone tree stood. He circled it and found two branches of about the same size growing from the trunk.

Krista looked back at Malpherities. "Thanks for the moral support," she scowled.

"Apologies. Your enthusiasm was . . . cute." A grin spread across the ghoul's toothy mouth.

Cursman ripped the branches off the tree and strolled back to their campsite. The tree let out a low groan, and Krista cringed.

"I suppose we could train to pass the time," Cursman offered.

Krista smiled and nodded. "Thank you."

Malpherities shook his head. "You have a lot of work to do, Cursman. She's inexperienced in everything."

Cursman plucked the loose ends from the branches and handed one to Krista. It was sturdy and would make a good walking stick.

Krista held the branch, feeling the texture of the wood. *It's kind of like William's training sword.*

The man stood and gripped his branch with both hands. "All right, I'm assuming you've never used a sword, either?"

Krista imitated his wide stance and the way he held the stick. "No."

Cursman lowered his guard and approached her. "Well, be sure to keep your guard up."

She relaxed her stance as Cursman walked past her. "I don't even know how to swing a weapon." She began to follow Cursman, seeing that he was ignoring her. "What do—?"

Before Krista could finish, the man spun around and with one low swoop of the stick, he tripped her by her calf, knocking her to the ground.

Krista yelped as she hit the dirt knees-first. "No fair!" Dust rose in the air and she waved the cloud away.

"I told you to keep your guard up." He dropped his stick and offered his hand to her.

She took it gracefully, only to be pulled up with vigorous force. Cursman brought her right up to his spare hand that was curled into a fist. The punch hit Krista in the ribcage and knocked the wind clear from her lungs. Krista gasped as Cursman let her go, allowing her fall to the ground again.

"That's just cruel." Malpherities shook his head.

"Kind of ironic to hear that from a ghoul," Cursman replied.

Krista began to whimper as she clutched her stomach in pain. She twitched a couple of times, fighting back the urge to cough.

"Come on, get up." Cursman lightly tapped her leg with his foot.

"It hurts," Krista managed to say after several gasps of air. "I thought you were going to teach me to fight."

"What is this?" a womanly voice shouted.

The noise alarmed all three of them. Fierel had returned with firewood in her arms, but she dumped the wood on the ground and marched toward Cursman.

"What did you do to her?" She pointed to Krista.

"She wants to learn how to fight," he shrugged. "I'm teaching her a valuable lesson."

Fierel grabbed the man by the chest and pushed him against the large stone beside their camp. "Beating a little girl is teaching her?"

"I'm okay." Krista carefully used both hands to get to her feet. "He's helping me." Now that the pain had eased, she understood what Cursman was doing. "He is teaching me to fend for myself and to keep my guard up, always."

Fierel shook her head and gave Cursman one last glare. "Carry on, then." She walked back to the pile of wood, picking it up piece by piece and bringing the armload closer to their shelter.

Krista leaned down to pick up her stick again and let out a deep sigh.

"Good first try," said Cursman, smiling while picking up his own.

Fierel brought the batch of logs and sticks to the group and began arranging them in a circular pattern. "The nights in Dreadweave Pass are cold, so stay close to the fire."

Krista lifted her stick and stood in the posture Cursman demonstrated earlier. "I'm ready."

Cursman straightened his vest and held his sword up. "Don't be ready."

She was confused. "Why?"

"Being ready now means you are expecting something, and you can't expect the unexpected." He pointed at Fierel. "When she let me go would have been a perfect ambush for you. Yet you didn't take the opportunity. Being ready now implies you weren't ready before and now you're expecting a certain outcome from me. You need to think like an opportunist; you're too innocent."

"That's why the Weaver wants her," Malpherities added.

"For now, let us focus on sword fighting and basic attack strikes. We'll work on your mind later." Cursman stood in a battle stance like Krista, this time pointing his stick toward her. "I'll strike first, so be ready to block."

"Okay."

This type of training was more what Krista was expecting, like what she'd seen William and the boys do back at the High Barracks. Cursman and Krista began exchanging blows, with Cursman ensuring her stance was right and her attacks were striking at efficient angles.

The two practiced for far longer than Krista expected. While they were on the road, she'd said she was tired and wanted to rest, but Cursman continued to push her limits. The blood-red sky darkened, leaving the world around them pitch black. Fierel's small fire lit their practice area.

Krista hoped that Fierel or Malpherities would intervene and call it a night. However, both spectators watched the two battle with interest. Eventually, the observers fell asleep, leaving her to press forward on her own. Malpherities stayed upright but his eyes drooped closed. Fierel kept her dagger in her hand while she pressed her body against the rocks.

Cursman was persistent and had her repeat the lessons over and over until she was proficient at attacking and blocking incoming strikes with her stick. She complained about the pain in her hands repeatedly, but he ignored her and struck with his branch, forcing her to block.

At least two hours after nightfall went by and the campfire had begun to die with no more firewood left. Finally, Cursman nodded. "That's enough."

Krista sighed gratefully. *I thought I'd never hear those words.* She wandered over to the campfire, sore and exhausted. Her body had numerous bruises that she did not notice until sitting down on the dirt.

She followed Fierel and Malpherities's lead in using the rock walls as protection against the light wind. Krista rested her cheek against a smaller stone.

"You did well," Cursman said. He sat across from her, beside Malpherities.

"Thank you," she whispered.

"I honestly do believe I belong here—unlike this paladin, who feels she was unrightfully punished," Cursman said, nodding at Fierel.

"How come? How did you die?" she asked, hugging her arms.

Cursman pointed at Malpherities. "It was partly his fault. When I first came here, he mocked me about it too, singing a tune of my story and imitating my voice."

"That's a little odd."

"He's a ghoul; they're like jesters of death. They enjoy the suffering of others." Cursman chuckled. "That's in the past, yet the song remains everlasting in my mind."

"Was it a nice song? I don't know many songs."

Cursman shrugged. "It summed up my pathetic state at the time." He licked his lips and took a deep breath before beginning to sing. Cursman's voice was soothing; a bit rough, but it put Krista in a gentle state. Soon, her eyes closed and she slipped into her dreams.

I once had a dream of a home filled with many possessions.

I had a wife who I loved with an obsession.

The joys of children shared between our minds.

However, these truths we could not find.

For the lords of old had to fold.

For a creature known as a ghoul tainted their once "minds of bold."

Passion for greed and fame.

The lords of bold now look back in shame

In all the things they had done!

They had taken from their people, quickly and relentlessly stealing their tools.

The ghoul used the lords of old like fools.

The lords of old laughed at the chaos they created.

The ghoul was elated!

. . . of the possibilities that he held.

For the lords of old minds could not be meld.

As for I,

All I could do is cry.

My home, I mourn the loss of its touch.

A place where my mind was at rest.
My home, I could never have too much.

My home is now in a place of gentle dreams . . .
A place where mountains roam.
. . . is nothing but a broken seam
A place I lost long ago.

For the lords of old had to fold.
For a creature known as a ghoul tainted their once "minds of bold."
Passion for greed and fame.
The lords of bold now look back in shame
In all the things they had done!

The lords of old demanded taxes or there would be a price.
The taxes grew, the ghoul ruled the lords of old's heads like lice.
My wife and I were driven broke.
We couldn't even pay a grain of rice.
We surely were to croak.

The collector for the lords of old came one fateful night.
With the moon being the only light.
The man demanded the payment that we could not give.
He threatened the price of life.
Threatening to kill my wife!

I drew my sword yelling for my wife to flee.
As she began a plea.

The fight was quick, filled with blood.
Surprisingly it was I who fell in the mud.
The screams of my wife were last I heard.
Until I saw the word.
"Awake."

Now here I am.
In the land of the damned.
Mourning the thoughts
Of my dear home.
Nothing left of it stands but the loam.
And my dear wife.
Whom I treasured with my life.

CHAPTER V

Big Time Hunting

Land of the Damned.
The sinful are put to perish.
Seven sins are free to flourish.

Specific sins corrupt the pure.
Beyond recognition of their former.
Giving birth to new.
Wrath is one.
Dangerous too.
For my bidding, plenty of fun.

Sinful games must wait.
As my master demands.
I come to him at the wave of his hand.

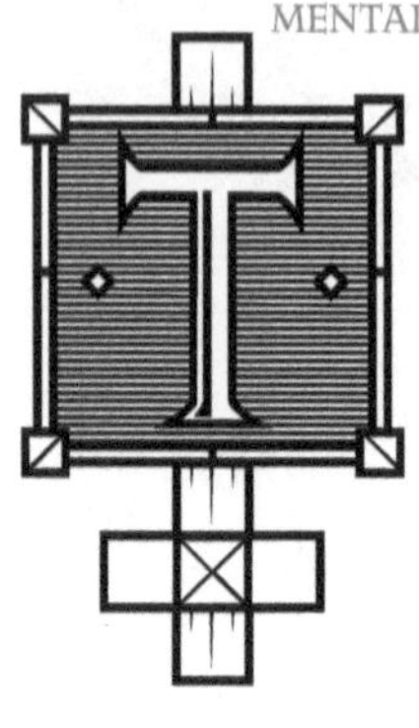hese were only a few of the thoughts that ran through an ungrateful mind, a mind that questioned his loyalty to the one he should be grateful to, questioning the passion of loyalty. He challenged the supernatural occurrences that led him to where he was, and the divine sins that brought him here. So many had fallen to sin, and not just mortals—gods and angels too.

These were the thoughts of a madman, the thoughts of one that suffers from a disease, a disease that most consider merely a state of mind: paranoia. It fills the mind with strange ideas and false beliefs. It can be the lead of perfidious acts. Paranoia is a sickness.

"Sir?" said a raspy voice.

The voice of one mortal who showed loyalty through his actions tore the pale-faced man free from his web of thoughts.

"Yes, lieutenant. Speak." General Dievourse ground his teeth and eyed his leather-armoured follower.

"What does the Weaver want to ask of you, my general?"

"He wants to know about the escape in the Blood Swamp." General Dievourse spat on the ground as they walked through the deep red stone halls leading to the Weaver's chamber. The halls were more like a cylindrical tunnel, with curved walls that seamlessly became the ceiling above and the floor below.

The general's armour clanged with each step he made, echoing down the empty passageway. "I can guarantee that it is nothing to be alarmed of," he said.

"Shouldn't we be, though? If it wasn't us who made the child disappear, then who?"

"I don't know Lieutenant. We'll have this investigated."

"We're at a halt until we find the child."

"We are."

The two came to the end of the hall and a large stone door decorated with carvings in ancient abstract glyphs. These were the glyphs the Weaver used to perform his necromantic rituals.

The lieutenant stopped in his tracks and folded his arms, leaving Dievourse to move on alone.

"I'll ease our master's temper with words to his liking," the general snarled.

"Of course," the lieutenant nodded.

Dievourse was aggravated by his master's paranoia. The Weaver being trapped in his prison left him alone in his thoughts and allowed his imagination to run wild. The Weaver didn't trust his creations who could roam free. Imprisoned with only his mind to keep him company, the Weaver would sit and calculate the possible outcomes of every mistake—such as the child who'd escaped the Blood Swamp.

As long as his paranoia doesn't provide insight into my own agenda.

Dievourse straightened his posture before pressing the stone door inward. He could feel the vibration of the door scraping against the floor. He stepped into the Weaver's dark chamber and the grey fog that obscured the floor from the knees down. The room was moist and warm compared to the cool hallway; he could feel moisture droplets forming on his forehead.

He squinted while adjusting to the lighting and marched toward a green glowing circle in the centre of the chamber—the only light in the room.

Dievourse stepped onto the glowing circle and kneeled, resting his arms on his leg. There were more glyphs written around the circle, these ones painted with what the general knew to be blood.

"My child . . ." The Weaver's deep voice elongated the vowels of each word, the sound bouncing off the walls of the chamber.

"Master. You summoned me?" Dievourse replied, crisp and clear, keeping his eyes facing forward into the darkness.

From the distance, long, extended pale arms slithered on the floor through the fog, toward Dievourse. The dim lights from the circle revealed hands that had an extra thumb opposite of the palm. The arms were veiny, dangly, and moved like snakes.

The hands arched upward and waved some fog closer together,

condensing it into a tight ball. Fingers stretched inward and out as the hands continued to wave around and around. The fog moved in motion with the hands, spreading outward as if the Weaver was finger-painting trees, steep hills, and pools of liquid.

The Blood Swamp.

"The child . . ." The Weaver spoke while the hands pointed at the image. "It's not here. Where is the child?"

Dievourse clenched his jaw. "I don't know, master."

"It was one of your squads that was supposed to deliver the child." The hands rushed down, separating the fog, then returned to the floor and slithered back into the darkness. "I tire of these shackles. I envy your freedom, general."

"I have no freedom. As long as you're imprisoned, so am I."

The Weaver laughed. "Your loyalty rides the line of disturbing and reassuring."

"You granted me life, therefore my services are to you." Dievourse took a deep breath. He was once grateful for what the Weaver had blessed him with, but his master had grown weak-minded over the years. His orders were questionable.

"The squad: where is it now?" the Weaver asked.

"I do not know. Their captain does not respond to me."

"He may be dead. Then, the child—where is it?"

"I don't know, master."

"These are questions you must find answers to. It greatly disturbs me that you have no control over your soldiers. Perhaps El Aguro would have been better suited for the task."

"I assure you, there is nothing to fear. I am in control, and my puppets will be punished."

"But the child!" the Weaver shrieked.

"The child remains in your realm; it will be found. You have nothing to fear. As you speak the gatekeepers reap more."

"No, fear is what I must indulge in. Reaping more, the gatekeepers may be doing, yet your captain does not reply? Why do you think that may be?" The Weaver's hand appeared again and pointed to the door. "Go, my general. Find the child and tell me what happened in the Blood Swamp."

"Yes, master."

Dievourse returned to his feet and left the chamber, careful not to look back even once. He exited into the cool, bright hallway where his lieutenant still stood. The stone door closed behind him and the general let out a sigh.

"What is the order, sir?" the lieutenant asked, bowing as the general approached.

"He wants us to investigate the Blood Swamp"—Dievourse gritted his teeth—"and find the missing child." The two marched down the hall side by side.

"Shall I go out and find it?"

"Not essential; such a meaningless task is not worthy of you. I'll send another."

"But who has such skills in tracking as my own?"

"Now is the opportunity to test Sporathun. He used to hunt Dega'Mostikas's demons when he was in the Heavenly Kingdoms. A child will be an easy catch for him."

"But sir, the fallen angel is unpredictable. The damage he caused when he was first banished from the Heavenly Kingdoms almost destroyed all of Dreadweave Pass."

"The damage was done to unappreciative mortals, so it is irrelevant. Besides, I was able to neutralize him."

"I am uncertain if he is going to co-operate."

"Sporathun could prove a valuable tool, if we can control his wrathful nature. A fallen angel of wrath craves anger and wants to feed his desire for destruction. Such is Sporathun."

"And what if he is not stable?"

"We'll send him on this hunt for the child as a test of his stability. But I assure you he is tame. He is convinced we have what he wants most in his pathetic life." Dievourse grinned. "If we could have his sincere loyalty, our power would be unmatchable."

"It would prove most useful. However, if he proves unstable once again, what then?"

General Dievourse released a drawn-out sigh. *The lieutenant worries about controlling every detail, a neurotic behavior that I admire in him. But he must understand that taking risks and loosening your control can play in your favour.*

"I suppose if he is unstable, I will have to restrain him as I did once before."

Dievourse led his lieutenant out of the hall and down several sets of spiralling stairs, going deeper into the Weaver's tower. They descended four levels until they reached a grey stone room with brick flooring, lit with torches on the walls. On each side of the room were circular extensions where the bricks spiralled inward and silhouettes of beings shackled by their wrists, hanging by their arms from chains attached to the ceiling. Some had additional cuffs around their necks and torso to restrain them. The long hall went on indefinitely.

"You have never accompanied me into the Chamber of Dishonored, have you, lieutenant?"

"I have not."

"This is where we keep Sporathun, among other beings of great power like fallen angels, demons and demi-gods." Dievourse extended his hand to the shadowed figures, who remained silent. "The Weaver does his best to control Dreadweave Pass. The souls who are too challenging to convert into puppets are locked up here. In this chamber they rot, waiting in darkness until they surrender willingly to the Weaver and he can convert them to puppets."

"Sporathun might never surrender."

"Sporathun is a unique case. His one desire in life is to find his lover again. When he was banished to Dreadweave Pass he was searching for her, for she too was banished for the sin of lust."

"Then the gods cast her out of the Heavenly Kingdoms and sent her to Dreadweave Pass."

"Indeed. Sporathun knew she was sent here, and went on a rampage in Dreadweave Pass to find her as soon as he arrived. I had to end his spree, threatening if he did not surrender I would order the execution of his lover. He surrendered to my bluff—and here we are, where I have the upper hand on Sporathun."

"Clever."

Dievourse led the lieutenant into the room, past the shaded, dangling beings. They were silent and breathed in inconsistent patterns; it was too dark make out details of the prisoners, but none of them mattered to Dievourse.

He marched forward to one of the chambers. It was reinforced with two sets of barred doors, bolted down with large, rusty hinges.

The general took a bronze key from his belt and unlocked the series of bolts and locks on the first door, then repeated the pattern for the second door. After the last lock clicked open, Dievourse swung the door aside, its hinges squeaking.

A high-pitched roar echoed from within the cell. A silhouette of a humanoid appeared, arms hung up by chains that jingled as the being tugged on them. "Dievourse!" the being shouted. "For too long, you have ignored me."

"Sporathun," Dievourse replied calmly, gradually stepping toward the fallen angel. "Are you ready to prove yourself for the one you love?"

The being stopped squirming and panted heavily. "Yes. Where is my Glamorous?"

Dievourse stopped just inches away from Sporathun, close enough that he could see the lean, muscular arms and torso of the fallen angel. He continued to circle around Sporathun, seeing the twisted muscles around his back, covered in massive white bumps. "She is safe." Dievourse shook his head. "You're so angry being locked up down here that it's taken a toll on your body."

Sporathun roared and yanked on the chains violently. "I will rip your head off!"

The malformed muscles and bumps on his back—nothing but pent-up stress. The life of a prisoner is eating away at him. "You want to release your anger. I can see it."

Sporathun let out a maniacal laugh. "How about you take these chains off me and find out?"

Dievourse smiled. "In good time—or perhaps not."

"Why not?"

"I know you have plenty of rage toward me because I know where your precious Glamorous is. But I assure you, if you lay a finger on me, she will be executed." *Lies come so easily,* Dievourse thought.

Sporathun growled, a deep sound coming from his very core.

"If you can prove yourself stable—and obey my orders—you will see Glamorous again."

"And if I don't?"

"We will bring you here again, and the cycle will repeat itself."

Sporathun inhaled deeply through his nostrils and exhaled from his mouth, seething with rage. "What are your orders, then?"

Dievourse smiled. "You used to hunt the most rebellious of demons, centuries ago. How about a warm-up hunt?"

CHAPTER V: BIG TIME HUNTING

CHAPTER VI

Everyone Knows

PATIENT: KRISTALANTICE SCALEBANE

DAY: TWO
ENTRY: THREE

The poor girl, I believe the illness has begun to consume her brain. It was obvious that she was lying about her symptoms when I first met her. The common effects of the disease were clear in her paranoid mannerisms; her answers seemed hasty and she wanted to leave my office so quickly.

Paladin had informed me over the night that she "wasn't acting normal," as he worded it. He took me to her room and we found her on the floor, rolling around uncontrollably.

As I expected, Stage 2 of the disease—the stage of Dreadweave Pass—had initiated. This stage of the disease is where the victims start to express excessive violence in their sleep. The second stage of the disease causes the victim to experience a loss of time when they wake from their rest. They gain mysterious wounds such as bruises and cuts all over body, which I initially hypothesized were solely the result of self-injurious behaviour. This is true in part, but I've discovered that even if they're tied down, the victims develop these bruises. In addition, their muscles either sporadically grow or shrink. From here on, the victims start to have suicidal ideations and as the days pass, they begin to spontaneously bleed through their orifices and feel tremendous pain. Kristalantice is still in the early period of Stage 2, beginning to vocalize in her sleep. She has whispered and shouted phrases such as:

Mal?

I want to go home.

Leave him alone!

Please.

Last night, her nightmare grew worse as the night wore on, and Paladin and I had to restrain her before she caused more physical damage to herself. She had bruised her ribcage by hitting herself, shouting, "Always on guard!"

It always pains me to see someone so young being tormented by a devastating disease. I'm puzzled how a powerful being such as God could see fairness in suffering such as this.

I'm certain that Kristalantice won't believe that she had a nightmare. The disease tricks the mind, convincing them what they see is real. She will believe she went to this Dreadweave Pass, regardless of how obviously unrealistic this belief is.

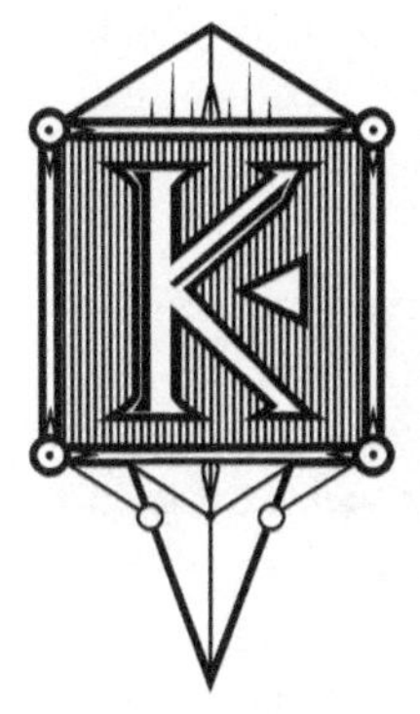

rista's eyes flew open, and she blinked several times to clear her vision. The grit that had developed in her eyes over the night hindered her sight. She had a skull-splitting headache stared at the grey stone ceiling, groaning. It was difficult for her to move, but she made an attempt to sit up anyway, only to discover her wrists and ankles were tied to her metal bedframe by chains. It was the bed she had in the High Barracks of Zingalg. In addition, there was a leather strap cinched around her mouth, and she realized her teeth were clenched down hard on the hide.

Krista tried squirming free from the chains, but they were too tight. Her voice was muffled but she screamed anyway, rattling the chains against the bedframe as hard as she could.

The wooden door to her bedroom swung open and a sturdy man with dirty-blond hair, a bristly beard, and a deep-red tunic came bursting into the room—it was Paladin. He rushed to her bedside. "Krista, calm yourself!"

She tried to speak through the leather strap, but her words were incomprehensible. *There's no way they can hear me.* She felt a tear roll down her face.

"Can she be untied?" Paladin looked over his shoulder at an older man with a shaggy grey beard who entered the room.

The doctor!

Dr. Alsroc cleared his throat then spoke. "Yes, she's awake now."

Paladin untied the leather strap from around her head and pulled a key from his belt. He then proceeded to unshackle the chains around her limbs.

Once she was freed, Krista leaped forward into Paladin's arms. "Please don't do that again," she mumbled into his chest. The chains were uncomfortably similar to the ones Danil used on her for his ritual only a week before.

Like when he cut my arm open.

All she wanted was a hug. She was exhausted and her brain felt like someone had cooked it. Her head was warm and the subtle throbbing wouldn't stop.

I feel like I haven't had rest in two days. She froze, suddenly confused. *What happened to Dreadweave Pass?*

"It's okay, Krista," Paladin said softly; his posture was stiff and he gently placed his hands on her shoulders. His awkward gesture reminded her of when she'd hugged the boy, William.

I don't think humans understand affection.

"Why was I strapped?" she asked, sitting back on her bed, taking in her surroundings. She recognized the open window to the far corner where blue sky was visible outside, the grey stone flooring and walls. *I'm back here, in the High Barracks. Maybe I was relaxed when I fell asleep and crossed realms!*

"You were having a nightmare." Alsroc stepped closer to her, arms behind his back.

Krista peeked over Paladin to see the doctor had a weak smile across his face, as if he pitied her.

"A nightmare?" she asked while wrapping her finger around the tip of her tail.

Paladin sat beside her. "You were injuring yourself again—and screaming." He wiped his face. "You woke many of the men here in the barracks with your racket."

"Sorry." Krista went to rub her head, but raising her arm spiked a sharp pain in her ribcage. She yelped and touched her side lightly.

The two men stood in silence, watching her.

Krista, frowning, began patting her torso and legs to feel more swollen spots all over her body. *Bruises.*

Alsroc spoke. "Do you remember anything about your dream?"

Krista shook her head. "A dream? I know I went somewhere, and it was horrifying. So much blood . . ." She closed her eyes, trying to shake the visions of the Blood Swamp away, remembering the trees, the abominations, Fierel, and Cursman.

"Your Mental Damnation is becoming more serious." Alsroc folded his arms. "Can you come to my office? I'd like to take some notes."

Krista glanced at Paladin, who nodded.

"Okay." She got off the bed to realize she hadn't taken off any of her clothes during the night and she was still wearing her trench coat.

What is going on? She brushed her scalp-feathers back and nodded. "Okay," she repeated. Krista felt very confused. *I seriously have not slept in two days. I spent a day with Marilyn, then I was in Dreadweave Pass, and now I am here.*

Dr. Alsroc smiled and led the way out of the room. Krista followed him slowly, with Paladin walking behind her.

Her headache began to fade now that they were moving down the halls finished with green running boards and arched ceilings. With each step, she could feel the blood flow through her body. Her mind buzzed with questions and confusion. Did she actually sleep? What happened to Dreadweave Pass? Is it real? Dreadweave Pass seemed so real while she was lying down, but now that she was walking, it felt more like a dream—like an intense nightmare.

"It was real!" Malpherities's black fog emerged from her shadow, followed by the blue smoke funneling inside the black until the fog moulded into the ghoul who floated beside her. The braces on his wrists clanged against each other as he folded his arms. "The doctor is an idiot. Tell him nothing! He is not worthy. Dreadweave Pass is not for him to know."

Krista glanced at Paladin, who kept his eyes on her. She winked at Malpherities, acknowledging him. She couldn't speak to Malpherities—Paladin was watching too closely.

The doctor took her down the stairs to the main level, leading her into his office. She took a seat on a stool beside the operating table she'd been on the first day in the High Barracks. Paladin leaned against the door as the doctor sat at his desk. On the desk was the same notebook he had during their first meeting and a feather in an ink bottle, ready to write.

"All right, Krista." Dr. Alsroc leaned forward. "I'm going to need you to be completely honest with me this time."

"I am," she replied, straightening herself on the stool, tail raised.

"You lied to me last time. I know what you're going through—I've dealt with Mental Damnation before."

Krista kept her lead low. *How did he know I was lying?*

Malpherities flared his nostrils. "He keeps notes on Dreadweave Pass from every case he has."

"All right. Before you went to rest for the night, can you tell me how you felt? Did you have any headaches?"

Krista crossed her legs and hugged her knee. "I can't recall much. Lots of headaches."

"When did you fall asleep?"

"I woke up several times in the night."

"How did your nightmare begin, then?"

Malpherities shook his head. "Don't tell him much. This paleskin is unworthy of the knowledge."

Krista shrugged her shoulders at Malpherities, unsure what to tell the doctor.

"Krista?" Dr. Alsroc asked.

Malpherities glared back at Krista, waiting for her to speak.

"I don't remember much," she lied.

"You told us earlier about a land of blood?"

"Yes, I partly remember. It was horrifying," Krista scratched the back of her neck. *Shit, lying is hard.*

"Would you mind describing the dream to me?"

Krista sighed. *He doesn't quit.* "I remember being drenched in blood, and almost drowning in a pool of it."

"The Blood Swamp is of no importance!" Malpherities flickered his black tongue. "Tell him nothing. No more."

"That's all I remember," she finished.

Dr. Alsroc nodded and continued writing.

Krista sat tall, trying to see the notebook. "What are you writing?" she asked.

"Nothing you need to see," Dr. Alsroc replied.

Krista glanced at Malpherities "Can you see?" she whispered.

The ghoul brought a claw to her lips. "Hush!"

"Can who see?" Dr. Alsroc asked.

Krista twitched away from Malpherities's claw and brushed her scalp-feathers aside. "Nothing. Sorry."

Malpherities floated over to the doctor's desk and hovered over the human, examining what he wrote. His fog channeled through the various shadows and cracks in the room while he hovered toward the desk.

"How long do I have to be here?" she asked.

Dr. Alsroc leaned back in his chair. "It seems to me you aren't quite remembering the dreams yet. I know they'll come clearer to you as time goes on. Try to remember them, even if you need to write them down in the morning."

"I can't write," she replied.

"Even pictures will do. I know we can help you, Krista."

Malpherities floated back to Krista, eyeing the doctor. "You can't help her, fool."

"Thank you," she replied while jumping from her stool. "Can I go now?"

"You may. But remember, my office is always open if you feel the need to talk."

"Thanks." Krista walked out of the office, politely smiling at Paladin as she walked past him.

Paladin didn't make eye contact and closed the door behind her.

"What did you see?" she asked Malpherities the moment the door shut.

The ghoul shook his head. "He was writing a lot down, mostly about your reaction to the questions. Not what you'd expect. He didn't care about your verbal responses." The ghoul lowered his head. "I thank you greatly for not telling him about me. I assure you, your life would be far worse if you mentioned me."

She smiled. "It's fine. We can trust each other, remember?"

The ghoul nodded.

Krista took a deep breath and let out a long, tired breath. "I feel exhausted. These bruises . . . I feel dirty."

Malpherities nodded. "Crossing realms takes a toll on your body."

Krista folded her arms. "Yeah. I'll see if I can take a bath. Clean myself up." She started walking to where she knew Marilyn worked—in the basement. The maid and Krista hadn't finished their work from the day before and she wanted to catch up with the girl first. "What happened? Why am I here, Mal? Did I have a restful sleep?"

"Yes, you managed to relax your mind. All the training you did with Cursman must have worn you out."

"So I left Dreadweave Pass? Why do I have bruises all over my body?"

Malpherities pointed to her ribcage. "Crossing realms is difficult. Our souls have deep roots in our current physical bodies. When the real you—your soul—changes realities, the soul has difficulty letting go of the ties it has made with this body. What happens in Dreadweave Pass will affect you here to some degree."

"Great. So anything that happens there is going to hurt me here?"

"Not if you can fully let yourself go of this world—leave the body."

"I don't know how, or how to control the realm-crossing."

"In time, Krista. In time."

Everything is about waiting, but I don't want to wait. I want to be done with Mental Damnation and find my way back home.

Malpherities followed Krista down to the narrow, torch-lit basement hallway leading to the laundry room where Marilyn was working, washing more clothes. The ropes with the wet clothes were gone from the day before, but the curved floor leading to the drain was still damp. Large piles of clothes still littered the room, giving off a nasty odour. The young, pale-skinned blonde girl, Marilyn, sat on a wooden stool beside a tub full of soapy water where she ran clothes along a scrubbing board. Her movements were sluggish, and she seemed tired; she had dark bags under her eyes.

"Hey, Marilyn!" Krista waved.

The girl looked up. "Good morning! I heard you woke most of the men on the second level last night."

Krista rubbed her arm. She'd hoped Paladin was exaggerating, and hadn't realized she'd been that loud. "Yeah . . . I would rather not talk about that."

"Fair enough. You've come to help?"

"Actually, I was hoping I could take a bath."

"There is a bit of work to do. Can it wait?" Marilyn asked.

"I guess so. What happened to the clothes we hung before?"

"The other maids came for them earlier in the day, taking them to finish drying in the sun."

Krista removed her trench coat and placed it on an empty stool, along with several other pieces of clothing she'd been wearing, exposing her light grey skin and sharp teeth. She didn't feel the need to hide her physical appearance around Marilyn; the girl didn't seem to judge her physical differences. The two girls began to clean from the clothes pile they left the day before, following their same routine: Marilyn scrubbed the clothes clean and Krista hung them to dry.

They worked in silence for most of the morning until Krista spoke up.

"So where are the boys training today?"

Marilyn smiled. "Why does it matter?"

"Just curious."

Malpherities frowned. "You wish to see that boy, William?"

Krista whispered, "How did you know?"

"You get a sparkle in your eye. You obviously enjoy his company."

Krista nodded and brushed her scalp-feathers aside. "He's nice to me. He reminds me of someone I knew in my home world, who took care of me in that harsh place." *Darkwing. He was always there for me.* Krista bit her lip; the thought of Darkwing made her heart sink. Where was he right now?

"I've told you before that William isn't helping you. You need to focus on Dreadweave Pass," Malpherities scolded.

"I'm not there now, though," Krista whispered.

"The problem there is very real and is still happening right now. You must not waste time here!"

"No!" she shouted.

Marilyn looked up at her. "You all right?"

Krista nodded. "Yeah, sorry. Just this clothespin is not opening. I'm okay," she lied.

"They're a bit tricky."

Krista sighed. "I like it here," she whispered, as low as she could. "I want to find William. I'd like something good in my life right now."

Malpherities folded his arms. "You need to learn about priorities."

Krista did not speak to Malpherities for the remainder of the morning. She didn't want to hear him complain about her choices.

All I want is a friend. Last night was scary and William makes me feel safe. I have all day to think about stupid Mental Damnation.

Marilyn got up from the stool and brushed her apron. "All right, we'll come back to this later."

"Okay." Krista hung the last shirt and grabbed her coat and extra clothing, then followed Marilyn out of the laundry room with Malpherities hovering behind her.

"We'll have our midday meal, then I'll review what is in dire need of cleaning."

Midday? How did the morning go by so fast? "Sure. How do you keep track of what needs to be done?"

"I have a pretty consistent routine and every week I do the same tasks. Every now and then it changes when something unexpected happens."

The two walked back up to the main level of the keep. Krista looked over her shoulder toward the black metal door leading outside—the door that Captain John (who the boys referred to as Jelly John)—had brought her through to meet Marilyn for the first time.

"Hey Marilyn, can I catch up with you? There's something I have to do."

The girl shrugged. "Sure. I'll just be eating in the dining hall."

Krista smiled. "See you soon." She waved goodbye, then began to dress herself in preparation for the sun.

Malpherities scowled. "Are you off to find your boy toy?"

She ignored his comment and tightened the scarf around her face, then opened the door to outside. The light blinded her eyes and she squinted, trying to block the bright sun. The first few steps into the daylight were impossible to see, but her eyesight started to adjust and she could focus on the gravel path leading off into the distance.

I'll try the training grounds first.

Krista walked down the dirt path, taking a deep breath, feeling the fresh air fill her lungs. *It feels so good outside. The air in Dreadweave Pass was so . . . stale.*

She walked down the path to where the training grounds were. The boys were walking up the path to the keep's entrance dressed in their red tunic uniforms. *They must be going for lunch.*

In the crowd, Krista spotted a red-haired boy trailing in the back of the group.

"Jeuth!" she shouted out to him, waving her hand in the air.

The boy stopped in his tracks and waved with little effort. He was covered in dirt and his knuckles were bruised.

She rushed toward him. A couple of the other boys—also covered in bruises and dirt—trailing from the group glared at her and walked ahead of Jeuth.

Krista brought her scarf down and smiled at the boy. "Hi."

Jeuth glanced around and nodded at her. He seemed afraid, almost embarrassed.

"Have you seen William? I don't see him here."

"Ugly child," Malpherities commented.

Jeuth shook his head. "We're clear of sword training today; this group was practicing hand-to-hand combat. I think William was assigned to be at the church."

"Church?" Krista squinted. "Where is it? Can you show me?"

The boy sighed. "Fine. Follow me."

Krista walked alongside Jeuth. He seemed ill at ease with so her close to him. He was slightly shorter than her, and had hunched, stiff movements. Krista couldn't figure out what he had to be intimidated by; most males of her kind demoralized her, and she wasn't used to being in the shoes of the terrorist. *It feels weird to intimidate someone.*

The boy stopped in his tracks and gestured off to the distance near the stables. "See? Over there." He pointed at the building Krista had briefly seen by the stables—a grey brick building with a curved staircase and a couple of statues of men with folded wings on each side. The roof was sloped, with red shingles that contrasted with the white stone cross on the bell tower above the arched entrance of the building.

"That's the church. He'll be in there, praying."

Krista smiled at the boy and lifted her scarf, covering her face. "Thanks again."

Jeuth nodded and began walking back to the rest of his group.

Malpherities hissed. "Disgraceful child. He showed no appreciation of you—or respect."

"That's okay. He's like me: afraid of something new."

"Being afraid is for fools."

Krista stared toward the church as she walked. As she got closer, she noticed that under the arched roof there was a second cross in the shade. She put her hand over her eyebrows like a visor until she was close enough to the church to see that the cross was made of copper and had a sculpture of a naked man pinned to it. Nails were jammed into his hands and ankles, and he wore a crown of thorns.

"Mal, what is that?"

"This is what the humans believe in: a single man who saved them from damnation."

"Mental Damnation?"

"They think they're free of all damnation of any kind. If that were true, beings like the Weaver would not exist."

Krista dashed up the stairs to the church and glanced behind her before opening one of the large doors. Malpherities remained at the bottom of the stairs.

"Aren't you coming?" she asked.

"This is holy ground," the ghoul said.

"Holy?" She was confused. "But this is only a human religion. It's just stories, right?"

The ghoul shook his head. "Holy ground of any kind is blessed. You naive mortals are constantly bickering over the small details of each religion, killing one another over the name you call your creator. Do you think a god that can create worlds cares about what a diminutive creature calls him? What you mortals fail to realize is all religions carry the same message."

Krista raised her eyebrow. "So you're not coming in?"

"Holy ground will burn me to ashes if I cross."

Krista frowned. "Well, all right, I won't be long."

The ghoul nodded reluctantly.

Krista regarded the large doors. They were at least twice as tall as she was, painted in the same red as the roof shingles. They had large, ring-shaped doorknobs painted in gold. She pulled on both of them, swinging the doors open. The wood creaked, echoing inside of the church.

Krista's eyes took in the detailed interior of the church, and she came to a dead stop, shocked. A red carpet in front of her led straight to a marble podium at the far end. Behind the podium were a series of frames that lined the wall all the way to the ceiling. Each frame held an ornate stained-glass design. The centre frame detailed a white cross with bright light shining behind it. The surrounding frames were filled with coloured glass tiles ranging from purple, to blue, to red. There was a stone staircase leading up to a second level to the left of the podium; to the right, another staircase led downward. Columns resting on flat, rectangular bases were on both sides of the red carpet—at least six on each side from the entrance up to the podium. Over a dozen black pews lined either side. The floor and ceiling were bordered with floral carvings and the corners had statues of more bird-winged men staring down at the entrance of the church. At the far left and right walls stood polished wood tables draped with red velvet sheets. They each held burning white candles that emanated a sweet scent. Behind the tables were rectangular indents in the walls, holding urns as tall as Krista with a single painting on each of them. The one to the left had a man painted on it: he wore black robes, a white collar, and a large black cap with a cross on it. The urn on the right had a painting of a woman dressed in white with long, wavy blonde hair.

Krista didn't understand any of it, but she loved it for its luxury. *At least art is always beautiful.*

Her eyes moved up from the urns to the stained-glass windows near the ceiling: the same pinned man from the cross in the front of the church was expressed on the glass, but this time he was surrounded by women crying.

The humans have strange beliefs.

Krista shook her head. *I'd best look for William; it is why I'm here.* She lowered her scarf and spotted some boys in the front of the church. Each boy sat in his own pew. There were a couple of brunettes, a black-haired boy, and in the very front there was a blond.

She felt her heart skip. *That's him.* She rushed down the red carpet and began creeping to the pew, sneaking up behind the boy.

"William!" Krista exclaimed loudly. It felt like she had not seen the boy in days. In a way, she hadn't.

Several of the boys glanced over. The blond boy jumped up and locked his widened blue eyes on her. "Krista! You startled me," he said, relaxing. "I was praying."

Krista bit her lip. "Oops. Sorry."

"It's okay," William said, smiling. "I'm sure the Lord won't mind."

Krista walked around and sat beside William, crossing her legs. It was thrilling to see his blue eyes and light hair once again. *It feels like way too long.* "The Lord?" She looked back to see the other boys were looking at her from the corners of their eyes, their heads lowered in prayer again.

William pointed at the cross behind the circular podium and above the stained glass to a statue of the same man, pinned to a cross mounted on the wall.

"A dying human?" She glanced around the church. "Why are there statues of him everywhere? Who is he?"

"He's our lord and saviour."

Krista looked confused.

"Don't your people have religion? What did they believe in?"

"We were told to praise our Five Guardians. They were kind of our saviours, when we were banished to the underworld."

"Did they free you of your sins?"

"Sins?" *He sounds like Cursman. It's like Dreadweave Pass all over again.*

He pointed at the cross. "That's what the Lord did for us—he died for our sins."

Krista nodded, not wanting to seem rude. "I see." *This sounds like nonsense, like how the Eyes of Eternal Life talked about the Risen One. But Cursman said sins were real. So did Marilyn.*

William stared at her, his blue eyes shining. "I heard Dr. Alsroc and Paladin rush past my room in the night mentioning your name. Some of the other boys said you were screaming in your room, too."

Krista looked to the ground, embarrassed. "Everyone heard?"

"Sounds like it. I didn't, though. What happened? There's not much that can get old Alsroc to run so quickly."

Krista began to wrap her fingers around her tail, looking down to the ground. "Um, I'm not quite . . . normal." Her shoulders tensed and her fingers combed faster through her scalp-feathers. *I don't want to tell William I have Mental Damnation when I don't really understand it myself.* She took a deep breath. "Dr. Alsroc says I have an illness." She felt her heart go heavy. *Maybe he won't judge me if I am honest.* "He says I have something called Mental Damnation." She felt a tear drop from her eye.

William bit his upper lip. "Is it contagious?"

"No, but it's pretty serious."

"I'm so sorry." He opened his arms and allowed Krista to fall onto him.

She cried softly, remembering Dreadweave Pass and the puppets. She inhaled William's scent; it was less strong and smelled softer, like soap. He must have bathed. She felt William's tight chest and stiff arms holding her.

Krista managed to giggle through her crying. "You can relax, you know."

William blushed and shifted his posture. "What does Mental Damnation do?"

Krista lifted herself up from his chest and sniffled. "It starts with this mark." She sat upright and slipped her jacket down, revealing the mark on her neck. "I have two of them—it's a long story. Dr. Alsroc says it is a bite, but I wasn't bitten." She unbuckled her belt and lifted her dress to show William her bruised ribcage.

William swallowed heavily, eyeing her exposed figure.

Krista was familiar with that look—the same desire she'd seen on Draegust's and Darkwing's faces when they saw her physique. Slightly concerned, she brought her dress down quickly. "He says I have nightmares that cause me to do things . . ." She buckled her dress then took his hand, guiding it along her ribcage. "They make me do things that hurt me."

William cleared his throat. "You'll be fine. I'm sure of it."

Krista put on a weak smile. "I would like to believe that." *What I saw in Dreadweave Pass makes me wonder.* "It scares me to sleep now."

"These nightmares, though—what are they about?"

Krista pressed both hands on her collar bones. "A horrible place. I hate it." Krista slipped her hands from William's and got to her feet. "When are you going to be done praying?"

"He finished when you arrived," a shaky voice interrupted.

The two turned to see an old man dressed in black robes emerge from a stairway leading to the lower level.

"Father Isaac." William got to his feet and bowed.

Krista looked back to see the boys behind them rise to their feet as well, hands behind their backs.

"Would you mind telling me who your new friend is?" Father Isaac asked.

William stood tall. "This is Krista," he said, lightly touching her arm.

Krista curtsied and smiled at the man.

The old man stared into her eyes. He showed no surprise, unlike the other humans who had looked at her. The wrinkly, bald man remained calm. His gaze seemed deep, though, as if he was looking through her eyes, beyond her flesh and blood, and into her mind.

At first she was afraid but then she found it soothing, only to realize that the moment ended a split-second before he spoke.

"It's nice to meet you, my dear." Father Isaac bowed his head. "When did you arrive?"

"A few days ago," she said and brushed her scalp-feathers aside. *Everything is so nice in this church. I feel so dumpy in these scraps.*

"You're clearly not from anywhere near here, and yet you found your way into my church—isn't that a coincidence?"

Krista glanced at William, who held his hands behind his back. She shrugged. "I'm not sure."

The father smiled. "I'm sure time will tell us. You boys are free to go; there's no need for you to be inside all day at such a young age. Go outside."

Krista moved closer to William. "I'll come, too."

William bowed. "Goodbye, Father."

The other boys wasted no time as they scooted from the pews and marched in a single line down the carpet.

"Bye," Krista called, waving and following close behind William.

Father Isaac waved at Krista. "Come back to God's house whenever you feel the need to, child."

CHAPTER VI: EVERYONE KNOWS

CHAPTER VII

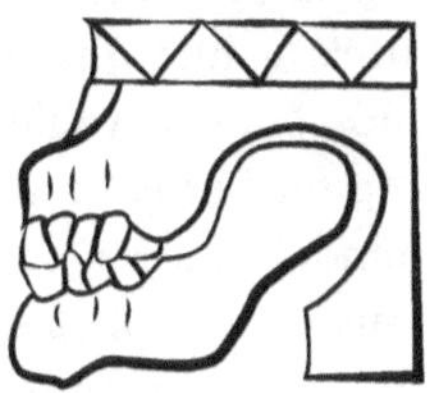

The Ghost

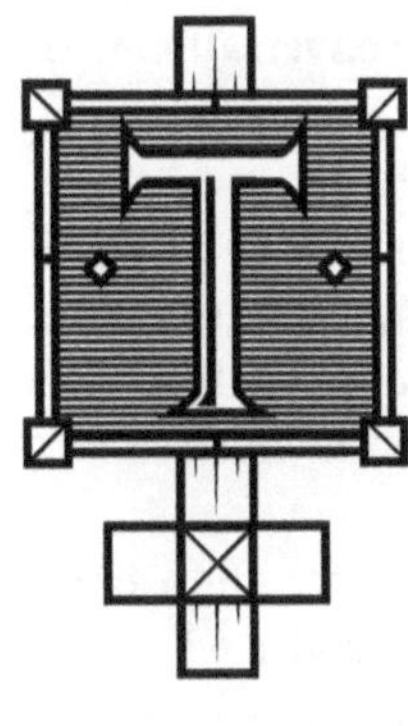

he dim light from several small candles cast soft shadows in the dark cave. Gusts of wind blew dust from the cavern's entrance to the shelving along the walls and around the black cauldron in the centre of the room. Five vazeleads stood around the simmering steel pot. One was Darkwing; the other three were his companions Alistind, Draegust, and Wrinkle Scale—with his reptilian pet, known as a shade—to his side. The fifth was the Corrupt named Fleerew who practiced shamanistic arts far from the City of Renascence.

Anger boiled inside of Darkwing as he stared at Fleerew's crooked smile. He wanted to save his dear Krista, and the best chance he had was to deal with a Corrupt—the only one who knew where the half breed, Abesun, was. Wrinkle Scale had informed Darkwing and his allies that the half breed knew of a path to the surface world, where Krista was. The longer she was away, the more Darkwing realized how much he missed her comfort. It took losing her just under a week ago to fully understand that she was the only treasure he needed. With each passing moment Darkwing spent here, he knew Krista's safety was further endangered. After all, she was alone on the surface world—a world ruled by humans.

Fear was another feeling that overcame Darkwing while he glared at Fleerew, who stared back at him. Just moments ago, the group had asked for her assistance, but she would not lend them her skills unless they did something for her first. There was no telling what type of quest she had in mind. It could be something life-threatening, or something reasonably simple. She was a shaman—which Darkwing knew nothing about except for her obscure fashion sense of tattoos, leather, bones, and painted eyebrows. What he did know was that she was a Corrupt, which were chaotic and unpredictable beings. After the metamorphosis fumes altered their people during the banishment, some vazeleads reverted to savages, resulting in the Corrput. This was the first time Darkwing had managed a reasonable conversation with one; usually, they just tried to rip off his face and eat it.

Fleerew gazed deep into Darkwing's eyes with her own glassy eyes—a clear sign of a Corrupt. It was a glare that scanned every detail on his face, as if she was trying to read his feelings. She squinted; maybe she picked up that he was exhausted, drained from the constant running around to protect Krista and now the hunt to find her. Not once had he been given a break.

Fleerew looked to the ground, still smiling, while strolling around the cauldron. Scraps of leather she used as clothing dangled with each movement. "Yes. Yes, there's someone I want ya t'see." She extended her tattoo-covered arm down to the rusty rim of the cauldron. "Y'see . . . I wanted t'live within the City of Renascence."

Draegust laughed while brushing his black scalp-feathers from his face. The sides of his head were plucked, leaving only the top portion of his skull with feathers. "And you think we could arrange that? The Five Guardians despise the Corrupt." He folded his arms, demonstrating the size of his muscles as he did.

Fleerew nodded. "Correct, my dear." The bone pierced through her nostrils twitched as she wiggled her nose.

Draegust folded his arms. "Who in their right mind would let your kind through the gates? It won't be the Renascence Guard, that's for sure. Let's get to the point here. What do you really want from us?"

Fleerew shifted her stroll toward him, raising her hand as if she held an imaginary ball. "I want the head o' my sister!"

Draegust and Darkwing exchanged glances.

The oldest, grey vazelead, Wrinkle Scale, cleared his throat. "Assassination? For you, Fleerew, that's a rather physical approach compared to your usual methods."

The Corrupt moved over to the old reptilian and ground her teeth as she spoke. "My sister Quilech has created a barrier—a barrier that blocks my nightmare potions, voodoo dolls, dust messages—none of 'em can touch 'er now!"

Alistind stepped forward. "Why would you want to kill your sister? She's your blood."

Fleerew staggered over to the girl, eyeing her vibrant, red scalp-feathers. The shaman's limbs twitched and she hunched, showing more resemblance to a Corrupt than a vazelead.

"She's in the military—up there, too—perfectly capable of lettin' me in the city. She could pull some strings. I've tried to communicate with 'er." The shaman fell to her knees. "She refused to answer me, and pretended I don't exist. So I tried to be rid of 'er to satisfy my rage and envy of 'er perfect life." She clutched her hands. "She abandoned me—her own blood! She's resisted my efforts." Fleerew chuckled. "Her head would satisfy me. Then I will lead you to the half-breed, Abesun."

Draegust leaned over to Darwking. "Our luck just gets better. Now we must find and assassinate a military-ranked Renascence Guard? Come on!"

"What's her rank?" Darkwing asked. He hoped she was a gate guard or something simple. He bit his lip at the thought of trying to assassinate a higher-ranked military vazelead. It would be difficult to locate her, especially if she was an officer. If she was, she'd be in the Citadel.

Fleerew rose from her feet. Her body jerked once and then she approached him. "She's a captain, an' I want her head!" She took a deep breath and sighed. "Then I take you to Abesun. Then you go to the surface."

"And exactly how are we supposed to find and kill a captain?" Draegust asked, his tail perking upward as he stared at her—eyes unblinking.

"That, I can assist with," Fleerew said with her crooked smile. "I know where her quarters are within the citadel, I know 'er routines, and when she rests at night." The shaman staggered over to her bookshelf and pulled out an old crumpled paper from the top shelf. "Finding 'er will be the easy part. I have kept good track of my sister." She walked over to Darkwing and took his hand, placing the paper in it.

He uncrumpled the paper and quickly examined the messy writing, organized into two columns.

This is crazy, he thought to himself. Darkwing had spent most of his life running from the Renascence Guard and now he had to go assassinate one for a Corrupt—another group he despised. What other choice did he have? No one knew the path to the surface world and the only being who knew how to find the half-breed was the shaman who stood before him.

"Head, or no deal." Fleerew folded her arms.

"That's a waste of our ti—" Before Draegust could finish, a voice interjected.

"All right." Darkwing stuffed the note into his pocket. "We'll do it."

"Darkwing!" Draegust exclaimed.

"Are you sure?" Alistind asked.

"Yeah, let's do it," Darkwing said.

Fleerew smiled with closed lips. "Good." Her smile twisted into a frown. "Now go!" She pointed to the door. "I've been waitin' a long while for my sister's death."

Darkwing eyed his comrades; Winkle Scale was the only one of the three who showed no surprise to his choice. He nodded at them and said, "Let's go."

The four exited the cave with Darkwing leading the way up the path of the mountain whence they came. Wrinkle Scale's shade, on all fours, kept to the rear. The black emptiness of the underworld beyond the mountain was quite the scene to behold once again. It was abnormal not to see even a single pool of molten lava that would project some form of light. There was only darkness, which made it rather difficult to see. Darkwing wanted to stare at it for hours and daydream about what else lay beyond Magma Falls, but he knew that he could not waste any time.

Draegust spoke. "This is suicide."

Darkwing pulled the paper free from his pocket. The paper had a listing of times and locations. "Not exactly." He ran his finger down the list of places. "This looks like a listing of her posts throughout the city and when she is supposed to be there based on the citadel clock. Plus, with the corruption of the Five Guardians, the Renascence Guard is scattered."

"How do we know this list is up to date, then? Maybe she was reassigned," Draegust said.

Wrinkle Scale chuckled. "I would not doubt Fleerew. When she is fixated on something, she perfects it. If you had not accepted her quest, she would have gotten someone else to do it."

"This is insane," Draegust complained. "We have to go all the way back to the City of Renascence? We travelled all this way just to go back."

"She is an outcast among the common vazelead. We had no other choice."

"We're going around in circles. I'd rather try and find this path to the surface myself."

Wrinkle Scale shrugged. "Be my guest. The underworld is a vast place."

Darkwing nodded. "Come on, Draegust, you know we don't stand a chance unless we can be guided by Abesun—who clearly comes and goes from the underworld as he pleases."

Draegust snorted. "This seems like a side step from our goal."

Alistind walked closer to Darkwing, lightly holding his arm. "Are you really going to kill her?"

Darkwing looked into her eyes, momentarily entranced with the slow, deep-orange flames that radiated from them. Looking at them made him want to say no, but knew he could not. This was his best chance at finding Krista. "I have to."

Alistind looked away and bit her lip.

He gently turned her chin toward him. "Why does it matter? We know nothing of Fleerew's sister and it's to save Krista."

"It's one of our own kind. There's been so much killing—so much blood. Can't we simply bring her to Fleerew?"

Darkwing laughed. "So she can do the killing for us? It's no better than slaying her ourselves."

Alistind shook her head. "I can't be a part of this." She broke free and moved toward Wrinkle Scale.

Darkwing sighed. He understood what Alistind was saying. Truthfully, it was what Krista would have said if she knew what he was about to do.

The old vazelead pointed back down the path. "Alistind and I will stay here."

Draegust shot a glare at the old reptilian. "Why?"

"Alistind is too young and may get in your way. I am old and wish not to take part in assassination."

Draegust shook his head. "Fine. Stay. Darkwing and I can handle this bitch's sister."

The old reptilain pointed back at Fleerew's cave. "We'll see if the shaman will let us stay with her."

"You sure?" Draegust raised an eyebrow. "That gal isn't exactly stable."

Wrinkle Scale nodded. "I know Fleerew. We will be safe."

Alistind looked to the ground. "This is barbaric."

Darkwing knew she was right, but what other choice did he have if he wanted to find Abesun? *It's for Krista,* he thought. "Hey, Wrinkle Scale. Can we take your shade with us?"

The shade hissed and glanced up at Wrinkle Scale while a voice projected into Darkwing's mind, presumably others as well. The vowels were exaggerated and drawn out. *I stay with my companion.*

Wrinkle Scale raised an eyebrow at the shade and turned to face Darkwing. "Shades do not like to be separated for long. Besides, I don't want him running rampant in the City of Renascence. I don't think you two can handle him."

Darkwing scratched his scalp-feathers. "Right." He had forgotten that shades could project thoughts into the minds of those around them. He presumed that the whole group heard what the shade had said. *The shade would have made this much easier.*

No, foolish mortal. The shade looked directly at Darkwing while projecting the words, *too much fear in your city. Less clarity.* Darkwing stared at its smooth translucent outer layer which was barely visible in the dark space, but the inner black core could be seen clearly. It brought back the memory when Darkwing and Krista had initially encountered the shade while attempting to steal a potion from Wrinkle Scale. There, the shade had demonstrated his attraction to fear. It was like a drug, and the creature could not resist the urge to attack.

I stay with my companion, Darkwing. The shade hissed.

Alistind spoke up, pulling Darkwing out of his gaze into the shade's astral form. "Be safe, Darkwing."

"Bye." Darkwing swallowed heavily while watching Wrinkle Scale, the shade, and Alistind walk back down the road to the cavern, leaving Darkwing and Draegust alone on the path.

Draegust shook his head. "They're useless," he bluntly stated. "Let's go get this head so we can find the half-breed."

Darkwing nodded and the two began to travel back up the mountain, remembering the path that they had taken back into the narrow, sharp-walled cavern. Normally a comment like that from Draegust would have angered Darkwing, but not now. *I have to focus on this task. It makes me sick, but I'm making progress in finding Krista.* He kept his eyes glued to the paper Fleerew gave him. *I can see an end goal now, even if the stepping stones are questionable.*

All they had to do was find Fleerew's sister, Quilech, then get her head so Fleerew would show them where the sun walker, Abesun, was. *Abesun will guide us to the surface world. That is, assuming we can get him to help us without doing another stupid task.* Darkwing shook his head. *One step at a time.* Now they had to come up with a plan to kill Quilech before they arrived at the city, and they had to know what time to arrive so they could execute it.

"Any idea what time of the day it is?" Darkwing asked.

Draegust shrugged. "My guess is, by the time we get back to the city, it will be well into the night. If we move quickly it should only take about a day and a half worth of travel." He pointed at the paper. "Check what she does after midnight."

Darkwing squinted, his eyes trying to read the scribbled notes. "Hard to read—the lunatic obviously does not know how to write."

"Do your best."

He scanned the two columns of notes as Draegust led him back into the cavern leading to Magma Falls.

The list was based on the ringing of the bell in the citadel clock tower and the times of the marketplace's rush hour, the two prominent time measurements in the underworld. Darkwing had never been exceptionally good at adding numbers together, but thankfully the times on the list seemed well spread apart and easy to add. *Based on the time we estimate to be back in the city . . .* He looked at the time on the first column: *1 ¾ Second Ring.* It referred to an hour and forty-five minutes after midnight—midnight being the second ring from the citadel tower. Over to the second column, it read *Citadel G12.* A letter followed by a number was commonly used among vazelead people to determine where a room was in a building. The letter referred to the floor and the number was the room or section on that floor.

He turned the paper around to see there was a second torn paper glued—with who knows what—to the back. This paper had a few paragraphs on it, speaking highly of Fleerew's sister's feats, achievements, and goals. *It might be some letter of recommendation. I'd be curious to know how Fleerew got her hands on this.*

NAME: QUILECH SWIFTTONGUE

RANK: CAPTAIN
SQUAD: VIOLET B

Quilech Swifttounge's passion is proving her dominance, so it was a natural fit for her to join the Renascence Guard in its early formation when the Five Guardians began to recruit warriors capable of keeping order in the new city. Quilech started as a low-ranked foot soldier, working with a squad to keep gangs and rebellious vazeleads away from the development of the gates dividing the Lower and Commoner's Districts.

After the gates were complete, Quilech's squad was reassigned to help clear out the Lower District from vermin. There, her hunting capabilities shone and her superiors promoted her to the captain of her crew. She led them ruthlessly into the streets, taking down groups of vermin twice the size of her squad. Quilech encouraged her men to show no mercy, kill, and even take pleasure with some of their captives before dragging them back to the citadel prison.

Years of cleaning the streets went by and Quilech's achievements in clearing portions of the Lower District did not go unnoticed. She was moved out of street-cleaning and promoted to the citadel where she would work alongside the tactical division of the Renascence Guard, planning the safety and control of the city.

Her courage and persistence in the ranks of the Renascence Guard have shown since day one. She has obeyed without question and even when given unclear directions she has shone through. If anyone is worthy of taking my place after I retire or perish in the line of duty, it would be Quilech Swifttongue.

~ FIRST LIEUTENANT DOUUL LONGTOOTH

Darkwing nodded to himself. *This should be fun.*

Draegust and Darkwing reached the entrance of the cavern, taking a short break by the stream in the entryway for a drink of cool water before proceeding.

Darkwing put the note in his pocket and splashed the water on his head, letting the droplets drizzle off his dirt-smeared face. He recalled this location from when he and Krista had tried to hide from Danil, before they joined the Eyes of Eternal Life.

What a stupid cult, Darkwing thought, recalling the ridiculous rituals they had to take part in.

Draegust cupped some water into his mouth and cleared his throat. "So. Any plans?"

Darkwing shrugged. "Judging from these notes, she's in fairly good shape. There's a letter of recommendation on the back here saying she's top quality for a First Lieutenant position."

"She is a female—we're male. One of us holds her down and the other cuts off her head. Simple. I don't care too much about her past."

Darkwing smirked at the idea; he liked the effortless plan. "From the schedule, it looks like her services to the Five Guardians are during the day, and at night she rests."

"So where does she rest?"

"Her quarters are in the citadel, G12. To get in, we'll have to disguise ourselves."

"That'll be the easy part," Draegust said with a smile. "The Renascence Guards are all over the city. Find one or two and we'll take their armour."

"I can't even fight one; us taking on two won't be easy. They're well-trained warriors."

"Then we'll ambush them."

Darkwing scratched his head while the two began to wander down from the stream, exiting the cavern. It was twice Draegust had come up with solutions to their problems. The simplicity of his plans astonished Darkwing. His mind buzzed with nonsense and worries, thinking about Krista and the potential dangers of their plan.

This is extremely dangerous—if I ever want to see Krista again, I can't slip up, Darkwing thought, feeling slightly discouraged. Here he was having to become an assassin, something he never thought he'd become.

The two continued on their path further down Magma Falls; the track had become less rocky and began to gradually level out. The waterfall to their right poured off into a scattering of streams that flowed down to the massive lava pool. The centre of the mountain was where the largest waterfall funneled directly into the lava lake, causing immense amounts of steam to rise, making the lower portions of the mountain misty and humid. The lava pool divided Magma Falls into two halves: the far-left half was where the smoother, flat ground was, which allowed farmers to harvest water from watermills and bring it back to the City of Renascence. The half to the right, where Darkwing and Draegust walked, was ridged, difficult to travel on, and impossible for the farmers to build on. The sharp rocks on the mountain of Magma Falls escalated high into the dark sky, disappearing into the darkness; it was rumoured that the rocks moulded to the ceiling of the underworld, making the mountain essentially a massive column. The path led the two of them closer to the centre of the mountain, where the main path away from Magma Falls resided.

"I'll admit, Draegust . . ." Darkwing said. "You said you wanted to prove your loyalty to me. I am still wary of you, yet I am beginning to trust you."

Draegust bowed his head.

"I know my head is a bit crowded right now, so if you could lead us on this assassination, I'd be grateful."

A grin crossed Draegust's face. "But of course. I've got nothing left here in the underworld, nor do you. The sooner we can get this head, the closer we'll be to seeing the surface world." He chuckled. "I can barely recall what it was like."

"Me either," Darkwing muttered. He knew they had to get to the surface world to find Krista but he didn't put a lot of thought into the actuality of it. They were on a mission to become the first vazeleads on the surface world since their banishment; it was history in the making.

The two walked in silence for the remainder of their journey, leaving Magma Falls and wandering down the red, sandy hills of the underworld back to the City of Renascence. Even though Darkwing was tired from all the travelling, the thought of killing two Renascence Guards for their armour excited him. He could feel the adrenaline surge through his veins.

Darkwing was uncertain how they would manage to bring down a pair of Renascence Guards, as they always travelled in packs of two or more. He understood that Draegust was a rebel his entire life and was fully capable of dealing with the guards, but worry spun in Darkwing's mind. What if they slipped up and Draegust got wounded? How would they finish their mission then?

Not often was Darkwing such a worrier. Before the corruption of the Five Guardians, life seemed so simple. It was just him and Krista surviving in the streets and his persistence to be accepted into the Blood Hounds. But now the world had turned upside down and the issues that seemed large yesterday were miniscule today.

Simpler times. I can't get lost in my thoughts; Krista is out there and she needs me, Darkwing thought as he stared at the long, rolling path ahead. The distant City of Renascence could be seen, easily identifiable by the specks of light that shined through the buildings in the three districts—with the citadel in the far end where Quilech would be.

CHAPTER VII: THE GHOST

CHAPTER VIII

Bigger Consequences

ozens of young men's feet stomped into the dirt in inconsistent motion. Their feet were covered in leather sandals wrapped up their ankles with straps. The friction with the ground caused dust to rise past their black trousers and red tunics that draped from their shoulders down to their upper thighs. Not much more than boys, they raised their wooden swords, ready to strike each other under the relentless sun. Their sleeves were rolled up to their elbows and their arms were covered in dirt and bruises.

The cracking of the wooden blades; the grunting and yelling with each strike the boys made—both were clear signs that the boys were focused. Their instructor, Paladin, had them swap battle partners frequently. He kept a straight posture, hands behind his back, while strolling through the training ground, watching every boy's move—studying to see where they could improve.

A large oak tree rested not far from the boys and their dirt training ground. The tree was surrounded by bright green and yellow blades of grass that blew with gentle grace in the wind. From the shade of the tree, Krista watched the action with Malpherities hovering over her shoulder. More than the swordsmanship, they watched intently the way Paladin eyed the boys like a hawk.

Paladin passed by two boys battling. The black-haired boy, Talif, trembled as Paladin lingered behind him. Talif's taller opponent seized the opportune moment to strike, knocking Talif to the ground with a forceful thrust of the wooden blade to the chest.

Paladin shook his head in disapproval. "Focus on what is right in front of you. Trust your other senses to aid you with your surroundings."

Malpherities sighed. "Foolish boy." He tapped Krista's shoulder. "You know, living between two worlds isn't going to be easy for you."

Krista squinted as the wind blew past her face; the tightly wrapped scarf kept her scalp-feathers in place. "What do you mean?"

"Think of it. You have two realms—that means two sets of problems."

"I have no problems here; this is my new home."

The ghoul pointed at Paladin, who was now yelling at Talif. "What of his offer to you?"

"What offer?"

"His offer to allow you to stay here. You are barely able to comprehend two worlds, let alone remember what is going on here. Paladin won't let you stay here forever. He wants information from you and he'll force it from you. Paladins are heartless." He pointed to himself. "At least I accept that I'm a monster. Paladins take no responsibilities for their actions. They justify everything in the name of the Heavenly Kingdoms—in the name of God."

Krista plucked a blade of grass and examined it closely. "I still don't understand the whole realm-crossing thing."

"What do you mean?" Malpherities folded his arms, the cuffs on his wrists clanging against each other.

"You still have the cuffs Fierel gave you, yet there's no blood on me. Even though I was just in Dreadweave Pass, it feels like a fading dream." She let the grass go and watched it fly away in the wind.

The ghoul chuckled. "You think you are a part of your body still, don't you?"

"What do you mean?"

"We both cross realms, but our spirits are the ones coming and going. Unlike you, who has a physical body in both realms, I can only view this world. The reason you can see me is because of your gift; your mind resonates at a higher level and now you can interact with those that are on that level, too—ones like me."

"If it was my spirit that crossed realms, why were my hands bruised when I first entered Dreadweave Pass?"

"We've gone over this. You had your bruises because you believe you're still attached to this body. Until you let go of this physical world completely, you'll still feel the senses that come with it."

Krista nodded. "Why do I get a body and not just be a spectre like you?"

"That is another gift you have. What the Weaver has given you is a second life in a new world. This is why I tell you to master the ability to cross realms on your own; then your soul will be able to let go of this body and your wounds will no longer affect both bodies."

"So if I learn, and one body dies and other stays alive, do I go to my other body?"

"Exactly."

"I have to get better at realm-crossing so if my body in Dreadweave Pass dies, I don't die here too."

Malpherities nodded.

"I'm confused about one thing, though. We spent at least a full day in Dreadweave Pass, but I know I was asleep just during the night here. The time doesn't seem to add up."

Malpherities nodded. "From your perspective, it may appear that way. The minds of mortals have a linear focus on time; your entire existence has been developed on this linear thought process that relies on physical objects to perceive movement and, inevitably, time."

"Time is faster in Dreadweave Pass?"

"No, it is constant like it is here. As you embrace your gift, you'll learn to stop focusing on the physical boundaries of this reality and the perception of time that you've created because of it. Your awareness will widen and your perception of time and space won't be dictated by your physical state."

"I really don't get what you said."

Malpherities smiled. "Time is just a series of observations in the same space. You have difficulty grasping this concept because your body is bound to a series of observations, which creates the time-driven conscious state. You know your body as being born, growing, and eventually dying. Letting go of this belief in your body and returning to your soul, the real you, you will see that the soul never dies and is not bound to a time-driven conscious state."

"I still don't understand this 'souls' business."

"Practice your realm-crossing gift; it is the first step to breaking your linear thought process."

This is too much for me. She appreciated that Malpherities was finally giving her genuine responses rather than riddles. However, they didn't make any sense to her. *Maybe I prefer the riddles.*

"Are you saying we have no idea how fast time will go when we go back to Dreadweave Pass?"

Malpherities shrugged. "Time is as fast as you wish to perceive it. Ever notice how the joyful moments of your life fly by and the times you are in despair seem to drag on?"

"Krista!" a female voice called from the distance.

Krista glanced around and spotted Marilyn at the top of the hill near the river waving at her, holding a basket in her other hand.

She smiled and waved back at the maid.

"Company is not what we need now." Malpherities poked Krista. "We need to plan what you are to do next in Dreadweave Pass."

Krista nodded. "I know, but if what you're saying is true, time is how I want to perceive it. Right now, I want it to slow down," she said and smiled.

Malpherities let out a deep sigh. "Why are you so naive?"

Marilyn walked down to the oak tree and placed the basket beside Krista. "How was your bath?" she asked.

"You waste your time with these mortals." Malpherities pointed at Marilyn's hunched posture, and the shadows under her eyes. "But we are friends—and as your friend, we can both see the girl is not physically well." It was true; Marilyn's skin was whiter than a dead man's.

Krista felt her stomach tighten at Malpherities's words. She smiled at Marilyn. "I didn't get to it—I ended up finding William instead."

"Of course you did. Feeling any better?" the maid asked, returning

Krista's smile as she sat beside her.

"What do you mean?"

"From last night."

Krista rubbed her shoulder. "I don't know."

Marilyn nodded. "I hope you recover soon."

"You too." The words slipped from Krista's mouth. *Shit.*

Marilyn squinted. "What do *you* mean?"

How do I reply to this? It's just so obvious she doesn't look well.

"You got into the hole, now climb out of it," Malpherities added.

"You don't look well," Krista spoke softly. "I don't mean to alarm you, but you're so thin and pale compared to the other humans I've seen."

Marilyn looked down at the grass. She nodded and inhaled deeply. "You're kind, Krista. We've just met and you already worry about me."

I do care about her, but I didn't think much about her health until Mal pointed it out. I just thought that was how Marilyn was.

Malpherities nodded. "Lesson one about being more observant, Krista. Analyze everything."

Marilyn pressed on her eyebrows. "It's complicated. I'd rather not talk about it, and there's nothing you can do for it, anyway."

"Paladin can help you, I'm sure he can." Krista sat closer to the girl. "He closed the wound on my arm, and now it's healed." She pointed at the arm Danil had cut open.

Marilyn smiled. "It's not like that." She patted the basket. "I thought we'd share some lunch before we returned to work."

"What kind of work?" Krista didn't want to do anything. *Paladin told me I had freedom?* She thought.

"Some of the floors need cleaning," she said, and opened the basket.

Krista paid closer attention to Marilyn's thin arms. The maid's hands shook lightly when she reached into the basket. *Be observant.*

Marilyn removed two sandwiches and handed Krista one.

"What's in here?" Krista asked, opening the sandwich.

The maid smiled taking a small bite. "Freshly fried chicken breast, and some vegetables."

"Don't know any of it." Krista sniffed the sandwich, smelling the oil that the meat had been cooked in. Krista took a bite, sinking her teeth into the soft bread and through the crunchy green vegetables.

Tearing off a chunk of the sandwich, Krista smiled as she tasted the mixture of tender meat and bitter plant. "The taste of the meat is good." She swallowed. "It's just about all we had in the underworld: meat, fungus, and roots."

"Must have been horrible. I couldn't live without any fruit."

"I wasn't always without fruit. Our people lived on the surface world when I was just a kid."

"That's right, your people were banished about two hundred years ago."

"Yeah, I remember eating lots of nuts and berries when I was young. I'd go picking them in the forests while I played with my friends."

"Are any of those friends in the underworld?"

"I don't know. We were all young kids." Krista swallowed heavily, feeling her stomach tighten. *But Darkwing is still in the underworld.*

The two ate in silence, watching the boys train in the field. As the sun moved through the sky, the exercises changed from dueling to one attacking and the other deflecting, then to group battles of three or four.

Paladin's voice boomed. "Finish the battle and lunch is yours!" He paced back and forth while shouting the names of the boys and grouping them in fours.

His shout reminds me of Fierel. Paladins are so aggressive.

"Sometimes they extend their morning routine into the early afternoon with a duel," Marilyn explained.

"Where's William?" Krista lost track of the blond boy when Paladin shifted them around.

"Ungrateful boy," Marilyn muttered.

Krista shook her head. "Why? He's nice to me."

The maid shrugged. "Of course he is. Look around you—what do you see?"

"Humans?"

"Men." Marilyn's face turned into a scowl. "Very few women ever come here; the High Barracks doesn't often accept females because they feel they can put them to more manual labor. We've had a few come through here, when they've proven in better condition than some of the boys. From what I have seen here, you and I are the youngest."

Krista didn't say anything.

Marilyn smiled. "Your world must have been different. These boys are at the age where they're curious—curious about women."

Krista nodded. "No, our worlds aren't different. I just didn't think—"

"Either way, it doesn't change the fact the boys are maturing, as are we." Marilyn sighed. "Just don't let William overtake you, all right? Men take what they want, and if it is a woman, they won't hesitate."

Krista giggled. "I won't. Trust me; I know how to handle curious boys."

Malpherities raised an eyebrow. "Except for when they overpower you."

"We'd best get to work," Marilyn said, lifting the basket as she rose to her feet.

Krista nodded. "I'm just going to see if I can find William."

"Be quick."

Krista ran out of the shade and down the hill to the packed dirt of the training ground. She watched the boys fight; it reminded her of training with Cursman. Indeed, their moves were like what Cursman had her doing: basic striking and deflecting techniques.

She scanned the groups until she spotted William, the only boy with blond hair. He was battling a larger boy, one with beefy arms and a shaved head.

"Go William!" she shouted with a smile.

Paladin came up from behind, his loud footsteps stomping in the dirt. He placed a firm grip on Krista's shoulder. "Krista."

"Hi, Paladin."

"May the gods banish you," Malpherities said, flickering his tongue.

"Keep your voice down when the boys are focusing," Paladin demanded.

"Sorry."

"What are you doing here anyway? I thought Madam Marilyn was supposed to keep an eye on you."

"You said I was free to wander the barracks."

"We all have to work here. I said you're free to wander, but I expect you to earn the right."

"You said that giving you information of my people would let me earn my right to stay here."

Paladin got down on his knees and lowered his voice. "I said that because things aren't going to get easier for you." He glanced at the boys, then back at her. "Have you considered my offer at all?"

"Not really," she admitted.

"I can't have you wandering around and not thinking about it. I don't want to banish your people to the underworld again."

Malpherities laughed. "It took a hundred paladins combining their holy power to banish the vazeleads. He could never do it on his own."

Krista smiled. *Mal is right.* "You can't do it on your own."

Paladin looked shocked for a moment, then smirked. "You're not a fool, Krista." He took his hand off her shoulder. "But the news of your coming is being sent to the king, and he expects me to bring him the information you give me. I serve the king, so I must do as he expects."

Krista bit her lip.

"If my king decides you're a spy because you're withholding information, he could order me to send you to the capital for interrogation."

Malpherities folded his arms. "He speaks the truth."

Marilyn walked up to the training ground, holding her dress out of the dirt with one hand and the basket with the other. "Is everything all right?"

Paladin nodded at her. "I just need a moment with Krista. Be sure to keep occupied all day, all right?"

Marilyn nodded. "Yes, Paladin. Come find me when you're done, Krista." The maid began to pace alongside the fence, watching the boys train.

"The king needs the knowledge you have about the underworld. It's a matter of safety for our kingdom!"

"But if I betray my people, what's stopping the humans from killing them?"

"The underworld is an evil place. We've heard tales of mortals from other races that have ventured there—those who returned had gone mad. It's for this reason that man dare not go there." Paladin sighed. "Did the underworld not make your people go berserk, too?"

Krista nodded slowly. *The Corrupt.*

"Think about it soon, Krista. It's important that you accept my offer. I can give you protection from the king as long as you share the information."

Marilyn returned from her short walk. "Sorry, sir, we have much work to do. Is Krista free to join me now?"

Paladin got to his feet and bowed. "Yes, my lady. Thank you for your time."

Marilyn bowed her head and hooked her arm around Krista's, forcing her to walk. "I haven't heard Paladin so upset in years," she whispered once they were away from the training ground. She let Krista walk free. "That's why I came down in the first place. I mean, I've seen him yell at the boys, but that is an act to toughen them up. He seemed genuinely angry with you."

"Thus, proving my point, Krista," Malpherities said. "You have problems in this world that you must take more seriously."

"What was he talking to you about?" Marilyn asked.

"Letting me stay here," Krista replied.

"What do you mean?"

"He wants me to tell him about my people and the underworld in exchange for my safety here at the High Barracks."

Marilyn raised her eyebrows. "What's the alternative?"

"Paladin said things could get much worse for me. It could get out of his control and his king could take me to the capital as a prisoner. But loyalty is important to my people and I don't know if I could betray them like that."

Marilyn nodded. "What are you going to do?"

"I don't know."

The two walked in silence until they reached the stairway up to the main entrance to the keep.

"The entrance hall needs cleaning at least once a month. Everyone has dirty shoes and we like to keep the High Barracks as tidy as possible."

Marilyn led Krista up the stairs and opened the wooden doors, letting Krista enter first.

Several steel buckets filled with soapy water were placed on the green marble floor. Two rags hung over the handle of one of the buckets. Krista looked around; the entrance area was about four times the length of the hallways. Four large marble columns stood in each corner and between them were smaller hallways. A large chandelier hung from the ceiling with about a dozen candles mounted on a silver spiral frame. *This will take a while.*

Marilyn walked straight to the buckets and took the rags. "I got the water ready for us earlier," she explained. "But back to our previous chat . . . I can see your point, but to be honest, you're just a girl. What can you know about your people's military or royalty?"

"Well, I know enough to let them know the state my people are in right now. And . . . I don't think I want them knowing that."

Marilyn bit her lip and passed Krista one of the rags.

Each girl took a bucket and the two got to their knees to scrub the stone floor. Mud and dirt was caked on the ground and it was obvious it would take several hours of hard work to clean it all.

Malpherities scratched his head. "It's a rather large problem. Not child's play. Paladin does not joke around."

Krista remained silent while scrubbing, trying to ignore the pain in her still-bandaged hands.

I don't understand why Paladin wants me to work so hard even when he knows I'm sick with Mental Damnation.

Marilyn dipped her rag in the bucket and rung it out. "I suppose you're going to have to decide if you're willing to sacrifice your loyalty to your people for your freedom—or possibly your life."

"I could run away."

Marilyn chuckled. "No one comes in or out of these walls unless Paladin says so."

"Then what should I do?" Krista felt defeated. "What would you do?"

Marilyn pushed the rag into the lining of each tile, scrubbing out the grime. "What would I do? I really don't know. On one hand, life is the most precious thing we have. On the other, sometimes one must make great sacrifices for the honour of their people—even if it is the greatest sacrifice of all."

They worked in silence, keeping on opposite sides of the hall to cover more ground. They spoke only to tell each other where they'd scrubbed. In places, the deep-green, stone floor tiles made it difficult to differentiate between the clean spots and the dirty ones.

Malpherities stayed nearby, watching Krista clean. "You'd better decide soon, Krista. You have many problems, and have much to learn if you want to survive in either world."

"I know," she mumbled, soft enough so Marilyn wouldn't hear.

"Good. Keep your mind busy with those thoughts."

"When do I go back?" Krista whispered.

"Back? To Dreadweave Pass? Soon, I am certain. Possibly the next time you rest your eyes," the ghoul said, smiling.

How can he find that exciting?

Marilyn spoke up. "I'd tell Paladin what he wanted." Malpherities and Krista looked over at the maid. "I would," she repeated.

"But to betray your own people?"

Marilyn looked uncomfortable, but the two were distracted by footsteps echoing down the hallway from the far left, ending their conversation. Eventually, two men entered the hall. One of them was Smyth, dressed in his black tunic, his curly hair bouncing with each step he took. The other man was dressed in armour from head to toe with a deep red kilt wrapped around his waist and a cape over his shoulders.

Marilyn stood, brushing the dirt from her apron, then curtsied before them. Krista got up and copied her actions.

"Good morning, madam," Smyth said.

"Master Smyth," Marilyn replied.

"I'll see you tonight, Madam Marilyn?" he added.

Marilyn frowned, but nodded. "Yes, of course."

He smiled. "Excellent."

The other man exchanged a bow with the girls.

Smyth glared at Krista before the two men continued down the right hall.

"What was that?" Krista asked.

"Nothing," Marilyn replied, swallowing heavily.

Krista wanted to ask again: what exactly did Smyth want with Marilyn? *Maybe it is none of my business. But he makes me uncomfortable, and I just know it can't be good for Marilyn.* She looked up at Marilyn. "But why would you betray your own people?"

Marilyn sighed. "When has my kingdom done justice for me? Or for that matter, what have your people done for you?"

Krista looked away. "I really don't know what my people have done for me."

Marilyn smiled weakly. "There you go—solved your problem. Will you stay here, then? I much appreciate your company."

Krista remained quiet.

"Say yes," Malpherities spoke. "It'd be best if you agree with Paladin, considering your circumstances."

"Yes, I think I'll stay." Krista said with a smile. *It would be nice to stay here with Marilyn, but what about my old life? What about Darkwing?* The thought of never seeing Darkwing again was chilling, possibly more upsetting than the thought of the Weaver.

Malpherities clapped. "Excellent choice. This is your new life. A better one than old life of thievery and gangs."

Marilyn smiled. "Wonderful to hear. I really need the help. It's a large keep and it isn't easy to manage. Besides, it would be nice to have some backup against all these boys!"

Krista laughed, then returned to cleaning the floors. Time passed quickly and they'd gotten most of the floor cleaned when the sun began to descend. Krista thought of Dreadweave Pass, knowing that night was nearing and chances were that she would go back to the nightmarish reality. What would happen next in Dreadweave Pass? Would she get hurt again? What if she screamed in her sleep and woke the humans here like she had the night before?

"Think we're done." Marilyn got to her feet, wringing the rag out into one of the buckets.

Krista dumped her rag in the bucket closest to her and took it over to the maid. Her arms were exhausted by the scrubbing and her knees sore from kneeling on the stone floor all afternoon.

Just then, a set of footsteps came from the right hall. Krista glanced over to see Smyth walking alone down the hall toward them.

Oh, great.

Smyth returned to the entrance hall, his eyes fixated on the floor. He did not acknowledge the girls and examined the green tiles closely, eyeing every corner. "Done?" He brought his hands behind his back and approached Marilyn.

"Yes sir," she replied, stepping forward to keep Krista behind her.

The man nodded, moving so close to Marilyn, he was practically touching her. "You think you did your best cleaning it?"

Marilyn looked to the floor. "I'm sure we did."

Smyth looked at the floor too; a small smudge of dirt could be seen in the filling between two tiles. "What do you call that, then?"

"Sorry, sir. I'll clean it." She spoke quickly while kneeling to the ground.

Smyth grabbed her arm, forcing her back up. The maid grunted.

"Just like that? Fix your mistakes because you couldn't do it right the first time? How would you explain your existence?" he growled as he continued to squeeze her arm.

Krista stepped forward but felt Malpherities's sharp claws on her shoulder.

"This is not our fight."

"Sorry, sir," Marilyn repeated. Her voice was weak and her eyes were wide. This was not the strong, independent girl Krista was used to seeing.

The man swung his other hand at Marilyn, slapping her across the face. "You laze around too much, girl! Do you expect the keep to take care of itself while you sit around on your disgraceful ass?"

Krista glanced around, embarrassed to witness the scolding. No one was around; the halls were empty to the very end and no one could intervene.

"What can I do?" Krista whispered to Malpherities.

"Comfort her when the man leaves. Entering the crossfire would be fatal for both you and her," the ghoul replied.

Smyth ran his hand down her arm to her wrist, rubbing with his fingertips.

Marilyn looked to the ground.

"What have you been doing?" He began to pull her sleeves back.

"No, please! Not without closed doors!" she begged.

Smyth didn't stop and tore her shirtsleeve, exposing her forearm. It was wrapped in bloodstained bandages.

Krista almost gasped at the lines of dried blood running down Marilyn's arm. *What happened to her?*

Smyth's face turned bright red, his eyebrows tightening and nostrils flaring upward. "Wrapping them up? Let it flow free! The tainted blood must drain from your body!" He slapped her face once again and let her arm free. "You dishonour your mother, you half-beast!" Smyth stormed away, stomping loudly through the hall.

Marilyn buried her face into her hands, sobbing where she stood. Her torn sleeve hung open, and the bloody bandages were still visible. Malpherities pointed to her. "There's your cue."

CHAPTER IX

Birds Fly Free

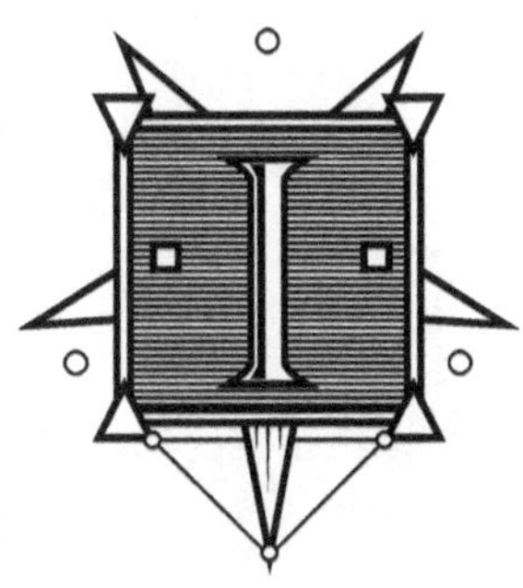

t is not easy to grow from child to adult. Life as a child means a less-conditioned mind, allowing one to see the world from a neutral point of view. The neutral mind is able to accept its surroundings from a blank perspective, like an empty canvas. A child's views are not altered by the events of the past—not influenced by the lives of others or permanently scarred by their own mistakes. This is a benefit when faced with any sort of event. An event is the constant, and the one thing we can change is our reaction to that event—leading to the outcome.

As adults, the way we react to events is often moulded by our state of mind, which is manipulated by our judgment and fears. A child is free of these weights and of the challenges others put on them. They are removed from the invisible chains we hold ourselves down with, whether those chains be doubt, or the thought that we need to achieve new heights of excellence, or the tension we give ourselves set by our friends, family, and the society we live in.

When one is born, they do not carry themselves with all the conscious and subconscious standards that bind us. As we age, we leave behind the beauty of the neutral perspective, the wonder we put into the unknown, the acceptance of what we do not understand. Rather than seeing something new as a discovery that we can learn and grow from, we put titles and names on the discovery before we take the time to learn about it and understand it. We judge a new object and draw assumptions. This predefined set of characteristics builds limitations in our minds about the discovery, preventing our minds from growing.

A youthful mind develops at a much faster rate and can absorb new information like a sponge. This constant stream of knowledge that a child consumes gives them a sense of naivety to the world; new things buzz by over and over. When we grow, if we do not nurture our ability to learn and accept, we become stale and we begin to deny anything new. We focus ourselves on controlling every aspect of our lives, continuously putting more weight on ourselves, all for peace of mind that we are in control. But in moments of clarity, we realize this control is just an illusion.

"I'm sorry I wasn't completely honest with you." Marilyn repeated the phrase several times while she and Krista sat in the shade underneath the Twisted Hermit.

The role reversal of the situation was odd for Krista, who'd always been taken into the arms of someone else. Krista had never expected to be the one comforting another being, yet here she was. Marilyn was now no different than Krista had been in the past: weak, helpless, and in need of affection. Like Krista, Marilyn was just a girl in a world bigger than her, bullied by those who had the power to abuse her weaknesses.

Normally, Krista turned to males like Darkwing or William for comfort and affection to help her cope with the difficulties of the world. But Marilyn was different: she was not opening up to a male—she was opening up to Krista.

"How long has it gone on?" Krista asked. A gust of wind blew some fallen leaves of the old oak tree away from the girls.

Marilyn stared blankly at her own arm. She had taken off the linen bandages that previously covered her many cuts and scars, leaving the old, the scabbed, and the fresh cuts exposed to the sunlight.

"As long as I can remember. Worse as time went on." She ran her fingers down her mangled forearm.

The two sat close to each other under the oak tree, close enough that Krista could pick up the girl's soft scent of sweat and flowers for the first time. *Marilyn's scent. I'm glad I can identify her by it now.* Krista put her hand on Marilyn's knee. "I'm here to listen." *She has no one, like when Darkwing abandoned me for the Blood Hounds. That seems so long ago.*

The maid rolled up her torn sleeve, revealing more scars on the upper half of her arm. She lifted the sleeve high enough to show a wide, jagged scar on her shoulder. Marilyn leaned closer to Krista. "That was the first one."

"But why? Who is Smyth that gives him the right to treat you this way?"

"He's my only living relative. Technically he is my third-generation cousin." Marilyn sniffled and brushed her knotted hair aside, then wiped some tears from her puffy eyes. "Earlier I told you it was a complicated story." She pressed her lips together and shook her head. "I understand why he does it, I suppose. My mother and father weren't meant to be together; it was unnatural and an eternal sin. That's why Smyth calls me a half-beast. My mother was a human—a paladin to be exact. So she was quite old, like Paladin, but did not show her age. My father was a shimen hunter. He brought food for his people from the wilderness."

"Shimen?" Krista squinted.

"They're a race shunned by humans, like your kind I guess—an ancient people that refused to adapt to the changing world dominated by man." Marilyn indicated her tiny waist. "That's where my thin body comes from. The shimen are tall, slim, and agile, with hooves and two coil-shaped horns on their foreheads. They venture through the mountains of Zingalg." She sighed. "Anyways, my father and mother fell in love, and I was born."

"Why was this forbidden? It should be celebrated."

"It's not . . . Well, it is. Paladin has taught me that the shimen's witchcraft practices are a form of necromancy. Paladin made it very clear that you do not turn to mediums of necromancy. They will make you unclean in the eyes of the Lord." Marilyn sighed. "My mother and father caused a clash of two worlds—complete opposites and mortal enemies. I don't know how they met, or why they risked eternal punishment from God. I suppose it was love, but there is no love greater than God's. All I know is my father was the first to die. The shimen found out quickly about his affair and they skinned him alive, forcing my mother to watch while they held her captive. Then the shimen let her go, knowing she would be hunted down by her own people. They were right; she had nowhere to go so she fled to Smyth. She knew her sin of lust was unforgivable, but begged her brother to hide her. Smyth's loyalties are to God and his plan for us, because in the end it is God's love that will set us free, so after I was born he brought her here to the barracks. She was executed here."

"What of you? What happened?"

"I was born at a farmstead not far from here. Smyth told me he left me with the farmer's family for several months before he came back to get me. I don't know how it all went, but Smyth saved me. He told me that if he could assist me in cleansing the tainted shimen blood from my body, I could revive my mother's name—my family's name." She swallowed heavily and her lip trembled before speaking. "But it hurts so much. Every week at the darkest hour of night, he cuts me open in the basement of the barracks and lets the blood flow through the drains and into the river so it can be washed clean by God. He gets angry when I try to mend the wounds because it prevents more shimen blood from leaving my body." The girl continued to break down.

Darkwing always held me when I cried, Krista remembered. She lightly took the maid into her arms and allowed her to lean against her as she sobbed. *It's what Darkwing would have done in a situation like this.*

It was awkward for Krista to take the role of the comforter—to be the adult in the situation. It was obvious that Marilyn was crushed and couldn't solve the problem on her own; she was possibly even worse off than Krista.

The maid continued to cry, tears soaking into Krista's jacket. "I don't know what to do. The pain gets to be too unbearable, but I want to rid myself of the shimen blood and redeem my mother's name."

Malpherities's smoke rose from behind Krista and the ghoul appeared. "I find this most interesting."

Krista looked up and shook her head.

He pointed at Marilyn. "If her mother was a paladin . . . that means the paladin's holy blood runs through her veins. But didn't Paladin tell you that he was the last living one? My question is, does he know about her bloodline and refuses to accept her, or did Smyth lie to him about her origins?"

Krista nodded. *He's right.*

"I never know where he will cut me, either." Marilyn pointed at her arm, her clavicle, her stomach, and her thighs. "He tries different areas of my body to make the shimen leave me, but it never seems to work."

"How do you know when the shimen blood is gone?" Krista asked.

"Smyth says he'll know; that we'll see the difference in my behaviour and appearance. I honestly have lost hope—it's a madman's dream." She lifted her arm and tapped her elbow. The elbow had no skin at the end, only a protruding black bone. It was worn down and covered in scabs, as if someone had dulled it with sandpaper. "As time goes on, the shimen seems more visible in me. I get aggressive when I shouldn't and Smyth and I are forced to hide the physical changes." She pointed to the bandana she had wrapped on her head. "Wondered why you never see me without this? Or why I am always covered from head to toe? It is to hide the shimen. Have you ever seen one?"

Krista shook her head. "No."

Marilyn sat up. "Horrible creatures—and to think I'm one of them."

Malpherities shook his head. "This problem is beyond you. It is none of our concern, really."

Krista ignored the ghoul. "In your heart though, Marilyn, do you believe Smyth is doing what's best for you?"

The maid shrugged. "I don't have a choice. If I let my body continue on its course, the shimen features of my body will continue to grow. Then what would I do? The humans would never accept me then; I'd be killed. But I don't know how much longer I can handle what Smyth does to protect me. We've butchered my body, and I don't think it can take much more." She opened her mouth, revealing a split tongue that was stitched together, along with her jagged, chipped teeth. "Shimen tongues are forked, their teeth sharp. I inherited those attributes . . . and we do our best to hide them. What I wear, the way my hair is fashioned, it's all designed to hide the parts of my body that resemble the shimen. All I want is to be normal; I hate being different. No one wants me for who I am."

"I don't see why Smyth criticizes you on your housekeeping, though. It has nothing to do with you being a shimen."

"I suppose he's still angry at my mother for having me, and she's dead so he only has me to release his hatred on."

"You don't think Paladin would understand your situation?" Krista asked.

Marilyn shook her head. "He's the one who executed my mother."

The words made Krista's stomach sink. *Paladin is colder than I thought.* He was capable of killing one of his own kind in the name of his beliefs, even if it meant leaving him to be the last paladin.

Marilyn looked down the hill where the boys were running in groups, increasing their endurance through the exercise. Paladin strolled alongside the jogging boys.

The maid scowled. "It means nothing to him. I'm sure he doesn't know of my bloodline and wouldn't favour me if he discovered it. When Smyth brought me here, he just asked Paladin to teach me the ways of God."

"You have me, though," Krista smiled softly. "I don't judge you for what you are on the outside. I try to see people for what they are on the inside."

Marilyn nodded and looked to the ground. "Thank you. It is nice to have someone who sees me for what I am. I did not mean for you to see Smyth act that way, or see the scars. It's not like Smyth to treat me that way in public; I suppose he doesn't think very highly of you either."

Krista smirked. "It's okay."

The maid pointed to Paladin. "I suppose you should tell him you accept his offer?"

"I forgot about that." Krista let out a long, drawn-out sigh, "Yeah, I should." *I can't leave Marilyn alone. She is an outcast like me.*

"You'll be glad you did it." Marilyn got to her feet and brushed the dirt from her dress.

"Yeah." Krista got up too. *I just don't know if I am doing what is right. I suppose if I kill Danil and get rid of Mental Damnation, I can leave here and try to find Darkwing again.* With everything happening around Krista, she found it difficult to plan more than a few minutes ahead. She liked it here, but she missed Darkwing terribly—his strong presence and kind smile. Every day seemed to bring another layer of complexity to her life. *Now I would feel guilty to leave Marilyn.*

Marilyn folded her arms. "Well, I've got to dust the weaponry displays on the fourth level in the keep. When you're done with Paladin, come find me."

Krista nodded. "Okay."

Marilyn looked to the ground. "Thank you again. For listening."

"That is what friends do."

The maid extended her arms to Krista, giving her a tight hug. "Thank you. It is nice not being alone."

"Likewise," Krista said, giving the girl one last squeeze then letting her go.

"See you in a while." Marilyn got up and walked away from Krista, slowly returning to the path down to the keep.

"The girl is doomed," Malpherities said.

"It's not fair that these humans judge her so harshly."

"The Kingdom of Zingalg is ruled by man, no other race, and they plan to keep it that way."

"Do you think they view me like a shimen? I mean, not Paladin, but the others."

"Unlikely—their views on the shimen are based on their lifestyle and beliefs. Most of these humans have hardly even heard of vazeleads. Your kind is ancient history."

Krista shrugged and the two began to stroll toward Paladin and his trainees. "I suppose so. I just want to help Marilyn; it isn't right the way she is now. How can someone like Paladin be so cruel?"

Malpherities kept to her side, his fog channeling from her sharp shadow cast by the sun. "Remember what I told you? I said paladins are monsters; they see no wrong in their actions. Why do you think I tell you that Fierel isn't good for our protection?"

"But she was able to kill those puppets in a blink of an eye. I think it's good to have her around."

"Yes, and she almost killed me, too. There's no telling what a paladin will do, especially a rogue paladin like Fierel. As for your friend Marilyn, she chooses how to live her life. If she wanted help, she'd ask you. As far as she is concerned, Smyth is helping her."

"But she seemed so upset."

"It's a sacrifice that she's willing to make."

Krista frowned. "Perhaps she doesn't know it's wrong . . . I can't see the shimen blood leaving her body forever even if they let her blood drain; it just doesn't make sense."

The ghoul shrugged. "Maybe not, but it is not for you to say."

Krista didn't reply since they were too close to Paladin. The boys were still on the dirt training ground, marching in rows of three, making laps around the training field. Paladin followed several paces behind them, letting them take the lead.

She smiled and waved at him. "Hi, Paladin." She found it difficult to make eye contact with the man. *He killed Marilyn's mother.* She just could not see him the same way now.

Paladin turned gradually while she sheepishly approached. He smiled, stopping in his tracks. "Krista. Good to see you again. What brings you to me?"

She glanced behind Paladin to see if she could find William. No luck. "I thought about your offer."

Paladin smiled. "I'm pleased to hear that."

She glanced back at Marilyn who was a speck in the distance, almost at the entrance of the keep. *I wonder how much I can get away with.* Perhaps she could find a way to help Marilyn.

"Don't do anything stupid, just stick with the original deal," Malpherities growled. "You won't be doing her a favour."

"I'll help you . . ." Krista spoke softly. The words felt like she was selling her soul, drilling an empty hole in her core. It was her loyalty to her people she was about to throw away. *But then again, like Marilyn said: what have they ever done for me?* "I'll help you so I can be here, safe with my friends."

Paladin chuckled. "You've been here so shortly and you have friends? I admire how you view the world and the people in it."

"Yes, I do have friends." She counted them on her fingers. "William, Marilyn . . ." Krista stopped, realizing she had no more, but she held her two fingers out at Paladin.

He raised an eyebrow. "It's a great privilege to know you want to share the knowledge I seek. Are you willing to talk now?"

Krista shrugged, "I guess so." *It's best to get it over with.*

Paladin turned around and shouted to the boys, "Keep with your laps! Captain John will be here to assist you."

The boys were halfway around the training field. Some of them looked over at Krista and Paladin. One blond-haired boy poked his head out from the crowd; it was William.

Krista smiled and waved.

Paladin scowled at her, then gestured for her to walk. "After you."

Krista curtsied and walked ahead. Paladin took a few quick steps and they were side by side. She liked that he didn't place his hand on her while they walked like he had done before; he had a strong grip that hurt.

The two remained silent, Krista keeping her head low and Paladin looking forward.

I wonder what he is going to ask me.

"Don't worry, Krista," Malpherities said. "Whatever you tell them is of little importance in the grand scheme of things. Your people, the barracks—they will all begin to seem so small. The important thing you must concern yourself with is Dreadweave Pass. There are bigger things at stake."

"Like what?" she whispered.

"Why do you think Fierel helps you? No one does something without gaining anything from it—not even Paladin helps you for free. Fierel wants something from you."

Paladin brushed his hair back after the first couple of steps up the staircase to the keep. "I hope you don't feel you are betraying your people."

Krista shook her head. "I don't know. It's a complicated situation. I don't think I even fully understand it."

"Fair enough," said Paladin as he opened the door for Krista.

Inside the keep, Paladin led the way. He took her straight through the main hall.

"The floors look good; you and Marilyn did an excellent job," Paladin commented, examining the tiles as he walked into the centre hall.

"Thanks," Krista said, and folded her arms as they walked. *Not according to Smyth.*

"Another lesson for survival: don't let your emotions guide you." Malpherities pointed to Paladin. "Concentrate on where you are right now, and be observant."

"Paladin is leading me where we can talk about my people," she whispered.

"Are you sure?"

"Yes, why wouldn't I be?"

"I am simply asking. My point is, never trust the words of someone. You can never be too certain."

Krista felt her muscles tighten. Malpherities's words made her worried. *I thought the world was an easier place than it's turning out to be.*

They passed a soldier walking the other way wearing armour and a red kilt. Paladin placed his hand on the man's shoulder. "Find Captain John and tell him to take over the training for the afternoon," he instructed.

"Yes sir," said the man, making a slight bow and marching away.

Paladin continued down the hall and up the staircase Krista used to get to the second level. This time, Paladin did not stop there; he kept moving up the sets of stairs, turning left to the next set at every level they reached.

Krista counted each new floor they went up. *Third floor . . . fourth floor.* With each level they passed, the interior design changed. The tiles on the higher levels had a polished finish, the lining was covered in gold, and the walls were made of marble. Paintings of men and women wearing crowns and draped in purple and red cloth hung from the walls on the fifth floor. The sixth floor had full sets of silver armour and a red carpet down the centre of the black-and-white-tiled floor.

Paladin stopped there, even though the staircase continued to go upward.

I wonder how many levels are in this keep.

"This is where we keep our most valued artifacts—armour and

weapons belonging to the greatest warriors in the known kingdoms. Scrolls and amulets abused for the demonic power they hold. Skeletons belonging to some of the most dangerous monsters the Kingdom of Zingalg has ever conquered."

Paladin marched down the centre of the red carpet, past two silver armour suits. They were outlined in gold and had engraved designs of two lions with crowns, and a cross in the centre of the breastplates. Outlines of trumpets were engraved in the shoulder pieces. They were both completed with a red cape, draping from a golden emblem of a lion's face on the right shoulder.

Krista stared in wonder around her, noting especially a couple of cabinets with necklaces and black leather books inside.

"You'd better keep up." Malpherities gestured to Paladin, who was already halfway down the long hall.

Krista rushed, careful not to slip on the rug. She ran past a number of other artifacts, skulls, swords, and armour, but didn't have time to pause.

Paladin stopped by a closed black door to his right. He pulled a key out from his belt and inserted it into the keyhole. After a twist of the key, Paladin pushed the door open to an orange-and-blue-tinted room. The coloured lighting came from the stained-glass windows that were lined up along the outward-facing wall. The pictures in the stained-glass were similar to those Krista saw in the church.

That dying man, pinned up again.

"This here is my private chamber. I let few people in here—Captain John and a couple others." He stepped into the room, and Krista followed.

Krista heard a sudden yelp behind her. She spun around to see Malpherities standing at the doorway.

"What's wrong?" she whispered, glancing back to see if Paladin was watching. No—he kept walking into the chamber.

The ghoul moved his hand past the doorframe and it ignited in flame. He hissed and quickly retracted his hand, shaking it to stop the fire. "How is this holy ground?"

"You can't come here?"

"No, this chamber is like the church. Paladin must have blessed this room. I can't go beyond here."

"But I need you. I might say too much."

Malpherities clenched his teeth. "Damn paladins! I truly can't pass, so you must handle this on your own. Just don't let him trick you; paladins are skillful in converting mortals to their faith by means of words and false hope."

"Krista?" Paladin's voice echoed through the chamber.

Krista nodded at Malpherities. "Coming!" She waved discreetly to the ghoul before following Paladin. "Sorry," she added, looking around at the room. It was large, and the ceiling was arched, much like the church. The walls were made of jagged charcoal-coloured rocks with a couple of black torches mounted on the windowed wall, currently extinguished. The floor was of a light-grey stone, tiled in large, square pieces—about Krista's length if she were to lay down on them.

Krista took off her scarf and brought her hood down while eyeing a stone altar at the far end of the room. It had a gold bowl resting on it, and a wooden cross was mounted on the wall behind it. This cross did not have an image of the crucified man on it. "It's a pretty room."

Paladin glanced around and nodded. "Thank you. Take a seat." He waved his arm at a deep red pillow lying by the altar.

She walked past Paladin with her hands cupped together and noticed a pair of glass cabinets to the left of the window. One held a gleaming suit of golden armour and inside the second were two claymores. She did a double-take—one had a curved blade. The weapon ended with a hook and the guard was carved into the shape of flames.

I know that sword . . . in Dreadweave Pass. Fierel had it. How is it here?

Krista stepped onto the pillow and sat cross-legged, confused. She shook her head and gazed around the room some more. Now she could see a row of crooked bookshelves filled with old torn paper and stacks of books at the opposite end of the room. Half-used candles rested on a splintered table with three short stools surrounding it. To the right of the altar was a glass frame mounted on the wall. Behind the glass was a silky deep-blue tabard with an ornate moon-shaped symbol in the centre. Below it was a brown paper scroll with swirled lines varying in weight along with outlined dots and straight lines.

"That's a pretty moon," Krista said.

Paladin bowed his head. "The moon crest of Karazickle, the last of the great Drac Lords. Below that is the shape-shifting formula he used to fool us into thinking he was Saule, the founder of the Paladins of Zeal."

"Why do you keep them?"

"As a reminder that he still roams the world. I will find him." Paladin sighed and sat on the stone floor facing her, also cross-legged.

"Reminders are good. I hope you do find him."

"Krista, I wish to learn why he banished your people to the underworld before I slay him. But sadly, there hasn't been any trace of him for quite some time now."

"I guess he is good at hiding."

"Too good."

Krista looked back at the curved claymore and swallowed heavily. *Mental Damnation must be messing with my head.* She turned back to face Paladin, putting the sword out of her mind again. "How come you made me work with Madam Marilyn?" Krista asked. Marilyn already told her why she had to work, but Krista wanted to hear it from Paladin himself.

Paladin nodded. "I know I didn't tell you that you'd have to do some labour. But I couldn't simply let you live here without earning it, could I?"

"I thought that's what our deal was for."

"The deal was to offer you protection from the king, not for earning your room and board."

Krista nodded.

"Krista, I brought you here so you can feel safe. This room is where I meditate and spend my evenings focusing on connecting with our Father. When we first met, Krista, you told me about the ritual you were a part of."

"Yes."

"I have mentioned to you that I want to keep our relationship honest. I want you to know that you have nothing to fear from me."

Except that you'll kill anyone, even your own people.

"Now, I will ensure your safety if you are honest with me. Let me know if your people are a possible threat to the Kingdom of Zingalg."

"Why would we be?"

"You took part in a ritual of blood." He rubbed his chin. "After I discovered you and brought you back to the High Barracks, I went back to the place I found you. There, I was able to study the aftermath of the ritual. It seems this ritual broke the holy shackles on your people to the underworld, Krista. Not just anyone can break those shackles; they are blessed by the Heavenly Kingdoms and exceptionally dark arts are needed to destroy them. I will be honest with you—knowing this puts me ill at ease about the safety of Zingalg. We had not heard of the vazeleads in two hundred years and I know you aren't capable of performing that ritual since you were the victim of it. I can't imagine who would be capable of pulling off a dark art of this level."

Danil, Krista thought while fiddling with the strands that ran along the stitching of the pillow. "What did you want to know?"

"I want to know more about your people. You've spoken about the mutations in the underworld that caused the Corrupt—what about those who are not the Corrupt?"

"They're fine." Krista rubbed her neck. *What do I tell him?* "They're like me—just trying to survive. My people built a city, so we aren't in small tribes anymore."

"All the vazeleads who were scattered throughout the world are one nation now?"

"Sort of. But we're in a big struggle among ourselves. We have a lot of gangs and rebels that reject what our leaders offered us."

"What have they offered you?"

"They unified our people. They're the Five Guardians. They helped us build our great city and formed the Renascence Guard. The Five Guardians helped us make a civilization and separated us from the Corrupt. But some groups of vazeleads disagreed with the Five Guardians and believed that they held a tyranny over the vazelead people."

"Is it true?"

"That they're a tyranny? No, I don't think so. I think they made us strong."

"So these Five Guardians: what do they have planned for the vazeleads?"

"They were trying to find a way out of the underworld."

"Were?"

"They would go out searching the underworld for a way to the surface, but two of them, guardian Cae and guardian Ast'Bala, found something else. I didn't really know what it was at the time but it made them go insane." Krista squinted. "I think it was Mental Damnation. It mutated Ast'Bala. He had bat wings"—Krista imitated wings with her arms—"and he gouged his eyes out, but it was like he could still see. Ast'Bala killed Cae, then he returned to our city and freed all the criminals from the citadel prison."

"Go on."

Krista looked to the ground. *This wasn't that long ago, either, but it seems like a distant memory.* "Ast'Bala saw me and said I had the innocence of a child." Krista rubbed her arms. "He picked me up by my tail and it was like he could see right into my thoughts and feelings. He burned the mark on my neck with his hand, and I fainted. Then the rest of the guardians tried to stop Ast'Bala, but he infected Danil—I think with Mental Damnation—and it made him go insane and chase me. Then guardian Zeveal battled Ast'Bala and they disappeared into the sky. But guardian Demontochai stopped Danil from getting me—at first."

"At first?"

"Yes. Danil was the one who cut my arm and killed my friend Saulaph."

"So Danil performed the necromantic ritual of blood," Paladin said, and clenched his fists.

"Yes."

"What was the outcome of the battle between Ast'Bala and Zeveal?"

"I don't know."

"Danil? Is he chasing you still?"

"I don't know. I don't think so—not after he gave me the mark on my palm. I don't know where he is."

"My guess is the ritual broke him free, too. I found a second set of footprints when I visited the ritual site."

Krista swallowed heavily. "But he doesn't need me now." *I need him, though, if he is the key to curing me from Mental Damnation.*

"When did all this happen?"

"A couple of days before I came here."

"So the Renascence Guard—they are the military of the vazeleads?"

"Yes. They retain order among our people, but they were pretty tied up with the escaped prisoners. Now that the Five Guardians have fallen apart, I think they're trying to maintain order in the city."

"Understandable. They have a lot to clean up." Paladin straightened himself. "How many Renascence Guards do you see in the city?"

"I don't know, they were everywhere . . . always monitoring our behavior, making sure we fell in line with the rules the Five Guardians placed."

"And what about you?"

"Me?"

"Yes, I don't know much about you as a person. I know you were in a cult for shelter—so you did not have a home?"

"No, I was street scum. No one wanted me—humans killed my family in the banishment to the underworld. But overall, my people are very ruthless compared humans. Beatings, thievery, and rape are a part of daily life. All of it has happened to me and I've tried to defend myself, but vazelead males are much stronger than our females. Thankfully, I wasn't always alone." Krista began to play with her scalp-feathers, wrapping her index finger around the longer ones. "I had a friend who protected me."

"What was your friend's name?"

"Darkwing," Krista's lips tightened. Saying his name made her heart heavy and a tear ran down her face. "I miss him," Her heart felt like it ignited with fire after saying the words. He was all she knew for so many years. *It feels like I haven't been able to think about him since being at the High Barracks, but talking about him makes me realize how much I miss him.*

"Where is he, Krista?"

"He's still in the underworld," Krista mumbled through her hands. She raised her head, "I was always a burden to him. He's so strong and kind. He did so much to protect me. That is why I joined the cult with him—it was his idea so we could hide from Danil."

"Was he all you had?"

"Yes," Krista sobbed, putting her head into her hands. "He is all I have ever had, and I really miss him."

She heard Paladin get up. "All right. Thank you for your time, Krista."

"Sorry?" She looked up at Paladin, tears running down her cheeks. *I never thought he would say that. I can talk about my people, but about me and my feelings are just too much right now.*

"You've done what I have asked of you."

"I'm free to stay here now?" Krista wiped the tears from her face.

Paladin smiled. "Yes, you may. If I have more questions, I will summon you again. You have a lot on your mind and are still taking in all that is going on around you."

Krista got to her feet and sniffled, "Thank you. Can I leave?"

"One thing, though."

"Yes?"

"You wouldn't mind if I shared your history with Dr. Alsroc, would you?"

Krista scratched her head. "Why does he need to know?"

"Do you honestly think he shouldn't? You've had a life of horror, yet you speak of it like it is ordinary. No child should have gone through what you have endured. Not to mention your case with Mental Damnation."

Krista nodded. "But they're my people, and it's the way we live. We see nothing wrong with what we do. We express ourselves physically more often than we do with words."

Paladin shook his head. "It makes me sick."

Krista looked to the ground, holding her hands. *Humans seem so stuck on their words.*

"It'd be best for Alsroc to understand your past—to help him cure your illness."

"Okay."

Paladin nodded, satisfied. "You may leave now."

She bowed slightly then slowly walked back to the open door. *Darkwing* . . . Krista felt herself conflicted; she was here at the barracks with new friends, but she missed her past life. The underworld seemed far easier: she looked for food, and was comforted by Darkwing. *Now I have two new worlds to worry about, and I am an outcast in both.* Krista peeked out into the hall where Malpherities waited.

"Did you hear any of it?" she asked.

The ghoul shook his head. "I cannot hear very far into holy grounds."

Krista and Malpherities walked back to the staircase leading to the main level.

"What did he tell you? What did he do to you?" the ghoul asked, eyeing her head to toe. "Did he baptize you?"

"What? No, nothing. He just asked questions of my past and my people. A lot of them were boring questions and I didn't know all the answers. I was a street scum among my people. I don't know about their politics or military stuff."

The two walked in silence for a while.

"Think we should find Marilyn?" Krista asked the ghoul. "I want to check in on William first, though—I know his training ends soon."

"I've told you my stance on the boy. He's a waste of time."

"I won't be long," Krista said with a smile. *Truthfully, I could use his comfort after talking about Darkwing.*

The afternoon had long passed and the sun was ready to set. The sound of splintering wood echoed in the sky from the hands of aggressive boys swinging wooden blades at one another. Captain John took the place of Paladin, watching the trainees fight in pairs, lashing at each other as if it were a fight to the death. He shouted at the boys who slacked in their fighting.

"Strike harder! Upon the battlefield, your opponent will not show mercy! Slack now and you might as well accept that you'll add to your opponent's death tally in the line of battle."

Krista watched from the distance as she walked. Malpherities had disappeared, not wanting to partake in her search for William. It was obvious that Malpherities did not want her to waste time with the boy. *Mal and I have been through it over and over, but sometimes I just need a break.* Krista was supposed to find Marilyn and help continue cleaning after meeting with Paladin, but a small break would not hurt.

Krista walked up beside Captain John. "Hi."

Her appearance caused him to jump and he smiled at her. "Hello."

"I'm Krista."

"I know."

She bit her lip. "I didn't think we were properly introduced, even though we know each other's names."

The man nodded at her and brought his attention back to the boys.

Krista moved past the captain and leaned against the fence, watching the boys fight. William was close to the fence, giving her an upfront view of him fighting. She could see every drop of sweat on his lean, muscular arms and the broad shape of his upper torso under the linen tunic he wore.

Her eyes widened when she noticed that he was fighting a much larger boy who swung his wooden training sword toward William with a single hand at lightning speed.

Black smoke channeled from up the shadows cast by the fence and Malpherities rested alongside the posts.

"The sun is setting," Malpherities said as he stared up at the sky. "Are you ready to rest? There are things we must do in Dreadweave Pass."

"I want to find Marilyn after this."

"You've abandoned her already for this boy. Why do you want to find her after? She'll probably be done cleaning."

"I'd like to watch over her."

"I guarantee you that we can stalk her another night, but today you have problems of your own. Don't worry about her."

Krista nodded. "I suppose I did choose to see William rather than Marilyn, and she has a really big problem."

"A problem you cannot manage now. Be patient; the girl is not going anywhere."

"How do you know?"

"If she has been letting Smyth do this to her for this long, I think she will be okay for one more night."

Malpherities was right: Marilyn's situation was a large and complicated issue. And Krista was finally accepted into the barracks. *That's one of my own problems off my list. Now I have to start on Dreadweave Pass. It's up to me to solve my problems.*

William dodged a downward strike from the brawny boy. He attempted to kick dirt in his opponent's eyes. The dirt did not raise high enough, and his opponent swiftly brought the sword up into William's chest, causing him to fall back and land on his rear.

"Slain!" Captain John shouted. "Well done, Lewin. The rest of the day is yours."

The large boy bowed to the captain and marched from the training ground, giving William a gleeful grin. William remained sitting and shook his head.

"Work harder next time, William." Captain John walked alongside the fence, patrolling the perimeter of the training field.

Krista glanced around the training field to see the boys who had finished their battles beginning to leave. She leaped over the fence and sat beside William.

"That was an intense fight," she said.

William looked up at her and smiled. "I made a mistake," he sighed. "I always make mistakes—just once I'd like to get it right."

Krista scooted closer to him and took his hand. "You'll win."

He shook his head. "I fail so often. If I keep this up, they'll remove me from the barracks."

"I thought they were going to train you to be the best."

"They're still in the process of elimination. Only two more rejections, then the squad will go into more difficult training and field experience."

"When are they going to remove another?"

He shrugged. "I don't know."

"Pathetic boy, isn't he?" Malpherities let out a deep chuckle. "I assure you that Cursman has taught you more about fighting in a few hours than what these boys have learned in all their months of training. They don't pay attention. You understand the survival need of training, and these boys have never killed anyone."

Krista patted William's hand. "Don't give up," she said and looked up at the sun. "Let's get you out of the heat; it's melting your mind." She helped him to his feet.

The two walked away from the dirt path and up toward the Twisted Hermit, underneath the cool shade. Krista noticed William grunt a few times as they walked; he had cuts and bruises on his arms from fighting.

Krista sniffed the boy's strong scent again, picking up on the sweat that emphasized his odour. It was still a desirable smell.

"Where do you want to go?" Krista asked.

"I need to rinse off. I'm covered in dirt."

Krista almost giggled but resisted the urge.

William pointed north. "We'll go by the river; there's a closed-off area that will give us shade from the sun."

They walked side by side down the hill toward the bridge he had taken her to. She helped support William as they walked—he was drained from the day of training and was sluggish in his movements. It was hard to resist smelling him; she brought herself close to him when he wasn't looking to catch a stronger scent, strong enough that it had a sharp sting. *How can someone smell so good?*

William led Krista past the bridge and up north, closer to the large brick wall surrounding the barracks. The river dipped inward, creating a ditch that was sprinkled with long green plants with brown fuzzy tips around the edges of the stream. Krista had not seen the plants in many years—not since she was a child. The water extended beyond the brick wall through a channel with metal bars, allowing the river to flow through. The sun had disappeared from the skies and made the area dark and secluded.

"Do you ever get a break from training?" Krista asked, sitting by the water.

William took off his sandals and rolled up his trousers. "Yeah, usually we get one day a week." He took off his tunic, exposing his bare chest in the dim lighting. He pointed behind Krista. "You should look away," he said, blushing.

She smiled and turned away. "I have no doubt you'll make it into the squad; you're strong."

Water splashed behind her. "I have to focus, though," he replied. "I don't see opportunities in a fight that the other boys see."

I wonder if he's wearing anything. She smiled, thinking of the boy naked. She had never seen a human with no clothing—not even without a shirt. It was common for her people to wear little clothing— it was a part of their tradition—but the humans rarely seemed to undress themselves and they were so pale and hairy compared to her people.

Just a peek.

It was too hard to resist. She glanced behind her shoulder, seeing the boy's white-skinned form turned away from her, wiping the smudges from his face.

Krista quickly looked away and giggled, muffling her laughter by closing her mouth. "You missed a spot, near your butt."

The sound of splashing water was heard. "I said no peeking!" William shouted.

Krista laughed. "I don't remember you saying that."

Silence.

"Honestly, it was just a joke."

Silence.

"Don't be mad." Krista turned around to see that William was right behind her. She screamed while he grabbed hold of her, pulling her into the water.

"William!" She fell into the cool river with the boy, landing in the shallow water.

The two laughed. Genuine laughter—something she hadn't done in a long time.

Krista and William panted as they sat up, William above her. Water dropped from the boy's body onto her face. Her arms were wrapped around his back, feeling the stern muscles under his skin. The two stared at each other. Krista looked into his bright blue eyes, and the stare he gave made her stomach tingle. The sensation of touching his skin was fulfilling.

Malpherities hovered over William's shoulder. "Let go of your toy and let's get to your room—the sun is set. Sleep is what you need."

Krista ignored the ghoul; she just stared into William's eyes. She tilted her head and gradually moved closer to him, lips opening.

"Put your primitive feelings aside!" The ghoul flicked her hand from William's back and her arm fell into the water, splashing both Krista and William.

"Oops," Krista muttered. *We almost kissed.*

The boy shook his head and rolled from Krista, reaching for his clothes on the shore.

Using her elbows, Krista supported herself upward, watching him as he dressed. "That's not what I was expecting."

William smiled as he put on his tunic. "Now you'll think twice next time you try to sneak a peek."

I want to be close to him again—his soft skin felt so . . . good. It was a strange urge that coursed through her veins, tingling throughout her body—a similar sensation to when she'd smelled him. *I really can't get enough of him and I don't know why.* It reminded her about her fixation with guardian Cae before all the chaos took place. She had felt strong feelings for the guardian, but nothing like this.

William brushed his hair aside. "You know, next time I might not be so forgiving," he winked at her.

Krista giggled. "That's not much of a threat."

He shrugged. "Never said it was." William helped Krista to her feet.

Krista extended her arms and let the water drip from her soaked clothing. "Look at this!"

William smirked.

The two began their walk back to the keep, Krista's drenched clothes weighing down her every step. Even though it was cold, the dampness was refreshing.

The two walked close to each other, taking their time to the road leading back to the keep. Krista smiled the whole way, keeping her head low.

Malpherities folded his arms. "You're falling for this boy."

Falling for him? Mal might be right.

The two entered the keep from the side entrance near the stables.

"That was nice," William said when they approached the stairway leading to the second level.

Krista nodded. "I think we both needed to relax. I honestly lost track of time."

"Me too," he said and glanced at the hallway. "I'm down this way—but we'll have to do that again."

"Marilyn warned you he was trouble," Malpherities commented.

Krista nodded. "We will."

They stood in silence, both knowing they had to leave, but not wanting to.

"Guess we should go. Good night." William waved and began to walk away.

Krista felt her heart race. "Wait." She snatched his hand, pulling him toward her, ready to kiss him.

Their lips were about to meet when a booming voice echoed in the hall. "Krista!"

The sound startled both of them and they pushed each other away.

A shiver ran down Krista's spine. *That's Paladin.* She spun around, seeing Paladin standing on the first set of stairs. "Paladin!" she exclaimed.

"What did I tell you?" he shouted, stomping down the stairs. "I told you to stay away from the boys! William is on the edge of being expelled from my barracks and I have you to blame for it!"

She shook her head. "No, sir. I'm sorry!"

"It's not her!" William defended.

"Hush!" He pointed at William. "Get some rest and prepare for double exercises tomorrow. You have no place with Krista," Paladin ordered, snatching Krista's arm.

William and Krista exchanged glances before the boy turned away and walked alone down the hall with his hands in his pockets. It happened so quickly and Krista was unsure what to do.

"You're one of two girls close to his age. These boys are being taught to place their desires aside and become disciplined warriors of our kingdom. I was already greatly disappointed with the boys who were brought to me to train and you're only making it worse!" His strong grip was causing Krista's arm to go numb.

She tried to jerk free but his hold was too strong. "I'm sorry," she whimpered.

"Just because I gave you freedom doesn't mean you can go soften up my soldiers and fill their minds with useless feelings."

"I'm sorry; he's just so nice to me."

Paladin looked down at her drenched clothing and let her arm go. "What were you two doing?"

Krista wanted to cry from fear. *But I can't.* If she wanted to survive in Dreadweave Pass, she would have to be strong. She had to take a stand. "It was nothing," she exhaled heavily.

"Explain yourself!" he shouted, his voice echoing.

"Nothing happened, honestly! William lost his fight and I wanted to cheer him up. He went to clean himself off in the river—I peeked and giggled. He threw me in the water—we just were playing," she said. "I wanted it to be more but William didn't, and nothing happened." She slouched over and her eyes began to water up. Her heart raced and her voice trembled. "Nothing happened." *Stay strong.*

Paladin let out a long sigh.

She sputtered and sniffled once, stopping herself from crying. *The night was ending so magically—how could it change so fast?*

Paladin gently placed his hand on her shoulder. "Let's just put this behind us. You know now that William cannot have such thoughts clouding his mind."

Krista said nothing. *I make the worst choices.*

"I wanted to find you before you went to bed. Dr. Alsroc thinks it'd be best to strap your arms to the bedframe so you don't hurt yourself again."

She nodded. "It scared me—it reminded me of the ritual."

Paladin patted her back, making her move ahead of him up the stairs.

When they reached her room, she glanced outside the window, seeing the stars in the dark blue sky. The view of the night reminded her of the darkness of Dreadweave Pass when she first crossed realms. Krista shuddered involuntarily; she knew it was to come again soon, in the depths of the night.

CHAPTER X

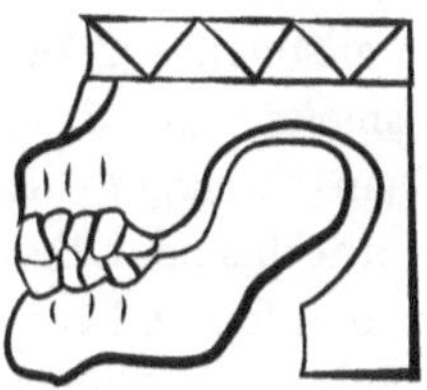

Hunters

arsh winds blew drastically lifting the red sand off the dunes and into the air, making it difficult to see further than a dozen footsteps ahead. The pitch-black sky made light scarce; only lava pools projected their dim orange light over the scenery. The nearest source was the massive lava pit at the base of a large mountain known as Magma Falls.

The waterfall funnelling into the lava pit was the only water source in the underworld. This made it dangerous with robbers, the Corrupt, or the various underworld beasts such as desert crawlers.

This is the last time we return to the city, Darkwing thought, who held out his forearm to deflect some of the wind. He was tired of the constant back and forth between the City of Renascence and Magma Falls. Never had he travelled as much until the recent downfall of the Five Guardians. What other choice did he have, though? He had to persist onward if he wanted to see Krista again.

I'll find you.

His travel with Draegust took an estimated day and a half of travel, as they had predicted. Making this hike numerous times before, Darkwing had a pretty good feel for how much time it would take. Besides, once the two reached the outskirts of the City of Renascence, it was clear that night was upon them. There were few lights visible in the districts, meaning most vazeleads had taken rest. Most of the fires that the rioting prisoners sparked only days ago had been extinguished, but heavy smoke lingered. The Lower District still had lots of activity from civilians moving in after the destruction of the Commoner's District. Even at this hour, they desperately tried to find new housing and restore their former lives.

Darkwing's legs felt numb, but he didn't see the need to mention that he wanted a break. It was pointless because they were far better off travelling. Any moment of rest meant Krista was further away. Besides, Draegust was in the lead now. If Draegust kept walking, Darkwing would walk. *No breaks. I've gotta keep going.*

"No fights—no screams," Draegust said as they walked down the centre of the Great Road leading into the Lower District. He placed his hand on the hilt of his blade. "Just the silence of the night."

"The Renascence Guard must be finally gaining order," Darkwing said, scanning the various side streets. They were littered with rubble, tents, and vazeleads taking comfort near fires. More vazeleads could be seen inside through the broken windows of the clawed buildings. He was not used to seeing the Lower District have so many people. Normally the rubbish buildings were abandoned and left to be used by the gangs.

I suppose the gangs aren't very relevant anymore either, Darkwing thought, recalling how Demontochai annihilated the Blood Hounds.

Draegust nodded up the road, leading to the distant black gates that divided the Commoner's District and the Lower District. "Keep your eyes open for patrols; we'll ambush them."

"In the open?"

"Play along when the time comes," Draegust whispered. "We'll trick them."

Darkwing kept his eyes wide open, glancing down every alley and road they came across. He felt his heart rate increase with each step they took. Normally Darkwing was the one being hunted by the Renascence Guard, not being the hunter.

His eyes were caught by the worn houses, the boxes that scattered the side streets, and the civilians that built shelter from scraps, clogging the roads of the Lower District. It reminded him of the times he spent with Krista, running for shelter when gang wars took place in these streets. He always wanted to offer her a better life—let her live in the High District, or even the Commoner's District would do. However, it was impossible for them to find fair work and they had always resorted to thievery.

"We'd best find the Renascence Guard in the Lower District," Draegust said while they approached the gate to the Commoner's District where two guards stood. "Too many witnesses otherwise."

"Right." Darkwing put his hand on his dagger, ready for a fight.

The two took a turn down a street and casually walked side by side, carefully watching every house they came across. The path was long, crooked, and narrow, which made each crossroad they passed more exhilarating at the thought of crossing paths with the Renascence Guard. It was odd that they hadn't found any patrols yet; the night was when crime was highest and the patrols were constantly on their feet to capture vermin.

Footsteps and clanging armour echoed from the next crossroad ahead. Draegust pulled Darkwing aside.

"The Renascence Guard," Draegust whispered as he pulled out his knife. "Cut yourself," he instructed with a grunt, slashing his own arm.

"What? Why?" Darkwing exclaimed.

Draegust growled and slashed Darkwing's forearm, cutting him lightly.

Darkwing hissed and examined his cut.

"Come," Draegust said while tucking in his blade.

He led Darkwing toward the crossroad while limping out into the centre road where two Renascence Guards with spears marched.

Darkwing mimicked the hobbling behavior and covered his forearm. *So this is how we will ambush them.*

"They wounded us! Help!" Draegust whined as he wobbled toward the guards.

The guards backed up slightly. One extended his spear. "State your name!" his raspy voice boomed.

Draegust fell to the street and groaned. "Ashen. Ashen Whisperton," he groaned.

"Saulaph," Darkwing said quickly. *Not exactly original.* He couldn't think of a name on his own and the albino vazelead from the Eyes of Eternal Life came to mind.

The guards lowered their spears and pointed at Darkwing. "Last name."

"We're in pain!" Draegust roared, lifting his gashed arm. "They assaulted us—the Savage Claws!"

The guards drew their spears without hesitation and pressed their backs to each other. "Where?" the raspy one demanded.

"We're far from their territory," the older one said.

Draegust waved at Darkwing to help him up. Darkwing assisted him and swung his arm over his shoulder.

"We need medical attention—they got me in the ribs too," Draegust grunted. "I think they're gone; we ran and ran—I don't know where we are or where they were. We come from the Commoner's District and are not familiar with the Lower District. We're blacksmiths."

The guards lowered their spears again. "We'll take you to the gates of the Commoner's District, and the guards there will deal with you."

The two guards moved past Darkwing and Draegust in uniform motion, taking a left turn down where Draegust and Darkwing came from.

Draegust broke free of Darkwing and stood upright with a wicked grin, too wide for his face.

He gets way too much enjoyment out of this.

Darkwing crept low and kept his eyes on the guards, who kept their gaze forward.

Draegust slipped his dagger from under his belt and held it tightly, creeping up on one of the guards. He kept a steady low posture, tiptoeing up on the two guards. His eyes locked on their armpits, a weak point in their armour. Draegust moved closer and closer to them, close enough that he had to step back to dodge one guard's swaying tail.

"What were you two doing out here at this time of night, anyway?" The raspy guard glanced behind his shoulder to see Draegust creeping up. "Look out!" he shouted.

Draegust leaped onto the older guard's back before he had a chance to turn. The knife plunged into the guard's side and deep into his lung.

The guard coughed and tried to shake Draegust off. Draegust pulled the dagger out and used his spare hand to pull the guard's head back. This time he stabbed the neck. Blood splattered out of the new wound like a fountain, spraying Draegust and the other guard.

The guard with the raspy voice stepped back and prepared to spear Draegust.

Darkwing pulled out his dagger and ran toward the second guard. He felt the pounding of his heart match the rhythm of his steps. After three strides, he leaped into the air, ending with a collision with the guard, the two crashing into the wall and sliding down onto the road.

"Help!" The second guard grunted as Darkwing landed on top of him.

Darkwing plunged his dagger down to the guard's helmet, putting his full weight behind the swing. The guard caught Darkwing's wrist, arms shaking intensely from the pressure.

Darkwing knew the stupidity of his attack: there was no tactical approach to his choice, but he had to buy Draegust time.

Draegust pushed the old guard to the wall; gurgling his own blood, he stumbled to the ground.

The former gang leader casually walked over to Darkwing with a smile. "Nice work." He leaned down with his dagger, pointing it toward the guard's face.

The guard ignored the second dagger and continued to focus on Darkwing's, which was perched directly over the helmet's eye slits. He was stronger and larger than Darkwing, and gradually he began to gain the upper hand in the struggle.

Draegust hissed and shoved the dagger into the guard's face, the knife fitting between the slits of the helm and piercing his eye.

The guard roared in pain while the fire around his eye flickered several times then extinguished. The shock caused him to lose his strength and Darkwing slammed the dagger down. The blade hit bone with a thud. Black blood oozed from the two wounds, seeping onto the sandy road.

Draegust laughed and pulled out his dagger. "Nicely done, kid."

Darkwing smirked at him. "Thanks."

Draegust pointed at the last guard killed. "Take that one. I've got the second."

Darkwing glanced at the body. Now he had to strip the corpse of the vazelead he killed. It seemed so savage—something he strived to not be. The constant anger he felt within himself was a struggle already, and now he was embracing the barbaric behavior.

It sure did feel good to kill again, though. He missed the satisfaction. Whenever Krista was not around, he could feel the urges, the desire to end another's life.

He shook his head. "Okay, let's get going." He got to his knees and began to unbuckle the armour from the corpse. He took each piece of armour one by one until the dead guard was left in his trousers and black shirt.

The two didn't waste any time and were dressed in their new gear within minutes. There had to be well over a dozen pieces of armour for them to put on, each with its own straps and buckles to keep the metal plates together.

They wore a layer of chainmail underneath the thick plating for extra support.

The clothing was weighty and awkward at first for Darkwing, but he quickly adapted to the change in mass. Strapping the dark plating onto his legs was strange. He had never worn a suit of armour before, but he was a quick learner and it didn't take him long to understand how it pieced together.

Finishing the suit, Darkwing buckled the deep-purple kilt around his waist.

Draegust looked down at his own kilt, then extended his arms. "Not bad, eh?"

"You would have fooled me." Darkwing took a stretch, feeling the extra weight pull on his arms. "It'll take a bit of getting used to."

Draegust leaned down and picked up one of the spears. "Yeah, it has been a while since I've worn a full suit of armour."

Darkwing grabbed the second spear. "First time for me."

"You'll get used to it. Your movements are delayed, so you gotta plan your actions a little more carefully." Draegust nodded to the road. "Come on, let's get this show on the road."

Darkwing took a sniff of air; the musty scent of the previous guard was still strong inside the armour.

I'll get used to it.

Darkwing marched alongside Draegust, the armour clanging with each step they took. The heavy weight and the limitations in movement forced them to almost waddle.

"Think we actually look as ridiculous as I feel?" Darkwing asked.

Draegust looked over to Darkwing. "Nah, it's all in your head. You're experiencing what it is like on the Renascence Guard side."

Darkwing held his spear tight while they walked. He was nervous. They had just killed two guards and taken their armour. From outside, they looked like every other Renascence Guard, which made a perfect disguise. *But how do I act like one of them? How do they socialize with one another?*

The two made it back to the Great Road and turned toward the Commoner's District.

Darkwing fixed his posture; the shoulder plates on the suit were weighing him down and he felt himself slouching constantly. He considered taking off the layer of chainmail; he knew he'd be far more flexible if he didn't have to wear it.

But I wouldn't look quite as beefy like the rest of the guards. I can't afford to stand out.

The two approached the closed gate where two guards watched on both ends of the frame. Darkwing felt his heart continue to pound. *What if they heard the other guard cry for help?*

Draegust pointed at the closed gate as they approached. "We need this open."

The gate guard bowed his head and then waved his hand up at the guard above in the tower. He nodded back and began to pull on the lever to the gate. After a couple of creaks, the gate began to push open with a loud crack.

Draegust and Darkwing marched toward the opening gate.

While Darkwing passed the gate guards, he examined their armour. Darkwing rarely inspected the Renascence Guard; to him, they were all the same. However, now that he was wearing the gear of one, he paid closer attention. The gate guard's armour wasn't polished like his own and the kilt was black. It was possible that the kilt identified military ranking.

Maybe there's more to the Renascence Guard than I first thought.

Draegust didn't thank the guard and he led Darkwing into the empty streets of the Commoner's District while the gates closed behind them.

Most of the barriers set up by the Renascence Guard had been taken down. The streets were still littered with stolen goods, broken wood, and the odd corpse.

Still a huge improvement since the first night the prisoners escaped.

The streets were dark. Light cast from the windows of a few scattered buildings, but the rest of the district was long asleep by now.

Darkwing glanced at the High District further ahead to see that the distant mansions had their windows open with bright colors flashing inside.

"Party monsters," Draegust said through clenched teeth. "The rich that have nothing else to do but drink and screw one another all night." He spat on the ground. "Let's keep our minds on the assassination."

Darkwing held his spear tighter, keeping his gaze on the road ahead. *I am a Renascence Guard.* He did his best to stand upright and imitate the commanding presence the guards had in the streets of the city.

The two walked past the marketplace, which still had craters in the ground from the battle of the four guardians. He remembered the horror on Krista's face when Danil smashed the packed dirt before chasing her.

Darkwing growled. *Focus.* Krista kept entering his mind wherever he walked. He had spent so much time with her in this city, and anything he looked at reminded him of her.

"We'll have to reach the citadel through the High District." Draegust pointed at the gates in the distance. "No point going through the prisoner sector."

Darkwing nodded. "That area is still a mess, anyway."

The two marched in silence, eyeing each street they walked past. They crossed paths with a group of three Renascence Guards in black kilts and the five exchanged nods and carried on their way.

I guess the guards don't socialize much.

Soon, the two reached the massive gates that separated the Commoner's District from the High District where two Renascence

Guards stood at their post. The black stone gates matched the high, solid walls that accompanied them, making it impossible to see into the other district.

Draegust stopped in his path, nodding at the two guards. "Open this."

One guard growled back at him and then waved at the doorman above the gates. Darkwing noticed the gate guard's purple kilt.

The guard scowled at Darkwing. He looked away and marched forward while the gates screeched open, allowing them to enter the district.

"I guess the guys we killed were high-ranked," Darkwing whispered.

"Probably. It's not something we want to be talking about, especially this deep in the city."

Darkwing shifted his focus to the district itself. There was a polish to the buildings' designs; their colourful paint was vibrant and fresh. Many were decorated with abstract artwork, designs of simple shapes overlapping one another. Each building had a unique design, complete with arches, curved entranceways, and balconies on the rooftops. The twisted streets were built with bricks and completed with tunnels and bridges. The roads were covered in more rubble like the other districts and majority of the buildings' doors were locked shut. Statues of vazeleads dressed in the double-breasted formal Renascence Guard gear were scattered along the centre divides of the wide roads.

The two walked by an intricately carved stone fountain in a plaza area where there was a bakery, a jewellery store, and a carpentry store. Beyond the fountain was a pathway leading to a park with blackwood trees, near the jewellery store.

"Man, they really don't have to ever leave this district. They've got bakers, tradesmen, and accessories." Darkwing said.

Draegust nodded. "Yeah, kid, high quality stuff too. This is everything you and I will never see."

Darkwing stared at the jewellery store. *Jewellery—something Krista was fond of. I treated her when I could find some, like the necklace I just got her.* He had found a necklace with a beautiful pearl while Krista was hiding from Danil at Magma Falls outside of the city. *Tracking Danil's whereabouts wasn't easy, but searching the city after the prisoner escape had some advantages.* Darkwing had taken the forgotten necklace from the floor of a looted jewellery store in hopes that it would cheer her up. *The orange pearl was identical to the colour of her eyes, and she adored it.*

Darkwing's gaze drifted over to the circular two-tiered fountain that bubbled in the middle of the three joined stores. They were obviously closed now, but they brought back memories from when he was at the marketplace, finding supplies for himself and Krista.

She loved luxurious things, he thought. To him, it didn't make a difference. A road was a road and the design of it had little appeal.

Draegust pointed further up the Great Road. "The citadel will be the hardest part for us to wander through. What does it say about where she is inside?"

Darkwing exhaled heavily, recalling the paper. "She's fairly high up; the paper said G12."

"A tough girl to get to."

Darkwing nodded. *Seventh level and in the 12th sector. We'll have a bit of walking to do inside.* "Let's hope our ranks are accepted that high into the citadel."

"Yeah, wish we had a better background on what the coloured kilts mean."

Darkwing continued to gaze through the High District, examining the fine arches along the doorways, the complex designs in the columns, and rich choice in colours. *Mind-blowing, the amount of effort put into this district. Seems so pointless.*

"Let's just get to the citadel and get out of here," Draegust snarled.

The two walked past the four-storey black-and-grey mansions with lights coming from the open windows and curved balconies. The sounds of fast-paced drums and laughter could be heard from down on the street.

"I can't say I've ever been to a party," Darkwing said.

"Not worth your time," Draegust replied. "People go there to let loose and make foolish choices. You only need to let loose if you don't have a goal in mind. If you got a plan, you don't have time for acting like a fool."

"Wise words."

About two hundred paces later, Darkwing and Draegust passed the last mansion on the outside of the neighbourhood and walked up a hill leading to the citadel. It was enormous in comparison to the mansions and conjoined with the side of the mountain. The citadel was made of the same black stone that the High District gate was built of. There were dozens of floors and hundreds of windows. The citadel had a massive dome-shaped roof in the centre, and underneath was a curved frame taking up numerous floors, complete with glass windows. The remaining citadel wings were flat-roofed, with the exception of some towers, including the clock tower which had a slanted roof topped with shingles.

Lights could be seen through several windows of various sizes.

Draegust pointed to a high tower beside the domed roof. "That is where Demontochai was. That sick beast is probably still in there."

"Let's try to avoid him."

"Good plan."

The two walked toward the first set of gates up the inclining road. The gate and fence were made of thick, black steel bars that ran from the mountain wall to the end of the Great Road.

There was one guard at this gate and he manually unlocked it as they approached.

Draegust nodded at the guard, and the pair kept walking. "That's the kind of service I like."

The main field of the citadel had blackwood trees spread throughout and large statues on each side of the brick road. They were statues of vazeleads—ones that Darkwing could not recognize. He did spot five large statues he could identify at the very end of the road. They were statues of the Five Guardians.

"Someone must have spent months working on these statues."

"Our people put the guardians in a high place of value—at least before all this happened."

The front entrance of the citadel was atop a long flight of stairs. There were two doors made of the same black stone as the walls, and two guards with purple kilts watched over the door.

Draegust walked ahead of Darkwing while they jogged up the set of stairs.

The two guards pulled open each door. Draegust did not acknowledge the two guards and he stepped into the citadel.

The interior was more polished than even the architecture in the High District. The floors were made of a dark marble and the halls had large, smooth pillars running along each side, spread apart by over two dozen paces. The walls were midnight black with mounted torches. The entrance-hall ceiling was finished with a massive silver chandelier hanging from three sets of chains underneath a bridge above. There were at least fifty candles in the chandelier lighting up the entrance, which hung from a bridge several floors above. The hall split off into smaller hallways on the left and right sides, and in the middle, a spiralling gunmetal staircase led up to the second level where there was another foyer, complete with black railings, overlooking the main entrance.

A deep purple carpet ran down the middle of the halls and disappeared into the distance.

Draegust nudged Darkwing. "Come."

Darkwing did his best to walk alongside Draegust, keeping the same pace as he did. He didn't want to get distracted by the luxurious interior. Krista fantasized about this type of life. *Not again.* It aggravated him to be distracted by her. He had to focus on the assassination; it was the only way to find her.

Draegust led Darkwing up the spiral stairway. The stairs were long and wide enough to allow six people to move side by side. Each step of their metal boots against the staircase clanged loudly.

They reached the second level and saw white-armoured Renascence Guards marching the halls. Their kilts were a light grey, they held long narrow shields, and walked two by two.

"By the guardians," Draegust whispered.

The second level had a similar layout to the entrance hall: a hallway on the left and right side and a staircase leading to the next level. The marble floor was lighter here, and sat above the large chandelier.

Darkwing and Draegust walked close to each other, moving up the second stairway. This staircase kept moving upward beyond the third floor, toward the next level.

The two kept climbing higher into the citadel. Darkwing kept his eyes on the stairs, keeping his attention away from any other guards who walked down the steps. *Don't make eye contact.*

Darkwing could hear Draegust count the floors. One by one, they passed each level until they reached the seventh floor. This floor led directly to the bridge overseeing the hall below. At the end of the wide walkway, there was a fork with two halls. Each wall on the outside of the halls had a plank of blackwood, one with white paint reading *12*, and the other, *13*.

"This is easier than we thought," Draegust muttered while turning down number *12*. This hallway had a low ceiling. The floor was made of polished blackwood and the walls were hung with paintings of various creatures found in the underworld, mounted on gold frames.

Every dozen paces, there was a new door on the one side of the hall with a bronze plate embossed with a name in the centre. The opposite side of the hall was finished with barred windows looking outside.

Darkwing could not resist and he peeked through the nearest window to see the vast open space and the City of Renascence down below. There were dozens of buildings from the mansions onward, getting smaller as they vanished into the distance of each district. The Lower District caught his eye; it was run-down, less colourful, and looked cluttered.

Draegust tapped his shoulder. "Let's keep moving."

Two black-armoured guards turned the corner from the other end of the hall. One was taller and had broad shoulders. He puffed up his figure while walking toward Darkwing and Draegust. The second guard was of Draegust's size and had a bounce in his step.

"Halt," the large guard ordered in his deep voice. "You don't belong here. Turn back."

Draegust flicked his tongue. "Let us pass."

The second guard glanced at Draegust's kilt. "You're not authorized to be here."

"We are if Captain Quilech orders it so." Draegust folded his arms.

The large guard let out a deep rumble. "What would Captain Quilech want of two street patrollers such as yourselves?"

"A personal issue," Draegust said with a light bow.

The large guard waved his hand. "Show proof, street cleaner."

Darkwing eyed the Renascence Guard's black armour. It was heavier than his own. He looked for the usual weak points in the neck and armpits. They were not there; the suit had no visible weak spots.

"We need no proof!" Draegust moved forward.

"Be gone, scum eaters!" the large guard instructed. "Wait on the first floor while I check with Captain Quilech personally."

Draegust remained still. "Fair enough."

The guard glanced at his partner. "Stay here," he said. He turned and strutted down the hall he'd come from. The second guard folded his arms and stood, legs spread wide.

Draegust and Darkwing watched as the other guard disappeared around the corner.

"We don't have time for this." Draegust flared his nostrils and with one shove, he lunged his spear at the guard's face at lightning speed.

The guard tried to dodge the attack, but the blade was swift and pierced through his helm into his mouth. He gargled and grabbed the spear with both hands. In a couple of moments his limbs collapsed and he tumbled to the floor.

"Go!" Draegust ordered as he pulled his spear from the guard's face and began wiping the blood on the blade onto his kilt.

"What about the body?"

"If the guard makes it to Quilech, she'll know we're lying and kick us out and we'll lose our chance of getting in there."

The two sprinted to the end of hall and turned the corner to see that the first guard was still there. He glanced back and shouted, "Hey!"

"Shit." Draegust mumbled.

"Did my partner let you by?" The guard drew a large claymore from his back and held it with both hands, swaying his tail back and forth.

"Yes. We bribed him," Draegust bluffed, raising his weapon.

"I'm not so easy to bribe, fools. My loyalties are to the guardians."

"The guardians are dead; your loyalties are to Demontochai, the tyrant of our people."

The guard scowled and gradually stepped closer. "You're beginning to piss me off, street cleaner." He stomped with each step he took, causing the paintings on the wall to shake. "You know these halls are the captains' quarters. If you disrupt their rest, we'll all pay for this!"

Draegust clasped his spear with both hands. "Then why are you stomping around like a fool?"

The guard stopped in his tracks.

Darkwing lifted his own spear, mimicking Draegust's posture. *He won't rush us—our spears have a longer reach than his sword.*

"Let us pass," Draegust demanded. "Quilech must hear our news!"

The guard shook his head. "Silence! They'll have our heads if we keep this ruckus up."

Darkwing didn't understand why they'd be killed over a little noise. He knew the military was strict to their people but he had no knowledge of how ruthless they were among one another. *It makes sense, though. Fear and punishment creates respect for authority.*

"Then let us pass or we'll all be dead." Draegust flung his spear against the left wall, opposite of the windows, smacking the stone.

The guard glanced around quickly. "You're insane! End this nonsense!"

A muffled male's voice came from one of the closed doors. "By the guardians, who is frolicking around in the halls?"

Draegust shrugged, eyeing the black-armoured guard. "Your choice: let us pass or face the consequences. Are your loyalties to your fallen guardians, or to reason?"

The guard bent his knees. "Enough!" He lowered his sword. "See her, then—and make it quick."

Draegust nodded. "Good."

The guard stepped to the side. "Pass slowly."

Draegust and Darkwing moved closer to him, with their spears held close to themselves in a defensive manner. Darkwing looked for an opening in his armour again. *Killing him still isn't a bad idea.* No luck, though; the armour was well-sealed.

They moved past the guard but kept walking backward, keeping their eye on him.

"He'll see the corpse," Draegust whispered.

"Then why'd you kill him?"

"It seemed like the best idea at the time. I'm making this up as we go."

"So now what?" Darkwing replied.

"We could use the captain as hostage when we get to her."

"So they'll follow us out of the citadel?"

"The citadel isn't easy to sneak into, Darkwing, let alone getting out of here. It may be our best bet."

"Shit," Darkwing hissed while glancing back to see the guard had turned around and begun walking back from where Darkwing and

Draegust came.

Draegust and Darkwing wasted no time and dashed down the halls, making several turns deeper into the citadel.

"He's going to come after us." Darkwing said. "We should have hid the corpse in a room."

"Not enough time," Draegust replied. "What room is this bitch in, anyways?"

Darkwing pointed at the doorframe to their left. It read *Viltor, Saltire*. "They're labelled, looks alphabetically to last name."

"What was her last name?"

"Swifttongue."

The two followed the last names on the doors; it took them down the hall a couple of turns.

U . . . T . . . S! The two stopped at a doorframe with the name *Swifttongue, Quilech*.

"We'll barricade ourselves in her room," Draegust pointed, "take her hostage, and plan our escape."

Darkwing nodded.

Draegust approached the door and raised his fist, tapping his knuckles on the door.

Silence.

He knocked again.

"Who dares disturb me?" a high-pitched voice shrieked from inside.

"Captain Quilech, we must speak. It's urgent." Draegust spoke clearly.

"Stay any longer and I'll personally obtain a Corrupt to eat you alive!" the captain replied.

Draegust rolled his eyes and tapped his foot. "Stuck-up piece of work, isn't she?" he said quietly.

Darkwing leaned closer to the door. "It's news of guardian Zeveal."

There was a long pause before the sound of rattling locks.

"Not bad, kid," Draegust whispered.

The door flung open and it startled Darkwing to see that the captain who opened it was a head shorter than he was. She was in a deep-purple nightgown that was low-cut and draped down to her knees. She looked young for a captain—a bit older than himself—with a lean, muscular body and brown scalp-feathers tied up in a ponytail.

"Why do you come to me with this information?" She eyed their kilts. "You're not even of my squad!"

Draegust dropped his spear and pushed the captain back into the room, clutching her mouth with one hand and grasping her neck with the other.

Darkwing grabbed the spear and closed the door behind them, locking it two sets of locks.

He placed the spears by the doorframe and turned around to see there was a wooden bed with a wreath made of bones hanging above the headboard. There was a dresser to its side that displayed a small shrine made of blackwood and a recently burnt incense candle, filling the room with a rich, bittersweet smell. On the opposite side of the room was a polished table, a couple of bookshelves, and a suit of armour with a rack of weaponry. A collection of small linen dolls hung by their rope-scalp-feathers dangled from the ceiling by the window.

Barricade. Darkwing rushed toward the dresser and began to push it toward the door, tipping it over on its side.

Quilech screamed through Draegust's hands as he slammed her down onto the bed.

Darkwing grabbed the table and dragged it toward the door, placing the legs over the dresser.

The sound of a yelp caught Darkwing's attention and he turned to see Quilech had broken free of Draegust—who covered his face—and she was rushing toward the weapon rack.

"No!" Darkwing snatched his spear and tightened his grip on the weapon before launching it into the air at her. The spear whizzed through the room to the captain, slicing her outer thigh.

The captain squealed and her leg collapsed, her knee slamming into the wooden floor.

Darkwing grabbed the second spear and marched toward her.

The head.

Quilech scurried to her feet toward the weapon rack and pulled out a short sword. Her leg collapsed again and she struggled to regain balance.

Darkwing held his spear out toward her, panting heavily.

Draegust shook his head and stepped beside Darkwing.

Quilech grunted. "She sent you, didn't she?"

Darkwing looked down at her wounded leg. A large amount of blood began to pour from her wound.

"Didn't she?" Quilech repeated.

The voice reminded Darkwing of Krista. *She's kind of her size, too.* Darkwing shook his head. *Get it together.*

Draegust snarled and charged the captain.

Quilech swung wildly but missed. Before Draegust could smother her, she dashed off to the side, limping when she put pressure on her wounded leg. The cut slowed her movement and she couldn't move quick enough.

Draegust snatched her tail and pulled her back toward him.

Quilech fell to the ground and turned around on her back. She lashed her sword at him wildly. "Back!"

Darkwing was unsure what to do. Stabbing the girl was not nearly as satisfying as he had hoped. He had thought bringing pain to the captain would boost his desire for violence and to find Krista. However, he felt regret for hurting her; he could see Krista in his mind—hear her cries. *Don't do it! Darkwing, please!*

The captain kept swinging her blade wildly. "I know she sent you!"

Draegust held her tail with both hands. "Get over here, Darkwing! Let's end this."

Quilech screamed. "Help!"

Darkwing moved over to Draegust. *It's just a head. Don't look at her.* He raised the spear and thrust it toward her neck, his eyes closed

The captain swung her blade at the spear, deflecting the attack into her forearm. The spear pierced through to her bone.

She yelped and dropped her sword.

Draegust chuckled. "This was easy. Some captain she is." He let her tail go and grabbed the blade on the ground.

Darkwing pulled the spear from her arm and shook his head. *Keep it together.*

Quilech rolled onto her stomach with a grunt and began to crawl away.

Draegust lunged down and pulled the bleeding captain up to her feet, holding her upper arm with a tight grasp. "Get dressed, missy. We're going for a stroll."

CHAPTER X: HUNTERS

CHAPTER XI

Second Dose

Child, I watched . . .
I impatiently wait.
Where were thou?
Not near you were.
Puppets arrived,
You refused the express.

Child, refusal . . .
Leads to hate.
Expected you to kneel,
Before me.
This I did not see.
Anger and paranoia, I must confess.

Child, changing plans.
I didn't wish for a twisted fate.
I send the one who was dismissed from his vow.

Your plot will stir.

Wrath is how he thrives.

You're pawns, in my game.

Child, time . . .

My forces of great.

Will make your allies kneel.

Before me.

You think it's unreal.

You're the key,

To freedom, from your pretty innocence.

rista had taken her damp trench coat and rested it on the bedframe. Her trousers and scarves were placed alongside it. She only wore her old black dress, but it was wet too. The sheets offered her warmth against the cold dampness of the cloth. Her wrists had been shackled to the bedframe, preventing her from moving during the night.

I feel like an animal. What if something happens and they forget about me?

A swift pain struck her head from behind. The headaches were starting.

"Not again . . ." Krista rolled her head from side to side. It felt as if her brain was swelling from the inside, starting from the forehead and branching off to the sides.

She let out a yelp and her chest thrust upward in a twitching reflex. Krista felt a lack of control in her arms as they began to shake like fish out of water.

"Make it stop!" Krista violently lashed her head. Her arms tugged on the chains, causing the bedframe to wobble.

Black smoke rose from the window-frame crack and travelled toward the bed. Malpherities formed from the smoke and placed his sharp claw on her forehead. "The pain of passing, my dear. Soon you will adapt to it."

Krista groaned as the swelling in her head became more excessive and her whole body seized up, the muscles tightening beyond anything she could physically control on her own. The tension was so strong it felt like her bones were being crushed.

The ceiling began to crack and pieces peeled upward one by one, showing the deep red sky behind it. The remnants of the ceiling began swirling around and flew into the sky, forming clouds.

Krista clenched her teeth. *It's happening again.* She could feel the blood pulsate through her skull faster and faster like an army of drums pounding on her head. Her body fell limp; she could only control her eyes, watching while the walls crumbled to dust, making the room less visible. The ground rumbled and particles of dust came together in the air, compacting and making crude shapes, eventually getting closer together until they made bark-like textures that formed into dead trees. The surface below her shifted itself into dirt patches and hills, moving up in portions and down, making rough terrain.

Krista's metal bed stretched upward and formed a canopy over her head, and it began to bubble until it transformed into a rough, rocky texture.

The chains turned bone white and the shackles around her wrists split apart four times, forming bone fingers. From under the former chains, muscle tissue and veins wrapped around the bones and pale skin followed around the muscle tissue and fingers.

Krista flung upward and screamed, panting heavily. The headache disappeared and she felt sticky and cool all over her body.

She glanced back and realized Fierel was holding her. "What's happening?" Krista tried to break free but the paladin had a strong grip on her. The movement startled her, and she realized she had control of her arms again.

"You're okay." Fierel rubbed Krista's shoulders. "You had a nightmare, and were twitching violently."

"I'm back here?" Krista looked around the wilderness, but the darkness made it impossible to see further than a few feet.

"Yes, you've been here the whole time." Fierel let Krista go and sat beside her.

Krista bit her lip. "How long has it been?"

"You were only asleep for a few hours; after all that training, I thought you'd be drained."

Krista rubbed her head. "I suppose I am."

Fierel squinted. "You all right?"

Krista nodded. "It's this illness I have. I'll get used to switching worlds."

"Right. You're not exactly dead in the mortal world." Fierel folded her arms.

Malpherities hovered closer to Krista. "You have a gift, not an illness."

"Why would it be called Mental Damnation, then?" Krista asked.

Fierel chuckled. "Don't bother with the ghoul; you're with me now."

Krista sighed. "How come you're awake, Fierel?"

"I prefer not to sleep."

"What do you do during the night, then?"

"Now? I keep watch, making sure we aren't attacked."

Krista glanced around the forest. "I thought you said the Lifeless Ones leave us alone?"

"They do, but other fiends roam the landscape and they're much more dangerous."

Krista hugged her knees. "Have you seen anything?"

"No. We're in a fairly remote part of Dreadweave Pass. The other areas are much more active." Fierel got to her feet. "Three of us are awake, so we'd best not waste any time."

Malpherities pointed at Cursman. "Our guide is resting. Some of us need sleep, unlike you."

The paladin walked over to Cursman, who slept with his arms crossed. She gave the man a kick to his shoulder. "Get up, sloth!"

Malpherities looked over to Krista. "How are your headaches of passing?"

Krista rubbed the side of her head. "Fine, I suppose. It's gone now."

"If it is ever too much, you must let me know. I've known of mortals who could not handle the force and have arrived dead in either realm."

"Dead? Could this happen to me?"

"It is possible."

"What can we do about it?"

"Keep you awake here for as long as possible. Or learn to let go of the burdens of the mortal realm."

"What burdens?"

"Your boy toy is a good start."

Fierel kicked Cursman again. "Up. We're ready to move."

"We just settled in, though," he mumbled.

"And we're leaving." She grabbed him by his jacket and lifted him up. "Let's go." She dropped him and he fell with a thud into the dirt.

"All right!" Cursman pushed himself off the ground, sizing himself up with Fierel. "You're a bit frisky, eh? You bring any of that fire in the sack?"

"Pig!" Fierel gave a swift smack over Cursman's head.

"Okay! Enough." Cursman brushed his hair aside and stretched his neck. "We ready to go? In this darkness?" His eyes scanned the blackness that surrounded their camp.

"Yes," Fierel said. "It will clear up in an hour. I've been watching the area; it is vacant and we are safe to travel."

Cursman smirked. "Don't be too sure, paladin. This place is full of surprises." He eyed Krista head to toe. "I'm surprised you're up."

"Nightmares." Krista got to her feet and smiled weakly.

Cursman exchanged glances with the group. "Shall we?"

Fierel extended her arm. "Lead the way."

Cursman leaned down and picked up his linen sack, swinging it over his shoulder. "Stay close; the night of Dreadweave Pass will eat you alive."

The four walked in pairs, staying close to each other, and hiked back up the ditch to the main road. Krista walked beside Fierel while Malpherities and Cursman took the lead.

Krista looked up into the blackness hoping to see any light, but there was nothing.

Fierel looked up too. "Don't be fearful of the dark; it never lasts long. Nights are short here, and days are long."

"Does Dreadweave Pass share the same sun as the real world? I mean, the mortal realm?"

"I can't say it does. The day here does have light but there never seems to be any source."

"What do you mean?"

"Well, in the mortal world, the sun is the origin of light in the sky. Here there is no focal point; the whole sky just lights up like a ball of fire."

"My homeland was deep underground—there was no sun either, just molten earth for light. But it wasn't like it was on fire."

"Well, we are in hell."

This place gets weirder the more I learn about it.

A sharp wind howled as it blew past the four, blowing through branches—at least Krista assumed that was what they were; it was a bit difficult to know for certain without seeing the sound's source. The noises caused the scales down her back to tingle.

It's scary, still. I have no idea what is ahead of me. How does Cursman know where he is going?

Krista watched the man lead. He walked straight and with confidence. He knew how to fight; perhaps that is why he walked with such courage, confident in his abilities.

At least half an hour passed and the sky slowly shifted into a deep red that cast enough light for Krista to see a way off into the distance. The wilderness had disappeared and the path was surrounded by blood-red mountains on both sides. They had sharp, jagged surfaces and were so steep that they looked impossible to climb. The mountains grew higher the further the group travelled. The road was still flat. It narrowed by a third and formed an uphill path into the rocky landscape.

"Watch the rocks; they're sharp," Cursman said and pointed to the mountainside.

Krista gasped as she saw the large, pointed stalagmites covering the steep sides of the mountains. They were arranged, at least two feet apart, in a zigzag formation up the mountain, disappearing into the clouds.

About ten paces away there was a human corpse pierced through one of the coned rocks. The flesh on the corpse was still plump, meaning the juices had not been completely sucked out by the atmosphere. The smell of the body was strong. Krista had to cover her mouth to avoid the stench.

"The body is at least a day old," Cursman said as he gripped the handle of his sword.

Fierel glanced behind them. "I thought you said the gatekeeper portal was abandoned."

"I did say that." Cursman marched toward the corpse. "This isn't a common style of execution out in the wild." He walked up to the side of the stalactite. "The fiends of Dreadweave Pass eat flesh, and this wasn't eaten."

The male—presumably human—corpse was naked, beaten, and bruised beyond facial recognition. It had been pierced into the coned rock from between its legs. The intestines had been pulled free and tied to a second stalactite. The sharp end of the rock could be seen poking through the gutted stomach. The jaw was dangling from one half of the face, tongue draping out.

Krista's eyes widened. "Who would do this?" She felt like she was going to throw up but she resisted the urge and took a couple of deep breaths.

Cursman walked closer to the body. "This kind of behavior is often seen in the Weaver's citadel, not among common folk. The butchering of meat is done to either extract knowledge or to use the flesh as pieces to assemble puppets."

"Or it could be angels," Malpherities added.

Cursman eyed the ghoul. "True. But angels don't kill mortals at random. The Heavenly Kingdoms would despise it."

"Ah, but you forget: we are in the land of the damned. Dreadweave Pass is where the gods send their rejected souls, both mortals and immortals alike."

Fierel pulled her sword from the sheath strapped to her back. "Keep on your guard. Whether it is some rogue angel or the Weaver, don't let your guard down."

Malpherities folded his arms. "Another possibility is that it's a warning message to the general public."

Fierel scanned the road ahead. "Of?"

"The Weaver might not want mortals up here to see the abandoned portal, if it is indeed abandoned."

Fierel shook her head. "I doubt it—the Weaver has never used a portal twice. We'll keep moving."

The four kept shoulder to shoulder, continuing slowly up the path. Krista felt an intense vibe run through her body, her heart pumping heavily.

Things are so much simpler in the High Barracks of Zingalg. I would much rather be dealing with Marilyn's issues than with this. Does the Weaver know I am at this gate? Did he place the corpse there?

"Fierel, do we have to see this portal?" Krista asked.

"Yes, we need to understand our enemy."

"What if there is a gatekeeper there?"

"We will be cautious with our approach. One moment." Fierel walked forward and grabbed Cursman's arm. "You sure this place has none of the Weaver's puppets?"

"Yeah, I've been up here myself."

"The corpse seems too new and too conveniently placed."

"I know," Cursman agreed, frowning.

Krista tapped Malpherities's back. "Think we can kill the gatekeeper?" she whispered.

The ghoul moved back toward Krista. "It's hard to say. Gatekeepers are willful beasts, able to pull off feats that are beyond any regular being. They are powered by the Weaver. A dozen men are needed to kill one."

"But the gatekeeper Danil was once a noble guardian—a leader of my people. Don't you think he'd help his own kind?"

"You betrayed your own people to Paladin, so who's to say he wouldn't do the same?"

"He broke the shackles to the underworld, so he must want to help his people. Paladin said that the cut Danil gave me purposely avoided my veins, proof he didn't want to kill me."

"It's possible he may want to help you. But remember, the key to a gatekeeper's portal—and to your freedom—is kept inside their chest. I doubt he would be willing to sacrifice his own life for you."

"There has to be another way."

"No, there isn't. If you want to get the key to your freedom that is in Danil's chest, we need to understand the gatekeepers, their gates, and what their weaknesses are."

"What if I learned how to let go of my body from both worlds like we talked about? So I don't get hurt when I wake up from here."

"But then you would have to die here. That is quite a risk to take when we don't know for sure if you truly have let go of your body in the mortal realm."

"Well, maybe Fierel has a plan we don't know about."

"She does. The question we have to ask ourselves is, what would a paladin banished to the first level of hell want with you?"

"Maybe she'll tell us once she has seen the gate."

"Just keep that question in your mind, Krista. You and I are friends, not you and her."

The group continued silently, this time with Fierel and Cursman leading the way. The two held their weapons tight, walking with extended steps in a battle-ready position. Krista tried to spot any monsters hidden among the jagged rocks, paranoid of someone watching them.

"Look . . ." Fierel nodded her head to a couple more corpses pierced through stalactites.

Cursman pointed higher above. "That's nothing."

Further up the path, most of the stalactites running up the mountain had corpses pierced through them. The bodies ranged in age and gender, but everyone was naked, withered away and dangling from the sharp rocks. The bodies spread along the rocks up the path and disappeared into the distance.

Malpherities grinned. "This here is an example of the Weaver's power."

Cursman waved his hand at the scene. "These ones I have seen before. Don't worry—they're old. They've been here since the gate was active. The gatekeeper, Hazuel, watched this land when he was alive, and was a bit rebellious to the Weaver's rules."

"How so?" Fierel asked.

"Hazuel was obsessed with his realm-crossing power the Weaver gave him. The Weaver wants gatekeepers to bring only a child back with them each time they cross realms to avoid suspicion from the Heavenly Kingdoms. But that wasn't good enough for Gatekeeper Hazuel. Each time he took a child, he always took one more mortal with him as a trophy, pinning them here."

Krista took a deep breath. "Thanks for the warning."

Cursman chuckled. "No problem. I've been in Dreadweave Pass so long I forget what some of these places must look like for newcomers."

Krista looked to the ground. "Yeah, it's scary. So Hazuel gave each of these people Mental Damnation?"

Fierel sighed. "It looks like it."

Krista peeked at some of the corpses as the group passed by. These ones had been shoved into the sharp rocks by their stomachs and chests, some through their necks. Most of their guts were in place, but some dangled out through bitten wounds.

The rocky path began to widen up the road and old circular bricks were embedded into the path. Dirt and gravel covered most of the bricks where they stood, but the bricks became clearer further up the path.

"It's just up here—the old gate," Cursman announced.

Krista looked up ahead. Just above the steep path, two black, polished, triangular peaks were visible. *This is it.*

Over the steep path, the mountains branched outward into a large circular opening.

Fierel and Cursman were the first to make it to the top of the hill, followed by Krista and Malpherities.

The path continued toward the centre of the opening, leading up a small set of curved stairs. Two columns were placed on either side. The columns were made from stacked blocks, with carved faces and hands with thumbs on both sides, along with crude abstract symbols. At the top of the pillars were the polished black triangles.

I've seen these before. Krista squinted, eyeing the symbols. "Mal, I've seen these pictures! They were in the cult temple Darkwing and I hid at—on the entrance and decorating the temple as paintings."

"The one that Danil performed the ritual in?"

"Yeah!" Krista brushed her scalp-feathers back. "The Eyes of Eternal Life must have had to do with the Weaver!"

"Sounds like he was interested in your people for longer than you realized."

Krista's eyes moved up the stairs where there was a twelve-foot circular doorframe. Portions of it had crumbled away, making it now incomplete. Black triangular spikes ran along the top of the portal and more abstract glyphs were carved into the front of the frame. Two columns were on each side of the doorway in a similar design to the others. A series of human-sized pillars—also black—formed triangles around the circular opening surrounding the stairs. There were at least a hundred that were aligned in each triangle and at least four of these triangles, two on each side of the road. Fierel and Cursman stood still, hands tight on their blades. Krista and Malpherities stayed behind them.

"It's abandoned," Cursman said.

"Never be too sure." Fierel took the first few steps forward.

"This is an old gate," Cursman said and followed behind. "When Hazuel died, the frame of the gate shattered and collapsed, which is why it is in pieces." He pointed at the gate. "We can see the other side of the gate because it has no gatekeeper assigned to it. Normally with active gates, you can see into the other realm through the doorway. Also, puppets have been known to guard this gate, dozens of them patrolling the perimeter to make sure no one came near. Not to mention the gatekeeper would likely be here."

Malpherities's eyes scanned back and forth over the ruins. "It's the work of a master."

Cursman gestured to the arrangement of structures. "The pillars on the outside work with the four large pillars and gate to create the portal. How it all works, I don't know; something to do with unifying frequencies. I do know that every pillar must be aligned perfectly to activate it."

"Does every gate have these pillars?" Malpherities asked.

"They're known as channel points—and yes, every gate has channel points in some form. Moving the channel points in different positions changes where the other side of the gate leads."

Fierel walked up the stairway and toward the gate, running her hand along one pillar. "What are these made of? I don't recognize the material."

"They're rumoured to be made from the same marble used in the Heavenly Kingdoms, but that's just talk," Cursman replied.

Fierel nodded. "What about these glyphs?"

"The Weaver's necromantic language. He writes the language to create what he wills. Not many beings know this language—it is a dead alphabet from the Book of Consulo."

"That book, I've heard of. I've just never seen the language in person before. So this gate led to the mortal realm? What if it was active and we were to pass through it?"

"We'd be brought to that realm. These gates defy the laws and judgments placed by the gods. They shatter the universal rules that were created. The Weaver has mastered a powerful technology. There's also been talk that the Weaver uses these gates to branch into other realms."

Fierel shook her head. "Other worlds?"

Cursman grinned. "Both. Gatekeepers currently hunt other worlds within the mortal realm, but there are other realms beyond that."

Krista shook her head, confused. "What type of realms?"

"We wouldn't know unless we went into one. The mortal realm isn't the only plane of existence. The gods rule many dimensions."

Fierel came a couple of feet from the gate and tapped the doorway with her blade. "It's solid."

Cursman smirked. "Trust me, there is no way you can break a gate unless the gatekeeper dies."

"But we can move the channel points?"

"That, we can." Cursman said.

"If we did, does that change where the gates go?"

"So I've been told. The channel points are aligned by the Weaver's engineers—puppets that retain intelligence to carry out sophisticated tasks."

"In theory, if these gates defy the laws of the gods, they could open into the Heavenly Kingdoms?"

"They could . . . If you can arrange the channel points in the right sequence. It's easy to move the channel points around and you can visit other worlds and realms, but to get the exact location you want is difficult. It requires the right alignment."

Krista walked underneath the gate, looking directly up. "So Danil and Ast'Bala have something similar to this?"

Malpherities floated beside her. "Correct."

She looked over to the ghoul. "Are there other gatekeepers?"

His eyes met Krista's. "There's one. I've never met him, but he is known as El Aguro."

Fierel walked around the gate, eyeing the ruins. "We need a live one." She moved past Malpherities and Krista. "We're leaving."

Cursman blinked twice. "We just got here, and now you wish to leave?"

"Yes, we've seen the size of it, we've seen what makes it work, and we've also learned what gatekeepers do for fun." She pointed at the stalactites. "I'm satisfied."

"So you made us walk all the way here just for a few moments at the gate?"

Fierel spun around. "I told you, I had to see one. Now that I have seen it, we must go. There is little more to be learned here. We need a live one."

Krista turned toward Malpherities. "Not just any live one, we need Danil's."

Malpherities stroked his chin. "That seems of little interest to her."

Cursman flung his arms in the air. "I could have told you everything you just saw, then taken you to a live one from the beginning!"

"Live ones are guarded by puppets. I had to see one that was inactive for myself to really understand what we're up against." She brushed her hair aside. "We return to Evergut and then we'll find a live one."

"I wouldn't mind leaving." Krista held her hands together. "Seeing that fresh corpse made me a bit nervous."

Cursman muttered to himself then sighed. "Fine."

The group walked together back down the road, Cursman taking lead. The four kept on guard, watching their surroundings, making sure no one was stalking them.

They walked by the walls of pinned corpses, followed by the fresh corpse. *There's so much brutality here. Is this really where Danil is now? Couldn't he have chosen someone else to send here instead of me?*

"It was your innocence that attracted him, Krista." Malpherities pointed at her palm with Danil's mark. "You were a little more naive only a week ago."

"Why does it feel so long ago?"

Malpherities smiled. "Time is what we make of it."

"Yeah . . . Mal, if Danil wanted me to live, why would he even send me here to begin with?"

"Most likely had to do with the Weaver's will. Not many beings can resist his influence once they have been confined to him. I'm most looking forward to meeting Danil, to see what he has to say about us needing the key in his chest. See what he thinks about our plan to kill him. Will he give in to us, or will he kill a simple girl for his own survival?"

I'm not simple. Krista clenched her teeth. "I don't want to kill him. He saved me, and freed our people."

"You'd rather be banished here? Be on the run from the Weaver forever?"

"There has to be another way."

The ghoul shrugged.

"I don't want to kill one of the Five Guardians. Whatever state they are in, they are still the leaders of my people. It is wrong."

"Morals restrict you."

A groan was heard from the side of the road. It caught Krista's attention to see that the Lifeless One from earlier was still wandering aimlessly.

She wasn't certain, but it seemed as if the Lifeless One's eyes looked up at her. Krista looked away, afraid to look into its drooping eye sockets. She kept her gaze to the ground, trying to keep her mind off all the corpses.

Her knees ached from descending the mountain. She had to focus on her balance to make sure she didn't stumble down the road. All the travelling was taking a toll on her and she simply needed to rest.

Hours passed and the four returned to the town of Evergut. The red sky lit up the street of the town and candles could still be seen burning inside each building.

"Now we can get some proper sleep," Cursman mumbled. "Let's take a day and we'll continue our hunt."

"We can't stay too long—it will only be a matter of time before the Weaver comes looking for her. After all, I slayed the squad that was meant to take her."

Cursman rolled his eyes. "It's one night."

They arrived at the inn, Gut Fillers, but this time they rented a larger room on the second level. The room was adjacent to Cursman's previous room. It was a bit larger and had two cots. Krista curled herself up on one of the beds; her legs were numb from all the walking.

Fierel kneeled beside Krista. "How are you? I haven't seen you eat since we've met."

Krista's stomach growled at the thought of food. It was odd; she wasn't hungry in the High Barracks, yet now she was hungry. *This two realms and two bodies thing is stressing me out.* "Yes, I am."

Fierel smiled and went to brush Krista's scalp-feathers out of her eyes but stopped her motion halfway and her smile faded. "I'll see what I can find." She clutched her hand and returned to her feet. "I'm going to get something for her to eat, but I'll be back soon."

"Got something for me to eat later?" Cursman smirked.

Fierel slammed the door.

Malpherities chuckled. "You haven't changed. Who does she think she is, anyway, taking command of us?"

Cursman lay flat on his bed. "She's a paladin."

Krista closed her eyes; her body was drained but her mind was very active with fear. The visit to the gate damaged her hopes of escaping Dreadweave Pass. *The gatekeepers are even more powerful than I thought.*

The room fell silent for several minutes. She could only hear her own breathing until Cursman spoke up. "Cute girl."

Is he talking about me? Krista remained silent.

"What is she?" he asked.

"Reptilian . . . vazelead," Malpherities replied.

"Not often do you see humanoids with tails. They must be an extraordinary race."

"Not from what I know of her people. She doesn't talk much about her past, though—not unless you ask about it. Which I don't."

"What do you know about her?"

"She was a street kid and wasn't treated well. Her past doesn't concern me . . . I am simply ensuring her protection."

Cursman's tone deepened. "What are you up to, ghoul? You ruin my life in the mortal realm . . . Our previous attempts to get out of this realm have all failed. You have never shown compassion for anyone, yet here you are, looking after a young girl."

"She wants to return home."

"So? So do I. How does this help you? Who wants you to do this? Goodwill is not in a ghoul's nature, and if you think you can have goodwill, you can't. We both know this—a ghoul's nature is to inflict pain."

"The girl wants to go home."

"I'm on to you, ghoul."

Malpherities let out a maniacal laugh. "On to me? I've done nothing to you since we've re-grouped. All I've done is protect this girl."

"The only reason we've re-grouped is because that paladin enslaved your soul. You tried to pass on some bull shit about a resistance force?"

"Did you think I wanted this?" Malpherities raised his arms, his cuffs rattling.

"Whatever you're up to, you better let me in on it at some point. After all we've been through to try and get into the Heavenly Kingdoms. Besides, I've seen you go to greater lengths to get what you desire."

"I must be going insane, then. A paladin has my soul. I'd be toying with my life! This Fierel character is dangerous—a walking bomb."

Cursman sighed. "That I can agree with."

"A paladin in the land of the damned . . . Total chaos, their power strengthens when there is more evil around. It's like a burning energy that they desire to release."

"Yeah, if she doesn't keep it under control."

"Is she really repenting? All that power just building up inside of her, and who is to say all this power won't turn her into the very thing she says she is fighting? She is constantly surrounded by evil; it is all she can hear, smell, and see in Dreadweave Pass. It will consume the mind if one is here long enough."

"She's a rogue paladin. Do you think she wants to slay the Weaver?"

"That theory is flawed. Note how she asked how the portals worked, specifically about the Heavenly Kingdoms? She's not a fool."

"Yeah, except you need to find an engineer puppet willing to work with you to align the portal. It doesn't make sense, though. If she was banished here, why are her powers still active? Fallen angels are stripped of their holy gifts when banished, so why not paladins?"

"Paladins are blessed with power as if it were a torch they hold. Angels are more closely tied to the gods, like strings to a puppet."

"Damn. In some ways they have it better than the angels."

"As long as their light doesn't burn out."

The two said no more and Cursman was heard rolling over on his bed.

They must be going to sleep, but I just can't. Their silence left Krista with nothing but questions. *What do Cursman and Mal have in common? I wonder if they have they tried to help others with Mental Damnation. And who is Fierel, really? Does she really care about me?* The thoughts made Krista's stomach tense.

A bloodcurdling scream erupted from outside.

"Bring me what I seek!" a growling raspy voice roared through the town.

Krista rose from her bed, eyes wide, scanning the room to see Cursman and Malpherities exchanging glances with each other.

"What was that?" Krista asked.

Cursman slipped from his bed while more screams came from outside, followed by the sounds of doors slamming shut. He crept over to the window and peeked from the curtain, only to swiftly move away. "Shit! It's Sporathun!"

Malpherities threw his head back in shock. "The vampyre? I thought the Weaver locked him up centuries ago. What is he doing out?"

"I'd rather not find out."

Krista walked quietly up to the two and kept her voice low. "What's a vampyre?"

Malpherities pushed her head down. "Fallen angels are commonly referred to as vampyres because their life force is sustained by committing the sin that consumed them over and over. If they, or others, embraced the sin, it would energize the vampyre with immense strength."

Krista squinted. "What is he doing here?"

"We don't know," Malpherities said.

"Who is he?"

Cursman bit his lip. "A disgrace to the gods." He gradually peeked through the window again.

"Why?" Krista peeped out the window for a moment to see a pale-skinned being standing at the end of the town. He was shirtless and wore a long, black, leather kilt. Two curled horns sprouted from his head and his eyelids were sealed shut. His lips were gone, but he had sharp fangs protruding from his upper and lower jaws. In both hands, he held large curved blades—blades at least the size of Krista—with the handles in the middle of each weapon.

"I seek a child!" Sporathun shouted, his long tongue licking his gums.

Cursman pushed Krista down. "Down. We'd best stay hidden until he leaves."

Malpherities squinted. "What for? So he can go door to door until he finds us?"

"How do we know he wants us?" Krista asked.

"Seen any kids around recently?" Cursman asked.

Krista bit her lip. "He is coming for me. The Weaver must have sent him."

"We must leave Evergut," Malpherities said.

A roar was heard from outside. "I smell you, girl! Young blood! It's all so sweet."

"We've got to leave now!" Cursman exclaimed.

Malpherities pointed to the door. "Take Krista and meet us at the Jawless Cavern."

"Mal!" Krista grabbed hold of his arm. "Where are you going?"

Malpherities yanked free. "I will assist Fierel in creating a distraction for your escape." The ghoul brought his arms together and he began to disintegrate into black fog, starting with his arms, his head, and then his torso fading into thin air.

"Where did Mal go?"

Cursman lifted Krista up into his arms. "He's bound to Fierel, remember? Let's scram."

Sporathun let out a deep growl, so loud it rumbled through the town. "Child! The Weaver demands your presence."

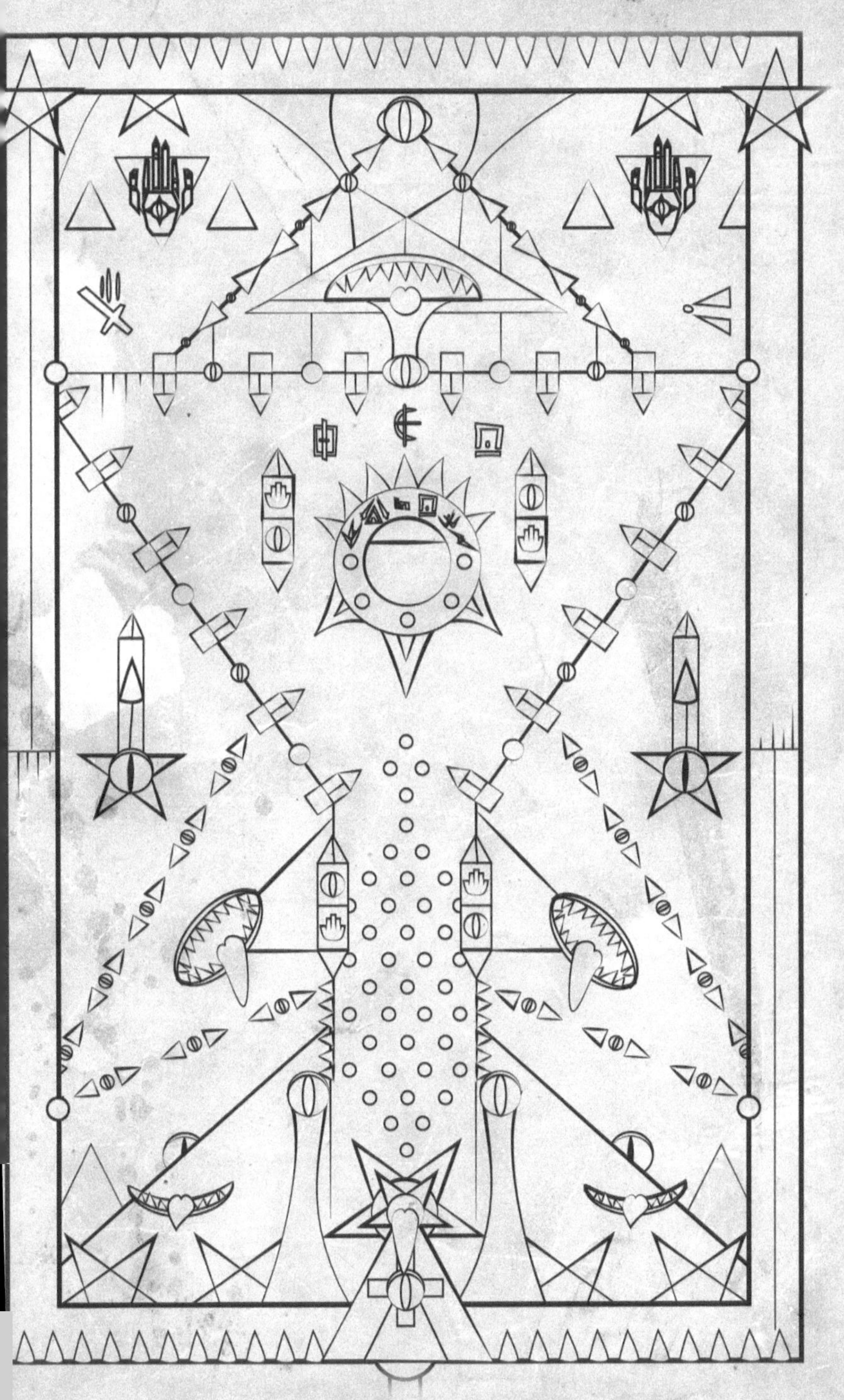

CHAPTER XII

Might, Rage and The Sly

esire is an act of impulse. It is a sensation that can surpass the control we have in our minds and bodies. Our thoughts may differ from what we are doing within the moment of desire, but thinking does not define what is actually happening. The action itself is how we are defined. When our actions are based on desire, irrational judgments are made without weighing the consequences. After the act, we often ask ourselves: why did I go through with this? Can I be forgiven?

Even if desire was a mistake, even if you should know better and you make a fool's choice—a pure sign of immaturity—it is still an error that can cause eternal banishment from the Heavenly Kingdoms. For example, if two beings are in love but it is forbidden, they cannot be together.

An impulsive sin has brought me here, in the land of the damned. Thought the paladin while she stepped outside of Gut Fillers, the wooden planks creaking as her metal boots clanged on the surface.

I once stood for the holy as defined by the gods, before that wretched

Truce of Passing. She shook her head. *I pray this girl will offer a case for the gods . . . or have my morals strayed too far from their agendas? Have I gone mad?* she thought, the same thought that she had asked herself countless times before since she was judged to live out her second life in despair in Dreadweave Pass.

I could truly go insane asking this over again. I have to feed Krista—keep her alive and under my wing until I can get us out of Dreadweave Pass and in the eyes of those who matter. She glanced up and down the road, the only road in Evergut. What could the girl could possibly eat in hell? A flash of Krista went by in the paladin's mind: the girl's dirty, blood-covered scalp-feathers. She'd wanted to brush Krista's feathers aside and comfort the girl in such an evil place. However, Fierel could see in Krista's eyes that she was frightened of her.

It was never the intention to scare Krista when they first met. The circumstances just ended up that way, and Fierel had needed to be cold-hearted. If it were not for the ghoul, Malpherities, it would be much easier to work with the Krista. But the ghoul was too close to the girl and there was no telling what influence he had on her.

The paladin crossed the road of Evergut where a line of log buildings rested. In the group was a butcher shop—one that she had visited before. She knew that Krista came from the mortal realm, the same realm she'd lived in, a place of peace where the food was rich. The food in Dreadweave Pass was nothing like the sweet fruit and freshly baked bread of the mortal realm. Here, for the most part, the food was disgusting—challenging to chew and barely manageable to swallow. Fierel had lost count of the number of times she'd vomited up her meals after finishing them. Mortal stomachs could hardly digest them. After all, the only things to eat here were the odd fungus, demons, and the living dead.

Fierel knew if she could find something, anything manageable to eat, she may be able to change the girl's mind about her. She could prove to Krista that she was an ally.

The paladin walked over to the butcher shop. It was made of the same wood as the rest of the town and was only distinguished by a single plank of wood with 'Meat' painted in black above the door.

She pushed open the crooked door, and the hinges creaked. The shop was no larger than their room in the inn. There were a couple of display buckets with a note above reading 'Freshly Cut.' Some flesh was kept behind barred windows, which were beside a counter and in front of the butchering table.

"Good day, dear," a man said.

Fierel glanced over to see a big, pale, balding man with a scruffy orange beard and a blood-stained white apron standing behind the counter. He held a large cleaver, which was wet with fresh blood.

"What can I do for yer, pretty lady?" he asked with a toothless grin.

"I need something that can suffice as a meal to a newcomer."

"Aye, something to ease the stomach into some of the heavier stuff, eh?"

"Correct," Fierel said. She leaned over, peeking into a barrel off to the right of the butcher. The barrel held shriveled-up skin, probably human. It wouldn't be the best food to introduce Krista to right off the bat.

"I got some dahk meat, probably the easiest to digest."

"Sure, I'll take it. What's your form of payment?"

The butcher leaned over and shuffled through the meat behind the barred window to grab three thin slices of purplish meat with a black crust. "I take blood coins. Three."

Fierel reached into the pouch that hung from her waist and pulled out three sticky, deep-red coins. They were actually dried-up blood that had rained from the sky. But not just any dried blood—they were compacted tight, pressed with an official seal to prove their worth, and dried. The coins could be used as long as they were not exposed to moisture, because then the coins would melt.

Not all merchants took blood coins. The currency was made by some of the higher-class mortals found in Dreadweave Pass—those who resided in the City of Blood. They needed a way to measure the value of their other goods.

Fierel passed the coins to the butcher and he returned a paper bag of the purple meat. "Thanks," she said. She carefully placed it in her pouch and began to walk out of the shop.

"Bring me what I seek!" A deep, growling voice echoed through the town.

The butcher gasped as he gripped his cleaver. "What the hell was that?"

Fierel rushed to the front of the store, keeping her shoulder pressed against the wooden wall, peeking through the side of the closed window. "I don't know. You're best to hide until it leaves, though."

The butcher nodded and tightened the grip on his knife.

Fierel used her finger to move the hide-curtain aside so she could scan the terrain. The road was deserted and the town was silent, except at the far end where her group had come from their visit to the abandoned gate. There stood a shirtless, pale humanoid. He held a bladed weapon in each hand.

"I seek a child!" the being shouted, exposing the razor-sharp teeth in his lipless mouth.

"Sporathun . . . the fallen angel," Fierel muttered. She had never seen him with her own eyes but his legendary story and horrific appearance was well known.

"The vampyre?" asked the butcher, eyes wide.

Fierel nodded slowly. *Damnit.* Sporathun had been banished from the Heavenly Kingdoms for being consumed by wrath—oddly enough, his story was similar to Fierel's. But in Dreadweave Pass, the fallen angel had caused too much destruction and he was captured by the Weaver's puppets to prevent further chaos. And now he was here, seeking a child. The only child Fierel knew of in Evergut was Krista.

Sporathun pointed at the inn and began marching toward the building. "I smell you, girl! I'm coming for you!"

Fierel had to act fast. She knew there was no way Cursman and Malpherities could handle the fallen angel. She looked up at the inn, seeing Cursman and Krista's heads duck from the window.

Fierel's necklace began to glow bright white around the cross pendant while it slowly levitated in the air. The white light acted as fire, projecting from the pendant to Fierel's side. Black smoke channeled out of the white flame, followed by blue smoke. The smoke compacted tightly together, forming the ghoul—Malpherities. The white fire vanished and her pendant fell back onto her chest.

Malpherities's cuffs glowed bright white, then the light gradually faded. Now that the ghoul's soul was bound to Fierel, they were connected—she could summon him to her at will.

"Paladin, Cursman and the girl are escaping for the Jawless Cavern. What is your course of action?" Malpherities glanced out the window.

"He's moving fast."

"We need to buy them time," she said and rubbed her forehead. "We have to slow Sporathun down."

Malpherities nodded. "As you command."

Nice to have the prick obey me for once. Normally Malpherities was resistant to Fierel and anything she said. But the ghoul also knew how dangerous a fallen angel was, so it forced an allegiance between them.

Fierel drew her sword from her sheath, gripping the flame-shaped pommel with both hands. "For thy Father who resides in our eternal home, give me the strength to shun those who have turned from you!" She barged through the front door, causing the frame to splinter. Her feet stomped onto the dirt road, red dust rising in the air while she charged toward Sporathun, her blade held high to her side, her shoulder facing the fallen angel for protection.

The twisted horns, sharp fangs, claws, lean muscles, and twin blades two-thirds the size of Fierel—she ignored them all. To her, it was simple: hold Sporathun back to give Krista time to escape. Fierel's fear of Sporathun did not matter; she had to have faith.

Fierel clutched her sword tightly with both hands while roaring fiercely, raising her sword, ready to strike. Sporathun turned. He tried to raise his curved blade to block the attack but her sword was quicker and the strike glazed down his arm, peeling back a layer of his skin.

Sporathun snarled and stepped to his side while Fierel swung upward for a second strike—a miss. Fierel wobbled in an attempt to regain her balance; she misjudged her strength and had thrown herself off-guard.

She looked over to her side. Sporathun dashed behind her, raising his blade at her. To her luck, black fog moved at lightning speed behind Sporathun. Malpherities sprung from the fog, his dreadlocked hair bouncing upward as if it were statically charged. He raised his claws, slashing down onto the fallen angel's back. Sporathun hunched over, grinding his teeth. "A creature of Death's Vortex!" He spun around, lashing both blades at the ghoul, swing after swing. The fallen angel's back was covered in twisted muscles and white bumps, now torn and bleeding a deep red.

Fierel regained her balance and guided her blade to strike behind

Sporathun's knees.

The fallen angel jumped, evading the strike and exposing his two-toed feet with extended claws from underneath his black kilt. Landing, he spun around, throwing his arms in an arc.

Malpherities and Fierel backed away from Sporathun's whirlwind of blades, avoiding the fatal attack as red dust kicked up in the air.

Fierel looked for an opening to strike, but the heavy swinging blades were too dangerous to even get close. She clutched her pendant and closed her eyes. "I can do all things through him who strengthens me," she said and stroked the pendant several times, expecting the holy fire to channel through her veins from her Heavenly Father's symbol.

Sporathun's whirlwind ended and the dust settled. He stood with one blade held high, the other low, and his legs extended far apart, keeping both Fierel and Malpherities to each of his shoulders.

Fierel swallowed heavily—nothing. The holy gift she relied on was nowhere to be found. Perhaps it fled her, or perhaps it was a test of faith. How would she handle a demoralizing situation with just her own will? It didn't matter why the holy flame did not respond; the fact was she had to rely on her own strength now.

Even the light is failing me. Why now?

Sporathun's eyeless face was trained at Fierel's pendant. He roared, his forked tongue coming out between his sharp teeth. "A paladin," he sneered. He sprinted from his stance, one blade still held high.

Fierel clutched her sword with both hands, standing strong as Sporathun lunged toward her, swinging both of his blades. Fierel retreated carefully, using her sword to parry the heavy arched blades that rushed down at her. Each blow he made chipped into her sword. The damage to her weapon startled Fierel, and she lost grip of the handle.

Sporathun swung down again, knocking the blade free from her hand. He shoved both blades toward her simultaneously. Fierel leaped to the side, landing heavily on the dirt.

Malpherities rushed toward Sporathun until the he turned around, blades ready to strike. The ghoul stopped in his path, glaring at the fallen angel.

Sporathun laughed hysterically. "A ghoul and a paladin? What a humorous couple. Stay out of my way if you want to live." He lowered his blades and began to march toward the inn.

Malpherities dashed over to Fierel's sword and picked it up, returning it to the paladin.

Fierel got herself up. "We can't let him close the distance on Krista." She rubbed her wrists; they ached from her hands being disarmed. "Hurry!" she snatched her sword from Malpherities and the two charged at Sporathun as one.

The paladin extended her sword, pointing it at Sporathun. He spun around and roared, crossing his blades. Fierel's blade locked in between Sporathun's; all three weapons were now stuck. Fierel tried to pull her sword free as Sporathun tugged on his.

Malpherities went around Sporathun and shoved his claws into the fallen angel's back again.

Sporathun broke his blades from Fierel's and ran his elbow back into Malpherities, pushing the ghoul away. He shifted stances to have each opponent to one side. The fallen angel swung his blades at each one of them, forcing them both to keep their distance.

His multitasking combat skills intimidated Fierel while she dodged his oncoming attacks. She couldn't see Malpherities well but saw he struggled to keep Sporathun's blade away.

Fierel struck low, hoping to throw Sporathun off his guard. "Seek the Lord and his strength; seek his presence continually!" She prayed in hopes the holy flame would come to her aid.

Sporathun stepped to his side and backed up; his movements were sleek and his stance low, ready to pounce. He glanced back and forth at Malpherities and Fierel, who were now both in his line of sight.

"The Father's offered strength is weak," he muttered.

Fierel was angered that her holy power was failing her, but she couldn't give up. She inhaled deeply and brought her attention to the holy flame her body was infused with.

Malpherities flicked his tongue at the fallen angel, his dreadlocks vibrating in tune with his hissing. "You seek a child who does not belong to you. Be gone!"

Fierel closed her eyes, trying to block out the two unholy beings around her and remember the light—the light of her Heavenly Father she had been following for so long.

The Father who betrayed you, a soft voice whispered in her head. The words hurt her, remembering that it was her Father's kingdom that was responsible for her banishment, responsible for taking her away from her desire.

They didn't like you; your faith in your Father and the gods failed. The voice continued in her mind.

Fierel blocked out the thoughts; whatever or whoever placed them in her mind was not of holy origin. Or perhaps they were—the words could very well be from the holy flame she relied on.

Don't be afraid. She reasoned with the words in her mind.

Such unholy strength all around . . . no faith . . . the whispers replied.

There is always faith; faith in our Father, beyond the gods, the faith in our own strength let me move on after being banished.

No! No more faith! Evil is getting stronger.

Do not fear. God is our refuge and strength, a very present help in trouble.

The voice did not reply and Fierel began to lose focus. Sporathun's beastly roar woke her from the short meditation, making her realize that time hadn't moved much—only by a few seconds.

"I will obtain the child!" Sporathun bolted at Malpherities.

The ghoul moved toward the fallen angel at the same time. Sporathun raised his blades, ready to attack, but Malpherities clutched his wrist and the two slammed into each other. They landed in the dirt, wrestling to assert dominance in the struggle. It didn't take long for Sporathun to gain the upper hand. He dropped one blade and used his hand to strangle the ghoul.

Okay, in faith of the Heavenly Father, above all, the voice whispered in Fierel's mind. Her pendant lit up with white flame, and the flame travelled up her necklace and into her skin. She felt her very core fill with heat and a burning surge coursed through her veins, reaching every inch of her body. The veins lit up white and moved down to her arms. It flowed up into her sword and the blade ignited in bright white flames, lighting up the Evergut road.

Sporathun slowly looked over his shoulder toward her, flaring his nostrils. "I may not see with my flesh-bound eyes, paladin, but I can sense your faith . . ."

Fierel held the flaming sword in one hand and pointed at the fallen angel. "God arises; His enemies will scatter and those who hate Him will flee before Him. His presence flows through those who follow, so the wicked perish at the presence of God. Fallen angel of wrath, be gone!"

Sporathun picked up his second blade, stood up from Malpherities, and turned to face Fierel. "Angel I'm not!" he shouted.

The fallen angel stomped toward her. Each step he took caused the ground around him to shake, dust and pebbles flying.

Fierel grabbed her sword with both hands.

Sporathun pounced, legs bent and weapons extended outward, aiming for the paladin.

Fierel held her sword tightly, remaining motionless while watching her opponent. She felt the holy flame from her body burn hotter. The presence of evil being so close was amplifying the fire's intensity.

Fierel let out a fierce cry as Sporathun came plummeting down. The two collided and skidded into the earth, tumbling while Sporathun's force pushed them several inches into the ground.

Their struggle ended with Fierel on top, lifting her blade and thrusting down toward his chest. She was expecting a scream from the fallen angel, followed by the holy flame consuming his body, much like what happened with the Weaver's puppets.

The blade pierced into his chest, but only with a dull sound of penetrated flesh and bone. Fierel looked down to see the blade had indeed pushed into his core, but it remained there. The holy flame was still on her sword and it did travel onto Sporathun's flesh, burning it. But his skin was rejuvenating at an unnatural rate and it healed over the holy flame, over and over.

Fierel pushed deeper in, feeling the blade hit the dirt underneath his body.

Sporathun grunted, blood splattering from his mouth as he snarled.

Fierel was out of ideas. She'd been certain her holy flame would be enough to slay him, but apparently not. Fallen angels were known for their rejuvenation abilities, but she had underestimated the speed. Even the slice on Sporathun's shoulder had sealed up, as if it were never there.

She pressed harder on the handle of her blade, twisting it to cause more pain.

Sporathun lunged forward, grabbing hold of Fierel's neck, squeezing it tightly and blocking her airway. Her eyes widened from the lack of oxygen. She used one hand to try and break his grip on her, but he was too strong.

Sporathun used her neck to pull himself up from the ground, drawing her blade deeper into his chest. His sealed eyelids twitched, and his blank stare seemed to look deep into her eyes.

Fierel let go of the sword and used both hands to try and loosen his grip on her neck, but no luck.

Sporathun stood, lifting Fierel high above the ground. He continued to squeeze her neck tighter, causing her to gasp for air. She kicked wildly, but her efforts were futile.

"Paladins . . ." Sporathun shook his head. "Mortals who think that they are angels." With his free hand, he pulled her sword out from his chest and held back, pointing it toward her head. "But in the end, you are still made of mud!"

Black smoke moved in the flash of an eye, twisting toward Sporathun.

The fallen angel redirected Fierel's sword toward the oncoming ghoul.

Fierel kicked Sporathun in the chest repeatedly, trying to throw him off balance. It was difficult to do; her body was running out of air and her face was turning pale. Her vision was blurry and she was exhausted.

Malpherities backed away from the sword, but not before the blade sliced him across the torso. He flew by Sporathun and Fierel, falling into the dirt and yelping in pain. He screeched as the holy fire from the wound spread around his body, burning him.

Sporathun sniffed the air and his face turned grave. "The child's scent! It is fading!" he shouted. "She is on the move!"

He lifted Fierel higher in the air and threw her hard into the dirt, then tossed her sword aside.

Fierel landed heavily on her ribcage, and her armour dented inward. She gasped for air while trying to endure the pain, which made the side of her body numb. It was too difficult to return to her feet.

"He . . . can't . . . continue . . . on," Fierel said, gasping for air after every word.

Sporathun picked up his blades from the dirt and began to run down the road.

Malpherities patted down the holy flame several times until it faded. "We can't stop him," he said. He clutched his wound while black smoke seeped from the cut.

Fierel watched as Sporathun sped away. The wound she'd inflicted by impaling him had sealed. She shook her head. "What type of vampyre is he?" She attempted to push herself up but stumbled back to the ground. "We can't let him go," she muttered.

"Don't be a fool." Malpherities hovered over to her.

"We can't let him get to Krista!" Fierel pushed herself up. She felt a sharp pain from her dented armour—she was bruised underneath. Glancing around, she spotted her sword a couple of feet away.

"Listen to me!" Malpherities argued.

The paladin ignored the ghoul and rushed for her blade. She had to buy Krista more time—Sporathun was still too close.

Grabbing her sword, Fierel sprinted onward. Her dented armour prevented her lungs from getting the full supply of oxygen she needed, but she ignored her breathlessness.

Sporathun stopped in his tracks and stood tall.

He can sense me. Fierel kept pushing herself to run, holding her sword low for an upper strike. She got nearer with each step she made until she was close enough to lift her sword. Before Fierel could swing up, Sporathun swiftly turned to face her, lifting his two-toed foot into the air. The claws on his foot collided with her chin, tearing open her skin and travelling upward to her nostrils.

The blow pushed Fierel backward, spraying her blood into the air. She dropped her sword and swayed side to side. She could feel her skin had been split apart down the middle of her lower face. The blood oozed from her open wound, dripping down to the soil. Her vision blurred and her hearing became fuzzy.

"You could have killed her!" Malpherities hissed.

"Stay clear of me, Malpherities!" Sporathun shouted. "Your previous offers were futile. The girl is my key now."

Fierel stumbled backward and landed with a thud. The last thing she saw was the blood-red sky before her vision blacked out.

CHAPTER XIII

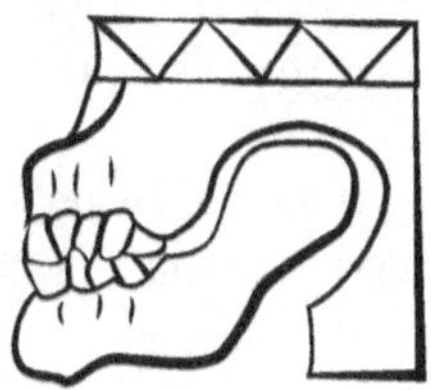

City of Blood

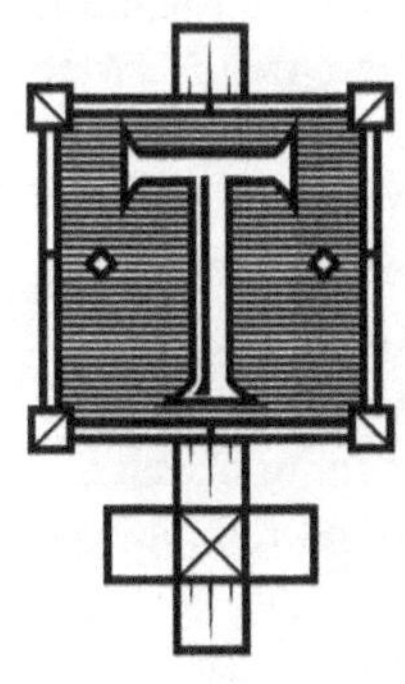wigs snapped and mud splattered as four feet trampled through the bloody forest. Two of the feet belonged to Krista. Her heart pounded as she ran alongside Cursman. She was afraid to get lost in the hellish wilderness; afraid for Malpherities's safety; afraid of the fallen angel who hunted her.

Krista felt doubt overrun her. Hiding in a cave didn't sound like a very good option; It didn't work very well for her and Darkwing at Magma Falls. Any time she hid from her problems, they eventually found her. Besides, she didn't trust Cursman completely—his history and scruffy appearance made her ill at ease. She wanted her ghoulish friend or even the paladin; they made her feel safe in Dreadweave Pass.

Cursman held her hand tight, keeping her up to speed with him while he navigated through the rough terrain of rocks, blood puddles, and sharp roots that sprouted out from the ground. She didn't like how he pulled her arm; the grip was tight and it cut off her circulation.

To their left was a red dirt hill covered in flat rocks with sharp edges. The top was difficult to see because of the tree branches blocking her view, but a dark opening was visible among the rocks. It had stalactites hanging from the narrow ceiling that reached down to the ground, forming the shape of a mouth.

Malpherities's words echoed in her mind: *Jawless Cavern.*

"Cursman," she grunted as they dodged a stump.

He didn't reply.

"Cursman! We are going the wrong way!"

"We're going the right way," Cursman replied.

She glanced at the cavern again as it slowly faded away behind dozens of black trees. "Where are we going?"

"Far, far away from here."

Her stomach felt like it twisted around from the inside. "We were supposed to meet Mal and Fierel here." Krista tried to pull free from his grasp but he was too strong. She stomped her heels into the mud, forcing Cursman to drag her through it. "What about them? What about Mal?"

Cursman let out a heavy sigh and stopped in his tracks, glancing at their surroundings before he turned to face to her. "We're dealing with a vampyre." He scanned their surroundings again, his eyes wide. "His senses are incredible. Our distance does not matter; he will still be able to track us. Malpherities and Fierel together cannot match his strength. Their sacrifice gave us a boost, but there's no telling how long they held him off. We have to keep moving!"

"Sacrifice? Are they dead?"

"I wouldn't put it past Sporathun after the chaos he caused last time."

"How can he track us? I don't understand. Why are these vampyres so strong?" Krista clutched her scalp-feathers and took a deep breath. *Why are there always new complications with this place?* "I'm scared," she wailed.

Cursman moved closer and took her hand. "You have to stay close and listen to me. You . . . This situation is far larger than Malpherities or Fierel first thought—whatever their real agendas were."

"Their agendas were to help me!" Krista whined.

He tightened his grip, ignoring her statement. "Now that ghoul has dragged me into it . . . You've attracted some big players in the afterlife kid. Not sure how you did it."

"I don't know, I just want Darkwing back." She whined, not thinking about what she was saying.

"Who?" He shook his head. "Listen: Malpherities isn't a fool—he wouldn't get himself killed just to buy us time."

"Fierel?"

"That bitch is irrational, so who knows."

Krista felt her eyes begin to water up and her lips shook. "I wish I was never brought here. Why me? Why did they pick me?" She started to lose control and sobbed.

"Hush, girl," Cursman said and took her into his arms, lightly stroking her scalp-feathers. "We've got a bit of a problem, but I don't quit. Now that I'm dragged into it, you're with me and we'll do things my way, all right?"

Krista nodded. "Where are we going?" She sniffled.

Cursman broke free, still holding her hand. "I never lose." He grinned. "We're going to a much bigger city—one that is a lot more populated. It is known as the City of Blood."

"What for?"

"To learn about Sporathun. I only know of the damage he's caused in the past. But if we can learn more, then we can formulate a plan to defeat him."

"What can we learn in a big city?"

"There's a chronicle that records the history of Dreadweave Pass. I know we'll find some answers there."

Krista nodded and brushed her scalp-feathers aside. The blood had partially dried and was now a sticky coating over her scalp-feathers. "Okay."

"We'll have to travel through the night. Are you fine with that?"

Her knees were sore and her feet numb from the excessive walking they had already done, but she nodded once again. "I'll manage."

Cursman smiled at her. "Good. We can't afford to waste any time." He held her hand tighter. "We must move."

Krista brought a weak smile to her face and they continued to move through the forest.

"What do we know about this vampyre, anyway?"

"Well . . . we've got some traveling to do. Here's some history for you: vampyre is the common-folk term for them. Sporathun is technically a fallen angel of wrath. When an angel commits a sin up in the Heavenly Kingdoms, they are consumed by it. Once they have done the deed, they become addicted to it, craving it more. So for Sporathun, his sin was wrath and he was banished from the Heavenly Kingdoms for his fury. The more he feeds his sin, the stronger he becomes. That means the more enraged he gets, the worse off we are. Fallen angels can recover wounds, have faster reflexes, and develop more endurance as they feed their sin. There's a catch, though: if they feed too much, they become overwhelmed by it and black out. Then their bodies are entirely controlled by the sin."

"Why is he so angry?"

"That's what we're going to find out," Cursman said.

"Why are they called vampyres, though?" Krista asked.

"Because they're like leeches. When an angel has fallen, their life force becomes their sin, meaning if they don't feed on that sin, they will die."

"How do they feed it?"

"There's two ways they can feed: they can feed off others' sins, or their own. As for Sporathun, if you are angry when he is around, or if he is angered, it makes him stronger and replenishes his wounds and overall health. But it must be genuine anger; he can't feed his own sin consistently unless he is honestly aggravated."

"What if no one is angry?"

"He will die. If vampyres can't feed, you'll start to see them get weaker and their skin gets dry and flaky. That is all I know about him, and vampyres in general for that matter. They aren't very common. We need to make a plan to defeat him."

"So now there's not just the Weaver I have to worry about, there's a vampyre after me? I don't understand why everyone cares about me so much."

"Nor do I. Maybe the Weaver sent him."

"The gatekeepers did say I was innocent."

"You don't seem as innocent as some of the other children the gatekeepers have brought here."

"I guess I'm growing up."

"Apparently. If only that were useful to us." Cursman led her to a hill above the main road, but they didn't travel down. The two stayed above, where the forestry provided camouflage.

"You see that?" Cursman pointed to the road.

"What?"

"The footprints." Looking closer at the dirt, dozens of fresh imprints peppered the road.

"Who are they from?" Krista asked.

Cursman slowed his pace and bit his lip. "The Weaver's puppets, most likely."

"Do they travel the roads quite often?"

"Yeah. The Weaver struggles with control over the mortals in Dreadweave Pass. There are so many who get sent here, it is nearly impossible to manage them all."

"Cursman?" Krista grabbed hold of her tail with her fingers.

"Yeah?"

"Why are you helping me?"

"Chances are Sporathun picked up on my scent with you. Even if I left you, he'd find me."

"No, I mean, why were you helping us with the gates before we discovered Sporathun? It's not like we have any money, if that even matters here."

"I suppose there's a streak of niceness in me after all."

"But why?" *It creeps me out that he's one of those . . . puppets.*

"Don't worry, sweetheart. I'm with you as long as you are a foe of the Weaver."

"I am worried. You said you worked for the Weaver. That scares me."

"I did. I was his personal assassin."

"You're a puppet."

Cursman chuckled. "Yeah. They are pretty creepy, aren't they?"

"You're not as creepy. I mean, you're not."

"I am. I get it. As long as I cover it up and people don't see it, they don't know. Most mortals transformed into puppets can no longer control their bodies; the Weaver uses them like drones. Few puppets keep mastery of movement—all part of the Weaver's design. General Dievourse, the leader of the Weaver's army, is one who has embraced his new state. He always came off like he was happy to be one. Other puppets who retained their consciousness are not so grateful."

"Like the creepy ones."

"Well, most of those don't have their consciousness anymore. I was lucky—the Weaver kept me in control of my body and kept my memories and my knowledge from the mortal world intact."

"Why?"

"He believed that the memories would keep me as cunning as I was before death. He was right about that much, but I'm craftier than the Weaver had anticipated." Cursman smirked.

"Are there others with their memories still?"

"Well, there is General Dievourse, then his lieutenant, and then the gatekeepers like El Aguro. I worked closely with all three of them. But they couldn't work together. Dievourse disapproves of El Aguro. Both are the most powerful, knowledgeable, and fully capable warriors to govern Dreadweave Pass. They are the Weaver's most brilliant creations. Both are obsessed with carrying out the Weaver's will and they're always trying to outdo each other in hopes that the Weaver will favour them. Thankfully, I never got wrapped up in the internal politics of the Weaver's army. I took orders only from the Weaver himself and the work I did was independent, with some technical assistance from Dievourse and El Aguro. The missions I had involved hunting down rebellions that were growing in Dreadweave Pass or taking out angels who learned too much about the Weaver's plan of vengeance against the gods."

"So you've dealt with fallen angels before?"

"Yeah. Well, more often with pure angels."

"That's good to know. Why did you leave the Weaver?"

"I knew the Weaver in person. I got to meet with him with each mission given. He's a fallen god, you know, and I saw his character firsthand, an honour only the four of us highest-ranked puppets—General Dievourse, the lieutenant, El Aguro, and myself—were given. Anyone else sent to the Weaver is destined for death. I've seen the irrational madness behind the ruler of Dreadweave Pass—the egotistical decisions made by the fallen god. I made the choice to abandon the Weaver, even though I knew that I would be hunted down by the puppets and killed if I was ever caught."

"What could you get from escaping the Weaver?"

Cursman put on a soft smile. "My wife."

"Where is she?"

"In the Heavenly Kingdoms, where I wish to be."

Cursman continued. "Like anyone in Dreadweave Pass, I wasn't among the good in the mortal world. I was vengeful, hateful, murderous, and destroyed hundreds of families. It was not until I found my wife that I realized what I'd been. She showed me a side of me I did not know was there, but I guess the gods didn't think I was worthy to be brought into the Heavenly Kingdoms."

"I hope you get to see her again."

"Thanks, kid. Me too."

Krista smiled. "Thank you."

"For what?" Cursman asked.

"For sharing your story with me."

"Yeah. You're welcome."

Maybe he isn't that bad.

The two walked in silence, only speaking to warn each other about the tricky path they walked on. Cursman led Krista over a creek of blood; they crossed over a rotting log to the other side. The creek went on for miles on both ends in a zigzag formation, disappearing into the distance. The two stayed near the road, but far enough away that they could not be seen from it. The forest dipped downward and the road was now on the higher ground.

The scenery was covered in a low white fog that spread for miles around. Several half-eaten, bony corpses were scattered in the dirt. Trees with faces, like those in the Blood Swamp, grew in the forest but were mixed in with thinner black trees. She spotted a few Lifeless Ones in the distance but they did not approach Krista and Cursman. Their eerie groans echoed sullenly as they disappeared into the fog.

"We'll cross the road now; it should be safe from any troubles," Cursman said.

Krista was worried about the word 'troubles' but didn't bother to ask him to clarify. *I have to trust him—he is really all I have right now.* She thought for a moment of Darkwing, but pushed the memories away. *Don't get sidetracked with wishes. You're in hell.*

The two walked up to the road. The hike was steep, making them rely on support from the nearby trees to push upward.

Cursman was the first to make it to the top and he extended his hand out to Krista. "Come."

Krista took his hand and was pulled up onto the road. "Thanks."

She scanned the road. It looked the same as every other road in Dreadweave Pass, with the exception of a stone statue to the far right. It was carved into the shape of a droplet, but large dragon-like wings sprouted from each side and the centre had a single reptilian eye. Abstract glyphs ran along the outer rim of the eye. Underneath the droplet were words carved into the stone.

"What's it say?" Krista asked.

"The glyphs? No clue."

"I mean the words below it. I know it's English."

"Oh, that is the City of Blood. It's a city built on top of the largest blood river in Dreadweave Pass. It's the only real city in hell. Even though it's under the Weaver's watch, he doesn't keep a close eye on it."

"Weaver's watch? I don't want to go anywhere near him!"

Cursman shook his head. "He doesn't live there. We will have to look out for his puppets, though—they're ruthless and I can't predict how they'll react to you." He examined Krista's exposed legs. "Try to hide your . . . more prime features. Maybe put your hood up or something so they can't tell your age."

Krista realized she was still wearing the short black dress that exposed her skin. She frowned and buttoned up her jacket. "Yeah." *I guess even in hell, males still have that behavior. It never goes away.* Krista flipped her hood over her head and nodded. "Okay."

The two walked along the right side of the wide road, large enough to have two wagons side by side. Several minutes passed and they came by a large, violent river filled with blood. There was an arched brick bridge going over it. On the other side of the river nearby was a black wooden gate with large, deep-red stone towers between it. A wall spread from each side of the tower, disappearing into the forest.

The two walked over the circular-bricked bridge, the sound of running liquid bubbling below. *I'd rather not look down to see any more deep pools of blood. I am so tired of blood.* Krista looked up beyond the two towers at the gate to see a much larger structure was behind the walls. It was a black castle that disappeared into the clouds. A range of cone-shaped towers were among the different tiers of the castle and a few bridges linked several of the towers.

"If it's not the Weaver, who's in the castle?" she asked.

"El Aguro," Cursman replied.

"I thought El Aguro was a gatekeeper."

"He has many roles; he is also the eyes and ears of the Weaver. They transported his gate here when the Weaver assigned him to govern the city."

"You know lots about the Weaver's military."

"I was there too, remember?"

"Right," said Krista gloomily.

"If it makes you feel any better, the Weaver is no less a child than you are. No offense."

While crossing the bridge, Krista couldn't resist the urge to look over the edge. Unlike the creek they'd passed earlier, the river was violent and the current splashed blood high against the rocks, staining them.

It gets stranger here every corner I turn.

"Don't get too excited—you're acting like you haven't been here before."

"But I haven't."

"The guards won't like that. They will sense you are a newcomer. We don't want attention."

Krista tried to keep her gaze forward, staying close to Cursman while they walked toward the gate. She had not realized how long the road was until she reached the opposite side of the river. It took them over a hundred paces to cross.

The gate was open, just a small crack, to allow one person in at a time. There was a single guard by the door who looked human. He was pale-skinned with stubble on his chin, and he wore a chainmail shirt and black trousers.

They remind me a bit of the Renascence Guard, watching their posts by the gates.

Cursman nodded at the man as he took Krista's hand.

The guard returned a bow and stepped aside to let the two pass.

They slipped behind the gate and into the City of Blood. Every building was a minimum of three stories tall, and others were much taller. Some were coal black, like the castle, and others were made of the dark-red stone seen on the towers. The roofs were covered in curved shingles and complete with gutters. The windows were finished with wooden louvres and the linings of the buildings were painted in black. Linen banners were draped over the roofs of the buildings. Some had a single eye on them like the statue on the road, and others had simple shape designs—squares, circles, and triangles overlapping—in vibrant colour schemes with more abstract glyphs surrounding them.

The narrow roads of the city were made of circular brick and branched off into a number of side streets and alleys. The long, straight road led up to the black castle in the heart of the city.

There were dozens of people, from what Krista could see—mostly human, while others had red skin or pointed ears. She didn't know what they were but they seemed humanoid much like herself. They wandered up and down the streets. They wore frowns on their dirty faces and their clothes were either black or stained red, much like the beings in Evergut. The people buzzed in and out of shops, some with baskets, others with wheelbarrows. The busyness of the city was familiar, like the City of Renascence.

The heavy clanging of armour caught Krista's attention and she scanned over to the side street on her left. Two heavily plated humanoids suited from head to toe were walking in their direction, eyeballing each person they neared. Their faces were concealed, but their chest plates had the same single reptilian eye on it, just like the banners. Their shoulder plates were moulded into the shape of bat wings and each joint in their armour ended in sharp points. They each wielded two-handed flails, and the spikes on the end of the weapons were at least a foot long. The beings held the weapons up and let the chains dangle down past their hips.

She tried to see into their cone-shaped helmets so she could identify their faces, but it was so dark inside them. In fact, it was so dark it was possible that there was no face inside the helmet at all.

I seriously would not be surprised with this place. Walking suits of armour don't seem so far-fetched anymore.

"Remain calm—we're only passing by," Cursman whispered to her while they walked deeper into the city.

The suits of armour stepped out onto the main road and began walking up behind Krista and Cursman. Their armour clanged louder the closer they walked.

Krista felt her back tingle as the sounds grew nearer. Were they going to grab her? Would it cause a large scene? What if they spoke to her?

The humanoids marched alongside Krista and Cursman, glancing at them as they walked past. Their eyeless stares felt cold, their heads so black and empty. An eerie wind picked up, blowing into Krista's hood, accompanied by a deep, steady whistling sound.

The moment passed in a couple of seconds. The wind died, the sound faded, and the humanoids looked away, continuing to march down the road.

Krista sighed. "Thank goodness."

Cursman slipped his arm around Krista's and yanked her to a side street. She had lost focus, staring at the sea of buildings. He brought her to a very narrow alleyway with a crooked road, only wide enough for two people. The buildings blocked most of the sky and Krista's eyes slowly adjusted to the change of light.

"Where are we going?"

"It's not exactly an advertised library, but I used to go here for intel. The chronicler doesn't like too much attention because he has secrets on just about everything in the Heavenly Kingdoms and Dega'Mostikas's Triangle." Cursman let go of her arm. "Come: this way."

The man took a right turn on the one crossroad they reached, leading deeper into the dark side streets. Krista followed without question, knowing he was all she had to trust. *I wish I had some guidance from Malpherities or Darkwing. It's hard to blindly trust Cursman.* She combed through her scalp-feathers several times. *Darkwing, if only you could see everything I've been through in such a short time.* She knew he would find her adventure fascinating. *He loves adventures. I'll have to tell him everything—if I make it out of here.*

Krista spotted a light midway down the alley from a window. She leaned to her side so she could see it from a better angle. There was a crooked wooden door that had a curved framing. A single window sat on one side of the door, and on the opposite, there was a wooden sign mounted with typographic characters she could not recognize.

She wasn't surprised that this was the library. Cursman stopped at the door and pushed it open, the hinges creaking.

"Stay close to me," he whispered while stepping through the doorframe.

Krista followed behind. The interior smelled of old leather and dusty pages, almost stale. It had a low stone ceiling, and held at least two dozen rows of black shelves. The library appeared to have several more columns of shelves further inside, too. Each shelf was jam-packed with books and binders lined up side by side. All of them varied in size and colour. Some shelves held stacks of loose papers. Every shelf was labelled with a small glyph.

The light-grey bricks of the floor were webbed with cracks, and the walls were made of the same stone as the exterior of the building.

"Hello?" Cursman spoke loudly, his voice echoing through the long hallways. "He has to be around here," Cursman mumbled to himself and started wandering into the aisles, glancing at a couple of the books.

Krista fell behind—she was mesmerized by the books. Some of the covers were made of linen, and other books had thick covers made of animal hides. The spines of each one were detailed with a painted finishing, laces, or writing.

Cursman shouted again. "Smelg!"

There are just so many different types. Her eyes widened. *If only I could read them, I can't imagine what they could tell.* She took a couple of steps to her side where a one shelf caught her attention—instead of books there was a range of sealed glass jars containing specimens. The samples ranged from organs in liquid, to bones, to dried plants. One particular jar caught her attention—it was the only one without a copper lid. The container was half filled with black bean-sized seeds with red stripes.

Oh god, I'm hungry. She instinctively took another step closer, reaching out to grab the jar.

A firm grip coiled around her wrist. Krista gasped and spun around to see Cursman.

"You don't want to consume those."

"Sorry."

Cursman eyed the jar of seeds before scanning the rest of room. "Don't get lost. The books will eat you alive."

Krista smiled. *I can see the books taking up lots of time. They're all so unique.*

A croaky voice called out. "Cursman?"

"Aye."

At the end of the aisle, a large white-and-brown bird stepped into the hall. He slouched and walked like an overgrown chicken on long, three-toed feet with sharp talons. He wore a deep-blue sleeveless robe lined with black. He had another set of three talons at the end of each wing which stuck through the large arm holes. The feathers were longest along his upper and lower wings. His extended face was narrow, ending with a curved black beak that was the same size as his skull. His head feathers extended far beyond his skull and draped downward. They bounced as he walked and perked straight up when he stood upright.

The bird stretched his beak while yawning and scratched his throat with the talons on his wings. "Cursman! You madman! What brings you here? The Weaver banished you from Dreadweave Pass, did he not?" His voice was croaky and difficult to understand as his throat animated rapidly to produce the sound of each vowel he spoke.

Cursman shrugged. "Not many places I can go when I'm trapped in his realm by the gods, are there, Smelg?"

Smelg nodded and glanced at Krista. His eyes widened and he hunched over, bringing himself down to Krista's eye level. "What is this?" He pointed at her with the talon on his toe. "You bring me a child?"

"We need your help."

"You're walking on thin ice travelling with one of such youth—and now you bring me into your problem? You know the Weaver's gatekeepers are the only ones who reap mortals of such a young age to Dreadweave Pass."

"We need to find information, and this is the place to find it."

The bird cackled. "You cannot ease me with flattering words."

Cursman raised an eyebrow. "Sporathun is loose." He placed a hand on Krista's shoulder. "And he wants this girl."

The bird squawked, raising his wings in the air, extending the full length of his wingspan. "And you come here?" he shouted. "Who's to say the vampyre won't come here too? You've drenched my home with your scent!" Smelg scowled, his red eyes boring into Cursman. "Why shouldn't I just turn you in now?"

"You and I both know the thousands of years of history in these books smother our scent. We could have easily gone into any nearby building."

The bird stared into the man's eyes for several moments and sighed. "All right, let's make this quick."

Cursman smiled. "Good. We need a history lesson."

"On Sporathun?"

"Correct."

Smelg motioned for them to follow and he led them down the next column of shelves. Krista scanned as many books as her eyes could manage while they walked. She was fascinated by how they were tailored and designed; it was too difficult to look away.

It's amazing that each book was made by someone. There must be thousands in here. She was never a good reader and didn't understand English well, even though it was only language she knew. *It makes me feel really stupid.* Everyone she knew had the ability to read. Even the boys at the High Barracks could read—they were far more educated than she was.

Seeing all these books reminds me of the underworld and the City of Renascence. I couldn't read much there either. Darkwing could read, though. She sighed. *Even through all of this I can't get him out of my mind.*

Smelg stopped at a series of shelves and began to mutter to himself, speaking the names of the books.

Krista strayed behind the two and began eyeing the titles on the shelf closest to her. The shelf was packed even tighter than the other shelves. On the far-right end at her eye level was a stack of books piled from the bottom up.

She glanced behind to see Cursman and Smelg were busy looking through a book.

There's no telling how long he will be. She looked at the stack of books and noticed one was easily reachable at the top of the pile. Krista grabbed the book and pulled it out, feeling the rubbery texture of the flesh-toned cover. The book itself was warm—quite warm.

Someone must have just held it. She ran her hands along the back, the bony spine, and front of the cover. As she continued to touch it, she realized the heat originated from the book itself. *It's like the heat is coming from inside.*

She turned the book face-front and squinted, trying to read the text. The cover only had red English words painted on it. The paint had faded, so she knew she wouldn't be able to read it even if she could read.

She began to pull open the cover just as the book sprung from her hand, lunging at her.

Krista shrieked while the book flapped about. The only thing that kept it back was her grip on the cover. There were no pages inside the book, just a mouth full of razor-sharp teeth and a long, slippery tongue that sprayed saliva over her.

The book growled and lunged at her again, tongue moving wildly while it attempted to open and close itself.

The book's force was too much and she let it go, dodging the book as it flew toward her face. The tongue of the book smeared across her cheek as it buzzed by before it landed heavily on the floor, spread open.

Her heart raced as she spun around, keeping her eyes locked on the book. It twitched on the floor, and the cover fell closed, thumping violently on the stone floor.

Cursman stomped over to the book, clamping it shut by the spine. "What did I tell you? The books will eat you!" He put the book on the pile it had come from.

Krista felt her cheek; it was covered in the slime from the book. She nodded at Cursman. "Sorry." Her hands shook from the adrenaline rush. She swallowed heavily. "I didn't think that would happen." *Although I should be ready for anything by now.*

Smelg clicked his beak together in disapproval, then raised his hands, revealing another book. This one was far larger and thicker than the one Krista had held. The pages were stained brown and the cover was a deep red with engraved text on the front. "The Fallen Angel Encyclopedia," he announced.

He took Krista and Cursman to a short table deeper inside the library. There were four chairs, and they sat at one end of the table with Smelg in the middle. He opened the book with the crisp sound of old, wrinkled paper.

Krista leaned against the table and looked at the words. They looked like English but the characters had dots on them and were shaped differently. *More things I cannot read.* She took notice of the pages; they were bound to the cover by a leather lace and holes punched in the pages.

"The Fallen Angel Encyclopedia is an ongoing record of all angels that fall from the light. I have written articles in here, and so have others. Now, Sporathun is free, you say?" Smelg flipped through the pages until he found the correct section. He pointed at the chapter heading. "Sporathun."

"Yes, it doesn't make sense. The Weaver had General Dievourse go through great lengths to capture and lock Sporathun away so he wouldn't cause any more damage to Dreadweave Pass," Cursman said.

Smelg nodded and cleared his throat before reading the text. "It states here that Sporathun fell from the heavens centuries ago." Smelg ran his claw along the words as he read. "Before then, he was once a stunningly handsome angel who served the gods in the Heavenly Kingdoms without question. He was known as Crasoe, meaning 'Handsome Creature.' Crasoe was a highly ranked military hunter, ensuring that Dega'Mostikas's demons did not cross into the Heavenly Kingdoms. The gods often sent him down into hell to exterminate targeted demons. He had complete freedom in the Kingdoms except, like all angels, he had to follow the single law all angels must conform to: No angel shall descend to man's plane, the plane of sin. Crasoe disobeyed the gods by breaking this law. To be exact, he broke it twice. There was a young angel named Glamorous. She served the gods as a vocalist, singing the most beautiful songs throughout the Heavenly Kingdoms, a voice that could soothe the deadliest of beasts. Glamorous and Crasoe met at the God Ha's chambers. Glamorous was there on duty to sing, while Sporathun was summoned to discuss tactics against Dega'Mostikas. Whether it was fate or design, Crasoe and Glamorous met.

Crasoe and Glamorous fell for each other, presumably in lust. The two of them often met in secrecy, knowing that their desire for each other was not accepted in the Heavenly Kingdoms—and the one law that they had to obey, they were breaking."

Smelg scratched his head. "Now, it doesn't mention how they were caught. But Glamorous and Sporathun's affair was not to last—the gods eventually discovered them. Glamorous begged the gods, explaining that it was love that bound her and Crasoe. The gods were not merciful and were convinced the two angels met in lust, so they banished Glamorous from the Heavenly Kingdoms, throwing her down into Dega'Mostikas's Triangle. They stripped her of her wings and tore out her vocal cords, leaving her mute."

Cursman put his hand on the page. "Wait. So Glamorous and Crasoe fell for each other, making them fallen angels of lust?"

Smelg nodded. "Correct, Glamorous is a vampyre of lust. Sporathun is an interesting case. Let me continue."

Cursman nodded.

"Crasoe's fate was soon to be judged by the gods. They thought of him as a valuable asset and were willing to rehabilitate him from the sin of lust. However, he was significantly enraged at the harsh treatment they'd given to his lover, Glamorous. The rage boiled inside of him, so deep that it began to affect his physical appearance. The anger building up inside tightened his muscles and they began to twist and cause white growths on his back. Horns began to emerge from his head, for his mind was filled with wicked thoughts. His eyelids sealed up and he was forever blinded by his anger because he could not forgive the gods for what they had done to Glamorous. At that moment, Crasoe was consumed by a second sin, wrath. To release his anger, he hunted Ha, waiting for when he was in deep meditation. He struck at Ha with his bare hands, beating him relentlessly to death then taking his decapitated head and draining the blood throughout his chamber."

"Why did Sporathun target Ha?" Cursman asked.

"He believed Ha was the one who had discovered the affair. He also believed Ha secretly was in love with Glamorous but could hide his emotions and was jealous of Crasoe. Regardless of why Crasoe killed Ha, the other gods acted quickly. They banished him from the Heavenly Kingdoms, now realizing he was consumed by his sins. Crasoe had fallen from the light, so they nicknamed him Sporathun, meaning 'Spotted Hunter of Wrath.' This name was given to him because of the hideous bumps on his back and his wrathful nature. They stripped him of his wings as well and threw him into Dega'Mostikas's Triangle. Specifically, they placed him in Dreadweave Pass because they thought he could eventually find his way from sin. His absence was a great loss to the Heavenly Kingdoms, so they put faith in his recovery." The bird lifted his finger even though there was more text to read. "This book only informs how an angel falls, not anything afterward. From here on it goes into the next angel to fall."

Cursman shook his head. "That's it? This tells us nothing of why he is free, or of his weakness. Why did his sin mutate him so greatly? Most fallen angels keep their angelic features."

Smelg shrugged. "Perhaps the feeling of hatred was too much and transformed him, or perhaps it is the duality of lust and wrath. Your guess is as good as mine."

"That doesn't explain how to defeat him, though, just his strengths. What about the fact that he has to feed two sins, lust and wrath?"

"Indeed, he can replenish himself with either sin or both at the same time. Doubly sinned angels are rare, and their sins stack, so they are twice as deadly."

"So what's his weakness?"

"Perhaps Glamorous? She was banished to Dreadweave Pass, too." He flipped to the earlier pages of the book and found her biography. "It says she was thrown to Dreadweave Pass to repent her sin. Her current location is unknown, but she can't be hard to identify from her angelic figure. The article here predicts she crashed in one of the three areas: first, the Ruins of the Mortals Run, which is an abandoned labyrinth used by fallen gods."

"Nearby . . . Just a short way from the city." Cursman said.

"It is and quite dangerous, if you recall."

"I know. Why might she be there?"

"The labyrinth was cast off to Dreadweave Pass around the time Glamorous descended. The Ring of Judgment potentially released them in the same area." Smelg said.

"Right. What else do we have?"

"Number two, the Weaver found her first when she came to Dreadweave Pass and is keeping her captive.

Cursman nodded. "So he can use Sporathun as a tool, promising he would release her if he obeys him."

Krista fiddled with her tail. "That would also explain why he is after me."

Smelg pointed at the article. "Yes, if that is the case. It also says she could have fallen into God's Tears, the only source of water in Dreadweave Pass, and she went downstream."

"There's no guarantee which one she is at?"

"No. They are all of equal possibility."

"So you think we should find her? What would that do for us?" Cursman brushed his hair with both hands. "Sporathun seeing Glamorous a vampyre will only feed his wrath, making him even more difficult to control. Not to mention his desire for her."

The historian closed the book and chuckled. "One's greatest strength is also one's greatest weakness."

CHAPTER XIV

Wrath

Our Creator, who watches over all.
Your child, I am.
Blessed to be in thy kingdom.
Created by you, with your endless grace.
While you provide endless love.
In this land of endless dire.
Deliver us from temptation.
Protect us in your eternal embrace.
Then thy will be done.

You are the way, the truth, and the life.
Without your guidance we will not find you.
So I beg you, Creator, lead me from false ecstasy.
For this temporary delight is no comparison to your distant light.
Its spark may die while dragging me.
If with your will I do not comply.
Creator, deliver me from the evil one.

men," came Crasoe's rugged voice as he sat cross-legged on the soft purple mattress in his chamber. The open windows on all sides of the bedroom allowed for a cool breeze to flow through. They also provided an exceptional view of the white sky and the endless sea of colour below the Heavenly Kingdoms—the mortal realm.

He raised his head and took a deep breath. "Creator, I have sinned," he mumbled while glancing over to see the pale white body of the angel who bedded with him. The purple, silky sheet covered only her pelvis, leaving the rest of her elegant figure in view.

Was it sin? Crasoe ran the question through his mind countless times after each encounter he had with her. After he met Glamorous in God Ha's chamber, he was moved by emotions he had never experienced before. The sensation he had while staring into her eyes, listening to the enchanting melodies of her song, her slim figure—all of it put him into a trance. Never before had he been able to numb his thoughts so easily. Previously, he'd have to spend hours in meditation to calm himself after a battle or, since the Truce of Passing and the lack of war, to retain control of his better self.

The mental damage of warfare affected so many angels, and those who failed to keep faith in the Creator fell to sin. Crasoe was strong-willed and could push the corrupting desire back. Just because he was a war fiend did not mean he couldn't function in times of peace . . . did it?

He swallowed heavily and stared out into the sky. *The sensation I felt when first meeting Glamorous—was it driven by love or by lust?* He contemplated the idea that his pent-up urge for violence was being transposed into dominating Glamorous for pleasure. Even though she was just as willing as he was, it did not change that he worried for his own status in the Heavenly Kingdoms. He had seen firsthand his comrades fall from the light and become vampyres. What if this was what he was destined to be?

After the first time Crasoe saw Glamorous, he found it difficult to get her out of his head. They had seen each other several other times in God Ha's chamber, exchanging glances but never speaking.

"Crasoe," Glamorous said softly.

Crasoe looked over his shoulder, where Glamorous was staring at him with her vibrant green eyes. She sat upright, raising her thin eyebrows. "What is on your mind?"

"I am recalling the events of how we met."

Glamorous smiled and leaned against his shoulder. "I think about it every day. When we finally found each other outside of God Ha's chamber we spoke so few words and expressed so much when we touched."

Crasoe looked to the ground. "Do you ever wonder what this is going to do to us?"

Glamorous raised her head. "What do you mean?"

"You and I: what are we?"

"We're in love, are we not?"

Crasoe leaned forward, pressing his hands together. "That is what I believe, but what we believe is not necessarily the reality. We could simply be blinded by our desire for each other."

"With love, it is. The Creator loves us—we believe that. How is our love any different?"

"But how will others receive this? Angels expressing this level of intimacy is forbidden, unless the interactions are guided by the gods."

Glamorous looked to the ground. "I pray, Crasoe. The gods may rule over the Heavenly Kingdoms, but I trust that the Creator's divine will can protect us and the gods will see the good that we have."

"You have proven good for me. My desire for war lessens with the time we spend together."

Glamorous smiled. "The time we've spent has been pure euphoria. But I do not deny the worries that you feel, Crasoe. There will be great backlash to what we have done. But what about your sister? After her encounter with Dega'Mostikas, she was left wounded and had never quite recovered . . ."

Crasoe nodded. "No, she did not. Her case was different, though; her interaction with Dega'Mostikas was not of her free will. The gods spent many years rehabilitating her mind."

Glamorous shrugged. "How is she? I have not had the honor of meeting her in person."

"She is fine, same as before. She struggles with inner turmoil—like myself—but her value to the Heavenly Kingdoms' army is irreplaceable and the gods do their best to try and break the mental link she has with Dega'Mostikas."

"She is so brave. I respect her greatly."

"As do I, but I fear she does not share the same respect for me."

"What do you mean?"

"If she discovered what we've done, she would take the right turn of action and report us to the gods, and we would be judged by the Ring of Judgment."

Glamorous frowned.

"She plays by the rules when they favour her." Crasoe stood up.

"Where are you going?" asked Glamorous.

"God Ha had demanded my presence."

"Again? What does he want to meet you for?"

"Hard to say—possibly a follow-up report on my research into the Weaver."

Crasoe turned and leaned closer to Glamorous, stroking the back of her head down to her jaw. "Until we meet again." He brought her head closer to his until their lips pressed tight against each other, embracing her touch and taste.

Crasoe stood up and fashioned his kilt around his waist.

Glamorous stroked her hair, watching him dress. "Goodbye."

He exited his quarters, located in an isolated tower in the first tier of the Heavenly Kingdoms. Looking back once, he nodded and spread his wings wide, leaping into the air and soaring through the kingdom toward God Ha's chamber, located in the centre of the tier.

The angel flapped his wings several times while arching upward to the balcony leading directly to God Ha's throne. His flight seemed long when in reality it was short; his mind was just clouded with many thoughts. Should he continue seeing Glamorous? What were the risks? If he ended his affair, how would she take it? If they were truly bound by lust, then if he no longer saw her, their desires to sin again would boil inside them, transfiguring them to vampyres.

Crasoe shook his head. *Snap out of it*, he thought while slowing his ascent to approach the balcony.

God Ha was standing tall waiting for him, his masked face staring out into the mortal realm below.

With one last push of his wings, Crasoe soared over the balcony railing, landing on both feet beside God Ha.

The god looked down at the angel. "Crasoe. It is a pleasure to see you again."

"Likewise." Crasoe stood straight, eyeing the god's masked face.

God Ha looked back out into curved streets below. "Normally we meet with an agenda in mind, Crasoe."

"Indeed; this meeting is a bit of a mystery to me." Crasoe put his hands behind his back and looked out at the scenery.

"How are you handling the Truce of Passing? With no war, it must be difficult for you to adjust."

"I am managing. With the Creator's guidance, I believe I can be rid of the memories that haunt me."

"How do you see him assisting you?"

Crasoe squinted. "I am uncertain; the Creator works in mysterious ways."

Ha chuckled. "Such a simple answer, isn't it?"

"Sorry?"

"When we are lost, we put our faith in the Creator—rightfully so. But the phrase 'mysterious ways' is open to interpretation, don't you think?"

Crasoe tilted his head slightly. "I'm no expert in the Creator's words, but when he provides us with a solution, it is something we feel is right."

"Indeed." God Ha placed his hands behind his back. "Perhaps he will assist you with a friend to relate with."

"Perhaps. What did you want to meet about?" Crasoe felt his palms sweat; the conversation made him feel ill at ease. *Is Ha referring to . . .?*

"Let us cut to the chase, then—how is Glamorous?"

"Glamorous? Isn't she personally scheduled in your chamber the majority of the time?"

"No, not as of lately. I've had to replace her because her schedule is too busy, she claims."

"No surprise. Her singing is well renowned throughout the

Heavenly Kingdoms."

"It seems odd to me that her schedule has only lessened in availability since you met her in my chamber."

"What are you saying?"

"I am a patient god, Crasoe. I understand being busy, but it has been far too long since I last had Glamorous' voice echo through my chamber."

Crasoe swallowed. "I don't know what that would have to do with me, Ha."

"Punishment! Impure! Fallen!" Loud chanting came from the ground level of Ha's chamber. "Punishment! Impure! Banishment!"

Crasoe leaned over the railing of the balcony to look down at the wide pathway leading up the stairs to God Ha's chamber. Down below, a crowd of angels with their wings folded back held spears pointed to one slim angel ahead of them, marching toward the staircase with beings in deep robes in front. The deep-blue robes were the traditional colours of the gods and angels who made up the Ring of Judgment. Their hoods were up and they walked up the stairs in uniform motion.

Who was the angel being brought to the council? Not once was it promising news when an angel was brought before them.

God Ha looked down toward the chanting crowd. "Then I suppose you would know nothing of the events that are currently taking place, would you, Crasoe?"

Crasoe squinted his eyes, trying to see who the angel below was.

"It is love!" came a cry through the chanting crowd. "We are not sinners!"

Crasoe felt his heart skip a beat; he recognized the soft voice. He glanced at God Ha, who continued to watch the crowd march up the stairs.

"I'm going to find out what is going on." Crasoe leaped over the railing and arched his wings back, diving downward at rapid speeds. It probably would have been wise for him to stay on the balcony with Ha and watch Glamorous be sentenced to whatever harsh sentence the Ring of Judgment gave her, but he couldn't. What he felt for her wasn't something he was able to shrug off. For the first time, Crasoe felt compelled to obey his impulse behavior. He was not in control.

Rahiie is in the Ring of Judgment, she will reason this out with me, he thought. It was the best plan he could think of in such short notice.

The wind picked up, blowing his hair back. He squinted to keep his eyes clear, watching as the last row of angels marched into the building, closing the door behind them.

The main floor of God Ha's chamber was the Ring of Judgment's meeting area, where they made decisions on the angels, gods, and mortals of the Heavenly Kingdoms that did not comply with the gods' laws. It was strategically built above three revolving gateways into Dega'Mostikas's Triangle. Each gate led into one of the three hells and was designed as a one-way path so the demons could not enter the heavens through the portals. The revolving gateways were constructed by the founding gods who engineered the Seven Heavenly Kingdoms millennia ago. It was no longer used for war, like it was originally, since the Truce of Passing was now in effect.

Crasoe spread his wings to soften his landing, but he was too reckless and landed with a thud on the marble staircase. His accelerated strength and heavy weight caused the stairs to crack, chips flying in all directions.

The angel rushed up the stairs and pulled open the large, gold-bordered doors to see inside the circular chamber. The ten hooded members of the Ring of Judgment were on the opposite side of the dark, torch-lit room. It was easy to spot Rahiie out of the ten members, as she was the only being with horns.

The angels were on the other side, closer to the entrance, still chanting, "Punishment, Impure! Fallen! Banishment!" The chamber sloped inwards about a dozen steps to the centre of the room where Glamorous stood, hands pressed against each other.

Crasoe rushed into the chamber. "Enough!"

The chanting crowd did not hear him.

The council member in the centre held out a scroll with his ghostly white hands.

God Lo, the head council member. Crasoe thought.

God Lo's piercing voice boomed: "Glamorous, you are summoned here by the Ring of Judgment for your treason against the Heavenly Kingdoms. Your act of lustful sin is a direct violation of the Seven Heavenly Virtues and you are hereby banished from the Heavenly Kingdoms for straying from the light."

"No, please! I have not fallen," Glamorous cried.

"Stop this!" Crasoe pushed the crowd of angels aside until he was at the front of the group, facing the gods. "This is blasphemy! Glamorous has done nothing."

"Crasoe?" Rahiie's eyes widened while stepping forward.

God Lo lowered his scroll. "Crasoe, you and Glamorous have committed a mortal sin and we are compelled to take action in the name of the Creator."

"We are bound by love!" Glamorous cried while falling to her knees. "How can you not see this?"

Rahiie swallowed heavily, staring at her brother for validation.

Crasoe exhaled heavily through his nostrils. "This is wrong!"

"We see the truth!" The council members' voices boomed through the chamber, silencing the chanting angels.

God Lo pointed at Glamorous. "The signs of a vampyre do not show physically early on but we are well aware of how you two met and what you continue to do. Because of this, we have made the judgment that your relationship with Crasoe is purely driven by lust."

"No!" Glamorous shouted. "That is a lie!"

All ten council members, including Rahiie, raised their right hand, palms facing Glamorous.

"Rahiie? Ring of Judgment, stop this!" Crasoe shouted.

Rahiie lipped the words, *sorry brother* before shifting her focus to Glamorous along with the rest of the group.

"Punishment! Impure! Banishment!" The angels and gods shouted again, slamming their spears simultaneously into the ground.

"No!" Crasoe shouted and jumped down toward Glamorous. In the moment of his leap, three nearby angels clutched onto his arms, preventing him from rescuing his dear love.

"Do not interfere with the will of the gods, Crasoe," one of the angels muttered in a gritty voice.

Crasoe let out a roar while tearing away from the angels, running toward Glamorous.

"Crasoe, don't be a fool!" Rahiie shouted.

A spear lunged from the crowd of angels, piercing into the back of Crasoe's knee, throwing him to the ground.

Glamorous spun around. "Crasoe! No! Do not interfere; it will be fatal for you."

God Lo snapped the fingers of his left hand, creating a smokeless flame in his palm. "May God have mercy on your soul, Glamorous." He brought the scroll to the flame and ignited it.

Glamorous screamed as her wings spontaneously combusted in a bright white inferno.

The god released the last scrap of the scroll to the ground as it burned, becoming ashes before it hit the ground.

Glamorous screeched one last time before gagging and vomiting blood onto the floor. She tried to shout while turning to face Crasoe, but no sound emerged from her throat.

"Glamorous!" Crasoe shouted, ripping the spear from his leg.

Several of the angels rushed toward him, one stepping on his fresh wound and the other two pinning his arms to the ground, forcing him to lay on his back and watch from below.

She tried to speak one more time but no words came out. She mouthed the words "I love you" through her bloody lips.

Crasoe ground his teeth and roared, using all his might to push the angels off of him. He got to his feet, throwing a swift punch to one angel's face before rushing down the stairs.

God Lo pointed toward Glamorous. "You are sentenced to Dreadweave Pass, where you will repent for your actions!"

The central circle Glamorous stood on split in two, both parts disappearing into the steps' edges, causing her to fall in.

"Glamorous!" Crasoe shouted again, leaping to the ground, extending his hand down into the hole. It was too late: Glamorous was beyond his reach and he could only see her burning wings descending beyond the thick black clouds into the red, rocky landscape of Dreadweave Pass.

The centre circle's halves closed back together, sealing the portal into hell.

Crasoe pounded his fist against the stone while breathing heavily as the chanting ended.

"It is okay to feel remorse, Crasoe," said a deep voice.

God Ha . . .

"Did you think your affair would have lasted? We were bound to find out."

Crasoe heard God Ha's footsteps walking down to the centre of the chamber.

The central council member cleared his throat. "You are a valuable asset, Crasoe, and we cannot afford to lose you. Even though we are in a time of peace with Dega'Mostikas, we can never relax our defenses. We need you to clean up those who violate the Truce of Passing."

God Ha's feet stopped once they were parallel with Crasoe's face. "We may have had a conflict of interest with Glamorous, Crasoe, but our relationship is far more valuable. Thus, I have convinced the Ring of Judgment to spare you."

Crasoe grunted and pushed himself up to his feet. He limped from the wound in the flesh behind his knee. His eyebrows curved downward as he felt his veins shake with fury. "You knew about this?"

"Of course I did. I am not a fool, Crasoe. This is why you and I make such a good partnership: my intellect and your field training."

"Did you order her banishment?"

"For the betterment of the Heavenly Kingdoms."

Crasoe roared from the depths of his throat, feeling his lungs burn from the energy he projected. The aggressive shout bounced off the stone walls as he swiftly turned to throw a punch to God Ha's ribs.

The god deflected the blow with one arm and gave a swift backhand to Crasoe's head, disorienting him. Ha kicked Crasoe's wounded knee, causing him to fall to the ground, rear hitting the stone floor first.

The Ring of Judgment and angels gradually left the chamber in silence—with the exception of Rahiie who broke free from the group and rushed over to her brother, moving past Ha.

"Crasoe." She spoke softly while extended her hand to him.

"No!" Crasoe slapped her hand away. "You betrayed me."

"Brother." Rahiie's eyes began to water. "It wasn't . . . I didn't."

"You turned your back on me!" Crasoe shouted, spit flying into Rahiie's face.

Rahiie remained petrified and stared at her brother.

God Ha shook his head. "Clear your head, Crasoe. Glamorous may have fallen into sin, but we can rehabilitate you like we did for your sister." God Ha placed a hand on Rahiie's shoulder. "You've done your duty. You may go."

Crasoe exhaled heavily, feeling anger boil inside of him.

"Dega'Mostikas really does flow through your veins, sister."

Rahiie gasped and quickly burst into tears, trying to cover her face with her mutated hand. She shook her head and darted out of the chamber, her cries echoing.

"You're a wreck, Crasoe. Take some time away to flush away your foolish thoughts of lust and strengthen your relationship with the Creator." Ha spoke while turning to leave the chamber. "It is what I did, for the same reasons as you."

Crasoe was left alone in the chamber to grieve over the loss of Glamorous and the betrayal of Rahiie. He leaned back against the second step's edge, arms sprawled out while looking up at the flat ceiling. His wounded leg stung slightly, but it was the least of his concerns. He was a soldier and knew how to handle physical pain. The emotional pain that coursed through his entire body was something entirely new and he did not know what to do with it.

How could an action that did not inflict any physical mark on me cause so much damage? Perhaps it was related to the intensity he felt when he first saw Glamorous. It wasn't just pain he sensed; it was now mixed with immense levels of rage. It was so intense that he felt his entire body shake.

He closed his eyes. "Creator, how could you?" he whispered.

Hours went by sitting in the Ring of Judgment's chamber as Crasoe soaked in his own misery. His mind was locked in replay of the day's events. It happened so quickly—he was lying in bed with his lover, and moments later, her wings were burning away while she vomited blood. *I've seen angels vomit blood before; it happens when the gods strip the angel of their prime skill. In Glamorous' case, it would be her beautiful voice.* If his theory was right, she was now a mute. And potentially, a mute vampyre of lust.

I do need to clear my head.

Crasoe limped his way out of the chamber, spread his wings and soared through the Tier of Temperance, eventually reaching the outskirts of the Heavenly Kingdoms. He didn't know why he travelled so far; his mind was numb and all his choices seemed questionable. He felt like a chunk was torn out of his physical being.

It's the effects of having emotions.

Not often had he gone this far, to the outskirts of the tier. Here there were fewer roads, which eventually ended, and smaller buildings housing mortals. After that, there was nothing but blissful emptiness.

Crasoe did not stop there. His mind still held an image of Glamorous' face as she lipped the words *"I love you"* before she descended to Dreadweave Pass. He did not realize that he was beginning to turn his flight downward, to the mortal realm.

Once he realized the distance he'd covered, the Heavenly Kingdoms were just a mere speck in space; not even the long distance between the tiers could be differentiated. The contrast between the white heavenly sky and the colourful space of the mortal realm was not as sharp. This close to the mortal realm, there were large boulders floating in the outer rim of space. Some were lively with trees and other plants, but the ones further down were cold and dark like the asteroids seen around the stars.

Crasoe slowed his speed to land on one of the bare rocks, where there was a small cave. The rock was not stationary like some of the platforms covered with plants; this one had a slow rotation to it as it floated through space.

The angel landed on his good leg and eyed the small surface; he was the only one here. Little did that matter to him, though. He was too focused on Glamorous burning, the gods and angels chanting, Rahiie and God Ha. *Rahiie betrayed me, Ha betrayed me. We had had a mutual understanding and protected each other through the politics of the Heavenly Kingdoms. Why would they both destroy my trust now? My own sister!*

Crasoe reached the small cave and fell to his knees, hugging them. "The gods betrayed me." Did they really? For a moment, he had clarity in his thoughts, recalling the questions he'd asked himself while Glamorous was in his bed. Crasoe was uncertain if they would be caught; now they had been and he was angered. To him, it was clear he was betrayed by the Heavenly Kingdoms and abandoned by the Creator. How could God allow for something like this to happen? Glamorous was the one being who kept his warmongering thoughts at bay.

The real anger I feel is toward God Ha. God Ha said he wanted to speak to his sister about her condition. Did he persuade her to betray Crasoe? It was out of Rahiie's character. Ha claimed it was through deep meditation that he restored his relationship with the Creator. Crasoe wondered why he had to restore it in the first place, and why he was so fascinated with Glamorous.

Time seemed to no longer exist to Crasoe as he squatted in the cave, watching the scenery around him rotate over and over. *The constant spinning of this rock . . . a reflection of my thoughts.* It was true; he could not take his mind from losing Glamorous, or Rahiie's and God Ha's betrayal. The pain, the anger he felt only escalated to the point he could physically feel the stress build up on his back. He felt massive bumps begin to raise all over his skin from his pent-up stress.

He continued to watch the rotating scenery, completely unaware of how long he remained motionless in the cave. *Hours, days, years . . . does it really matter? I have no control over my own life; the gods dictate what I do and don't do.*

Crasoe suddenly punched the rocky ground several times. "I did not wish for this!" he shouted. "I did not wish for any of this!" He ran out of the cave and stood tall, looking up at the pure white sky. "Creator! Why have you done this to me?"

His voice echoed for miles around, only to be answered by silence. There was no reply; Crasoe was alone. Even the Creator did not respond.

"Why?" Crasoe shouted. *None of this would have happened if God Ha had remained my ally. He took Glamorous away from me. He filled my sister's head with lies.* He paced back and forth on the rock, tugging at his hair tightly. *None of this would have happened if I had not pursued Glamorous.* He roared and tore out a chunk of his hair. "No! Glamorous was a blessing! It was God Ha who took it all away from me!"

Crasoe knew that it was Glamorous who could cure his desire for violence. His countless decades of meditation did not compare to the sweet smell and gentle touch of her body. *How I miss it.* With her gone, there was no soothing his craving for war. *Unless I start my meditation practice all over again, spending years to try and rebuild what I had.* He had found his remedy for the war the gods forced him to take part in. *Then God Ha took her away from me!*

Crasoe spread his wings wide. "Ha!" he roared while tightening his fists. "I am coming for you!"

He leaped into the air with several massive flaps of his wings, eyeing the Heavenly Kingdoms far into the distance.

Ha, you will pay for what you have done.

The streets of the Tier of Temperance were clear, and the skies held few angels flying. Those who were, were on their way to either rest or meditate for the day. The skies may never see darkness, but a waking and resting cycle took place.

This is why I wait. Crasoe flapped his wings in motion to keep hovering along the side of God Ha's chamber. He had kept himself out of sight from the skies and the roads of the city, waiting for the rest cycle to begin. He knew there would be less possibility of anyone catching him during his act of vengeance.

His heart raced as he tried to control his heavy breathing. He could feel the rage inside him was desperate to get out.

Crasoe took one deep breath and swooped forward, spreading his wings for a soft landing on God Ha's balcony. He quickly looked around to see if the god was awake.

At the far end of the chamber on the circular extension, God Ha sat cross-legged on his throne with his palms facing upward.

The angel stood tall in the middle of the entranceway. God Ha did not move.

If the god was awake, he would obviously see him. But there was a possibility that he was in meditation.

Or he may be acting, waiting for me to make the first move.

Crasoe stepped forward quietly, not sure which one of the scenarios he was in. His fist clenched tighter the closer he came to Ha. Seeing the god again, the rage that boiled inside him only grew stronger with each step he took closer.

I will rip out his throat.

The god was only a dozen steps away when Crasoe came to a halt, scowling at the tall being. Ha's breathing was slow—calm—as if he were unaware of the situation.

The angel remained motionless, breathing quietly through his nose to avoid any sound. He stood there for several moments to see if the god would make the first move.

He could hear his own heart pump with each beat that it made. Time seemed to drag on, but the god was perfectly still.

That's it. Crasoe decided he would make the first move. The angel rushed forward, hands straight out, aiming for the god's neck.

In the blink of an eye the god's hands moved upward, grabbing onto Crasoe's.

"Did you really think I was meditating, you fool?" Ha growled.

Both pairs of arms shook vigorously, trying to get the upper hand in the struggle.

"I grew tired of standing," Crasoe snapped back. "I've come to seek vengeance for Glamorous." The angel rushed forward and head-butted the god's mask, cracking the wood.

The blow was enough to allow Crasoe to jerk free from Ha's grasp.

God Ha kicked his legs out, his bare feet knocking Crasoe in the chest.

The blow threw Crasoe to the ground, rolling backward until he gained balance upright again. He looked up to see that the god was now charging toward him.

Ha jumped upward, spinning, swiftly extending his one leg for a lethal hit.

Crasoe dashed to the side, crouching low and waiting for the god's next move.

Ha landed and turned to face him, standing tall, fists clenched. "You disappear for over a decade just to attempt an assassination? You're making a grave mistake, Crasoe. If you go down this path, you know there is no return."

"I've made up my mind, Ha . . ." Crasoe was caught off-guard. He had no idea how much time had passed while he was on the spinning rock. To him it had been merely hours. ". . . and it has been set on vengeance the moment Glamorous descended into hell."

"What of your sister?"

"The one you turned from me? I will not show you mercy."

"I see sin has consumed you . . . So be it." Ha shifted his position to a defensive stance, waiting for Crasoe to attack.

The angel roared and threw a swift kick toward Ha. The god deflected with his forearm and lunged his knee at Crasoe.

Both Ha and Crasoe extended blows with their fists and feet, attempting to strike each other. They had known each other for countless centuries and could reach each other well.

Crasoe was a speedy, tactical fighter, but God Ha was larger and one solid hit would be devastating.

God Ha swiped his leg out for a low strike and cupped his hands, slamming down with a heavy blow.

Crasoe leaped back while flapping his wings, hovering until he was head-level with Ha.

"Quit hovering, you fly!" Ha threw an uppercut.

Crasoe dodged the attack while rushing toward Ha's side.

The god attempted to step back but Crasoe managed to grab Ha's upper arm and neck, his legs clamped across the torso. His grip was tight and he pulled together, restricting Ha's ability to use his arm.

They swayed side to side, each trying to gain dominance. God Ha roared and leaped backward to crush the angel on his back.

Crasoe jumped off just as Ha slammed onto the floor, denting the ground. The angel swooshed downward before the god could stand upright. He aimed for Ha's neck with his fists but was deflected by the god's arm.

The god used his other arm to throw a punch to Crasoe's ribs. The angel managed to stop the blow with both of his hands. Crasoe lunged the heel of his foot forward under Ha's arm and rammed into the god's neck.

The hit caused God Ha to gag, paralyzing him momentarily. It was just enough time for Crasoe to push God Ha's arms away and rush forward, grabbing his head with both hands. Crasoe clamped down, digging deep into the god's bald skull. The angel lifted Ha's head up as the god attempted to push him away with all his limbs. Crasoe slammed Ha's head back down into the metal floor. The blow dazed the god and his arms relaxed.

Crasoe lifted Ha's head again. He slammed it down multiple times, until blood started to pour from the back of the god's skull. The angel let go, inhaling heavily as he ran his hands down to the god's neck and clutched the skin, thumbs pressing onto God Ha's jugular notch.

The god gagged and tried to push Crasoe away but the angel's grip was fueled with all the rage that had boiled inside him since Glamorous's banishment. He could feel the air gradually being sucked out of Ha.

While he squeezed, Crasoe clenched his teeth, pulling on the god's head and lifting with all his might.

Ha's arms moved wildly, trying to gain some control while his spine began to crack. His struggling turned into twitching just as his neck snapped. The muscle tissues then easily tore and his skin peeled apart until the head ripped free, causing blood to flow onto the ground like it was coming from a hose.

Crasoe roared while lifting the head high above his own, fluids raining down on his face.

"Enough!" came the powerful shout of a female.

Crasoe growled and spun around to see three silhouettes of angels at the entrance of the chamber. The light made it challenging to see their details, but the two on the sides held their spears outward. The centre angel's figure had horns; she pointed at him with her large three-clawed hand.

Rahiie.

The glimmer of a tear shone on her face, running past the spikes on her cheekbones. "Brother. What have you done?"

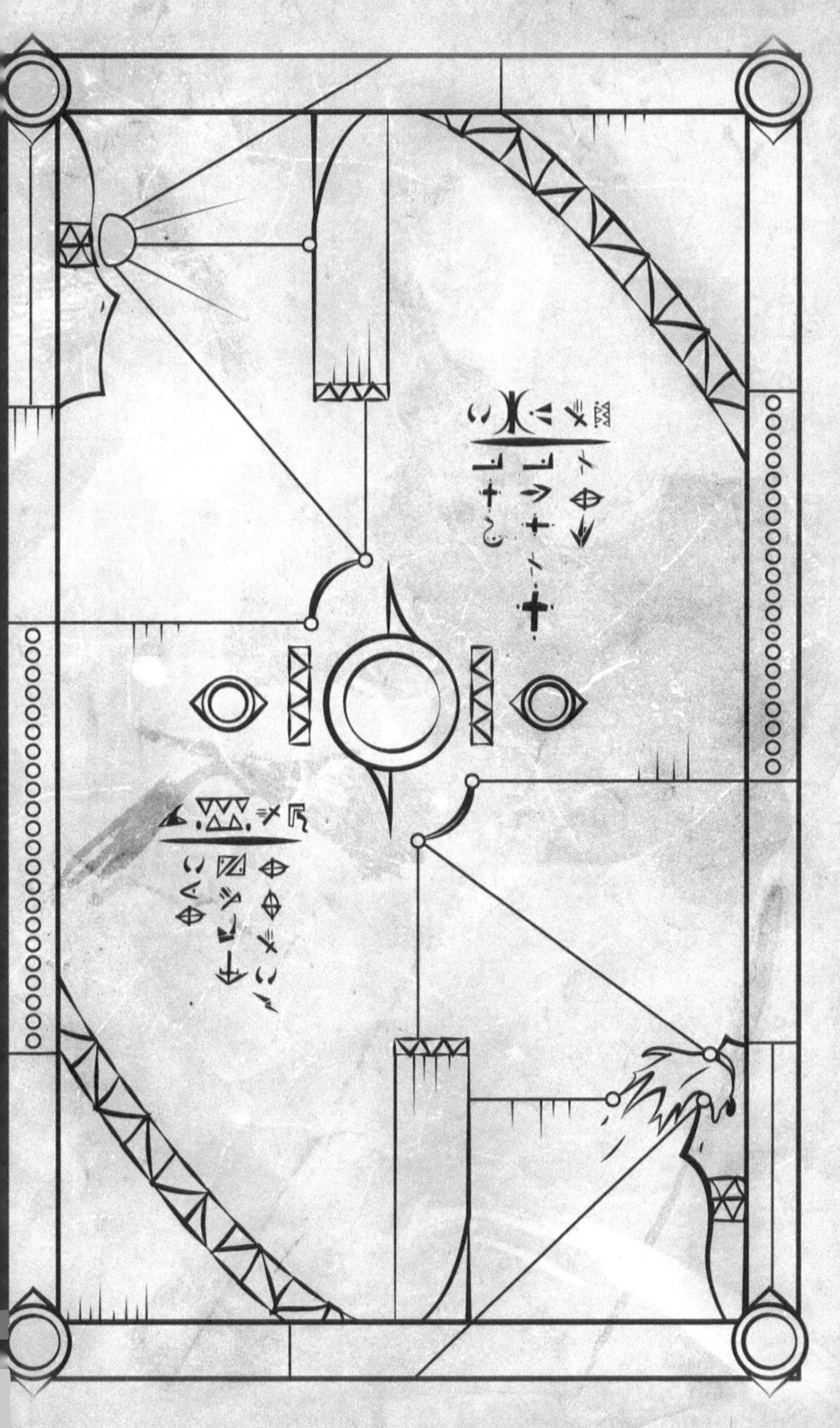

CHAPTER XV

Biological Chemistry

PATIENT: KRISTALANTICE SCALEBANE
DAY: TWO
ENTRY: FOUR

It has been my second day back in the High Barracks of Zingalg. After two days of knowing Kristalantice, she still is quite distant toward me and does not wish to share any of the experiences she is having with Mental Damnation. This is common in patients and I am certain that over the next week I will gain her trust, when the hallucinations become too overwhelming.

The disease is most likely projecting visuals that are the early effects of schizophrenia, convincing the poor girl that what she is seeing is real. When she realizes that these other characters in her head are not looking out for her best interest, she will likely turn to me as her last resort. I can only hope she doesn't come to this recognition too late.

Kristalantice's case is complex. She may also

be having trouble adjusting to the social and environmental changes she has endured in leaving the underworld and coming to the surface. Thankfully she has warmed up to Paladin, and he has informed me that he is developing a stronger relationship with her. Paladin told me that she is sharing with him the nightmares she is experiencing with Mental Damnation. His first session with her gave us a clearer understanding of the harsh background she had living on the streets of her people's city, which seems to be exceptionally violent. Kristalantice is beginning to express aggressiveness, a trait seen in many cases of the disease. Perhaps her history will aid her in facing the psychological challenges she will go through.

From what Paladin shared with me about Kristalantice's people, it sounds as if Mental Damnation affected her people's leaders shortly before she was infected herself. This information supports my earlier hypothesis that Mental Damnation originates from the underworld. If this is indeed the case, I would learn much if I could see another vazelead with Mental Damnation and compare their case to Kristalantice's. The way Kristalantice describes her people's violent nature, she may be an anomaly. There is a possibility that they could even manage the disease better than she does.

With human victims who have become deceased, dissecting the brain has provided valuable insight on how quickly the disease grew, where it was located in the brain, and how deeply it rooted itself into the organ. Having never seen a vazelead brain before, if Kristalantice proves to be another casualty (I do pray she lives through this, of course), I will have an opportunity to see a vazelead brain, and to understand how one with Mental Damnation behaves.

I hope to learn more from Kristalantice the more

Paladin speaks with her. He was not able to give me as much knowledge as I had hoped about her dreams from last night. Now that she has passed into Stage 2, the stage of Dreadweave Pass, she will continue to be subjected to the harsher effects of the disease, which means Paladin and I will need to keep a close eye on her. If she does have a violent outbreak we can analyze the events leading up to it.

Now Kristalantice's second night has begun and I have requested that Paladin restrain her again. After the events of the first night, I would rather not take the risk of her causing damage to herself or others.

r. Alsroc placed his pen down in the bottle of ink, eyeing the journal he kept. He wanted to write more about Krista, but had nothing else to add.

He let out a deep sigh. *It is only the second day. In the days to come I will observe her more frequently. Perhaps tomorrow morning I will touch base with the girl.*

The door handle to the entrance of his office rattled and the door flung open. Paladin stepped into the room, face painted in a wide frown and hands clenched. The man was clearly frazzled.

"Paladin." Dr. Alsroc leaned back as his visitor dropped onto the chair opposite the desk. "What brings you here?"

"I just escorted Krista to her bed."

"Oh? Did you restrain her to the frame?"

"Yes, I did." Paladin folded his arms and exhaled through his nose.

"You said escort? Was she not willing on her own?"

"No, I found her on the main floor, with William."

Dr. Alsroc reached into his drawer, pulling out a pipe. He kept a small wooden box in the drawer as well, containing his dried tobacco leaves. "Can't she have a conversation with beings of similar mental age?" He tapped the edge of the wooden box, allowing the leaves to gracefully fall into his pipe. He then lightly packed them into the chamber with the corner of the box.

"Talking is one thing, but she is taking an erotic interest in him."

Dr. Alsroc brought the pipe to the lit candle on his table, and with his other hand, tilted the candle slightly, transferring the flame onto the leaves in his pipe. "She is of age." He inhaled while gradually placing the candle upright. "Do you know much about her background with males of her species?"

"A little. I know she had a strong bond with one named Darkwing. She did not say how deep the relationship went, but I could tell she was emotionally involved with him, perhaps like a brother, or maybe she felt more. Other than that, there were times she had been . . . overpowered by males."

Dr. Alsroc took the pipe from his mouth. "She may have a fear of her own species and seeing a human is stimulating her suppressed natural desires."

"It's not natural unless God wills it so."

Dr. Alsroc smirked. "Then how do you know when God wills it?"

"God gives them a sign and it grows from something purer than what William and Krista are experiencing."

"They are both in their flourishing age and are curious of the opposite gender. It is natural what they want."

"What they want will create anything but something natural. Krista is a distraction for William and he is struggling to keep up with his training. Females should be the last thing he is focusing on—especially one of an ancient race."

"Is that why you have Krista working with Marilyn?"

"Partly. I also want her to earn her place here. Now that I know more about Krista's past, I can see why she and Marilyn get along so well. Krista comes from a twisted background and Marilyn is obsessed with dark topics."

"Why do you suppose that is?"

"I don't know. But like I mentioned yesterday, I want to dedicate more time with Marilyn." Paladin let out a sigh.

"There's not enough of you to go around," Dr. Alsroc commented.

"No, and I am short-tempered lately. I made Krista cry when I found her with William."

"Not often do you lose your temper with anyone."

"I have a lot on my plate." Paladin stood up. "Speaking of which, I must begin writing my report to the king regarding the knowledge Krista shared with me."

"Remember to stall him. The longer we can keep Krista here, the more we can learn from her."

"Exactly. The king's men will only frighten her and there is no telling how she will react, with her current infection. Not to mention there has been no sign of this Danil character whom Krista said performed the ritual. Smyth and I had checked the ritual site and found nothing. I've sent some men to search the nearby forests and there is no sign of him."

"It is hard to say." Dr. Alsroc waved goodbye. "Try to calm your inner fire tonight, Paladin. You've got a strong will and these are a lot of tasks stacking up. Rest will provide clarity."

"Thank you for your concern." Paladin bowed and exited the office, his posture less tense.

Dr. Alsroc always held his friendship with Paladin in high regard, despite their different stances on many topics. They respected each other and always worked toward the same end goal, even through all the bickering and cheeky remarks they made about each other's beliefs.

He took the final puffs from his pipe and placed it down on the table.

I have some of my own preparation to do for Kristalantice, he thought as he stood from his desk.

There was a new remedy he wanted to give Krista that would help numb her mind. He had previously used the mix of skullcap, wild lettuce, and a few additional herbs for insomnia. It didn't necessarily stimulate any of the joyous portions of the mind, but the plant mixture was enough to make one's brain less active, which would not be in the disease's favour since Mental Damnation needed energetic minds to feed from. Numbing Krista's brain would be quite helpful so she didn't generate so many nightmarish visions.

Dr. Alsroc gathered the herbs from a couple of cupboards in his office, balancing out the quantities in several white sheets of paper before pouring them into a single jar.

Once the mix of leaves was complete, he sealed the jar so he could grind it up the next day and provide it to Krista in a tea form.

Now my job is done. It had been a long day and Dr. Alsroc needed rest.

He extinguished the candles lighting his office and locked the door on his way out, placing his key in his front pouch. He had barely left his room the entire day, spending most of it reviewing his previous notes about Mental Damnation, seeing if there was anything he had missed.

Reviewing his past cases was something Dr. Alsroc did frequently. There just weren't enough clues to pave a clear path on how to cure the diagnosed, and with each case he had he grown less hopeful.

Each case just gives me more garbage to sift through. However, I mustn't give up hope. Perhaps one of the days he reviewed his notes, he thought, there would be a eureka moment that would put Mental Damnation to an end once and for all—and before it takes Krista's life.

CHAPTER XV: BIOLOGICAL CHEMISTRY

274

CHAPTER XVI

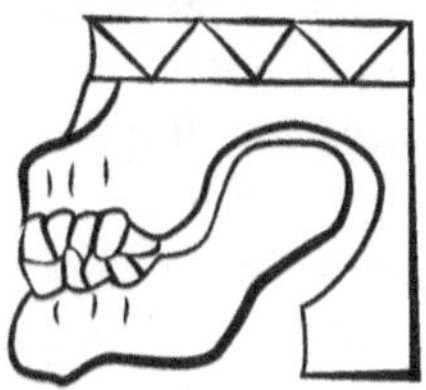

The Dawn of Hope

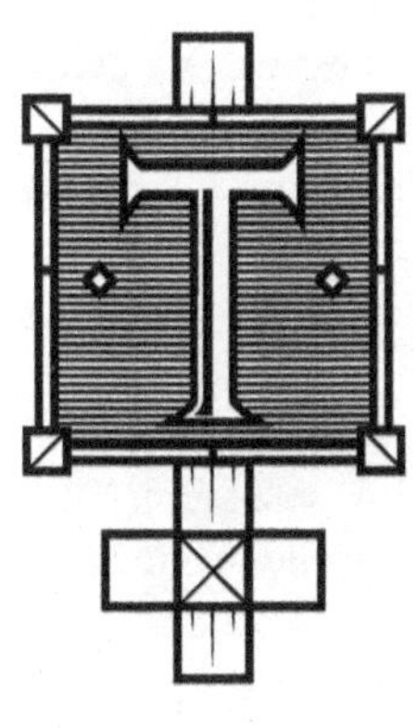he girl's gown was drenched in black blood from the waist down. Two large puncture wounds oozed blood from her scaly back. Her legs trembled while she walked around the bedroom filled with polished blackwood furniture. The blood travelled down past her waist and onto the floor, leaving a trail of where she had been as she limped over to the glass cabinet that housed the bronze-and-purple Renascence Guard armour.

Two intruders accompanied her. One was Darkwing, who watched his prisoner, Quilech, scurry around the room to get herself into her armoured suit. He was captivated by the fact that she was no older than he was, which made her not much older than Krista. Unlike Krista, though, Quilech's scowling face and tightened brow ridge above her hate-filled eyes painted a picture of experiencing lots in her young age. She lacked the innocence that Darkwing adored in Krista.

Besides the eyes, watching Quilech put on her chest piece gave Darkwing a clear view of her physique. Her slimness, size, and even her skin tone were similar to Krista's. It was ridiculous that every female he saw, he could relate to Krista in one way or another. He knew he longed for her so badly that his mind was trying to cope with the loss by finding any similarity to her in others. Even though the relations were slim, he couldn't resist the urge to embrace them. Thinking of Krista—her smell, her skin—it was very similar to Quilech, and he now found himself mesmerized by the Renascence Guard captain.

Quilech grunted while reaching to her side to buckle the straps on the breastplate. She moved on to buckle together the rest of her well-shined armoured suit complete with engravings of teeth around the purple outlining. Red jewels of varying sizes were crafted into the centre of each plate piece. The kilt was stitched with black thread and was the same deep purple as the outlined plating. Needless to say, it put Darkwing's and Draegust's pilfered armour to shame.

"It's my sister, isn't it?" Quilech asked while adjusting the pelvic plating of her armour.

The two remained motionless. Darkwing wanted to answer but he found it difficult to say yes.

The girl groaned. "If you scum won't answer me, at least have the dignity to turn around as I dress!"

Darkwing bit his lip and turned his head away.

Draegust laughed and folded his arms. "You think we're fools?" He glanced at Darkwing and slapped his shoulder, forcefully turning him around. "We're not turning our backs to you so you can scheme."

"The guardians will punish you greatly in your death!" Quilech's tongue flickered at them.

Draegust thrust the spear toward her. "Get dressed! We don't have a lot of time."

"Where are you taking me?" Quilech put on her upper-thigh plating.

"None of your concern. If you don't obey us, I'll sever your head right here!" Draegust growled.

The captain clamped the plating together on her boots and stood, grunting as she gently pressed on her back wound.

Darkwing looked to the floor to see blood was still dribbling from the cracks in her armour.

"I know you're here because of my sister. What else could she do?

Her witchcraft can't touch me now that I've surrounded myself with charms and pendants that can resist her unnatural practices. The only thing she could do was send two goons to get me."

Draegust stepped forward and snatched her arm. "Quit your complaining. We must leave now." He yanked her toward the door.

Darkwing was surprised by the girl's cooperation. She was injured, but that would only make Darkwing fight harder if he were in her shoes.

Maybe she fears death, he thought. The girl was young and had most of her life ahead of her, so ending it now would be a shame.

"You're keeping me alive, though," Quilech muttered while Draegust pushed her.

Darkwing rushed to the door and dragged the furniture he'd used as a barricade aside; afterward, he leaned down and picked up his spear.

"Fleerew would want me dead. I'm betting you aren't her allies, either."

Draegust nudged her wound through her armour. "Enough chatter. Open the door and get us out of the city. We're going to see your sister."

Darkwing shook his head. "Just work with us, we'll figure something out."

Quilech nodded and took a step toward the door.

Draegust leaned closer to Darkwing. "Don't get soft, kid."

Darkwing squeezed the handle of his spear, feeling the suspense surge through his veins. *Here we go.*

The girl extended her hand and twisted the knob, pulling the door inward, revealing the empty hallway on the other side.

Draegust kept close to her. He pulled out his dagger and kept it pressed against her armour, pointed to where her wound was underneath. "Keep moving."

"I promise you, whatever you want, I can offer you far greater," Quilech bargained.

Darkwing walked alongside his partner as all three stepped out into the hall.

"Release her!" a deep voice boomed.

The three spun to their right to see the large black-armoured guard with his claymore drawn, accompanied by several others in gunmetal armour. Their tails perked upward, swaying side to side.

Draegust poked the girl with his dagger.

Quilech grunted and raised her hand. "They're with me," she spoke through her sharp teeth.

The large guard lowered his sword and shook his head. "They killed my partner!"

"You were both fools for not letting them pass!" Quilech shouted. "Did they not say they had to see me?" Her voice trembled.

She's in a lot of pain, Darkwing thought.

"Let us pass," Draegust sneered.

The guard slammed his breastplate. "They talk above me, these street cleaners. They aren't even of your squad, Captain Quilech."

"They are my personal men," Quilech coughed.

Darkwing glanced at her wound. The blood was still dripping to the floor.

"Spies?" the guard questioned, tail raising.

"You're quick, aren't you?" she replied.

Darkwing poked Draegust with his tail and lightly motioned the bottom of his spear to the blood.

Draegust cleared his throat and pushed Quilech lightly. "We must be going—important matters."

Quilech nodded. "Move." She stepped forward in a straight and stiff motion. Darkwing and Draegust kept inches away from her, the dagger still pressed against her armour.

The large guard and his comrades moved aside and lowered their weapons, remaining silent as the three passed.

The large guard shook his head and growled. "Your captain won't always be here to protect you!"

Quilech turned at the corner in the hall and stumbled, slamming against the stone wall.

Darkwing leaned over and helped her gain balance. "She's losing a lot of blood."

"Let's get her out of here." Draegust grabbed her other arm and the two jogged down the hall, practically dragging her feet across the ground.

Quilech cursed under her breath, "The guardians will smite you."

"All five of them, eh?" Draegust chuckled.

"I'll spit on your grave if you do not cooperate with me."

"You're going to have to have a miracle on your side if you think you have the upper hand here, missy."

Darkwing sighed. "Just stay with us. You're not well."

Draegust squinted. "What did I just say to you Darkwing?"

The two hurried through the halls with their captive, retracing their steps to get back to the staircase that led to the main floor. They passed a pair of Renascence Guards in white armour who paused in their path and stared as the group buzzed by.

Darkwing felt his heart pound inside his ribcage. Here he was, breaking into the citadel, taking a captive, and sneaking out right under the Renascence Guard's noses. It was inconceivable among the vazelead people. Then again, the Five Guardians collapsing was never a worry either.

The three crossed over the bridge and reached the staircase leading to the main floor, taking each step carefully so they did not drop Quilech.

"How are you holding up?" Darkwing whispered.

"How do you think?" she mumbled.

Darkwing shook his head. "What's your game?"

"Game? I have none. I am just praying there is an ounce of decency in your scum blood."

Draegust nudged her back. "Move faster. This girl is just a coward, like the rest of the Renascence Guard. Once we are out of here, we'll finish this."

"It doesn't make sense, though," Darkwing persisted. "There were plenty of opportunities for an escape, yet you ignored them all."

Quilech's bit her lip. "It's not like your ally made it easy for me to do anything without wounding me."

The three gradually made it down each flight of stairs. Darkwing counted each floor they passed out of suspense—he wanted to get out of the citadel as quickly as possible. They were lucky to sneak in at night, while there were less guards coming in and out of the halls.

Most of them are probably sleeping now—it's just the guards on night duty who worry me.

The group reached the main floor after several minutes and picked up speed through the corridor.

Quilech's panting could be heard with each step she took; her head was wobbly and her path swerved between her captors.

Darkwing extended his hand to pull open the large entrance door. He yanked on the handle and used his whole body to leverage it open. *I had no idea it was so heavy! Damnit.*

The same guard from when they first entered was still outside. He turned around and nodded at them.

"Safe travels," he waved.

Draegust nodded and kept marching out of the citadel.

The three rushed down the main road leading back to the Great Road in silence. Darkwing felt the weight fall from his shoulders with each step they took away from the citadel. *I have been under stress before, but nothing like this.* This was a new feat for him. As stressful as it was, he couldn't help but feel a level of accomplishment.

Draegust snickered once they reached the hill leading down toward the mansions, his laughter bouncing off the buildings. "I can't believe we managed to walk in and out practically undetected. A little more exciting than potion shops, hey Darkwing?"

"I need my wounds mended," Quilech mumbled.

Draegust pushed her shoulder. "You're pretty demanding, aren't you?"

The captain stumbled to the ground, her chest hitting the dirt.

Darkwing leaned down and gently pulled on her arm. "Come on, get up." He turned to Draegust. "She's right—she is going to die."

Draegust shrugged. "Don't we need her head? I'm pretty sure that will make her dead, too. If she dies from blood loss, so be it."

Quilech pointed down the alley to the far end of the street, her hand shaking. "There's a medicine shop not far from here. Take me there. Please, whatever Fleerew is offering you, I can offer better."

"We can't kill her here." Draegust sheathed his dagger and leaned down beside her. He yanked on her arm, forcing her up. "The High District night life is way too active."

Darkwing and Draegust pulled her down the path that became the Great Road. The subtle sounds of traditional vazelead tribal drums could be heard from several of the nearby mansions.

It's like all the higher class does is party, Darkwing thought while eyeing an open window of a three-level mansion. The window showed a group of vazeleads chatting among one another with glasses of wine, dressed in vibrant clothing.

"We've got to find an alley or somewhere less obvious." Darkwing spoke.

"I promise you . . ." Quilech panted. "We can arrange something. What did Fleerew offer you? Dracoins? Jewels? I can provide that."

"Hush." Draegust let go of her arm. "I'll take lead and scout ahead. Keep hold of her."

Darkwing bit his lip and gently took hold of the girl. *Something about this just doesn't sit right. I've killed Renascence Guards before—I don't know what makes her different.* Perhaps the fact that she was female and bore a resemblance to Krista made him pity her. Or maybe Alistind's words had sunk into him and he knew that this was barbaric. *Krista, what would you do?*

"Sorry," Darkwing whispered.

"Excuse me?" Quilech leaned her head back while squinting through the pain to see him.

"I thought hurting you would have made me want to kill you, but it didn't. Normally it does, but it just didn't this time. I'm sorry for hurting you. I see how much pain you're in."

Quilech lightly coiled her tail around his leg. "Thank you." She put on a weak smile. "There wouldn't be any way I could convince you to not bring me to my sister, would there?"

Darkwing felt his heart race and he looked to the ground. "If there is a way not to kill you . . ."

"Can you help me?" Quilech's tail tightened around his leg.

He nodded. "I'll try." *What am I thinking?* His main goal was to find Krista on the surface. To get there, he needed the half-breed, and only Fleerew knew his whereabouts. Fleerew only asked for her sister's head in return; it was simple. But here he was, beginning to make this complicated.

Draegust pointed up the road. "The gate will probably still have guards. Keep our girl presentable and make sure she doesn't collapse."

"Right," Darkwing replied.

"Talk to me," Quilech whispered.

"I want to find the half-breed," Darkwing replied.

"The half-breed?"

"Yes, he knows the path out of the underworld."

"You're a madman. There's no reason to go to the underworld entrance. We're stuck here, remember?"

Draegust glanced back and stopped in his tracks. "What the hell are you doing, Darkwing?" He stomped toward them. "Get your whorish tail off him!" Draegust unsheathed his dagger, pointing it toward Quilech's throat as he stomped.

Darkwing tightened his grip on her arm, forcing her behind him. "We might not have to kill her."

Draegust's nostril's flared as he came to a halt inches away from Darkwing. "She's fucking with your mind, boy, just as Alistind does, and even your Krista. At least when I fuck I toss them aside."

Darkwing took a deep breath, feeling fury brew inside of him. *Yet he is right.* Despite Draegust's harsh words, he knew he'd let every female he'd known manipulate him. It wasn't intentional, but the company they offered him was welcoming. Even Quilech was beginning to soften his resolve.

"I need you to focus. Remember why we're doing all this?" Draegust said as he lowered his spear. "I'll escort her if you take lead."

Darkwing nodded and let out a long, extended breath. "All right." He let go of Quilech and Draegust snatched her arm.

The girl grunted. "Please don't do this."

"Make any noise and I will kill you here and now," Draegust snarled.

The three marched in silence toward the gates leading to the Commoner's District. There was only one guard on this side of the gates and he nodded at them while they approached.

Within moments, the gears to the gates began to turn from the lever above and they opened with loud creaks.

Darkwing walked with his chest extended out, trying to imitate the proud Renascence Guard posture.

The streets were still deserted in the Commoner's District and it took little time for them to reach the Lower District gates. These gates had two guards on each end of the frame. They did not bother with questions either and the gates opened when the three were close enough to walk through.

Darkwing held his spear tightly while walking down the road into the Lower District, feeling conflicted. *Draegust might be right; we probably do have to kill Quilech. But there must be another way.*

The three arrived at the outskirts of the city after about an hour of walking. Darkwing's legs were numb and Draegust was practically holding Quilech up while she attempted to stand on her feet.

Draegust shook her arm. "Quicken your pace."

"I can't," she murmured.

"Don't play games with me. You may have Darkwing coiled around your lies, but I remain strong." He glanced around the few remaining buildings on the outer rim of the Lower District. "Well, Darkwing, it looks like we executed our stealth mission well." He put on a wicked grin and lunged his foot into Quilech's back, launching her to the ground.

She yelped as she fell onto her hands and knees. The captain attempted to get to her feet, and her arms shook while she pushed up.

"Let's find out if she has anything of value to say. You knew Fleerew would send us. How?" Draegust shouted.

Quilech got to her feet and tried to run to Darkwing, but Draegust grabbed her by the tail and pulled her back.

"You didn't run then, yet you run now?" he laughed. "Run because you're scared?"

"Let me go!" the girl screamed while Draegust wrapped his hands around her neck from behind, locking her in place.

"Coward! The Renascence Guard makes me sick. No honour or respect for your own people."

Quilech groaned as he put more pressure on her neck. "Enough, please!" She clutched his forearms, trying to break free.

Darkwing stood stiff; his body was frozen. *I want to say something, buy some time so I can think—but what for? I barely know Quilech, and I'm putting myself on her side while Draegust has risked his life on this mission. Why am I making this complicated?*

Draegust used one hand to pull off his helmet then clutched Quilech's scalp, bringing his face closer for a long, slow lick along her neck. "There's many ways we can handle this, girl. Where should I start?" Draegust turned her head and clamped down on her cheek, his teeth puncturing her skin.

Quilech screamed.

"Stop!" Darkwing shouted and rushed toward the two.

Draegust spat out a mouth full of blood. "We both know she's hiding something. I think she wanted to be captured."

Darkwing shook his head. "This is barbaric! Let's just get back to her sister and we can sort this out."

Draegust let the captain go with a push, throwing her to the ground again. "You keep defending the bitch. I'm losing my patience." He chucked Quilech aside and stomped past Darkwing, bumping his shoulder.

Darkwing ignored the urge to hit Draegust and leaned down to help Quilech up. "Did you want to see your sister?"

She took his hand and got to her feet. "The half-breed, you said?" Blood oozed down her face and neck.

Darkwing put her arm around his shoulders and the two followed behind Draegust. "Yes. I need to save a friend, and the half-breed is the only one who can help me."

Quilech kept one hand on her cheek to stop the bleeding. "Where did your friend go?"

Darkwing leaned closer to her ear. "The surface world."

"Excuse me?"

"Danil shattered the holy shackles the paladins cast, and now my friend is on the surface world. Fleerew is helping us."

"And she wants my head." Quilech looked to the ground.

Darkwing sighed. "I can't see a squad of guards assisting me. Your sister is the only one who knows where the half-breed is."

Quilech nodded. "I know. Just help me think of another way. Let me see my sister—let me talk to her."

"Yeah, sure." *Demontochai was at the temple though, perhaps he hasn't figured out that the shackles are destroyed,* he thought.

The three walked in silence for several hours through the sand dunes leading to Magma Falls. Darkwing felt his legs grow increasingly tired. *I can't imagine what Quilech is going through.* She put less effort into walking as the energy seeped from her body, making her heavier to carry the further they walked.

She's not going to make it.

Eventually, the group reached the bottom of a large sand dune and started the hike up the hill.

They hiked up the dune and panted once they reached the top. The City of Renascence and Magma Falls were about equal distances now.

"Not bad, eh? Even with this deadbeat slowing us down." Draegust wiped some sand from his scalp-feathers. "You did well, kid."

Darkwing leaned down, gradually placing Quilech down on the sand. Her eyes were closed and she breathed heavily. "Thanks," he said while taking his helmet off. The gust of wind that blew by was refreshing to inhale without the stale smell of the helmet.

"We got her out." Draegust pointed at the captain. "Before we return to Fleerew, we need to have a plan."

"What do you suggest?"

"You tell me. You're the one who wanted to save her!" Draegust laughed. "I would have been fine killing her the moment we left the city. Hell, even in her quarters, and we could have battled our way out of the citadel."

"Keeping her alive, we can bargain with Fleerew." Darkwing rubbed his hands. *Shit. I need to come up with something fast.*

Quilech opened her eyes, blinking a couple of times. "Please let me see what I can do with my sister."

"Why?" Draegust raised an eyebrow.

Quilech spat some blood from her mouth and sat upright, a mixture of blood and saliva drooled down her lips. "It is the only thing I have on my side at the moment. I want to earn your trust to live, and I can see you two know what you want. Who is crazy enough to sneak into the citadel? You want to find the half-breed?"

Draegust's scalp-feathers stood straight up as the blood rose to his skull. "You told her our plan?"

Darkwing stood. "I told her our situation. Krista would not have wanted bloodshed over finding her."

Draegust huffed and put his hands on his hips. "You honestly care what your Krista has to say about how we find her? She's lucky we've even gotten this far." He slowly walked toward them, bouncing his gaze back and forth from Darkwing to Quilech. "This girl is hypnotizing you." Draegust coiled a fist and rushed toward Quilech, his knuckles ramming straight into Quilech's nose. The metal gauntlet crushed her cartilage and her body flung backward, skidding in the sand.

Darkwing pushed Draegust aside. "You're going to kill her!"

Quilech grunted and attempted to scurry away. Darkwing wasted no time and rushed to her side. "Calm down!" He snatched her arms and shook them slightly.

Draegust pull out his dagger and sneered. "Stick to the plan, kid."

Quilech reached for Darkwing's hand as he helped her get to her feet.

"Your female companions are making you weak!" Draegust shouted, dagger pointed toward Quilech. "Quite frankly, it's testing my nerves."

"We can find another way," Darkwing argued.

Quilech tried to speak but her mouth was filled with blood. She looked away and spat the black liquid out. "He told me of your situation," she said and pointed at Darkwing. "The surface world, the half-breed, the girl . . . This is a great historical event for our people. Let me live, and we'll find the half-breed and your friend."

Draegust chuckled. "You don't even know where to look! Your sister is an outcast like the half-breed—she will take us where we need to go."

"What of your own people?" Quilech shouted. "Letting us return to the surface would be a massive contribution to our people. We would be free of the Corrupt, of the metamorphosis fumes, and the underworld! You would be considered heroes!" The girl closed her eyes, trying to ignore the pain.

"You honestly think I care about our people?" Draegust frowned. "I tried to bring justice to our kind, free them of the dictatorship we're in." He lowered his collar and revealed a Blood Hound scarification on his neck. "Yet it served no use—your guardians' strength cannot be matched. They'll drive our race into hundreds of years of depression, and the Renascence Guard like yourself will assist them every step of the way!" Draegust roared and charged the two of them. His metal armour clanged with each stomp he made into the sand.

Darkwing's heart skipped a beat and he widened his stance, blocking Draegust's path to Quilech.

The gang leader sheathed his dagger and slammed into Darkwing, causing them to fall into the ground. Dust flew in the air as they impacted, Draegust on top.

Draegust coiled his fist again and slammed it into Darkwing's face. The metal gauntlet hit his eye and his head rebounded against the ground.

"I am doing this for your own good, kid. You're too soft." Draegust got off his feet and turned to face Quilech.

She screamed and turned to run in the opposite way.

Darkwing fought his spinning head to get to his feet. His vision was blurred, his head was pounding, and his balance was wobbly. He could feel blood drip from his spiked brow.

Where are they? he thought while glancing around the top of the hill. The other two were nowhere in sight.

"Leave me alone!" Quilech screamed.

"Your end arrives!" Draegust bellowed.

Darkwing pushed himself up from the ground and shook his head. He could barely see, but ran in the direction he had heard Quilech scream from.

Her shrieks were cut short by the sound of flesh being punctured several times, gargling, coughing, and more stabbing.

Darkwing ran down the hill to see that Draegust had pinned Quilech to the ground with her chest pressed to the sand. Draegust had her head lifted with one hand by her scalp-feathers and his other hand used his dagger to carve into her neck. Black blood spewed to the ground from the open wound like a water hose.

"Draegust!" Darkwing shouted.

"Don't come closer, kid. Alistind and your Krista bring you nothing in life! I'll assist you in finding Scalebane as I promised, but Quilech's life is over!" Draegust pulled on her scalp-feathers, stretching the remaining attached scales until the girl's head ripped free. Her severed head dripped blood as the gang leader stood upright, turning to face Darkwing. "Listen to yourself! You joined the Blood Hounds to create a better tomorrow for you and your Krista. I saw the potential and the passion in your eyes. How does sparing the life of this worthless Renascence Guard help you achieve anything you've aimed for in life?"

"She was just a girl."

"She didn't have anything worth offering us and was just trying to buy herself some time. Think of it from a logical approach: our original plan or this girl's plan? Just because Alistind told you it was barbaric you got all soft. Who do you trust more? An outcast who can find another outcast, or a Renascence Guard whose kind have hunted you over and over? I want to see the surface, Darkwing; this bitch or your weak will is not going to stand in the way of that."

Darkwing looked at Draegust and then at Quilech's decapitated head. Her tongue dangled from her open mouth. The fire around her eyes had faded, leaving the large black pupils wide open.

Draegust nodded and lowered his posture. "That's what I thought. Let this be an emotional lesson for you, Darkwing. You still have much to learn."

CHAPTER XVII

The Lifeless Ones

eing alive is something that we all experience—at least the basic definition of being alive. Our brains are active, we have a pulse, and we eat, sleep, and breathe. This is being alive. But are we actually living life? Being alive and going about your day and interacting with the world around you is living from your perspective. Living life is when you bring your existence to your fullest expectations and push the limits of your understanding of what can be done, embracing something new. Now how can you live life? This will differ for everyone. Some relish the high points of excitement, or adrenaline, if you will—points in time that can only last a few seconds but are such captivating experiences that the moments can leave imprints that last a lifetime. Does that define living? And if intense imprints in life define living, does being chased by an overpowering force define living as well?

Cursman and Krista left the City of Blood several hours after they met with the historian, Smelg. After learning a bit about Sporathun's history, Cursman—musing out loud—had unwittingly formulated a plan to defeat the fallen angel. The plan involved finding Sporathun's lover, Glamorous, and using her to lure him.

Cursman was convinced that Sporathun was not going to stop hunting Krista until he caught her. Why did Sporathun want her? That part was uncertain. What they could count on, though, was that Sporathun's sins—lust and wrath—revolved around Glamorous. From the information in Smelg's book, it was clear she was the one being the vampyre desired. It seemed logical that his need to feed his sin would overpower him at the sight of her and he would almost certainly lose all interest in capturing Krista.

The first step to this plan was finding Glamorous at one of the three rumored locations.

Whether Glamorous was at God's Tears or not, Krista wanted to visit there. The lack of anything to drink in this land of blood and the dirtiness of her clothes made her feel wretched. Thinking of fresh, clear water was impossible to resist. To their luck, Smelg was kind enough to leave Cursman and Krista with a small sack of food for their travels. Krista ate a couple of the purple slices of meat in the bag that Cursman identified as dahk. The texture of the meat was tough and rubbery, and it tasted like a bitter fruit. But she ate it regardless of the flavour; her stomach was famished and she needed energy.

Cursman took Krista back out into the forest leading over the blood river.

Krista grunted and tried to keep up to the man's speed.

"You all right?" Cursman asked, slowing his pace.

"Yes, I'm just really tired. Can we please take a break? Hide in the City of Blood?"

"We can't stop now. We have a plan, and we need to act quickly before Sporathun finds us."

"I know, but we've been on the move forever." She rubbed her legs.

"I mean, it is nice we're travelling on the road now, but I really don't think I can keep walking." Krista stopped and looked down to see her legs were trembling. "My legs shake as I walk!"

Cursman spun around. "We can't stop!" His eyes were wide and the veins bulged from his face. "I'm tired, too! Don't you think I need rest? You and that paladin forced me to show you the gatekeeper's portal and go back again to Evergut with practically no rest!" He rushed closer to Krista, so close she could smell the sweat on his body.

"Stay back!" She took a couple of steps back and reached into her belt, pulling out her dagger. "Stay back," she repeated. Her hand shook as she held the blade with an extended arm.

The two stood still, eyes locked on each other's. Krista felt her heart pump faster in her ribcage while staring at Cursman's wild eyes.

A cool breeze blew past them and Cursman shook his head. "I'm sorry," he said and brushed his hair back, taking a deep breath. "You have to trust me, girl. I've been here for so long, and I know the dangers of Dreadweave Pass. This is big—much beyond anything you've probably dealt with."

Krista lowered her dagger and rubbed her arm. *The stress of Dreadweave Pass is making me act crazy.*

"We just have to keep moving." He waved for her to follow. "We have to act fast if we want to stop Sporathun from catching you." Cursman turned around and started to walk, but at a pace Krista could keep up with.

Krista tucked her dagger in her belt and took a deep breath before walking with Cursman. "Are we going to God's Tears?"

"Might be best—it's closest to here. We can search for Glamorous and bathe."

"I'd like to clean myself," she said with a smile. "Rid myself of this blood."

Cursman nodded. "Aye. I haven't seen the river myself in a few weeks. It would be nice to dip into the cool water while we're in the area. We'll have to be quick, though. There's a good chance the Weaver may have put out a bulletin on you to his abominations."

"Why is it called God's Tears?"

"The tears from the Creator himself pour from the heavens and create this river."

"I don't understand—humans talk about gods and then about God. What's the difference?"

"Well, there are a number of demi-gods in the Heavenly Kingdoms. Those are the ones we call 'the gods.' Then there is the Father, and supposedly the Father is God, and he is the Creator."

"Creator of what?"

"Of this," Cursman extended his arms. "Of me, of you—the one who built the building blocks of life."

"So God made the gods?"

"Yes, so they could manage the elements and the more complicated aspects of life."

"So he made a world too complex and he needed help?"

"Sort of. They help him manage everything. He oversaw the construction of the Heavenly Kingdoms, then eventually he made the angels to do the grunt work. He built the realms and the worlds inside them."

Krista scratched her head. "So where are the Heavenly Kingdoms?"

"Supposedly above all realms, watching over what we do here."

"You said God's tears; why does God cry?"

"You sure ask a lot of questions, don't you? They say it's because he is shameful for what he created, yet does not have the heart to destroy it."

A gust of wind blew by Krista and Cursman, and the leaves on the trees ruffled. The wind felt icy cold, as if Krista's skin was being bitten all over. "It's freezing," she said with a shiver.

Cursman looked up to the sky. "We might have to set up camp after all. The night winds are very cold, and you're not dressed for it." He scratched his head. "Come to think of it, I'm not dressed for it either, and neither is Sporathun. He'll be slowed down from the cold—there's nothing around now to stimulate his sin, like he would have in battle. I may have been too quick to judge how fast we should move."

Krista hugged her arms and looked up, seeing that the blood-red sky was darkening. *Finally. All I want to do is rest.* "So where are we going to rest?"

"We'll find some decent coverage in the forest. There's no way we are going back to the City of Blood—we'd lose some of our distance. We'll keep on the road for now, but we'll want to turn off at a spot where there is less activity in the forest."

Krista looked over into the trees. A low, white fog spread over the area, making the ground impossible to see. "How can you tell it's active?"

"The fog wasn't here when we first came to the City of Blood, and the dirt was littered with footprints of Lifeless Ones and dahk."

"Oh, you're pretty observant."

"You've gotta be if you want to survive in hell."

"Cursman, when we find Glamorous, what are we going to do?"

He shrugged. "When we have her? Use her as bait."

"I mean, is she going to cooperate with us?"

"Damned if I know. She is a vampyre of lust. She is going to be batshit crazy, like all fallen angels. All we need is for Sporathun to see her."

Krista nodded. "What about Mal and Fierel? Will we go and find them?"

Cursman did not reply.

I hope they are okay, especially Mal. Krista sighed. She realized they were planning to set up camp, meaning she would be resting soon, meaning she would return to the mortal realm. *If I am at the High Barracks, that means Mal can find me—if he is still alive.* The High Barracks would be a nice change from what was going on here, but how could she relax at the High Barracks when Sporathun was after her in Dreadweave Pass? *It is so hard to balance these different worlds with different problems.*

A low, gargling groan echoed in the distance.

Krista gasped and moved closer to Cursman. "Where did that come from?" She glanced around, but saw nothing but empty forest on both sides of the road.

"Don't be scared." Cursman pointed off to his right. "It is only the Lifeless Ones; they sense weakness."

Krista scowled. "I'm not weak."

Cursman grinned. "They seem to think so."

She swallowed heavily and walked closer to Cursman, her shoulders pressed against his arm. "Well they're wrong." *Shit.* "They should go away."

"Be strong," Cursman said and placed his hand on the hilt of his sword. "They never tire; they will wait for their prey to be at their weakest. You've got to stay strong."

They must be sensing my legs—my body's exhaustion. I can do this. She took a deep breath. "Okay."

Krista could feel her heart pump steadily; her senses were heightened as the daylight continued to fade. *The forest is going to get pitch black and we're going to stay in there. I can do it.*

Another groan trailed from the forest. This time, Krista could pinpoint the sound and she spun over to the origin off to her left. In the distance, a humanoid silhouette stood. It was slouched over, arms dangling forward, its head slanted as it limped slowly toward her.

"Why is it coming toward us?"

"You're scared, Krista. Don't be."

A third grumble was heard, this one coming from Krista's right. She turned to see another Lifeless One limping from the opposite side of the road. It rather skipped, trying to drag its one dead foot.

Krista grabbed onto Cursman's arm. "Where are they coming from?"

"They wander the forest. Sometimes they lay on the dirt until they sense someone coming near them."

"They should piss off!"

Another deep groan.

Her spine tingled and her scales stood upright. "I'm trying to be strong, Cursman!"

Cursman grabbed hold of her shoulder and brought her to his torso, her head bumping against his tough, bony chest. She held her breath and tried to look around without moving. Cursman was motionless.

A high-pitched shrill roared through the forest.

Krista's eyes widened; she had heard that sound before. It was the same deathly shriek the abominations made at the Blood Swamp.

"Get off the road." Cursman mumbled.

"Puppets?"

"Quickly, get off the road!" Cursman pushed Krista toward the ditch while the sound of a dozen footsteps rose from further up the road.

This is like a bad dream.

She dashed off the gravel and skidded down the ditch into the foggy terrain. The ground was moist and it was difficult to see two steps in front of her from the fog, but she kept running. Krista felt like a scared animal; she instinctively ran as far as she could until the sound of footsteps from the road began to fade.

"And why was returning to the City of Blood a bad idea?" Krista glanced back to see Cursman, but no one was there.

She stopped in her tracks and tried to find the road, but it was not visible, either. The ground was invisible under the white fog, and most of the details in the forest were blacked out like the night sky.

Krista's tail perked up. She felt her senses go into overdrive while she listened intently for danger, and her eyes scanned every inch of the forest for Cursman.

There was nothing but the dark silhouettes of trees and hills. She saw the one Lifeless One limping toward her several paces away, but no other humanoids.

"Cursman?" Krista called softly.

Another gust of wind blew by, this one colder and sharper. She did her best to keep her coat wrapped around her tightly until the wind died out.

The Lifeless One groaned.

"Cursman?" She backed up to a tree, watching her surroundings. She slowly pulled out her dagger from her belt. *Be strong.*

It was easier said than done. Her heart would not stop pounding, and she could feel it vibrate up into her head. Her legs shook and her muscles burned from the sprint. She was alone in a forest in hell with walking corpses all around her.

She tightened her grip on her dagger. "Cursman?"

A shriek came from deeper in the forest, not quite as aggressive as the puppets.

Krista gasped. Was it a Lifeless One or a puppet? Or something else? *I'm not going to find out.*

She brushed by the tree that exhaled as she pressed against it, causing her scales to tingle and she dashed away from the shrilling noise. Krista was unsure where she was running to, but the sound was enough to make her run.

Just don't be scared.

As she ran, she shifted her gaze quickly up and down to make sure she didn't bump into any Lifeless Ones ahead and that the ground underneath her didn't have something she could trip on. She could hear herself panting while running, fingers coiled around the handle of her dagger. Her leg muscles burned from exhaustion.

After several minutes, Krista slowed her pace to catch her breath. She sniffed the air. It was stale and rotten, much like the air at the road was, or even in the City of Blood.

How can I identify anything here if it all smells and looks the same? I can't take any more of this blood.

Krista took a deep breath and rested her hands on her knees, looking around the forest. The wind was more consistent, just as cold and it blew loose leaves around her. Several brushed by her legs.

"Where am I?" She stood upright. *Did Cursman set me up?* It didn't make sense—there were a dozen ways for him to set her up if he wanted to and this didn't seem very practical. So where had he gone? Krista hadn't run that far from the road when she lost track of him.

Where did the road go, anyway? I swear I didn't run that far. She coiled her tail around her ankle in an act of stress. "Shit, this really is like a dream. Nothing really seems to line up."

Another gargling groan came from the forest. This one was closer and louder.

Krista whirled around, dagger drawn. There was nothing there, just the forest as dark as the sky, so dark that even Krista—with her sharp vazelead eyesight—had difficulties seeing.

The nights here are unreal.

The groan was heard again, close enough that Krista felt the excess of breath against the side of her face.

Krista screamed and lashed her dagger to the side. The blade hit something soft and warm—flesh. Penetrated, the flesh sliced open.

What did I hit?

She looked up to see a naked man, missing his nose, in front of her. The pale skin was peeling away from the muscle in various parts of its body—a Lifeless One.

It groaned, opened its crooked jaw, and rushed toward her, sharp rotting teeth going for her face.

Krista leaped backward to avoid the Lifeless One's attack. She lost her balance as her foot hit the ground and she stumbled. She landed with a splash into the mud and rolled backward; the ground was sloped, and she began to tumble down.

She lost grip of her dagger and rolled violently down the slippery descent. Her face collided with dirt several times and her legs struck the rocky borders of the slope. The fall was manageable until she flew off a bank and her head slammed into a sharp boulder, making a long, jagged slice on her forehead.

Krista was dazed and the rest of the fall was a blur. She inevitably hit bottom in a thick pool of mud. Her head dunked first and sunk a couple of feet in, enough to bring her back to a conscious state.

It's not just mud. She pushed herself to the surface and gasped for air, feeling sandy droplets drip into her mouth. It tasted like a mix of dirt and salty metal. *Blood!*

Rolling around in the liquid, she managed to stand upright, the pool as deep as her chest. Krista spat and brushed her scalp-feathers aside. She shook her head, trying to clear her blurred vision.

The collision with the sharp rock impaired her sight; all she could make out in the fog were nearby trees and a trio of naked humans standing about a dozen paces from the pool—more Lifeless Ones.

My dagger!

The Lifeless Ones groaned at different pitches, some for longer and others in short bursts, all three limping toward her.

Krista panted heavily, trying to lift her leg from the mud—but it was too thick, and her left foot had sunk deeply into a soft spot. She grunted and pulled with all her strength, feeling her joints crack from the force.

Krista let out a huff. No luck.

One of the Lifeless Ones groaned.

I can't give up.

She tugged on her foot again, trying to break it free from the mud, but it wouldn't budge. Krista tried over and over, tugging at her limb to get it free.

"Break out, damn it!" She dipped her hands in and pulled on her thigh.

The three Lifeless Ones' groans grew louder until they were only a couple of steps from the blood pool.

Krista glanced up; she saw that two were male and another was female. One of the males extended its half-bone arm, trying to reach for her.

"No, please no." Krista cried. *Mal, please help me.* It was a foolish wish. She knew he was nowhere nearby. She was alone in this situation and she couldn't push her own fear away.

The Lifeless One groaned and dropped its arm, realizing she was too far to reach. It took a step forward and its foot sunk into the blood pool.

"Please don't let it end like this." Tears ran down her cheek as she sunk herself slightly in the pool. *I'm stuck.*

The Lifeless One took another step into the pool, slowly wiggling toward her. The other two took their first steps into the pool, gradually moving closer.

"Krista!" a raspy male's voice shouted.

The sound caught the attention of the Lifeless Ones and they let out a confused gargle.

Footsteps pounded in the dirt and a new silhouette with long hair and a muscular structure rushed from the fog to the pool, long claymore in hand.

A smile spread across Krista's face. "Cursman?"

The humanoid held his sword with both hands held high, skidding to a stop at the blood pool. With a single swipe down, he brought the sword onto the first Lifeless One's skull, splitting it in two.

Krista sniffed the air. Through the intense rotting smell of the Lifeless Ones, she picked up on Cursman's scent.

She watched in awe as he swung his sword rapidly, chopping off a Lifeless One's head and plunging his blade through the last.

Cursman looked up around the forest, checking to see if any more Lifeless Ones remained. "Looks like we're safe now," he said as he sheathed his blade.

"Thank you, Cursman! Thank you!" Krista cried with joy.

"Where did you go?"

"I ran from the road. I'm sorry. I got scared."

"I lost you in seconds. I've never had someone able to run from me like that."

Krista let out a laugh of relief. "I grew up on the streets. I'm good at running."

Cursman shook his head. "Try to stay with me next time."

"I'm stuck. Can you help pull me out?"

The man nodded and took one step into the blood pool, making sure he didn't go too deeply in. He extended his arm toward her, resting his other arm on his knee.

"Oh, thank you." Krista reached her arms out to him.

Their hands locked onto each other's forearms and Cursman began to pull.

"Thank you, thank you!" she repeated while pulling on his arm to help wiggle out.

The two struggled for several seconds. Krista could feel their arms shake from the force. Her ankle had twisted slightly in the mud from their pulling.

She yelped. "It hurts, stop!"

Cursman tightened his grip. "Hold on," he said through clenched teeth.

Krista screeched from the pain. "Shit, make it stop!"

Bit by bit, Cursman kept pulling and Krista's ankle felt like it was beginning to tear. However, gradually the suction gave way, the surface of the blood pool broke, and her ankle slipped out.

The sudden pop startled the two and she was thrown from the mud and into Cursman's arms. They stumbled backward into the mossy ground with a thump.

She held onto him tightly. *I never thought I'd be happy to see Cursman.* Krista buried herself into his chest, her arms clutched around his neck.

Cursman patted her softly. "All right."

She rubbed her head along his chest while her tail coiled around his ankle. "Thank you," she repeated. "I was so scared and you saved me." *Being in his arms is too comforting.* It reminded her of Darkwing and the relief he gave her when he held her close.

Cursman got up and used his arms to hold her. "All right," he repeated.

"I was scared," she mumbled into his shirt.

The man shook his head. "We have to work on this."

Krista looked up at him. "What did I do?"

"You need to stand on your own two feet—defend yourself."

She broke the grasp on his neck and slid from his arms. "I can."

Krista limped while she walked. Her left ankle was aggravated from the pulling.

Cursman kept his arm around her. "No, you cannot. What just happened is a perfect example, and so is the way you're acting now."

She frowned and brushed some mud from her scalp-feathers. "Sorry."

"The Lifeless Ones would have left you alone if you'd stayed strong."

"This place is horrifying. I tried my best." She rubbed her hand along the cut on her forehead, feeling it had swelled up.

"In time . . ."

"Did the puppets see us run in here?"

Cursman shook his head. "No, they don't follow you into the forests."

"Why?"

"They patrol the road. They don't have time to manage the wilderness."

The two walked into a clear patch in the forest, a spot where the road could be seen above the ditch.

Puppets or not, I'm so glad to see the road again.

"We'll rest here for the night."

The words were most satisfying. "Thank you," she said with a smile.

"We can't have a fire, though."

Krista hugged her arms. "But it is so cold."

"We don't want attention from others."

She nodded and sat herself down beside a sloped tree trunk.

"I take it you lost your dagger?" Cursman asked while scanning the terrain.

"Yes, I wish I had it back there."

"We'll find a couple of branches, then."

Krista squinted. *Training again?* "I hit my head against a rock. I don't think training would be good for me."

Cursman kneeled beside her. "Let me see."

She leaned forward and pointed at her forehead.

He brushed her scalp-feathers aside to see the wound. "Did the pain last long on your head?"

"No, but it left me in a daze."

Cursman nodded. "You did hit something sharp." He returned to his feet. "But it doesn't look too bad. We'll wipe it off and keep watch on it until we make it to God's Tears. But for now, we need to work on your ability to fight—running isn't always the answer, as you've seen today." Cursman offered her a hand.

Krista sighed. "Okay. You're right. I really don't want this to happen again." She accepted his help and stood on her feet.

The man pointed at a tree with some lower branches. "We'll review what we practiced last session."

Krista limped over to him. "It's kind of tough to practice when my leg is in pain."

Cursman grinned and tore off a branch. "That makes it good practice."

CHAPTER XVIII

Animals Can't Dream

rista lay on the rough ground, exhaling heavily in response to the throbbing pain in the sides of her skull, her breath puffing the dirt away from her face. A warm tingling sensation sunk into her skin and the warmth surrounded her innards. It was a familiar sense. *Like the sun, that made me spit blood.*

Her eyes shot open wide. *The sun?* Krista raised her head to see she was on the cool floor of her bedroom in the High Barracks. Her pillow lay on the ground, along with sheets and her clothing spread across the floor. Her blood smeared the sheets and the ground near the cot—which was now on its side—near where she lay. Her wrists had raw imprints from the straps on the bed.

The sun shone a bright, warm light through the window directly onto her skin, casting a sharp shadow behind her.

What happened here? She brushed her displaced scalp-feathers from her face and examined the bedframe. The straps were unbuckled, which would explain why she was on the floor.

Krista sat up using both arms, moving out of the sunlight. *Malpherities had to have done this.* It wasn't possible for her to have caused so much havoc in the room.

She rubbed her eyes and grunted, keeping her weight on her other arm. Her body ached in every joint from her head down to her feet. Her wrists and ankles stung and were lightly swollen. She felt her one arm lose its strength supporting her, so she crossed her legs and sat upright.

It's like I didn't even sleep last night. Krista ran her fingers along her forehead, feeling a rough diagonal scab on it. The scab was slightly sticky; it was fresh. Memories came flooding back. *I hit a rock when I was running away from the Lifeless Ones.* She looked around the rest of the room, but it was bare. *Cursman saved me from the Lifeless Ones and we were training, then we went to sleep, yet now I'm back here in the High Barracks.* She felt mentally exhausted. *This realm crossing stuff is strenuous.*

Krista got to her feet, pressing her hands on the ground to lift herself. Her hands were still bandaged, but they were not as sore as the previous day; thankfully, vazelead wounds healed quickly. With a single wobble, she got herself upright. She took notice of her arms—they didn't look the same as the ones she remembered. These arms were lean—toned. Krista pressed her fingers against her arms, testing their firmness. *My arms have more muscles on them, but how?* Krista ran her hands along her stomach and upper legs. Any spot that felt sore was firmer than before.

This isn't my body. "What happened while I was sleeping?" She looked outside to see the sun was still low on the horizon. It was morning.

Krista shook her head and began to touch her arms again; the muscles were indeed there. It was not a hallucination. She remembered the changed appearances of Danil and Ast'Bala and frowned. *Maybe it's the Mental Damnation.*

A cloud went by the sun, blocking out the light and darkening the room.

I have to find Mal—I need to know if he is okay and find out where Sporathun is. She scurried around her room to pick up her clothes and dressed herself, putting on her trousers, her coat, and her scarf.

A knock came from the door.

Krista jumped. "Coming!"

"Coming?" came Dr. Alsroc's shaky voice.

He's right. Paladin strapped me to the bedframe last night for my own safety. She licked her hand and rubbed the cut on her forehead, wiping the blood. It was swollen and rough like the one she had in Dreadweave Pass.

The doorknob began to twist. "I'm coming in, Krista."

She dashed to the door and finished turning the knob, pulling the door open. "Hi," Krista said. She tried to keep her body covering the doorframe, hiding the mess in her room.

"Good morning, Krista," the doctor replied pleasantly, taking a slight bow.

She smiled and placed her hands behind her back, hiding her swollen wrists.

"I wanted to see how you were doing—you have slept most of the morning away."

Krista scratched her head. "I'm doing fine, thank you."

The doctor held his hands together. "Some of the men from across the hall heard you during the night."

Krista swallowed heavily. "Really?" *What could have they heard?*

"They said you screamed several words. I'm curious about one in particular: 'Malpherities.'"

Don't tell him anything. The memory of the ghoul's voice echoed in Krista's head. She folded her arms. "I'm sorry, it doesn't mean anything to me," she lied.

The doctor nodded. "All right. Now, did Paladin help you get out of your restraints this morning?"

"Yes, I had to excuse myself to the restroom." *Is that the best I could come up with?*

Dr. Alsroc nodded again. "Any bad dreams?"

"No."

The doctor stared at her for several seconds, his eyes moving back and forth. He shook his head. "Well, I'm glad you're doing well. Thank you for your time." He stepped back from the door.

Krista smiled at him and slipped out into the hallway, closing her door behind her.

"Remember, Krista." The doctor paused, waiting for her to turn and face him. "They're only dreams."

A nice thought. She smiled. "Thanks."

"I'll be in touch, Krista." Dr. Alsroc walked past her, keeping his hands behind his back.

Krista let out a deep sigh. *I hope he bought the lie. Now to find Malpherities.*

She began to stroke her scalp-feathers while glancing around the halls; they were empty except for the doctor, who was walking away.

Krista looked out to the closest shadow. "Mal?" she whispered.

Silence.

Krista frowned. *Maybe he will show up when I least expect it, like he always does.* What could she do about Sporathun? There wasn't much she could do right now in the High Barracks. Even though she was exhausted, she couldn't go to sleep. Dr. Alsroc and Paladin were keeping too close an eye on her. *If I try to go to sleep, they'll think something is wrong with me. Maybe I'll wait until I hear from Mal; he can help me.* She tried to remember where she'd left off on the surface world. *I was with William. It seems so long ago now.* The events in Dreadweave Pass made it tough to remember the details of the previous day.

Krista waited for Dr. Alsroc to be out of sight before rushing downstairs to the main level. *I'll try to find William—see how he's doing. That seems to bring Malpherities around.* She exited the keep from the nearest entrance and ventured down the path to the training ground. Her hood was over her head and her scarf was covering her face, adjusted to hide the new cut on her forehead. Krista could feel the warm sun beat against her heavy clothing, but felt no tingling in her guts.

In the distance, she could see the training ground, but there were no boys in sight. Where else could they be? It was too early for lunch, meaning they had to be elsewhere in the High Barracks. The next likely place would be the Twisted Hermit—she had found William and his friends there before.

Krista wandered up the road away from the training ground, toward the hill where the Twisted Hermit spread its branches.

She could hear boys' voices and the sound of clashing wood up the hill. There was a deep voice and a whiny voice that were both recognizable: William's friends Talif and Jeuth.

Krista walked up casually to the oak tree. Normally, seeing William had her excited. *But today I just can't get my mind off Dreadweave Pass. I'll just be back there tonight and anything that happens here really won't matter when I'm there struggling for my life.*

The boys were spotted in the shade of the Twisted Hermit, training with their wooden swords. William and Talif were fighting each other while Jeuth sat on the grass cross-legged.

"Hi." Krista waved at the boys.

William smiled at her and waved, and the other two boys acknowledged her with a nod.

She sat herself beside Jeuth and sniffed the air to pick up his scent, sweet and ripe. *Cursman has a much staler smell to him. It must be his age.* "Don't you ever get tired of training?" she asked.

"We have to train; it's our future to serve the Kingdom of Zingalg," Jeuth said as the other two clashed swords.

Krista watched the fight with wide eyes, studying the way the boys swung their swords. They were wild and careless. It was unlike how Cursman had her focus on where she placed her attacks, drive her energy toward each move, and constantly keep herself defended. *These boys really are sloppy. I'm starting to see what Paladin is saying.*

"Why don't they put more energy in their attacks?" Krista whispered.

Jeuth shrugged. "We're tired; it's tough to focus all the time."

"I hear you." It was hard to focus her mind on anything else while a fallen angel was right on her tail in Dreadweave Pass.

William swung up at Talif, leaving his torso wide open. *That was a foolish attack.*

She expected Talif to take advantage of this opening, but he didn't. Instead, the boy backed away from the wild strike and the two continued to throw feral blows at each other.

I could even take on these boys. The thought startled her. Malpherities had said the same thing to her the day before. Normally she wouldn't have thoughts that involved challenging someone. *Normally I just want to get away from people, survive, and be in peace.*

"You're doing it wrong," she spoke up.

The boys stopped their fighting and the three stared at her.

'What?" Talif asked.

Krista eyed all of them and got to her feet. "William, you left yourself open." She positioned herself where she saw his mistake, pretending to hold a sword. "Talif, you didn't take advantage of this, either." Krista shrugged. "It just surprised me that both of you made those mistakes."

The two boys exchanged looks and lowered their swords.

Talif put his hand on his hip. "What do you know about fighting?"

William nodded. "I didn't know you knew how to fight."

Krista looked down at Jeuth, who stared at her. She scratched her head. "I do know a few things, I suppose."

"Show us," Jeuth smirked.

"I don't have a weapon."

The red-haired boy pulled his wooden sword from the tall grass and handed it to her. "Show us."

Krista hadn't even seen the sword in the grass, but took it slowly. The wooden blade was a bit heavy and the handle was finished with a worn leather wrapping. She gripped the blade with both hands carefully and took a deep breath. *Maybe I should have kept my mouth shut.* "All right," Krista said and extended her legs in a battle-ready stance.

"I'll fight you." William stood, sword pointing toward her.

"I don't want to hurt you," Krista said, frowning.

The other two boys laughed.

Talif pointed at William. "You probably would hurt him—he's always making mistakes."

Jeuth shook his head in disagreement. "She's just a girl. William here is turning into a man; he'll win."

Krista stared into William's blue eyes.

He smiled and pointed his sword toward her.

I don't want to hurt him. She relaxed her grip on the sword. "Maybe we shouldn't fight."

Jeuth smiled. "See? She's a girl."

Krista felt her veins boil from the words. *Everyone always thinks I am weak. Just because I don't think violence is the answer.*

William shook his head. "No, we'll do this." He stood wide-legged.

"We'll just take it easy."

William's smile faded; his expression was now blank, staring at her with focus. She glanced at the other two boys who scooted away, leaving room for her duel.

There weren't many options for her—Krista had to fight. If she said no, she would have only humiliated herself. Besides, Cursman was right—she had to be stronger if she was going to survive Dreadweave Pass. Practicing with the boys was a safe way to improve her skills.

No one is going to take me to the Weaver here, or try to bite my face off.

William tightened his lips and inched closer toward Krista while she remained still. He seemed sheepish in his movements, as if he was being careful not to get too close.

Gradually, Krista brought her sword up on an angle and she stood sideways, a position that Cursman had taught her. She was uncertain of her skills in an actual fight; Cursman had only spent two nights practicing with her.

But these boys are sloppy and they were long nights.

William dashed forward and swung low. The attack was slow, and he left his backside open with the wide swing.

Krista bolted to the side, dodging his attack, and with one hand, she lunged her forearm toward him, her wooden blade jabbing William's shoulder. The wooden blade made a thud on his back and rebounded back to Krista.

William grunted and spun around, this time keeping his feet circling around her.

Jeuth's and Talif's eyes widened.

Krista remained where she stood, in the same position, waiting for William's next attack. She knew how eager he could get and it wouldn't take long for him to strike again.

Never let your guard down. Cursman's words replayed in her mind.

William let out a shout and rushed toward Krista, both hands tight around his blade as he raised it upward.

The boy was inches away, and Krista lifted her sword as William struck down, their weapons colliding and locking in place. Both of their arms shook from Krista pushing up and William pushing down, the wooden swords grinding against each other.

William let out another grunt and leaned forward, pressing his upper body weight down on the sword. Krista's arms wobbled and she began to feel the boy's weight overpower her.

Shit.

She eyed her surroundings: William was less than a foot away and pressing in on her. She was losing the blade lock and she would have to pull out, risking getting struck by him.

Or I could improvise.

Krista eyed the boy's open torso. She shifted to her right allowing William to push forward and the blades slid away. Krista lunged at the boy with her knee, ramming into his ribcage.

The blow stunned William, leaving his front open.

Krista lifted her blade in an uppercut at the boy's chest and chipped his jawline. In a fluid motion, she forced the blade around on William's upper back, throwing him to his knees and knocking his sword from his hand.

The two boys roared with laughter while clapping.

Krista ignored them and got to her knees, placing her hand on William. "Are you okay?"

William nodded. His eyes were lean and eyebrows tense. "I'm fine. Good fight."

He's mad.

Talif held his sword up. "It seems you do know a bit about fighting, hey, Krista?" A wicked grin spread across the boy's face. "My turn."

Krista glanced at him and back at William, who nodded at her before crawling over to sit beside Jeuth.

Great. Here we go again. Krista held her sword up. "Okay."

Talif twirled his sword once and began to circle around her, shifting his legs to keep focus on his opponent. He breathed heavily and tightened his grip on his handle.

Krista began to follow his path, moving in his circular pattern. *I'd best mix up my style a bit. Talif saw how I beat William. Darkwing would always change his moves when we were on the run from the Renascence Guard.* She gripped the sword with both hands and kept her stance low.

The boy roared and rushed toward her. His size was menacing and startled Krista.

Talif let out a wide sideways swipe.

Krista leaped backward, the tip of the wooden blade scraping against her collarbone.

Her opponent continued to rush forward, swinging his blade at her a couple more times in a crisscross fashion. He was too far away for the first strike and the second was easy for her to dodge by moving to the right side.

While Talif ended his last strike, Krista lifted her blade up and struck down with both hands, her blade slamming into the boy's shoulder blade.

Talif let out a cry and stumbled to the ground, dropping his sword as his hands slammed into the dirt.

Krista panted and positioned herself for a second strike but remained still.

Jeuth and William burst into laughter.

"Nice one, Krista!" William chuckled.

Jeuth pointed at Talif. "She made you eat the dirt!"

Talif tried to get up but his arm twitched.

Krista dropped the sword and rushed to the boy's side, gently placing her hand on his shoulder. "I'm so sorry. Let me help you up."

The boy grunted as Krista offered her his hand and she helped him to his feet.

"What was that?" He whined while rubbing his back. "No one has ever hit me that hard before."

"I'm so sorry. I didn't mean to." She clutched his hand tightly.

Talif squinted his eyes in confusion. He jerked his hand free. "It's fine, just was a shock to me."

Jeuth scratched his head. "You seem so kind and soft all the time, sometimes scared of us."

Talif rubbed his back and grunted. "We didn't see it coming."

Krista couldn't help but smile; she didn't even know her own strength. Perhaps vazeleads were stronger than humans. *Maybe I can actually defend myself. Wouldn't Darkwing be impressed?* "I know a few tricks. I'm scared all the time because the males of my people are far stronger than I am, and violent." She looked down to the ground. "They often take that as an advantage."

The boys nodded and looked to the ground.

William scratched his arm. "I'd hate to see one. They sound horrific."

Krista fiddled with the tip of her tail. "I hate to see them too; it's nice to be away from my people. I never realized how forceful they were until I came here. Your people seem to deal with problems more with words than with action."

"We consider ourselves civilized," Jeuth said and sat upright with pride.

Talif grunted again as he reached for his training sword. "It's going to bruise," he mumbled.

"Sorry," Krista said softly.

"Where did you learn to fight?" William asked.

Krista wasn't sure what to tell them. *It was from an assassin in hell— because that's a good thing to tell him.* "I guess I picked it up from my people," she lied.

The boys nodded.

"Fierce warriors, then." William leaned down and picked up Krista's dropped sword. "Those are some tactics Paladin might want to know about."

Krista shook her head. "I'd rather not. I don't want to fight." She rubbed her arm, feeling the growing muscle again. "It's not me." Her voice softened. *I've never been a fighter; there was always Darkwing to protect me. But with him not around, I have to change.* The new muscles, her ability to fight, it disturbed her; it really wasn't her. She continued to grow stronger and faster, and her mind was challenging the world around her. *Since this disease, it hasn't felt like my mind or my body.*

"We'd best get back to training." William brought the sword to Jeuth.

Jeuth took the sword and got up from the grass. "All right, let's do this. Maybe we can take on Krista at some point." He said with a smile.

Krista smirked while sitting herself down beside Talif. She didn't pay much attention to William fighting; instead she was in awe at her own fighting ability, going back over the mock battles. *I've only visited Dreadweave Pass twice and I feel like I'm a changed person.* She seemed to analyze her surroundings more, and she judged people by their actions. *I feel when I come back here I'm a different person. What will I become if I'm in Dreadweave Pass for a week? Or a month? How much time passes here?*

Talif sighed. "I hope to learn some of the techniques you know. I'd like to become a fighter that Paladin can be proud of."

Krista nodded. "I'm sure you will. Just focus on what he teaches you." She scratched her head. *Where is Mal?* Her thoughts were empty without the ghoul to assist her in the daily problems she faced. *He really does help guide me in making the right choices.* With him as her friend and constantly by her side, it was easier to make decisions.

With or without Mal, I will be going back to Dreadweave Pass, where the Weaver and Sporathun are after me. The fallen angel's figure entered Krista's mind—the horns, his torn-out lips. He was possibly the most dreadful being Krista had ever laid her eyes on. *Not even the creatures of the underworld are as frightening. How could he be so disfigured? They said he was once beautiful. His conversion into a vampyre seems like a fairy tale.*

"Hey, guys . . ." Krista looked up at the sky. "What are vampyres?"

William and Jeuth stopped dueling and stared at each other.

"Bloodsuckers?" Jeuth panted.

"They can't walk in the day—they'll burn," Talif added.

William shook his head. "No, they just fall asleep when it's day."

"Not true," Talif argued.

"What about the vampire who attacked the farmstead not too far from here?" William said. "The farmer said he fell to the ground in a slumber when the daylight came."

"I don't remember that."

"Well, it happened."

Jeuth scratched his arm. "Either way, vampires still suck blood."

The boys nodded at one another in agreement.

"I remember the one that was rumored to be living in the City of Courage, right under the king's castle," Talif said.

"They caught it, didn't they?" William asked.

"No one really found out."

Krista shook her head. "They suck blood? What about wrath vampyres?"

The boys exchanged glances and shrugged.

William sat down. "What do you mean?"

"I mean, what about vampyres that feed on sin?"

William shook his head. "Never heard of them."

Jeuth joined the group on the grass. "Are they from another kingdom?"

Krista shook her head. "No, vampyres: angels that fell to sin. Blood isn't a sin, is it?"

The boys shook their heads.

Talif folded his arms. "No, vampires aren't angels. They were once people."

William pointed at his neck. "Bats bite them and they're transformed."

Jeuth shook his head. "I heard they made a deal with the devil. We might want to ask Father Isaac to clarify about vampires."

Krista smiled at the boy. "Thanks for the idea. Maybe I'll go do that."

Jeuth nodded.

She got to her feet and brushed the grass from her legs. "Well, it's been fun." Krista waved at them. "I'm going to talk to Father Isaac."

William waved back. "See you later."

Krista walked down the hill leading toward the church at the far end of the High Barracks.

With or without Mal, I need to solve my problems in Dreadweave Pass. The best thing I can do is try and learn about my enemy, like Cursman and I did at the library. Those boys just made this more confusing.

Krista had her arms folded and kept her head low. She felt forlorn without Malpherities and was hoping he'd appear on her long walk. *Please, anytime would be good, Mal. I think I am finally understanding what you mean by me needing to focus on Dreadweave Pass.*

She moved closer to the church and slowed her pace in case the ghoul decided to appear. Nothing. Krista approached the stairway and knew that he was not coming.

"Father Isaac, here I come." Krista rushed up the stairs and pulled open the large front doors to the cathedral. The large empty hall echoed with the squeaking hinges while she entered the building.

Krista lowered her scarf and hood and she stepped onto the red carpet.

At the end of the hall, Father Isaac was kneeling, facing the altar and cross on the stage.

The old priest rose from the ground, casually turning to greet Krista. "Welcome, child," he said with a smile.

Krista took a curtsy once she approached the front pew.

"I was expecting you," Father Isaac added.

"Why?" Krista asked.

"Wonder filled your eyes when we first met." Father Isaac chuckled. "Curiosity of a child." He shook his head. "Yet it surprises me today; your eyes tell me a different story."

Krista blinked. His stare seemed to look past her physical appearance and into her thoughts. *It's uncomfortable.*

"Your eyes are sharper today, more focused, your mind less open."

Krista nodded. "I suppose."

"Then what brings you to me?"

"Vampyres." Krista looked at the priest's bright green eyes.

The priest leaned back, frowning.

She shifted her position. "I need to know about them, specifically about vampyres of wrath. Does that mean anything to you?"

"Someone so young wants to know of dark creatures such as vampyres. Then to speak about vampyres of wrath. The youth know only about the vampires from folklore—the ones who drink blood."

"Bloodsuckers?"

"Correct."

Krista pointed at the entrance of the church. "I was talking to William and his friends; they mentioned them. Jeuth told me to talk to you about wrath vampyres."

"What interests you about them? Not often do people ask about real vampyres, let alone someone so young."

Don't tell anyone anything. Mal said so. Krista sighed. "It's a problem— for a friend." Her shoulders tensed up and she clenched her teeth.

Father Isaac folded his arms. "Your friend isn't a vampyre himself, is he?"

Krista smiled, finding the idea amusing. "No, of course not."

"Then what is this friend's problem?"

"Just some research for him," Krista lied.

The priest nodded. "Paladin?"

"Yes, he's busy and needs my help. He doesn't want people to talk about his research." She scratched her head. "I'm from the underworld, and I don't know much about the surface."

Father Isaac raised his eyebrow. "The underworld is quite the unholy place."

Krista nodded. "I know. It changed my people."

The priest waved for Krista to follow. "Come." He began to walk toward the spiral stairway. "Paladin is very busy; I know of the underworld's shackles being shattered. There's no telling what horrors this may bring to Zingalg."

Krista let out a sigh. *Lying is becoming too easy.* "Paladin knows I'm from the underworld and hopes I can help him."

Father Isaac led Krista down the staircase to the basement of the church. The basement was not as gloriously decorated as the surface level. The room was dark; light came in from barred windows near the top of the stone wall. A series of bleached oak bookshelves lined one wall, and a small desk with candles and a pile of books on top sat adjacent to them. A couple of wooden stools rested nearby, complete with red velvet cushions.

"Paladin is a good man, but he is lost in the past." Father Isaac began to scan through the books on the shelves. "A man who must realize his days of bloodshed and redeeming land have come and gone." He pulled a green book from the shelf and placed it on the table. "Yet when problems like the underworld arise, we need heroes of old such as him. Unfortunately, he is the last of his kind." Father Isaac sat on the stool in front of the desk.

Krista dragged a second stool closer to the priest and sat on it. She leaned closer to the book to see that it was very different in shape, size, and texture from the books in Dreadweave Pass. This book was complete with a linen covering; it was large with tan pages.

The alphabet was different, too: the words were in English, like Dr. Alsroc's books, nearly identical to the characters that the vazeleads used.

Father Isaac scanned through the book, flipping page by page until he reached his desired section and pointed to an illustration showing an angel falling from the skies, wings burning. "Vampyres, otherwise known as fallen angels. The name 'vampyres' was given to them by common folk who were frightened by their sharp teeth and energy-leaching ability."

Krista nodded. "I know that much, about their corruption from sin. I just I don't know much about their weaknesses, or strengths."

Father Isaac turned the page and pointed at a table in the book. "Fallen angels turn corrupt by one of the Seven Deadly Sins." He pointed at the second column. "They are consumed by the act of the sin. In the case of wrath, a vampyre of wrath channels anger. They embrace the act of hatred."

Krista leaned closer to the table trying to read the faded text, but it was too difficult. She squinted her eyes trying to make out the words, but didn't recognize any. "What do they mean?" she asked.

"Some vampyres have an easier sin to fall under, such as lust and greed. But these sins are harder to gratify and the fallen angels must work hard to feed their sin—or in other words, feed their life force. The fallen angels who are consumed by the more difficult sins such as wrath and sloth are able to feed more frequently."

"What?"

"Well, don't you find it easier to get angry than it is to constantly be greedy? Even if you were greedy all the time, could you act on the greed more often than act on anger?"

"I guess not."

"With wrath, it is easy to act on the sin, making it easier for these types of vampyres to feed. They're able to sustain themselves merely by the thought that makes them aggravated."

Krista swallowed and looked up at the priest. "So they feed themselves, which means they can't die from hunger?"

"As long as they keep their body and mind focused on their sin, they'll never tire."

Krista nodded. "What about a vampyre that has fallen from two sins?"

Father Isaac shook his head. "That can have both good and negative results on the vampyre. They can feed their life force from both sins, but if they only feed from one, they will start to perish."

"So how can you kill one?" she asked.

Father Isaac raised an eyebrow. "You want to kill one?"

"Paladin needs to know."

"Well . . . of course, you can prevent them from feeding their sin, but that doesn't always work because it can take centuries for them to decay. A more guaranteed result is through a crucifixion. You can damage a fallen angel with physical attacks, even chop them up into a thousand pieces. But this won't kill them—not right away, at least." Father Isaac turned the page showing an illustration of a burning cross. "A crucifixion burns a fallen angel's corrupt soul and cleanses it from the sin that consumed them."

"How do you do one?"

"Only beings blessed by God can: a priest, a paladin, or—technically—another angel."

Krista took a deep sigh. "What if you're not blessed?"

"What can you do about it?"

"Yeah."

Father Isaac smiled. "Pray."

Krista raised an eyebrow. "That's not very helpful."

"With faith, anything is possible."

"Right . . . what if the vampyre fulfills their sin?"

"Fulfill it? They never will. Sin continually rots away at them, as it does to everyone. They will never be satisfied."

So is finding Glamorous really going to help? Father Isaac's words were unsettling. "Thank you for the insight."

Father Isaac nodded. "I'm glad to be of assistance, my child."

"So why don't you tell children about real vampyres? Why do you call bloodsuckers vampires?"

"Bloodsuckers are just people who have been infected by the venomous xephile bats. Actual vampyres are such an old piece of our history. There hasn't been a recorded fallen angel in well over a thousand years. The ones who have fallen are still around, but they're trapped in hell where they belong."

"So why aren't children told about them?"

"Children don't know about every demon in hell, or how many hells they are. There's no need to clutter their mind with darkness from another generation. They only need to know that the Heavenly Kingdoms will save them. The moment they learn about fallen angels, they'll start asking about why they fell and may even question their own faith."

Krista lifted herself from the chair. "Makes sense. Thanks again; I'm sure this will help Paladin greatly." She lifted her hood and tied up her scarf.

Father Isaac smiled, "I'm sure it will help *you* greatly."

Her eyes widened and she shook her head. "It's not for me."

The priest closed the book slowly. "There's no need to fear your problems, child. Secrets never stay hidden forever. To solve your problems, you mustn't deny them."

Krista swallowed heavily. "Sorry."

He rose from the chair and placed the book back to the shelf. "Dr. Alsroc has dealt with many patients before. I've learned to understand the symptoms of the disease that he's dedicated his life to. He believes it is a mental issue; however, the stories I've heard from his patients are not the effects of an illness, but of a spiritual battle."

"But you're a human priest—you teach about human religion." She scratched her arm. "Mental Damnation isn't a religion."

Father Isaac smiled. "You'd be surprised, Krista. They're not very different."

Krista shrugged. "Maybe not."

Father Isaac waved his hand. "Run along now, child. I am certain Madam Marilyn will need your assistance."

I completely forgot about her. Krista nodded and bowed before the priest. "Thank you."

"Remember, Krista, this church is a safe place. Even from the invisible demons you're fighting."

Krista put on a weak smile. "Thanks again."

She scurried up to the second level and marched down the red carpet of the church, arms folded. *So Father Isaac knows about Mental Damnation? Does he know about Mal? What about the Weaver?* They were questions she was afraid to ask Father Isaac. If he was friends with Dr. Alsroc, it meant anything she told him, the doctor would find out. *I should keep quiet.* If Malpherities was here, she would be able to make a logical choice. *I just want more information about how to survive and escape Dreadweave Pass.*

She pushed the front doors open, the sun temporarily blinding her. Shortly, Krista's vision returned and she marched down the stairs. *I hope Marilyn isn't mad that I abandoned her today.*

At least she'd put her time in the High Barracks to some use. *Anything I can learn about Sporathun is good. He still sounds dangerous and, by the sounds of it, my only chance to kill him is with Fierel's help. If she is still alive. But maybe with Glamorous, he won't want to hunt me anymore.* It was a longshot but she didn't have much else to work with.

Krista began to walk down the stairway of the church and heard a yelp come from her side. She glanced downward to see a puff of black smoke evaporate in the air from a crack in the step.

"Mal?"

Krista hurried down the steps until she was on the gravel road.

The black smoke rose from her shadow.

"Mal!" Krista exclaimed.

The ghoul unfolded from the smoke and hissed. "Careful where you go! My soul could have been burned alive when I spawned on the holy ground."

Krista clutched her hands and smiled widely. "You're alive!"

Malpherities glanced around. "Don't acknowledge me so noisily among the humans. Do you have a wish for them to lock you within prison doors?"

Krista frowned. "No. Sorry." She began to twirl her index finger around her tail. "I was just glad to see you again."

Malpherities shook his head, dreadlocks waving side to side. "What joy would you have to embrace me again?"

Someone is in poor spirits. "We're friends."

"Yes, of course. That is of little importance right now, though. Fierel and I were unable to hold Sporathun back for long. His strength is beyond what we are capable of dealing with."

"What do we do?"

"Krista!"

Krista glanced up the road to the garden. Marilyn waved at her while holding a woven basket.

Malpherities let out a brief sigh. "She seems paler today."

Holding her dress above the dirt, Marilyn rushed down the road toward them. "Krista, what are you doing here? I've been searching for you all day."

"Sorry," Krista replied.

The maid glanced at the church. "Don't your people have their own religion? Or are you finally confessing to God?"

Krista scratched her shoulder. "I just wanted to talk to your priest." Krista kept her eyes on Marilyn's skin; it was indeed paler. The dark bags under her eyes were larger and her eyes were bloodshot, too.

She really isn't well.

"Come, we've got work to do." Marilyn walked past Krista.

She followed behind the maid but slowed her pace. "We need to help her," she whispered to Malpherities.

The ghoul hushed her. "Mustn't talk to me, girl." He eyed Marilyn from head to toe. "She must have lost a lot of blood to be so white." Malpherities lightly pushed Krista. "Go, walk with her. We have time to discuss Sporathun before you rest again."

Krista obeyed and hurried to the maid's side. Marilyn's pale skin made Krista's stomach twist. She couldn't understand how Smyth could treat her so ruthlessly and justify his actions. *I know he believes it is in the name of God, but how could a god be so cruel to such a nice girl like Marilyn?*

Krista glanced at Marilyn's frowning face. "How come you let them treat you this way?"

"I have to, Krista." She took a deep breath. "I've told you, Smyth will cleanse me from the shimen blood." The maid looked over at Krista with her weak eyes, eyelids hanging low. "I want God to accept me, and I want to reclaim my mother's honour."

Krista's heart felt heavy while staring at the girl's tired eyes; they screamed for mercy.

"Marilyn is no different than you, Krista." Malpherities folded his arms. "She wants freedom from her mother's curse and you want freedom from Dreadweave Pass."

Krista bit her lip. "I understand."

The two walked in silence as they entered the keep. Marilyn had the lead, taking her to the basement where they washed the laundry of the High Barracks.

Krista stayed behind Marilyn while she led her through the hall.

The maid glanced back. "I overreacted last time we talked about this." She opened the door to the laundry room. The smell of dirt, human, and soap filled the air. "Smyth is cruel, I'll admit, but he has to be to cleanse me of the shimen."

"Why can't you make peace with yourself?" Krista replied, taking a seat on a stool near the tub and a pile of clothes.

Marilyn laughed—a weak laugh that ended in a grunt. "I tried. And like I said, I overreacted. Smyth is trying to help me; he wants me to revive our family's name." She sat on the opposite side of the tub with her own pile of clothing, using a scrubbing board to clean the clothes.

She actually believes Smyth is doing the right thing? Krista felt anger run through her veins. How could Marilyn be so naive?

The maid handed Krista a dirt-filled blue shirt. "It's for the best, and if God wishes to forgive my mother for such an unholy birth, he'll clear the shimen of my body."

"Otherwise?"

"I will die trying. Maybe God will have mercy on my soul in the afterlife."

"That's ridiculous!" Krista's shouted and rose from her seat.

Marilyn gasped.

Malpherities chuckled.

Krista glanced at the ghoul. "This isn't funny." She turned back at the maid. "How can you even consider worshipping a god who doesn't accept you as you are?"

The maid looked down and began to wash a tunic in the tub.

Malpherities spoke up. "She's used to abuse; she has been beaten verbally and physically enough times that she just takes it now."

Krista took a deep breath and sat down. "You're my friend." She dunked the shirt in the tub and ran it along her own scrubbing board. "I want to help you."

Marilyn shook her head. "You make things sound so simple, yet they aren't. I appreciate that you want to help me, but it's of no use. I need to do this."

Krista bit her lip. *How do I reply to that?*

Malpherities moved closer to her. "It is easy. I minimize my involvement with others. This removes emotional investment from myself and impractical drama mortals cause from their desires."

Krista glanced up at him while the ghoul nodded. She repeated his statement word for word to Marilyn.

The maid nodded. "Those are defensive words, Krista."

The ghoul shook his head. "She's a hopeless being. She may have inherited a shimen's appearance but she also inherited the useless thinking process of a human." Malpherities chuckled. "You really know how to pick friends, Krista. Even your friendship with Darkwing. Perhaps that's why your life has been such a mess from day one."

The words ignited Krista's veins. She was already steamed over Marilyn's ignorance, and now Malpherities had insulted her oldest friend, Darkwing.

She spread her lips showing her sharp fangs and pushed the ghoul. "Don't say that!" she shouted.

"Don't touch me, girl! The maid is here." Malpherities folded his arms.

"Krista?" Marilyn asked.

Krista jumped onto the ghoul and the two fell to the ground. "She's not stupid, you take it back! My life is not where it is at because of my choice in friends!" She slammed the ghoul's hands onto the stone floor. "I've struggled my whole life!"

"Krista!" Marilyn gasped.

Malpherities roared and lunged both arms at Krista, throwing her away and knocking her against the tub.

Her body hit the metal rim hard enough to collapse the walls into the tank, and the water poured out onto the dirty ground. The impact stunned her and her vision swayed side to side.

The ghoul got up from the ground and towered over her. His pupils constricted and his tentacle-like hair flew wildly in all directions.

Krista tried to get up but her body was indented into the frame and her spine ached. She kicked her legs trying to push up, but it was no use.

"I can only talk to you, girl! We can't interact in this world—I've told you this." Malpherities shouted. The inner blue of his body glowed brightly and the fog from his waist down began to expand, swallowing up the room and leaving him and Krista in pure darkness.

"Oh, Christ!" Marilyn voice quavered. "I'll get Dr. Alsroc." The maid could be heard dashing out of the room, leaving the door wide open.

Krista grunted and tried to back away from the ghoul again. "Mal, I'm sorry."

"Do you think I enjoy being trapped in these realms?" He raised his shackled wrists. "I've got places to go. I want freedom!" Malpherities picked up a stool with one hand and chucked it against a wall, shattering it into a dozen pieces. Veins bulged from his muscular arms and, breathing heavily, he pointed his extended claw at her. "You judge me so quickly by my words but little do you know about what I have done and what I have endured. I don't deserve this entrapment! Your age holds no comparison to my own. I've had enough time in several worlds to understand what a hard life is—and the truth about allies." The ghoul snatched Krista by her scarf, lifting her up into the air until their noses touched.

She gasped for air and choked while the scarf pressed against her esophagus. She kicked her legs violently at the ghoul, trying to break free.

"Please! I said I was sorry!"

Malpherities shook his head. "I don't understand your childish mind, girl. This maid is a bane to shimen and humans. You defend the weak and waste your time. You befriended a blond boy, yet I told you to stay clear of him. I was able to deal with your weak, primitive needs of comfort from a male and friendship of another female . . ."

Krista gargled and sputtered. She felt her lungs burn from the lack of air and her limbs began to lose feeling.

"But assaulting me, in your own realm? I've had nothing but patience with you to protect you here and in Dreadweave Pass. I've sacrificed my freedom to a paladin for you. All you do is bitch about wanting to go home . . . Then you go and jeopardize your own freedom by attacking me? You spoiled, ungrateful brat." Malpherities raised her higher, the scarf putting more pressure on her neck.

Krista coughed and her vision began to darken.

"Do you think you're going to die? You'll only be free of this realm and then your final passing to Dreadweave Pass will be complete!" Malpherities let out an ear-shattering roar, lifting Krista higher in the air. "I'd be doing you a favour to end your misery once and for all."

"Leave her, Malpherities!" Dr. Alsroc's voice boomed. The ghoul glanced at the doorway.

"Krista!" Paladin's voice came.

"But I need you with Mental Damnation, alive. There's more at stake than your little escape from Dreadweave Pass, Krista. You present a major political advantage against the Truce of Passing, being in hell and not technically dead. You defy the laws set in place by the gods. This makes you the key into the Heavenly Kingdoms." Malpherities's grasp faded as Krista's eyes closed. She fell to the ground and her head hit the metal tub, knocking her consciousness clear.

CHAPTER XVIII: ANIMALS CAN'T DREAM

CHAPTER XIX

Denial

Child.
You didn't wake?
This worries me greatly.
You feel I'm fake?

I assure thee.
Realism shall return.
You try to flee.
What for?

The sin will find you.
Our meeting to follow.
That is true.
End your games!

Resisting what's real.
Only does you harm.

Let me feel.

So we can master the worlds!

o!" Krista shouted, rising from her rest. In mid-rise she was caught, her arms restrained by leather cuffs.

She fell back down onto the bed with a thud. The fall spiked the pain from the bruises on her back, even though the mattress was soft. Her head throbbed on both sides; her veins pulsated with each beat of her heart.

Krista grunted and turned her head around to examine her surroundings. The bookshelves and desk off to the far-left corner, the stone walls, and windows near the ceiling—it was Dr. Alsroc's office. Her bed was the operating table, with a mattress, a pillow, and a couple of soft, loosely woven linen sheets draped over her body.

Krista tugged at her arms; they were buckled down at her wrists by black leather straps.

"What happened?" Krista muttered a curse under her breath. *I really made Mal mad.*

She shifted her body, trying to ease the tension on her back. She closed her eyes and relaxed her head on the pillow. *He'll come back. He didn't kill me, he said he wouldn't.* The vision of Malpherities grabbing her by the neck flashed through her mind and she shook her head. *Don't think about it.*

An itch rose on her neck and she attempted to scratch it but her hands were caught by the straps and she couldn't reach. Krista whined, trying to lift her hands several times, inching her neck closer to her hand, but it was of no use.

The sound of the door creaking destroyed the silence. It was Marilyn; she held her hands together and her face had a long frown. She held a basket of strawberries, a mug with steam coming from it, and a damp rag draping from the basket's edge.

"Thank God, you're awake." She rushed over to Krista's bedside. "I was going to leave these for you, for when you woke." The girl's eyes were wide. Her movements were sheepish as she leaned down beside Krista.

What did Marilyn see when Mal attacked?

The maid pulled up a nearby wooden stool with a green cushion and sat, placing the basket on her lap. Her knees were close enough to touch the edge of the operating table.

Krista sat herself up as best she could, using her elbows for support.

"Why am I strapped down?" Krista asked. *I probably know the answer—it is for my own safety.*

Marilyn shifted her eyes to the ground. "It's a safety reason." She took the red fruit from the bowl and held it out for Krista.

She stared at the strawberry. *It makes me feel like an animal.*

"I'm not too hungry." Krista lied back down and grunted from her sore back. "I can eat them later."

Marilyn nodded. "All right." She placed the fruit back into the basket. "Feeling better?"

Krista shrugged. "I suppose. What happened?"

The maid sighed. "I'm not sure if I should be telling you. I suppose you'd know, though. Dr. Alsroc told me about your . . . condition."

"Mental Damnation?"

"Yes, that one. I've met his patients before; they've horrified me with their talk about hell and blood. Father Isaac has tried exorcisms, and they've never worked. Everyone sees it as just a disease."

"That's what I'm told."

"Krista . . ." Marilyn looked to the ground. "Can you tell me what caused you to spontaneously react the way you did?"

She wants to know about Mal. Krista opened her mouth to speak. *Should I tell?* She trusted Marilyn and Malpherities had been rather harsh to her. It was also possible that Dr. Alsroc was using Marilyn to try and get the information from her. *Mal said that if Dr. Alsroc found anything out about my Mental Damnation, he'd make my life far worse.*

"I can't really explain," Krista lied. *Half a lie.*

"It looked like you were fighting someone." Marilyn clutched her hands together. "The doctor told me that your illness causes . . . schizophrenia. I'm talking to Krista now, am I?"

Krista smirked. "Yes, you've always talked to me. Who was I fighting?"

"Why, yourself." Marilyn scratched her nose. "I've never seen such force in someone before. You crushed the tub we were using . . . It was made of iron. You got up from your seat and pushed yourself into it with your back and started to strangle yourself. It looked almost supernatural."

Krista shook her head. "I'm not that strong."

"You're not—Dr. Alsroc said your illness causes temporary bursts of strength from the infected parts of the brain sending the wrong messages to the body." Marilyn placed her hand on Krista's own. "You'll be okay."

Krista stared into her eyes; they were still wide, with slanted eyebrows. *Her eyes say I won't be okay.*

Marilyn patted her hand. "I'm here for you."

"Thank you."

"Dr. Alsroc said you are most lucky to even have a working back. That iron tub is exceptionally solid. He said your body's endurance is beyond a human's; you should heal at a decent rate."

Krista sighed. "It hurts, though."

"It should. Dr. Alsroc said that amount of force would have paralyzed any man."

"It doesn't make sense. I just want to be left alone." *She doesn't know what I'm talking about, but I needed to get it out.* "Does Dr. Alsroc have anything to stop it?"

Marilyn shrugged. "I don't know. He said you're not opening up to him. He can help you if you'd tell him your problem."

Black smoke rose from underneath the operating table. Krista's eyes widened. *It's Mal.* The smoke began to mould into the shape of the ghoul, the blue smoke funneling in the centre of the shape.

"Krista?" Marilyn leaned closer.

Krista shook her head and looked away from the smoke. "Nothing."

Malpherities's smoke climbed higher than Marilyn until he was about two heads above the girl. "The doctor won't assist you. His medicines mean nothing." The ghoul cracked his knuckles.

"It would do you a lot of good, Krista," Marilyn added. "You need to tell someone your problems. It might not be the doctor, or me, but let someone know. Holding it in will only hurt you."

Krista nodded. Her eyes swayed back and forth between Marilyn and Malpherities.

The ghoul folded his arms. "The maid speaks nonsense. No one can help you here."

"I'll consider it," Krista replied.

Marilyn smiled. "Please do so." She got to her feet then placed the basket and mug on the doctor's table. "I must return to work, but you'll be assisting me again soon—I'm sure of that."

"Bye." Krista gave a slight wave, hindered by the restraining cuffs.

Marilyn waved back and exited the room, quietly closing the door behind her.

Malpherities watched as the door closed then spun his head to face Krista, his dreadlocks flying in the air. "Fool!"

She shook her head, "Mal, don't hurt me. I'm sorry."

The ghoul growled and moved closer to her. "You assaulted me first. I told you not to interact with me while others were around." He slipped his claw between her hand and the leather straps. "This is what happens when you do—they lock you up."

"Marilyn said I'll be helping her soon. I won't be in here long."

The ghoul lifted his claw, forcing the leather straps to snap. "Of course she did. She expects you to tell the doctor your problems and about your little adventures in Dreadweave Pass." He moved his claw to her other wrist and snapped the second strap.

Krista sat herself up and rubbed her wrists.

"Think about what happened when you attacked me."

"Yeah, it put me here. Do you really think you should be breaking those straps? What will Dr. Alsroc think?"

The ghoul shrugged. "He'll assume you broke them, just like the other cuffs and the iron tub. I think he's aware that things tend to break around you because of your realm-crossing. Just don't escalate it by attacking me."

"I didn't hurt you, did I?"

The ghoul let out a croaky laugh. "No, but you hurt yourself. Then the tub—I can't see them letting you do anything after that."

"But you pushed me! I didn't do anything."

"And they'll believe you?"

Krista crossed her legs and slouched, staring at her sheets. "What am I supposed to do?"

"You got yourself into this mess."

"But you told me you'd help me!"

Malpherities poked her bare shoulder. "I also told you not to interact with me while others are around. You're getting too aggressive."

Krista glanced at her uncovered shoulder and noticed she was just in her black dress. Her other clothes were gone.

"I say you're getting hostile," said Mal, "because when we first met, you told me we were friends."

Krista relaxed her position, lowering her hands. "We are."

"Do friends attack each other? When you first told me we were friends, you were more naive, even if it was only a handful of days ago. Now you're growing, moulding into the adult you are meant to be." The ghoul folded his arms, his wrist shackles jingling. "Dreadweave Pass is toying with your mind."

"It's not my fault." Krista looked to the ground again. "I am changing, but I don't mean to. I just never get any rest anymore. It's messing with my head."

"Don't be ashamed. You need to strengthen your spirit and mind in order to survive in any realm. These are growing pains."

I still don't feel fine. I miss the days living in the City of Renascence and being with Darkwing—having him take care of me.

The ghoul gently placed his claw under her chin, lifting it up. "Be proud of yourself, girl. I know you're testing your strength; attacking me is an example. But you have to understand that you have limits."

Krista took hold of his claw with her hand. "I'm so sorry. You're my friend and I don't treat you well."

Malpherities broke his claw free. "Nor do I to you, yet we understand each other." The ghoul glanced around the room. "We'll get you dressed."

She watched him float around the room, his fog still attached to the mattress. It always amazed her, seeing how he managed to move within this realm compared to in Dreadweave Pass, where he just floated around freely.

Malpherities found Krista's clothes by the doctor's desk. He took them into his arms and floated back to her bed. "Get your clothes on.

We're leaving this office." He placed the clothes on the bed.

Krista obeyed and started to dress herself. "Where are we going?" she grunted while putting her trousers on; bending her back spiked the pain.

The office doorknob began to twist and the door flung open. Dr. Alsroc entered the room, wearing a white apron and a deep blue shirt.

Krista finished buckling her boots and sat upright.

"Krista!" Dr. Alsroc glanced at the torn leather straps. "What did you do?"

She glanced at Malpherities.

"They were slightly torn to begin with, and you were frightened so you ripped them," the ghoul answered for her.

She repeated his words and continued to dress herself again.

The doctor stared at her for a couple of moments then nodded and walked to his desk. "Your back is in surprisingly good condition for the impact you made on the tub. You'll heal quickly."

"We need to make this conversation quick," Malpherities said. "Fierel and I could not find you or Cursman at the caverns. We need to meet up again. Where did you and Cursman go?"

"Fierel is alive?" Krista muttered.

"We were both wounded from the battle with Sporathun, but are capable of mending ourselves."

Dr. Alsroc sat at his desk. "I know you're going through much more than you can handle."

Krista turned around on her bed to face the man.

"Your Mental Damnation is a complicated disease that will trick your mind to drain your body of its energy. It creates illusions that will convince you that they are real to stimulate more activity from your brain." He leaned forward on his desk. "Who attacked you while you were with Madam Marilyn?"

Krista remained silent, hoping Malpherities would answer this for her.

"I know you've been untruthful to me. I've dealt with this illness for a long time and know that you're hiding your nightmares and imaginary friends from me."

"What do I do?" Krista whispered through her breath.

Malpherities flared his nostrils. "He knows you're well into

Dreadweave Pass and understanding the realm-crossings. Lying to him is becoming harder to do."

"I don't know." Krista put on her leather coat carefully so she did not stretch her back.

Dr. Alsroc stared at her, his eyes studying every movement she made.

"I hear voices," Krista said as she finished putting her coat on. "They tell me things that I don't always like to hear."

"Like what?" Dr. Alsroc leaned back in his chair.

"They were commenting about Madam Marilyn."

"Is that why you attacked . . . them?"

"Yes."

Dr. Alsroc nodded and opened a drawer from his desk, pulling out a paper. "Come take a look at this."

Krista got off her bed with a grunt. She wobbled over to his desk, using the operating table as support until she had to walk on her own. With her slow motions, it took her several moments to reach the desk.

Dr. Alsroc pushed the paper toward her, tapping it once.

She eyed the doctor then the paper to see a crude crayon drawing of Malpherities. The two types of fog, the horns, and dreadlocked hair—yes, it was undoubtedly Malpherities. His fog in the picture was attached to a poorly drawn boy who had short hair and a frown.

Dr. Alsroc put his hands together. "Are you sure it was . . . 'them'? Or was it him?"

The ghoul moved closer to Krista and glanced at the paper. He took it in his claws and squinted. "Looks nothing like me."

Krista yanked it from his hands. "Don't touch it."

Malpherities raised an eyebrow and pointed to the doctor.

Krista looked up at Dr. Alsroc who was watching her with squinted eyes.

He's trying to read me.

"You seem to recognize it." The doctor folded his arms. "Was it the creature you attacked?"

"Yes," Krista replied.

Malpherities growled. "Don't tell him anything." He poked her head several times. "Think!"

Dr. Alsroc got up from his seat and stepped toward the shelf behind him. "I've got an herb that might help calm your nerves down." He pulled a jar from the shelf and placed it on the table, pulling several leaves out. "This character calls himself Malpherities. I've seen him appear in a number of cases before. He accompanies you during the day and in your nightmares. He is mischievous. To be honest, Krista, I believe he is just the negativity, fears, and doubts of an individual being conceptualized into a figure through the disease. Your feelings manifest as something you recognize so you will stop fighting the sickness."

Malpherities shook his head. "What a fool."

"This is what the disease does. It starts to tear your mind apart, splitting portions of your personality into different sections and characters. It must have horrified you, attacking Malpherities; it takes a lot of courage." Dr. Alsroc walked past Krista and to the far end of the office where there were a couple more shelves. He took a polished wooden bowl and steel rod, then dropped the leaves in the bowl and started to grind them.

Krista scratched her head. "I suppose."

"You have to understand this illness feeds on fear. Once you accept that they're not real and it is just you, they cannot harm you." The doctor walked over to the basket and mug at the table. He carefully poured the ground leaves into the steaming mug.

Mal never hurt me until I physically attacked him. It was possible that the doctor knew more than what Malpherities claimed he did. *But then again, Mal did scratch me with his claw when we first met.*

"His tea will make you drowsy," Malpherities said. "If you need help walking anywhere, I'll assist you."

The doctor placed the bowl and rod on the operating table and took the mug from the stool, walking over to Krista. She stood tall as the doctor approached her with the drink.

"Here. Take this and you'll be free to go."

Smiling, Krista took the cup with a slight bow of her head. She sniffed the mug and quickly snorted from the strong, bitter smell of vegetation.

"Guzzle down," Malpherities said with a wicked grin.

Krista took one deep breath and tipped the mug back into her mouth. The water was not exceptionally hot and she did her best to let it bypass her tongue and go straight into her throat. A bit of the liquid skimmed over her taste buds and she picked up on the flavour, which was exactly how it smelled. The last few gulps of the liquid were the most repulsive: chips from the leaves had sunk to the bottom and got caught in her throat.

She coughed once and then finished the last gulp. Krista tried to wipe the taste from her tongue with her hand but it was of no use; the strong bitterness was stuck there.

Dr. Alsroc took a slight bow. "Take care, Krista. I'd like it if we could have a session every second day so I can keep track of you." He moved behind his desk and opened a cabinet, taking out a black-painted walking cane. "Take this until you can walk comfortably."

"Okay," Krista said. She took the wooden cane and used it as support while limping over to the door.

"Your illness changes with you," Dr. Alsroc added. "Be cautious of what your voices say."

Krista smiled weakly at him then turned to open the door.

"Or of what Malpherities tells you."

Krista remained motionless at the door for a moment before opening it. "Thanks." She twisted the knob, pulled the door open, and limped out of the office.

Malpherities and Krista began to walk down the hall slowly. "He knows of you?" She grunted after taking an awkward step; it was difficult to use the cane and adjust to her bruised back.

Malpherities's fog now followed her shadow. His presence so near made her feel alarmed, afraid he might attack again. "The doctor and I have dealt with each other before."

"You've helped others with my illness?"

"It's not an illness, girl! You're blessed! I've told you this before."

"Sorry."

"I've attempted to save several others, most of them human and far younger than you are. You're different, you and your people."

"What do you mean?"

"The Weaver has not come across a race like your own before—such strong mortals and capable of great power."

"Is that why my people's guardians were turned into gatekeepers?"

"Correct. Right now, though, we must return to important matters—Sporathun is closing in on you and Cursman. You must return to Dreadweave Pass. Cursman must know that he has to backtrack to Fierel and me. So, where did you two go?"

"We went to a large city." Krista scratched her head, trying to recall where Cursman had taken her, but her mind could not place a name.

"The City of Blood? It's the only civil city in Dreadweave Pass." The ghoul tapped his chin several times. "If that is the case, we need you and Cursman to circle back to a place called the Ruins of the Mortals Run. It's about midway between the Jawless Cavern and the City of Blood. It will also give us cover against Sporathun. With any luck, we will meet up before you encounter him."

Ruins of the Mortals Run—that name sounds familiar. But her mind was too clouded to think anything of it. "I will, but when you caused me to black out . . . I wasn't awake in Dreadweave Pass. I heard voices; they always speak to me before I cross realms. But this time I did not go to Dreadweave Pass. Why?"

"Interesting that you heard voices. They were not mine."

"Was it the Weaver?"

"Most likely."

Krista shook her head. "Why did I not cross?"

"Perhaps your mind was ill at ease and could not activate your realm-crossing abilities."

"I have been pretty stressed out," she admitted.

The two turned down a hall where windows were visible. Krista could see that it was about midday and she still had plenty of time to kill. *It'd probably be best to find Marilyn.* Paladin expected her to obey his rules if she was to stay within the High Barracks. *I don't know how much I can do in this condition, but I might as well try.*

Krista found the stairway leading to the basement and she remembered the location of the laundry room.

This time, it took Krista twice as long as usual to reach the laundry room. She carefully limped down the staircase, and the steps seemed extra deep. *Or maybe they just feel that way now that I am injured.* Eventually, Krista and Malpherities reached the laundry room, where Marilyn sat on one of two stools beside a white-enameled tub that was chipped in the corners, showing the copper base.

"Hi," Krista said with a grunt.

Marilyn waved. "I didn't expect to see you so soon, and walking at that."

Krista shrugged. "It wasn't so bad. I've had worse in my home world."

"Must have been tragic, living there."

Krista began to walk over to the empty stool when an invisible wave brushed past her, her vision swaying side to side.

"It's the tea." Malpherities held her with both hands. His grip felt unusually soft, as if she were being supported by pillows. "Just keep walking. This tea numbs your senses." His voice was faint.

"Okay," she whispered.

The two took their time walking over to the stool. Her vision continued to wave back and forth as if she were seeing reality through rippling water. Her whole body had a tingling sensation and her other senses were dulled. *It's kind of soothing in a way.*

Krista sat herself down on the stool and she rested her cane on the ground. "I suppose it was a horrible life." She spoke slowly. *This tea is calming.* "Yet I didn't know any better until now."

"This tea might give you what you need to calm your mind and return to Dreadweave Pass, Krista," Malpherities said. "To relax and cross realms, clear your thoughts that cloud your new ability."

Krista nodded. *He's right.* Cursman had to know the news of Malpherities and Fierel. *I'm not a fan of Dreadweave Pass or what is waiting for me there, but I can't ignore it.* If Sporathun found her, there was no telling where she could end up. *Maybe I would be brought to the Weaver.*

"If I cross realms when I am relaxed, why did the doctor give me this soothing tea?"

"Like I said, he is a fool and doesn't understand what he is dealing with."

Krista shook her head and eyed Marilyn. "Let's get to work, hey?" She rolled up her sleeves while wiggling her fingers. They were more flexible today.

Marilyn smiled and tossed a grime-covered red shirt at her, then took two scrubbing boards, placing them in the tub.

Krista caught the shirt despite her dizziness. She dunked it into the new tub, scrubbing it against one of the boards. She could barely feel the water as it touched her skin.

Focus. She used one of the scrubbing boards and worked vigorously, cleaning the clothes as quickly as she could to tire herself out.

One shirt done.

Krista reached over to the pile of clothes and grabbed a few items, placing them on her lap. There was a mixture of poorly woven linen shirts and rich silky shirts of bright colours.

These probably belong to Paladin, Smyth, or some of the other higher-ranked humans. Either way, they all needed to be cleaned.

Krista took one of the silky white shirts and dunked it in the tub, scrubbing aggressively where there were dirt spots. She barely noticed her bandaged hands in the warm water; perhaps the tea was numbing them too.

Marilyn got up from the stool and used a bucket to grab the dirty water. She took the bucket and poured it into the drain in the centre of the room. She then took another bucket at the far corner of the laundry room that had fresh water in it and carefully tipped the bucket into the tub.

"What's your hurry?" Marilyn asked as Krista pulled the white shirt out of the tub.

"No reason," Krista said, trying to keep her back straight so it would not hurt.

"I've never seen you work so intensely before."

Krista looked up to the ceiling. *I do want to return to Dreadweave Pass. But if we finish before nighttime, I still have time in the day.* The image of William's blue eyes and white smile entered her mind. "I'd like to find William again."

Marilyn shook her head as she pushed her dry hair aside. "I told you about boys. He only causes trouble."

"He's nice to me."

"Perhaps, but what about the little scene with Paladin the other night?"

Krista felt her vision become clear and the tingling in her body froze. "You heard that?"

Marilyn raised her eyebrow. "Nothing stays hidden around here for long, dear. There are at least a hundred people in the barracks. We hear things."

Krista groaned and dropped a pair of black trousers in the tub. "What have people been saying?"

"There are various versions of the story," Marilyn said with a wicked smile. "I know they're all false, of course. He was naked in the water, though, wasn't he?"

Krista nodded.

Marilyn giggled.

Malpherities rolled his eyes. "We don't have time for this kind of talk."

"Did you see his ass?" A grin spread across Marilyn's face.

Krista sighed again and shook her head. "I know your people see physicality as something a little more serious. I thought nothing of it. Nothing happened and it's nothing abnormal among my own people to either be naked or to react physically. I forget your customs are different here."

Marilyn nodded. "You've got a lot to learn." She bit her lip, trying not to grin. "So, did you see him from the front? See any of them prime jewels?"

Krista giggled. "No!" She threw a shirt at the maid and the two laughed.

"In all seriousness, though, the people here aren't making any judgments about me, are they?"

"What do you mean? They already judge you for your race."

"Calling me names?"

"I'm sure they have. They don't talk dirty around me, though, or around most women."

"There are other women here? Our age?"

"They're all fairly older. Easily could be yours or my own parents and grandparents. Well, perhaps not. Smyth and I are uncertain how I'll age with the shimen curse in my blood."

"It's not a curse."

Marilyn continued to scrub a pair of trousers against her scrub board. "I respect your opinion, yet you haven't confessed your sins to the Lord and I can't accept your words."

"I don't need to confess sin. I never did anything wrong."

The maid smiled.

Malpherities tapped Krista's shoulder. "You killed someone, Krista. You don't think that is sin-worthy?"

"I don't know . . ." she whispered.

Malpherities paused. "Don't waste your time with confessing sins. It is something the weak do to justify their actions. Humans need religion to feel strong; they need the reassurance of a fatherly being watching over them."

Religion was something Krista could still not fully grasp. She believed in the Five Guardians, but never considered them a religion.

The two worked in silence for a couple of hours, the pile of dirty clothes gradually diminishing. Krista felt the effects of the tea began to wear off as the hours passed and she gained her senses back. *I liked the way the herb made me feel lightheaded. I wish it would have lasted a little longer.* The tea made her feel content with the moment.

Eventually, the pile of dirty clothes was gone and all the clean clothes were hung from the lines of rope, water droplets dripping to the floor and running down to the centre drain, waiting for the other maids to take the garments away.

Krista slid off the stool and leaned down to grab her cane, feeling her back ache while it stretched.

"Well done." Marilyn stood.

"Thanks." Krista took a deep breath in and out. *Still in pain, and my body is tired, but I don't think I could get a solid sleep yet.*

The maid put her hands on her hips. "Well, time to make a round through the shower halls. There will be plenty of used towels."

"Are the boys showering now?"

"Most likely done now—they clean every three days after training."

Krista scratched her head. "Do you need help or can I skip?"

Marilyn winked. "Just this one time. I am still a bit behind on work, but your assistance has sped things up greatly—and you are hurt." Marilyn nodded her head to the exit. "Go play with your boy toy."

"My what?"

She rolled her eyes. "Never mind. I've got to finish up putting things away here. I'll catch up with you later."

Krista waved and limped her way out of the laundry room, staggering back to the main level. Malpherities followed her, gently keeping his claws on her one arm for support.

"You must rest now," Malpherities ordered.

"I know."

"You don't have time for this William."

"I can't rest right now, though. I honestly don't think I would be able to go to Dreadweave Pass."

Krista took each step of the stairs with care; the flight of stairs was more of a challenge while keeping her back straight and lifting the cane. After a couple of minutes, they reached the main level. The lighting was orange and the halls were mostly vacant, except for a couple of armoured men marching in opposite directions. Krista glanced outside to see the sun was setting. "I don't see why I need to go to sleep just yet." She broke free from Malpherities's grasp. "I hope seeing William will calm my nerves. It's worked before, hasn't it?"

The ghoul growled. "Yes, it has. But you need to learn to find your own ground and not rely on boys for your mental foundations."

Krista stepped toward the nearest exit, the same doorway Captain John took her through the first time she met Marilyn. She lifted her hood while she leaned her body against the door to open it. "William should be done training now."

She slipped out into the daylight where the sun blared directly at her through the orange haze. The ghoul followed behind her, staying in her harshly cast shadow. The air was crisp and cool, refreshing from the staleness of the keep's basement.

"Krista!" a deep, commanding voice boomed.

It startled her and she dropped her cane. She glanced around to see Paladin was approaching her from a few paces down the road. *I didn't even see him from the blaring sun.*

Krista kneeled to pick up her cane. "Hi."

"How are you recovering? After your injury?" Paladin walked over to her and offered her his hand.

Krista took it with grace and returned to her feet. "It's no big deal."

"It was quite the blow." Paladin folded his arms.

Malpherities eyed Paladin up and down and snorted.

"How are you handling your . . . condition?"

Krista squinted. "Condition?"

"Your mental illness."

"I'm fine. Nothing is wrong." She glanced down at her appearance:

her clothes were smudged with dirt and she knew her scalp-feathers were tattered and her face probably showed exhaustion. Krista put on a toothy smile and attempted to groom her scalp-feathers. "I was cleaning clothes."

"Let's walk." Paladin extended his hand.

Krista nodded and gripped her cane tighter. *I don't want to talk to him right now. He's so grumpy lately.*

A slight breeze blew past Paladin and toward Krista. She could pick up Paladin's scent for the first time. It pleased her to actually place his smell; it was how she recognized beings. The smell had no relation to other humans. Often, they had a strong scent of sweat and dirt, like Cursman. Paladin was clean, with the same strong scent of a male, but it reminded her of the fresh spring mountain smell of Magma Falls.

"When I first found you, Krista, you were a small, injured girl. When we discovered your illness, I've noticed that in the short time you've been here, it has changed you greatly. Not just your physical strength and posture, but your personality."

"Thanks?" Krista scratched her head.

"You're losing your innocence," Malpherities added.

"I've also been informed you're skilled with a sword."

"How do you know?" Krista's eyes widened.

"Talif informed me, shortly after you defeated him and William."
That little shit. "It was a fluke."

"A fluke? Those boys train daily to be the best the kingdom has. You've told me of your past and it consists of no combatant training, unless there's something you haven't mentioned."

Krista shook her head. "I told you everything. Well, I learned a bit from living on the streets I suppose."

"Dr. Alsroc told me that your illness can cause the body and mind to learn complex skills in a matter of hours—skills that would normally take years to learn."

"Fools," Malpherities said. "Cursman is just an expert swordsman; he's only spent hours with you."

"Maybe that has something to do with it." Krista looked to the ground.

"Are you scared of this illness?" Paladin stopped in his tracks.

Krista glanced at Malpherities then looked off at the distant barracks walls. "Yes." She felt her heart fall heavy. The thought of Dreadweave Pass and Sporathun horrified her—the terrors of being in hell. "I'm scared of dying from all this."

Paladin placed his firm hand on her shoulder. "You won't die, Krista."

She looked up at the man, the sun positioned behind him, blacking out his face and body.

"You're in my prayers."

Malpherities snickered.

"Thank you, Paladin." Krista coiled her tail around her own ankle. *Whether religion is real or not, I am glad someone has nice thoughts for me.*

He patted her shoulder. "You'd best get some rest, Krista. You've had a busy day."

She nodded.

"Your back should heal soon; when it does, you must share your sword skills with me."

"Okay." *So much for finding William with Paladin out here.*

"Good." Malpherities grinned.

"I'll see you tomorrow, Krista. Dr. Alsroc and I will keep a close eye on you during the night." Paladin waved.

"Thanks." Krista waved back and turned toward the keep. *I really don't want to go back to Dreadweave Pass yet.*

"You're bringing too much attention upon yourself, girl," Malpherities said as they reached the keep.

"I don't mean to—I just want to see William."

"Your fascination with him is pointless."

"No, it's not!" Krista protested. "He cares for me."

"You may be maturing, but you are still so naive in many ways."

Krista bit her lip while she opened the barracks door. His words made her angry. *But I shouldn't argue with him. Remember last time . . .*

The ghoul sighed. "Think about it for a moment, girl. What do you think this William is going to bring for you? You seem to run from one boy to the next. What if this blond boy doesn't work out? What then? There's plenty of pickings here if you need another male's company. At first you told me it was to keep yourself safe because you thought you were weak. However, if you keep nurturing this behavior as you grow, it could turn you into a whore."

The last word stabbed deep into Krista's heart, sending a chilling tingle through her spine. That word had been thrown at her by Draegust, the Blood Hound leader, along with many others within the City of Renascence. She stopped walking and took hold of her chest.

Malpherities flared his nostrils. "I say this to assist you."

She spoke softly. "You hurt me." It was true she did hide among males; they made her feel safe when she could be protected behind their brute-like behavior, like with Darkwing. But with William, this was the first time she had started to identify with erotic feelings. "Their bodies don't enter my thoughts." She folded her arms.

"Somehow I don't buy that."

"I've never opened myself willingly for something like that. It's not me. William is the first time I've started to feel this way. Well there was guardian Cae but I didn't really know him, you know? It was not the first reason I wanted to see William either. I like him because he shows me affection and doesn't use me—something no one in my life has done for me. It makes me feel wanted."

"You've just met him! You cannot make a judgment so early on."

"Maybe it's a leap of faith."

"Then you're no better than these humans who blindly base their entire lives on their faith."

CHAPTER XX

Rats in a Maze

PATIENT: KRISTALANTICE SCALEBANE

DAY: FOUR
ENTRY: THREE

The Mental Damnation spreading through Krista's brain is evolving even as I write this. All of the symptoms of the first stage of the disease—Initial Takeover—are there. She has the puncture wound on her arm (and, oddly enough, her neck too), her sleeps are restless, and even though she doesn't say so, it is obvious she is having headaches. However, I would have expected more symptoms to start showing after her first day of being diagnosed with Mental Damnation. I arrived after Krista first appeared in the High Barracks of Zingalg. Perhaps vazeleads have a higher tolerance to the disease.

This is my first opportunity to see the disease in another race and, so far, the symptoms that do occur seem fairly similar to those in us humans. Yet from what I have seen in previous cases with older victims, the disease is less potent to begin with and inevitably the victim dies. So perhaps it is the vazelead's age that is slowing the development of Mental Damnation.

It's too early to tell, but there is a possibility that she is the key to finding a cure, whether it is her mental state, her blood, or, possibly, her diet before coming to the High Barracks.

Her people, the vazeleads, are a robust race. They have withstood tremendous amounts of heat in the underworld—this illness often causes great rise in temperature during the night like a fever. A wild theory is that perhaps vazelead blood injected into a victim of Mental Damnation could fight off the disease.

Again, a wild idea. A hope. Like I said, it is still too early in her illness to make radical theories. Sometimes it has taken a number of weeks for the illness to destroy its host and other times, mere days. Only time will tell how Krista will handle the disease as it progresses. Human victims after four or five days would start to claw into their own skin and throw pieces of their flesh against the wall. She has had just a few scratches and bruises.

But her reaction toward the drawing of this Malpherities character is of great interest to me. He has appeared plenty of times in past cases of this illness. There have been several other characters that the victims have developed, such as the Weaver and General Dievourse. I believe that the disease attempts to rewire the mind, alters the host's senses and thought processes in a way that suits the illness so it can feed off the brain's overstimulated activity. It has been my strongest theory yet, that Mental Damnation needs brain activity to feast on. Projecting fear into its victims' brains causes awareness to heighten, thus giving the disease more to feed on.

I have had the chance in the past to inspect the

corpse of a victim to see how the disease grows. However, I have written about it before, and do not wish to repeat myself, as I have been apt to do lately. Perhaps it is old age, or maybe I am going mad.

Time will tell how Krista's mind handles Mental Damnation and I can only hope she opens her thoughts to someone. Mental Damnation is not a disease anyone should have to face alone.

rista's body pressed into the soft mattress, her head sinking into the feather-filled pillow while she curled up in the warm sheets. She had taken off her heavy clothing and remained in her black dress; it was all she really had to wear for bed. But she didn't see a need to complain—Paladin had not come by to strap her to the bed.

At least, not yet. Krista rolled to her side, clutching her blanket. *What if I wake up strapped down? Or bruised?* The uncertainty made her feel sick to the stomach.

I have no way of knowing until I wake up again. Right now, she was left to face crossing into Dreadweave Pass. Malpherities had left her at the stairwell leading to the second level of the keep.

I'm glad we're friends again. Mal would make a scary enemy. The memory of Malpherities strangling her flashed through her mind—his strength, his anger. But at least for now, she was alone in her room where it was quiet and safe. The sun had set and the moonlight cast a dim glow into her room with crickets chirping from outside in the fields.

She rolled over to face the window, staring at the blue-tinted bricks around the window frame. Krista liked the dark. Despite the cold, it was far easier on her eyes and gave her less of a migraine.

After several moments—or possibly hours—of staring at the window, Krista took a deep breath and her eyelids gradually closed over her eyes. *Mal said I have to clear my mind to cross realms. I need a clearer head to go to Dreadweave Pass.*

Dr. Alsroc told her that Dreadweave Pass was not real, but the doctor had never experienced it. He has never felt the dusty road or crawled stickily out from one of the blood pools. He hadn't met the strange people in Dreadweave Pass. *He hasn't seen that they are people who have been banished, like my people were banished from the surface world.* She didn't want to leave Cursman alone in hell with Sporathun close behind them.

I'm coming back, Cursman. Krista took a couple of deep breaths. *In and out; just breathe.*

She didn't know exactly how long she repeated the words in her mind, but eventually her thoughts vanished and she just breathed. The feeling of inhaling and exhaling began to fade with each breath she took and transformed into a tingling, surging pulse in the same pattern as her breathing, travelling from her head downward. She felt her muscles loosen on her back and the sounds of the crickets began to lessen until the only sound was her own breath. It sounded muffled. The tingling sensation heightened with each wave and slowed into fewer sequences, each surge erupting from her head and travelling down her body, stinging each muscle it passed.

Child . . .

Krista pressed tighter on her eyelids, feeling the pressure in her head pulsate down her body. The sound of the room collapsing and reshaping filled the silence, followed by the high-pitched shrieks of abominations.

Child, willingly you go.

To save your friends from below.

The mattress began to rumble and the feathers inside scurried around on their own, compacting together to make the surface much stiffer. The mattress stretched around her body, curling up along the side of her face and moulding to cup her head.

Child, from one world to the next.

Our distance will close.

When the sinful kills your friends and returns.

Because it was you I chose.

The pulsing in her brain stopped but was replaced by the steady rhythm of footsteps that were in sync with the mattress's wobbling. Krista opened her eyes and looked around to see thick branches buzzing by, covering a blood-red sky above. She raised her head and jumped at the sight of arms around her body; she was pressed up against a man's chest.

"Calm down, girl!" came Cursman's voice.

She glanced up to see his whisker-covered face. "Where are we? How long have we been travelling?" Krista rubbed her forehead, which still ached from the pulsating. *Even after the third time, crossing realms is awful.* She looked down at herself to see that she was fully dressed, her clothes coated in dried blood.

"You've been asleep for many hours, and we had to stay on the move. You wouldn't wake; it made me wonder if you were alive. I assume you crossed into the land of the living?"

"Yes."

"Any news? I know Malpherities can talk to you there."

Krista scratched her head. "Mal and Fierel couldn't hold Sporathun back for long. They're alive, though."

"Good. Any idea where the vampyre is?"

"Mal told me that he's closing in on us."

"Tell me something I don't know."

"Mal also said we should circle back toward him and Fierel."

"Is he insane? We could run directly into Sporathun!"

"He said if we met at a place . . ." She scratched her head until the words came back. "Ruins of the Mortals Run."

Cursman shook his head. "I'd rather not go there."

"Why's that?"

"That place is not safe. I mean, we can do it—Glamorous might be there too—but I can't carry you anymore."

Krista struggled in his arms. "Well, put me down and let's go!"

Cursman let her go and she fell with a thud on the gravel path. The bridge from the City of Blood was nowhere to be seen. *He must have been travelling for a while.*

Cursman ran a hand through his hair. "We need to move quickly. We can't run into Sporathun." His arm fell to his side and he picked up his pace, pointing to their left where a dirt path led into the forest. "This will take us to the ruins."

Krista followed behind Cursman while he steered their route off the large road. "I'll do my best to keep up." Her head ached, and her body was sore and covered in small bruises. *That's right; in this realm, I had trained with Cursman. I'm the Dreadweave Pass me.* Krista panted, trying to keep up with Cursman's pace.

"You all right?" Cursman asked.

"Yeah, I'll make it. This realm-crossing isn't easy for me."

"It shouldn't be for anyone; it's unnatural."

Krista swayed to the side of the dirt path to avoid a root that stuck upright from the ground. "Can't we stay on the road?"

"No. We can't let anyone see us. Remember the puppet squad we almost ran into? Besides, our scent is covered better in the forest, making it harder for Sporathun, and the camouflage gives us a tactical advantage."

"Okay. Speaking of Sporathun, I learned a bit about vampyres in the living world." *Maybe he'll see I've got some use.*

Cursman smirked. "Good for you. So, you're going to find us an answer to defeat him?"

Krista frowned. "I learned about wrath vampyres . . . although I didn't get all my answers."

"All right, try me. What did you learn?"

"Well, I kind of asked myself a question. Everyone says he is a great hunter, but what makes him such a great hunter if he's so angry? Shouldn't it cloud his judgment?"

"He was part of the Heavenly Kingdom's military, so he has the training from there. Plus, being of angelic roots, he sees the world differently than you or me. Their sight is said to be more like dozens of single strings moving in waves, looking past the physical boundaries that we face. Instead, they can see the essence of an object, like a spirit. They can also see the energies left behind by beings and follow the energy trail through the string waves, so to speak. Or think of it like a ripple effect."

"So he knows where we're going based on some invisible trail we leave behind?"

"We all leave a mark wherever we go. Like our footprints, our hair, or our blood. But we also leave a stronger essence based on our emotions. Like with the Lifeless Ones . . . You were scared, weren't you?"

"Yes, horrified."

"Your emotions were strong then, marking that location with your impression. It's like how a haunted house has an essence. You understand that?"

Krista nodded. "I think so. The underworld where I come from had creatures called shades. They could pick up on my feelings."

"Well, then this is very similar to that. If someone—like an angel—can tune into these hidden messages, they can pick up on these imprints. Angels are more tuned to pick up on it because the gods needed them to sense and hunt Dega'Mostikas's demons."

"Wow. I wish I could do that. Can anyone sense the trails?"

"Yes, technically."

"Can you teach me?"

Cursman laughed. "I'd like to learn it myself, but I'm not humble enough. I doubt you are, either. We're alike, Krista—both eager and relentless."

Krista blushed. "I wouldn't exactly say I'm relentless."

The man shook his head. "I see it in your eyes, and in your words. You're a survivor—a warrior at heart."

"Mal said the same thing about me."

"Do you trust him?"

"I suppose."

"Well, then, I think the only thing holding you back from your natural state is yourself."

Is he right? I always survive, but does that give me the heart of a warrior? She knew that pain, suffering, and murder were not her favourite things, but since Mental Damnation, she had begun to want to fight. Krista wanted to survive and didn't want anyone to hold her back anymore.

"I'd like that—to be a warrior and defend myself like you or Fierel."

Cursman chuckled. "You need to convince yourself, and understand that you have nothing to fear in the heat of battle. That will scare the shit out of your opponent."

"But what about pain and dying? Or losing someone you love?"

"A warrior is nothing without all three. Pain should encourage you, and death is the one time you will have rest—it will come when the gods demand it so." He sighed. "As for loved ones, a warrior's path is an icy cold road. Taking loved ones with you will seal their death."

"If I am naturally a warrior, does that mean pain and death is my fate?"

"I believe that what we can greatly influence the outcome of our lives and those around us. I wasn't exactly a pleasant man myself for most of my living years. When I met my wife, she changed me, but I suppose the gods didn't see I was worthy of redemption so they took her from me and sent me here."

"The gods killed your wife?"

"I brought her down a warrior's path." Cursman's lips tightened. "Her death is on my head. But they brought her into the Heavenly Kingdoms, I am sure of it."

"What about me? I've done my best to be a good person, yet my luck keeps failing and I end up worse off with every choice I make."

"Perhaps it is a message."

"Message?"

"For the short time I've known you, I've seen that you are a runner. Running away from confrontation and living your life in fear. Malpherities and I both say you're a warrior at heart, yet you run from that, too."

"I do not." Krista folded her arms.

"Then what are you doing?"

"I don't mean to. Malpherities hurt me in my realm."

"He's a ghoul. Hurting people is all he knows how to do."

"I tried to defend my friend, but he was too strong and I couldn't use physical force. How can I be a warrior when I'm so small?"

"You're trying; therefore, you're not convinced that it is possible for it to happen. Trying is for those in fear. In the moment, you must act and trust your actions. In time, you won't have any doubt in your heart and mind that you can indeed follow the path of a warrior."

Krista thought for a moment, then put on a wide smile. "Thank you." *Maybe he isn't so bad after all.* Just because he was in hell didn't mean Cursman was evil.

"For what?"

"Talking to me. My life has been such a race for survival that I've never had time to reflect on who I am."

"You're welcome. In hell, reflecting is all you have time to do."

It is exactly what I want to be—a strong fighter like those I always go to for protection. She thought back to her first kill, back at Magma Falls when she had first met the half-breed, Abesun. The experience was terrifying; she hated murder and found it hard to see how she could become a fighter. But believing in herself was a good place to start.

"So why don't you want to go to the ruins?"

"It was built by fallen gods."

"Kind of like the Weaver then?"

"Yeah. They made a game that was shunned by the Heavenly Kingdoms and the gods banished them to Dega'Mostikas's Triangle."

"A game? Like a toy?"

"A labyrinth. They used mortals as playing pieces. In the Heavenly Kingdoms, it was an unholy betting game because it forced mortals into the maze against their will. Eventually the gods banished the demi-gods and descended the labyrinth into Dreadweave Pass."

"You sure know a lot."

"Yeah, I got my share of history from Smelg when I was the Weaver's assassin. I did my research before I went on a hunt."

"What happened to the gods?"

"They didn't last long here; it is believed it happened around the same time as Sporathun's banishment. Sporathun and the gods were both enraged about what happened and took their anger out on each other. They fought to the death."

"Sporathun killed them?"

"Yeah, he did kill God Ha, remember?"

"That's right. I don't want him to do that to me."

"This is why we cannot let Sporathun find us—he's insane. The benefit for us is the ruins are also one of the locations where

Glamorous is rumored be."

Krista's eyes widened. "I remember now! Do you think she's there?"

"It's possible."

"Could we search for clues while we're there?"

"It's hard to say. We may not even know what we're looking for—I've never seen the crash-landing site of a fallen angel."

The further the two walked into the forest, the more the vegetation altered, with deep red vines dangling from the trees and small, knee-high bushes covering most of the dirt path. Cursman swatted the branches away as he walked, clearing the trail for Krista.

The stems and leaves of the plants were soft and warm. The line patterns in the leaves were deep red, as if they had blood running through them.

Krista was tempted to stop and investigate the plant life; she wanted to know more about the forest. *But that could get me into trouble. I'd best stick with Cursman.*

Their travels led them out of the forest and into rockier wilderness, much like the terrain that surrounded Evergut.

It makes me wonder if we're just going in circles in Dreadweave Pass.

The rocks were slightly different from the ones in Evergut. The ground had red moss growing on it and the rocks dripped slime from the edges. A white mist was in the distance, too, limiting their visual perception to only a hundred paces.

"So, Cursman . . ." Krista ran her index finger through her scalp-feathers. "Why have we only seen the Lifeless Ones here? Why don't we ever see any animals? The ones Fierel was worried about."

"This isn't a zoo. Any wildlife you'd see is the kind you wouldn't like. It's not like the surface world—most don't wander the open lands or the forests. They often stick to the historical areas."

"Like the old gate we visited?"

Cursman nodded. "Yes, that one is fairly new and I'm certain it will be inhabited soon."

"Why do they want to live there?"

"Either they have some sort of attachment to the location or they know others do and they know eventually someone will come by."

"So these animals can eat them?"

"Possibly. Dreadweave Pass is a pool of rejects, Krista. Fallen angels, gods, mortals, and even Dega'Mostikas's rejected demons wander this realm."

"Why don't others try and escape like we are?"

"Because escaping from the Weaver is a suicide mission—but then again, no one has ever had a paladin on their side before. Or myself, one who knows the workings of the Weaver's army." Cursman pointed toward the white mist. "We're nearing the ruins; they're just up ahead."

Krista smiled. "Good. I hope Mal and Fierel are waiting for us." She wanted to see Fierel again, even though the paladin frightened her. It was comforting to have someone with such powers on her side.

A deep growl broke the silent air, echoing throughout the open dunes.

Krista felt her stomach sink. "What was that?" she asked.

Cursman scratched his nose and looked around. "Sounds like that are everywhere in Dreadweave Pass. It's hard to say, but keep on your guard."

"Could it be one of the animals?"

"By animal do you mean a demon or an actual furry critter?" Cursman smirked.

Krista rolled her eyes.

"Stop your running!" A hoarse, high-pitched voice echoed across the landscape.

Cursman stopped in his tracks and looked back. "Now that is not an animal."

Krista looked around the landscape to see nothing but open space of rock and white mist.

"The hunt is ending!" the voice boomed.

"Sporathun!" Cursman pushed Krista without warning. "No more joking. Get moving!"

Krista felt her legs start to collapse after the push but she managed to regain balance and sprinted across the loose gravel. She peeked over her shoulder to Cursman, who now had his sword drawn and continually glanced behind them, watching to see if Sporathun was near.

Two pyramid-shaped columns appeared in the mist on each side of the road. At first, their size was difficult to estimate but as Krista neared them, she realized they were at least twice her height.

Cursman and Krista passed the pillars and came to a steep hill sloping downward. Further down the hill was a circular building with no roof. It was least double the size of the gatekeeper's portal and was filled with a series of curved walls ranging in length. Some of the walls were in L-shapes and others linear. Many halls ended with entranceways leading into corridors disappearing into darkness. The walls that were closer to the centre were not as long and were more curved than the outer walls. In the centre was an open space where a crude face—just round eyes and a triangular mouth—was carved into the ground.

"That's it!" Cursman shouted. "Go!" He pushed Krista to spur her forward.

The steep road's loose gravel chips made an all-out sprint out of the question. Cursman and Krista slid down the path and took careful steps to pick up their momentum.

Krista was lighter and found it fairly easy to keep her balance as she skidded down to the bottom.

A screech filled the skies from above the hill and echoed for miles around.

Krista glanced back to see that Cursman was at least twenty paces behind. "Hurry!" she shouted.

"Keep going!"

Krista bit her lip and looked at the ruins ahead. The blue matte stone walls were about twelve feet tall and the paths were as wide as the road. She turned back to look at Cursman. *I can't just leave him.*

A figure stepped out from atop the hill. The white mist masked the details, but Krista could make out horns, a long kilt, and a lean, muscular body. It could only be Sporathun.

"Cursman!" Krista shouted.

Cursman reached the bottom of the hill and glanced up. "Let's move it, Krista! I've got your back."

Her heart pounded in her ribcage. She pushed her left foot into the pebbles and hastened for the Ruins of the Mortals Run. Krista's dash was wobbly on the inconsistent ground, but she kept her balance upright.

Someone help me. She panted the closer she got to the ruins, feeling her lungs burn with each exhale she made. The muscles in her legs hardened like rocks and her hands clenched into fists. *Dare I look back?* Krista reached the entrance of the ruins and skidded to a stop to check behind her.

A three-fingered claw snatched her arm and dragged her behind the wall.

Krista yelped and struggled to break free from the grasp.

"Calm down, girl!" Malpherities shouted.

Krista glanced around to see the ghoul, who held her, and Fierel standing behind him with her sword drawn.

Cursman dashed through the entrance. "He's still up on the hill!"

"He's just standing there?" Krista asked, trying to catch her breath.

"Keep running!" Fierel ordered. "We're not in any position to combat him here."

The group picked up momentum, sprinting deeper into the curved hallway.

"We can't outrun him!" Cursman shouted.

Krista hid herself between the three while they raced through the maze of walls.

"This is the labyrinth?" Krista asked.

Cursman shook his head. "This is just the top. The labyrinth is inside."

Malpherities spoke up. "There's a player's entrance near here."

Fierel bit her lip. "A player's entrance? We will become part of the game, and who knows what horrors those two fallen gods had set up in there. Are you mad?"

"Glamorous might be in there," Cursman added.

"Who the hell is Glamorous?" Fierel asked.

"Sporathun's lover."

Sporathun roared, his voice bouncing off the walls. "Who are your comrades, girl? I sense them . . . They waste their time. You will be mine."

The group made a turn down a long hall that forked into two paths. The right led closer to the centre of the maze and the left path ended in a narrow, dark tunnel with a curved frame and a human face with its mouth open as if it were screaming carved into the top of the arch.

Malpherities pointed at it. "That's it, the player's entrance."

The group ran together, getting closer to the fork.

"Let's take the entrance," Cursman ordered.

"I disagree. We'll be trapped in the labyrinth," said Fierel.

Loud footsteps echoed behind them along with scraping of stone. "Girl!" Sporathun roared.

Krista glanced back to see Sporathun burst from the corner with his head low, blades in both hands. He dragged their edges against the stone walls, creating sparks.

"The entrance!" Krista shouted.

Fierel sheathed her sword and snatched Krista's arm. "We're out of options."

The group dashed to the left side of the fork to the player's entrance. Inside was complete darkness, making it impossible to see what lay beyond. They came to a halt at the narrow doorway.

"Malpherities and I will hold guard. You two first." Cursman held his blade while Malpherities raised his claws.

"Hold my hand," Fierel ordered.

Krista clutched at Fierel and turned back to see Sporathun closing in.

Fierel tightened her grip on Krista's arm. "Hold on." She pushed Krista in through the doorway first, still holding onto her. The two instantly fell down the moment they passed into the darkness.

Krista's shoulder hit a rough stone wall, slowing her fall. She tumbled into Fierel and the two clutched onto each other while they plummeted into the abyss. Several seconds later, they hit bottom and began to slide down a spiralling, greasy slide.

Fierel grunted and grabbed hold of Krista around her waist, with Krista sitting in front.

The two accelerated downward as the slide spiralled around and around.

Krista's stomach felt like it was going to heave. Her scalp-feathers blew back from the funneled wind.

After the eighth spiral, the slide ended with a hole in the ground and the two slammed into the end wall, falling for a few seconds before hitting the moist dirt below.

Krista hissed as mud splattered into her face. She wiped it off with her hand. Fierel got up and extended her hand to Krista. "You all right?"

Krista groaned and reached for Fierel's hand. "Yeah."

The paladin lifted her upward. "We need to move—in case Cursman and Malpherities can't hold him off."

"Is this the labyrinth?"

"Yes," Fierel said, turning around. "I've never been here before, for good reason."

The two had landed in what appeared to be a hallway that mimicked the surface. The walls were the same height as the matte blue walls outside. Stalactites two times as large as the walls covered the wide-open ceiling of the underground cave. The air was humid and cool with a dim light coming from the centre of the ceiling, where what looked like foggy glass made up the reverse side of the face Krista had seen at the centre of the building from above. The ground was covered in mud and some of it was smeared along the solid stone walls. Rocks and boulders were scattered across the path.

"Are we going to look for Glamorous?" Krista asked.

"Entering the maze wasn't my idea. Stay close to me." Fierel extended her hand outward again, reaching for Krista while keeping her gaze on the wall to their left.

Krista stared at the wall. *What is she looking at?* "Okay." She slowly took the paladin's hand. It was the first time she noticed the texture of the paladin's skin; it differed from the humans in the High Barracks: rougher and cool.

Fierel checked over her shoulder to see Krista. "Come on." She turned back, holding her sword upright.

"It's cold here." Krista's legs shivered. *Even colder than the surface world.*

Fierel scanned the floor, the ceiling, the walls, and up ahead. "This place is unholy."

"Cursman said that it was a game for the fallen gods."

"That's correct. It isn't safe here." She cleared her throat. "In any shade of the sun, you are my lamp, Father; you turn my darkness into light." Fierel extended her arm with the sword. The pendant on her necklace lit up white, the light channeling through the chain in a single beat. It moved onto her skin and travelled up her arm into the sword. The blade lit up bright as if it were hot metal recently forged.

Krista squinted; their path was brighter and they could make out more details of the mud and smooth, solid stone walls.

"What type of game is it? I mean, I know it is a maze, but why is it unholy?"

"The fallen gods put a demon in the middle of it. The demon is known as the centre beast."

"Demon? Is it like a vampyre?"

"No, demons are the children of Dega'Mostikas, who is the root of evil."

"So worse than vampyres?"

"That all depends. Sporathun is far superior to many demons you'll encounter in Dega'Mostikas's Triangle, and I am certain the centre beast cannot match his power."

"Can you kill it, the demon?"

Fierel smirked. "I'm a paladin. I am designed to kill anything tainted with evil—I just need the right opportunity to perform an exorcism and always keep faith in God to guide me."

The paladin walked close to any walls that were discoloured or cracked. Fierel inspected each closely for several seconds before moving forward. She led them through at least a dozen halls, all ranging in length. Each one had two to four doorways scattered on either side, leading into new hallways. Fierel walked carefully by each doorway they passed, carefully examining the walls before making a decision.

Krista too tried to inspect the walls, looking for anything special about them. *Maybe she sees a pattern or a language on them.* Each wall Krista looked at looked the same. *Just normal wear and tear.*

"So, Krista . . ." Fierel's voice echoed through the labyrinth. "Neither of us knows much of the other, except the lies Malpherities spreads about us. What's your last name?"

Maybe she wants to get to know me after all. "Scalebane."

"You're a vazelead, right?"

"Yes."

"So sorry for what happened to your people."

"You know about the vazelead banishment?" Krista's eyes widened. "Were you there?"

"Yes. I was young during your banishment to the underworld, one of the few to survive the Drac Lord Karazickle's attack on the Paladins of Zeal at the top of Mount Kuzuchi. After he destroyed our people, the paladins who remained went our separate ways. The vazeleads are still in the underworld, right?"

"The shackles were just broken. A vazelead gatekeeper used me to free my people. Now when I'm in the living world, I am in the High Barracks of Zingalg."

"I hope they're taking care of you. We humans are an ignorant race."

"Most beings are, not just humans."

Fierel bit her lip and looked back at Krista. "I'm not your enemy Krista. I know Malpherities and Cursman have talked to you about me, saying you cannot trust me."

Krista looked to the ground. "Yes, they have."

"I'm not one for words—I prefer action. Children aren't my specialty, as it was forbidden for paladins to breed. I . . ." Fierel stopped and leaned down to read one of the walls before continuing in the maze. "I want you to feel safe with me."

"Thanks." *At least she is trying, but she is still a little scary. I don't know what she is going to do.* Paladins hadn't exactly earned Krista's trust in the past. *They always justify what they do by talking about their god, like with my people's banishment and Marilyn's mother.*

"When did you die?" *Well, that sounded better in my head.* "I mean, you died and ended up here, right?"

"That's a common question around here."

"Were you alive to know of a man named Paladin?"

Fierel squinted. "A man who goes by the name Paladin?"

"Yes."

"He is a paladin?"

"He said he's the last one."

"Just him?"

"He saved me. Did you know him before you died? What's his real name? How many paladins were left before you died?"

"It was a long time ago, and a rather long story. But this Paladin character—yes, I knew him. His name was Zalphium, and he was a legend."

A groan echoed through the halls, the sound bouncing off the walls, making the location difficult to pinpoint.

"What's that?" Krista held the paladin's hand tighter, glancing at the doorway a couple of paces ahead to their right.

Fierel pointed her sword outward. "I think the centre beast knows we're here now."

"Is it coming?"

"The legends say it cannot move from the centre." Fierel spun around, checking both ends of the hallway. "However, its arms are long and, according to the stories, they can stretch for miles throughout the maze."

Krista reached for her dagger before she remembered she'd lost it. "I don't have a weapon."

Fierel tightened her grip on her sword. "I'll protect you."

"I want to go out!" Krista cried softly. "I have nothing to defend myself with! Where's Mal? Where's Cursman?"

"We're meeting them in the centre." Fierel extended her legs and bent her knees in a defensive position. She let go of Krista's hand and placed it on the hilt of her sword, eyes scanning down the long hallway, her body perfectly still.

"But that's where the demon is! How do we know Mal and Cursman are going there?"

"The signs on the walls lead us directly there—it's the easiest place to meet up again. Malpherities will know."

"What signs? Isn't there a path out?"

"You aren't looking close enough, and the way out is past the centre beast."

Suddenly, two gangly, three-fingered hands rushed from around the doorway, attached to long, tentacle-like arms. They were a light brown and moved like snakes while turning the corner toward Krista and Fierel. The hands hovered about five feet above the ground— around Krista's height—travelling toward them at an accelerating rate, fingers spread outward.

Krista screamed and pointed.

The paladin jerked Krista behind her and held her sword close.

The arms spiralled around each other, alternating positions while funneling toward Fierel.

The paladin spun her blade once and lunged upward at the oncoming hands. Her blade collided with one of the limbs, cutting the hand clean off from the wrist and spraying black blood into the air. The arm wiggled uncontrollably and dragged itself away.

Fierel heaved her blade in a downward strike, cutting into the second oncoming hand, splitting it in half down the middle from the palm.

Krista gasped as the arm fell to her feet. The split hand twitched and left a blood-smear trail as it was dragged back around the dark corner.

"There will be more." Fierel grabbed Krista's arm and the two continued deeper into the labyrinth, following the bloody path of the retreating arms.

CHAPTER XXI

Reunited

Once I thought worthy.
Oh, foolish I was.
To think such falsity.

My eyes no longer blind.
Reality sunk in.
I see, that I am not free.

Gods, fallen and high.
See themselves fit to judge.
I will no longer let this be.

Come for me,
here I am,
In the land of the damned.

A knuckle bone rattled back and forth as the blood-red metal gauntlets fiddled with the object, moving it between the fingers. The bone was only one piece from an entire skeleton that lay on the ground in a pile of rubble. It was once a man, or a woman. The disfigured mess was impossible to identify. It had been cracked, crushed, and scattered across the ground.

They are simply part of the dirt now, as I will do to all, Dievourse thought while he stared down at the knuckle, casually walking forward. He had picked it up on his travel. Normally he wasn't one to fidget, but he was experiencing a mixture of emotions and felt a need to distract himself from it. Often, he was fueled by hate at a subtle level where he was still able to think clearly. Now, jealousy also evoked him.

All of this is driving my hate, he thought. "El Aguro already waits for me, Lieutenant." Dievourse spoke as he marched down the familiar red hallway leading into the Weaver's chamber.

The Lieutenant accompanied him as per usual, leading to the end of the hall where the stone door leading into the Weaver's chamber resided. "Yes, as you expected."

The two reached the end of the hall and came to a halt. The Lieutenant routinely stopped a few steps back, knowing he was to wait.

Dievourse stopped fidgeting with the knuckle and stared at it. "Yes, that is what we wanted. He just pisses me off." He chucked the knuckle to the ground and exhaled heavily. *Remain resilient.* "We knew this meeting would be called after my outlandish claims of summoning all the puppets to the Weaver's chamber."

"Of course, knowing that El Aguro and the Weaver will deny it."

"That is the purpose of this meeting. Keep them on the cautious side and ultimately prevent more children's souls from being reaped. The Weaver must stay in his chamber."

"Any word from Sporathun?"

"Not yet. The child must have someone supporting her; this is rather unexpected."

"Who could have killed the puppets in the blood swamp?"

"I don't know. We may need to investigate. Sporathun is taking too long and I'm sure Gatekeepers Ast'Bala and Danil are growing impatient."

The Lieutenant nodded and turned his gaze to the wall. Now was Dievourse's time to meet with the Weaver. He stepped over to the stone door and pushed it open, allowing the familiar grey fog to seep out into the hall. The subtle mist fell onto his face, as it did with every visit to the Weaver.

The general stepped into the dark room leading to the central green glowing circle where he always stood. This time, there were two circles. A secondary being kneeled on the circle to the right; feathers could be seen from the arms and skull—El Aguro. Even while his eyes adjusted to the darkness, he could tell it was the gatekeeper by his distinct figure.

That feathered monstrosity . . . how I look forward to bringing an end to his existence. Dievourse marched to the glowing circle to left and kneeled, not losing his eye contact on the blackness that faced him.

El Aguro remained silent, head lowered, staring at the glowing green glyphs around the circle. He remained motionless, like a statue.

"My children . . ." came the deep familiar voice of the Weaver. "My dear children." He repeated while his snake-like arms extended from the darkness and into view. The palms of both hands were open, showcasing the double-thumbs on each hand. "Why do you bicker so? We all share the same agenda, do we not?"

"I share only your vision, master," El Aguro said.

Dievourse nodded. "Of course, we are all trapped here until you are free."

The hands moved downward and scooped up some of the low-lying fog and lifted it upward. The hands' index fingers twirled around, moving the fog with it. The hands moved up and down, painting with the fog out of thin air. As the Weaver formed the fog, the image he was creating became clearer: two gates with rays of sunlight.

"The Heavenly Kingdoms remain unaware of what I do. I must thank my supporter from above for her cooperation."

Her? That is the most I've heard about this immoral angel he shrouds in mystery.

"Yet, I fear it won't be long until she cannot steer the gods' view away from Dreadweave Pass. There are tasks that have left me concerned. Dievourse, you have yet to address my fears. El Aguro, I require updates from the gatekeepers: why are they so slow in the reaping? I demand my freedom!" The Weaver's hands clenched into fists and slammed down into the fog, crushing the image of the heavenly gates. "I want to wreak havoc on them."

El Aguro looked upward, clutching his claws. "Master, Ast'Bala and Danil aren't quite what I had hoped for."

"Elaborate, you must. You promised me they were different." The

Weaver pointed at the gatekeeper with his hand. "You promised that they had five leaders. One is dead, two are ours; where are the other two? Why are they not gatekeepers yet? This is slowing the reaping."

"Ast'Bala fails to answer me. He spends most of his time through his portal into their world, presumedly looking for them. I do not have time to chase him."

"Assumptions do not satisfy me, El Aguro. Send your crows. You disappoint me."

Dievourse smirked. *If only they knew why their newfound gatekeepers are not performing to their standards. Ast'Bala and Danil chose wisely to ally with me.*

The Weaver's hands relaxed their posture. "The two showed such promise. I would like to see this proven. Where is Danil?"

"He continues to hunt for more souls to reap. As do I, while I govern the City of Blood and cooperate with General Dievourse. We are encumbered with duties."

Cooperate? Lying shit, Dievourse thought.

The Weaver remained silent for several moments, thinking about what he had heard. "All right, that is fair. The three of you are spread thin as gatekeepers being tasked with so many more items. It is quite important for Ast'Bala to convert the remaining two guardians into gatekeepers. It must happen. The reaping must accelerate!"

El Aguro nodded. "I will work tirelessly to fulfill your desires my master."

The Weaver's hands moved to Dievourse and extended forward, open palms. "General Dievourse, my first creation. I cherish you."

"As I do you, from the moment I kneeled before your awesomeness, my master."

"Yes, for by me, all things are created in Dreadweave Pass, visible and invisible." The Weaver's hands moved backward. "Yet, Dievourse, I fear that what I have shaped is being tampered with. What of the Blood Swamp? The Child?"

"I have sent Sporathun on a hunt."

El Aguro shook his head, "The fallen angel? He caused much trouble."

The Weaver's hands made a horizontal slicing motion. "Silence, gatekeeper. I spoke of you; I now speak of Dievourse."

El Aguro lowered his head. "Of course, master."

Dievourse nodded. "El Aguro is right, the fallen angel has proven to be troublesome in the past. I assure you I have his obedience, though. He believes I have the one thing that matters to him."

"The fallen angel Glamorous? You lie, Dievourse. This is another reason I embrace fear: where is she? What if Sporathun finds her? We do not have this vampyre. My puppets should not be dead in the Blood Swamp. Paranoia clouds my thoughts."

"If he finds Glamorous, which he won't, he'll have questions. He will come to find me and I will deal with him then. Despite his destructive behavior, he can be reasoned with. I proved that when he willingly surrendered to me."

"You take risks, general. This is where we fail to find common ground. This is why I do not place you in charge. I have to divide responsibilities so I do not have all my bets on you."

Dievourse gritted his teeth. *Do not lash out.* The words angered him greatly; he knew the Weaver was referring to El Aguro. It was the start of his disloyalty, the Weaver expressing his distrust in him. *I bowed before him—I showed my utmost loyalty but that was not enough. Instead he tossed it aside.*

"I have little choice now, general, other than to trust in your plan. This makes me ill at ease."

"I promise you, master, you have nothing to fear. Sporathun will show loyalty by obtaining the lost child and I will personally see to what really happened in the Blood Swamp."

"Good." The Weaver's hands extended to both of his servants. "Now what of you two? General, you proposed a rather ambitious plan of summoning the puppets. What for? So the Heavenly Kingdoms can see a mass army gathering? The gatekeepers have yet to reap the required amount of souls to allow the ritual to succeed."

"I am only acting in preparation. Let us start the war with the heavens."

"I cannot. I want my freedom! I've expressed this numerous times my child. You must respect his."

El Aguro nodded. "This is what I had said, Dievourse. We must put our faith in our master's original plan."

Dievourse shook his head. "The original plan was to destroy the

Heavenly Kingdoms."

"And free our master."

The Weaver's hands pressed together. "Yes, El Aguro. Very good. Now I hope we can resolve our differences and work together. We are not summoning the puppets yet. We will keep them patrolling Dreadweave Pass is small numbers, among the mortals in camouflage. Dievourse, resolve these mysteries. El Aguro, get control over your gatekeepers. Now, are we able to work as one? Before me, you are all equal, my children."

Lies, Dievourse thought. *I know very well he is a perfectionist and does not see me as his finest work. He praises his gatekeepers.*

"We are close, my children. El Aguro, you must persist with the other gatekeepers to reap more children. I can feel the collected blood of the innocent; we only need a few hundred more. We are down from the thousands we once had to collect. This excites me!"

"Of course." El Aguro nodded.

"General, times are changing from when we first began this quest. Things seemed easier. Less players involved in our metaphoric chess game with the gods."

"That I agree with, my master. It has grown political—something I prefer to avoid."

"As time has progressed I have kept as much to myself as possible because of your distaste for negotiation. I fear this is now tearing us all apart."

"What are you proposing, master?"

"That we work as one." The Weaver extended his hand, pointing toward the door leading into the chamber where Dievourse had come from.

The door opened on its own as the stone scraped against the ground, echoing through the chamber.

Dievourse and El Aguro shielded their eyes while adjusting to the cool brightness from the blood-red hallway. It was difficult to see further than a few steps beyond the doorframe. Walking straight through the middle of the doorframe was the silhouette of a female figure.

Her hips swayed side to side with each step she made into the chamber, her long black skirt moving with each motion, brushing against the fog. Her left hand was atrocious in size and consisted of three large claws. Spikes pierced out of her shoulders and two long horns erected from her forehead.

No . . . Dievourse thought, eyeing the approaching female. *The horned silhouette, I've seen her before.* A brief memory of his after-death experience at the gates of the Heavenly Kingdoms ran through his mind. *The heavenly gates—she was there. She judged my soul.*

The Weaver's hands pressed together and tilted forward in a bowing motion. "My children, meet the angel Rahiie."

CHAPTER XXII

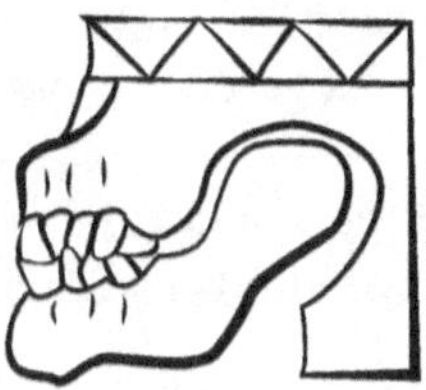

Crooked Allegiances

ain: a sensation felt all throughout the body that is transmitted to the brain. Without the mind's ability to process a nerve's reaction to a hostile touch, we might never know if our body is in danger. Pain is a strong defense mechanism that can also trigger other chemical reactions throughout our body, such as adrenaline and heightened senses. Emotion is strictly psychological, and because of this, if a conscious mind was disciplined enough to control the nature of the mind, one would be able to, in theory, tune out the brain's natural response to the nerve signals of pain. The advantage of this? Controlling pain would give a sense of clarity in a time of fear, uncertainty, or when a logical perspective is needed to carry on.

What the hell have I gotten myself into, thought Cursman while he gripped the leather handle of his blade firmly.

The plan was supposed to be simple. Fierel and he had a mutual understanding: wanting to exploit the Weaver for bringing the souls of children into Dreadweave Pass. Now that they had Krista, there was a possibility of bringing an end to the Weaver and his hold on Dreadweave Pass.

Such a coup for the gods would surely earn Cursman a place in the Heavenly Kingdoms with his beloved wife. Now, things seemed a little more difficult.

I should have known the Weaver and General Dievourse had a trick up their sleeves . . .

The vampyre sprinted in the loose gravel, kicking up dust and closing in, only metres away from Malpherities and Cursman. A normal man would have felt their legs tremble and the hair on their skin would have stood up, but Cursman had seen death before, and he knew what to expect.

It's not my day to die again. He took a deep breath. *Vampyres are all the same, blinded by their sin.*

"Make the first strike," Malpherities whispered.

Sporathun roared and raised one of his large curved blades at them.

Cursman swung his sword diagonally underneath the blade as he leaped to the side of the vampyre.

Sporathun jumped backward, avoiding Cursman's long blade. He moved too far back and Malpherities lashed his claws onto the vampyre's shoulders, ripping downward into his back.

Sporathun barked and made a wide swing with both blades at the ghoul.

"Go!" Malpherities ducked and sprinted toward the labyrinth's entrance.

Cursman sheathed his sword and the two dashed simultaneously toward the door, knowing they had a fraction of a second before Sporathun recovered from Malpherities's attack.

The ghoul was the first to dive into the entrance, followed immediately by Cursman, who kept his head low while he leaped into the darkness, colliding with a wall. His back and shoulder scraped against the side of the pit for the whole fall until he landed on slanted ground. He scurried to sit upright while he slid down the slippery, spiralling slide. It was steep and he spent several seconds sailing downward until he saw a faint light coming from a square-shaped exit at the end. Cursman took a deep breath as his speed increased. The slide came to an end and Cursman flew out into the labyrinth, landing in the mud, slamming into the ground so hard he left an imprint.

Cursman leaped up and snatched the handle of his blade, eyeing the long, smooth, matte stone hallway of the labyrinth.

Malpherities was only a couple of feet away and he examined the ceiling of the labyrinth. "It's been a long time since I've been in here."

"Why doesn't it surprise me you've been here?" Cursman eyed the ground but saw no fresh footprints, expecting to some sign of Krista and Fierel. "Does the entrance drop us off in different locations?" Cursman asked, scanning their surroundings.

"Correct. After a player enters the labyrinth, it shifts the starting location. Sporathun should not enter here because he didn't step into the doorway with us."

Cursman looked up at the square entrance he'd fallen from. "Well, we haven't heard from him, so I think we're safe for now."

Malpherities moved closer to the wall furthest from them and ran his claw around it.

"What are you doing?" Cursman asked.

"I am reading the directions—to find the centre of the labyrinth. We must not waste any time."

"But the centre beast is there."

"It's the easiest way to group up with the girl and Fierel. I am bound to the paladin, remember? I know that is where she will go." Malpherities pointed down the path to their left, where a fork offered the choice of opposite directions.

The two began to venture carefully into the maze, examining the floor, walls, and ceiling. "If needed, I can return to Fierel whenever I please, yet that would leave you lost here."

Cursman rolled his eyes. "Nice to see you are such a caring soul. Taking care of the girl in both Dreadweave Pass and the mortal world, and now making sure I am safe in the labyrinth. You're a real charity worker now, aren't you?" Cursman had known Malpherities for decades and knew the ghoul always had more in mind than doing a simple good deed.

"Times have changed," Malpherities replied.

"What? Your days of conquest and terror are over? Ghouls are nothing but plagues. I know you better than that. You still have that craving to make the world rot. You're hiding something from all of us. Protecting the girl isn't what you want, and being shackled by Fierel must be part of your plan. There's no way you would dare allow anyone to own you like a slave."

"We don't have time for this. Focus! We must press forward."

"Don't think I am not on to you." Cursman dropped it, though. Malpherities was right: finding Fierel and Krista before Sporathun did was important. That was, assuming the vampyre had even entered the labyrinth.

The sound of a tumbling body echoed nearby. It was close, possibly the next wall over. "That was under fifty paces away." Cursman drew his sword and he and Malpherities exchanged glances.

"Make haste," the ghoul whispered.

The two dashed to the right fork in the road and came across a hallway twice as long as the first. Both sides of the walls had at least four entryways leading elsewhere in the maze.

Cursman trailed close to the ghoul, who paused at each new entry they came across, examining the walls around it. After the third examination, Malpherities pointed at the new hall and guided them into it.

"Where's the girl?" Sporathun shouted.

"He's near." Cursman scanned the first path they passed in the new hall.

"Closer than you think!" Sporathun shouted back, the source coming from behind.

Cursman spun around, looking down the hall, but saw nothing.

Malpherities bellowed, "Above!"

Cursman looked up to see the vampyre crouching on top of the walls.

"Damn it," he muttered. *His acrobatics are greater than I anticipated.*

Sporathun stood upright, his lean muscles highlighted in the dim light of the maze. His large twin blades were buckled onto each side of his belt. He inhaled heavily and let out a loud roar that shook the walls, saliva spewing in all directions.

Malpherities and Cursman sprinted forward while Sporathun leaped from the wall. The vampyre collided into Malpherities and they toppled into the dirt.

"Shit!" Cursman turned to face the vampyre, sword held with both hands.

Sporathun jumped from Malpherities like a wild cat and rushed at Cursman, back arched low.

Cursman lifted his blade and thrust down with Sporathun inches away. The vampyre dodged to the right and hopped from one foot onto Cursman, pinning him to the ground with a clawed foot on his chest.

Sporathun pushed Cursman deeper into the dirt. "Where's the girl?" he shouted.

Cursman coughed from the pressure, feeling his thick, layered sternum crack. "How should I know?"

Malpherities groaned and rose from the dirt. "You're a fool. We're in a labyrinth. It's impossible to know."

The vampyre unbuckled one of the blades from his belt and pointed it at the ghoul. "Take me to her."

"Can't you read the walls yourself?"

The vampyre ground his teeth and stomped his foot on Cursman, the force knocking the wind from his lungs. Cursman hacked while his vision blurred, but he could still hear.

"I should have killed you in Evergut, ghoul!"

"You and I both know it wouldn't have served any purpose. We need each other."

Sporathun buckled his blade and lifted his foot off Cursman. "What of this one?" He leaned down and lifted Cursman off the ground, slamming him against the nearest wall. "His scent is strong, yet I don't recall him."

The vampyre's saliva splattered across Cursman's face. He resisted the urge to wipe away the thick ooze and took a deep breath. *Keep calm, if I want to survive.* Cursman had never been so close to a vampyre before; seeing that dry, flaky skin up close, feeling the intense rage radiate from Sporathun's body.

"Silent one!" Sporathun slammed Cursman against the wall again. "Take me to the girl!"

"What for?" Malpherities challenged.

"The Weaver demands her."

"Clearly, yet what do you get from it? You're not exactly his ally. The Weaver's general locked you up."

"Take me to her!" Sporathun shouted again. "Or the man dies!" He grabbed hold of Cursman's neck, putting pressure on his windpipe.

Cursman sputtered and glared into Sporathun's closed eyelids, where the skin had fused together, preventing them from opening. The lids twitched and attempted to open while he sniffed Cursman.

"What's your story?" The vampyre snarled wickedly, showing every sharp tooth in his mouth.

"Bad luck," Cursman grunted. "Having a drink in a bar and Malpherities lands on my lap with the girl—then you show up."

Sporathun flickered his tongue and touched Cursman's bony chest with his other hand. "You're puppet?"

"Yes." He glanced behind the vampyre to see Malpherities, who folded his arms. *He knows Sporathun . . .*

"How many lives have you crushed in your lifetime?"

"I've lost count."

Sporathun let go of Cursman, letting him fall to the dirt. "My life was crushed by beings like you, who show no sympathy. You only carry out orders, mindless drone!"

"I have free will. Not like other puppets."

Malpherities grinned. "What are you doing now for the Weaver, Sporathun?"

The vampyre stomped his foot on the ground, hands shaking vigorously. "Don't test my patience, ghoul!" He lifted Cursman up from the ground, tearing the neck of his tunic. "You may have destroyed lives, but that does not matter. What I want is the girl!"

"You're not too different from a puppet yourself, being despised by the Heavenly Kingdoms," Malpherities said.

The vampyre clenched his teeth and let out a shriek, dropping Cursman to the ground a second time. He slammed his hand into the wall, cracking the stone. "I did not wish for this!" His breathing picked up rapidly, grunting with each exhalation.

Malpherities floated closer to Sporathun. "You knew the consequences of mating with another angel, weakling. You so easily gave into primitive desires."

Sporathun slammed his other hand into the wall, pebbles flying from the rock. "I wished it not!" The vampyre pounded both fists into the wall repeatedly.

Malpherities rushed toward Cursman. "His anger is amplifying; he is having a breakdown," he whispered.

Sporathun pounded his forehead against the stone. "I never wished for this, my dear Glamorous! I long for you."

Cursman shook his head, remembering what he and Krista had learned at the library. "He'll black out in any moment, and he'll kill anything he sees! Do you pray for our death?"

"Read the walls. Let's split to distract him—now!" Malpherities pulled Cursman away from the vampyre and darted down the nearest exit.

Cursman got up and grabbed his sword, rushing down the opposite hall from Malpherities. He glanced back before turning the corner, watching Sporathun begin to punch his head with his one fist. "I wished it not!"

Cursman sprinted down the hall, taking the nearest turn. There had to be a dozen paths to turn down in each new hall he came across.

"Read the walls? I don't—" Cursman stopped at one of the entryways and examined the wall's edge closely.

"My Glamorous!" Sporathun yelled.

Cursman ran his hand along the wall, squinting to search for clues on the smooth surface. At first the wall looked identical to all the others.

"The ghoul has set me up for my death." He bit his lip and looked closer to the edge of the wall. "Or not." He ran his hand along a small engraving in the wall. To the untrained eye, the markings would look like cracks and wear, but Cursman was familiar with the language. It was the same one used in the books of Smelg's library, an older alphabet used by gods, angels, and demons alike. Engraved in the wall were two glyphs reading: *hall beast*.

"Just gotta find the centre." Cursman swallowed and held his sword high. "Sounds easy enough."

CHAPTER XXIII

Painful Beauty

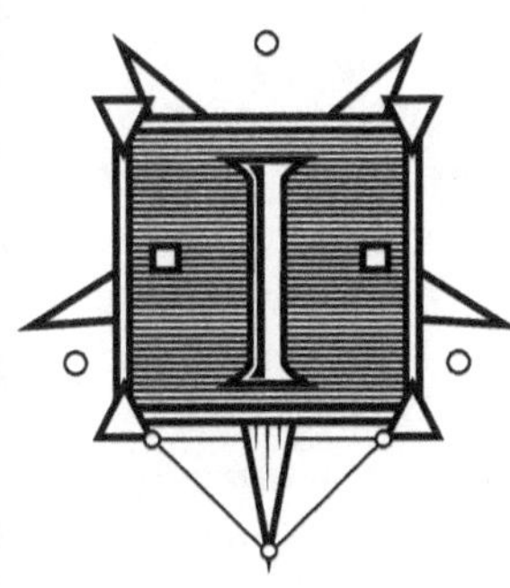*f a harmonious love has been shattered, one feels great levels of agony—a psychological soreness so great, it is felt throughout the whole body. How can something that is purely based in the mind cause so much hurt and harm to our physical being? Love comes in many shapes and forms. It can exist as unconditional or it can be defined as a family trait, as seen with a mother and her child. Love can be expressed through romance between two souls. This should not be confused with the primitive desire of lust that our bodies express. No, love is said to reach beyond the flesh and bone of our bodies. True love can carry on where the body can never reach.*

Yes, there is a fine line between romantic love and lust. Often, the lines blur and it becomes difficult to judge which is which. This is a question that has troubled souls for centuries: Are they simply acting on sin, or are they embracing something pure? Not all beings are capable of this self-reflection, though—even those of the heavenly kind.

Her feet were numb from the endless hours of walking, her body was weak from the lack of food, her head ached from crossing into Dreadweave Pass, and she was being hunted down by Sporathun. Like all the beings Krista had met since she was infected by Mental Damnation, Sporathun really had nothing to do with her. She presumed he was after her because the Weaver ordered him to and, from the history of Sporathun, she figured he simply wanted to find his former lover, Glamorous.

But it is just a theory Cursman and I came up with, Krista thought while following inches behind Fierel. *We can't be sure that he wants to find Glamorous. He is chasing me, not her.*

Cursman and Krista's entire plan was based on the idea that the fallen angel was seeking Glamorous, and they were going to use that to their advantage to strike Sporathun down.

We really have no idea if this is going to work, but what choice do we have now? They were trapped in an underground labyrinth with no guarantee that they would escape from the demon in the centre.

"Did you ever have a doll when you were little?" Fierel asked. Her hand extended the light from her blade, casting a clear path down the long, curved hall.

"No, I didn't own much. I was always on the move and only kept what was on my back."

The paladin nodded. "Nor did I. We were taught not to sentimentalize meaningless objects."

"Why do you sentimentalize me, then?"

Fierel shrugged. "For one, I don't see you as meaningless—or an object."

"But I really am meaningless in all of this. I did nothing to anyone, yet everyone in Dreadweave Pass has some interest in me."

"You're one of a kind, Krista. Your character is pure and your spirit is filled with so much potential. There's also the fact that you're not dead but are in the afterlife."

"If my own people saw me that way, maybe I wouldn't have been street scum and ended up here."

"What happened in the past is written. You can only mould yourself into who you want to be in the future."

"Like a warrior?" Krista asked, remembering her conversation with Cursman.

"It is possible."

"Why do paladins strive to be so heartless? Do I need to be cold to be a warrior?"

"We were the hand of God, bringing righteousness to the mortal realm. We had to be cold to face Dega'Mostikas's trickery."

"If paladins did so much good, why doesn't God, or the gods for that matter, bless more beings with their gift?"

Fierel sighed. "I suppose they don't need to since the Truce of Passing."

"What do you mean?"

"Dega'Mostikas's Triangle and the Heavenly Kingdoms have a truce now. There is no need for warriors in a time of peace."

"This is a time of peace?"

"Hard to believe, isn't it? The truce was created to allow the holy and the unholy alike to walk side by side in the Heavenly Kingdoms or in Dega'Mostikas's Triangle. The idea of the truce was to allow peace between the two factions during the eternal struggle for dominance. It would allow the souls of the mortal world to be judged without interruption."

"Everyone was okay with the truce?"

"Not everyone—including me. The Truce of Passing was made official, but not accepted by all. Rebels continued to follow the old ways, both in the Heavenly Kingdoms and in Dega'Mostikas's Triangle. Some rebels hunted and killed their foes like in the time before the truce. Other rebels had the impulse to act on their desires. If the Heavenly Kingdoms were going to change what was considered right and wrong, like making a truce with hell, it made me and others question if the gods even knew what was right."

"What happened to the rebels?"

"Some are still around. Others ended up here or in Death's Vortex. I suppose I am lucky to be here."

"What did you do that put you here?"

"I wrongfully loved someone not of my kind, or of my beliefs."

Krista raised an eyebrow. "Not of your kind?"

"No." Fierel sighed. "His people were known as shimen, and they practiced dark arts. Witchcraft, if you will."

Krista opened her eyes wide. "Wait. Did you have a daughter?"

"Look out!" Fierel shouted and blocked Krista from the new entryway to their left.

Krista ducked as three demon hands came darting out from around the corner, curving out in three separate directions and diving toward them.

Fierel swung her blade with both hands at the one to the far left. Her sword's tip punctured the skin of the forearm, tearing into the bloodstream. She pulled the blade free, tripling the size of the wound. She struck at an upward angle into the next hand, cutting it clean off from the wrist.

The hand to the right arched around Fierel and aimed for Krista.

"Fierel!" Krista shouted.

The hand extended its sharp claws and reached out for her. Inches away, Krista leaped to the side. The demon's hand shifted closer to her, buzzing past her outer thigh, the claws slicing into her leg.

Krista yelped and fell to the floor, clutching her oozing wound.

Fierel rushed to stand over Krista and struck down on the arm while it attempted to circle away from the paladin. Her blade severed the arm and it fell to the floor, the detached limb landing on Krista's chest.

Krista shook it off and noticed the first hand crawling on the floor. Blood drained out of the open forearm wound as it crept up behind Fierel.

"Look out!" Krista shouted.

The paladin twirled her blade around and downward. The sword hacked into the palm of the demon's hand, getting lodged in the middle of the bone.

Fierel pulled her blade back as the hand twitched once and went limp.

Simultaneously, all three dismembered arms slithered away on the dirt floor and around the corner, leaving a bloody trail behind.

Krista put pressure on her open wound with both hands, her black blood squirting between the cracks of her fingers. She squealed and took several long breaths; the outer edges of the wounds felt like they were on fire.

Fierel leaned closer to the wound. "How bad is it?"

Krista opened her hand so Fierel could look, but exposure to the air made the wound flare with pain. She whimpered and put her hands over it again.

Fierel hushed her. "Let me take a peek." She sheathed her sword and used her other hand to move Krista's.

Krista clutched the moist dirt and clenched her teeth. *Think of a happy place. Like my home—like Darkwing.*

"It's not that bad," the paladin said.

Krista looked at Fierel's wide eyes. She had the same shocked look on her face that Marilyn had shown after Malpherities attacked her. "You're human." Krista couldn't resist a smile. "Horrible liars."

"You will live."

"Can I walk?"

"You will; let's just stop some of the bleeding." She took her dagger from her ankle belt and tore a strip of fabric from the end of Krista's coat. Carefully, she wrapped the cloth around the wound several times.

At first, Krista didn't feel the cloth touch the wound until Fierel tightened it slightly, causing Krista to yelp.

"It's better than nothing." Fierel tucked her dagger back, stood up, and grabbed Krista's hand, forcing her to her feet. Krista shifted her weight to her better leg to avoid putting pressure on the wound.

"I'll help you." Fierel rested Krista's arm over her shoulder.

"Can't you fix me?" *Paladin healed the scar on my arm from Danil.*

"I can with a prayer. But I need time and meditation, and this is no place to do it with a vampyre and demon on our trail. We need to keep moving."

Krista groaned as they took the first step, her mouth hanging open. The two wobbled sideways and paused. Fierel nodded to herself and gradually took a second step, this one more stable and they built up momentum.

"Okay, let's keep on the move. Staying here isn't safe."

With each step they took, Krista felt a portion of her energy deplete. She resisted the urge to stare at her leg, feeling the blood drizzle past her knees. The leg felt weaker and it was too difficult to put any pressure on it.

Keep focused. I can't lose my strength now. The shock of the wound hit her stomach, thinking of the clawed hand slicing into her thigh and the sound of flesh tearing open. Her guts twisted and she gagged, leaning over to the side.

"Hold in there, Krista." Fierel rubbed her back lightly.

Krista took several inhalations through her mouth and exhaled through her nose, resisting the urge to vomit. Her injured leg began to shake with each step she took. The muscles in her arm that wrapped over Fierel's back fell numb.

"Will it stop bleeding?" Krista asked.

"Yeah." Fierel glanced at her, then the leg. "Just don't stare at it." Her words were quick.

She's stressed. Krista felt responsible for the strain. *If I wasn't so scared, if I was more of a warrior, this wouldn't have happened.* But she wasn't; she was still a girl and was still learning how to become strong. *If Fierel was not here, I do not know what I would have done.*

The two continued to travel for what felt like hours—or perhaps it wasn't so long. It was difficult to tell exactly how much time passed. Krista could barely pay attention to walking. She kept her mind focused on breathing: inhale, then exhale. The steps she took were in rhythm with each breath she took.

"I wish it not!" a voice echoed in the distance.

"What was that?" Krista asked.

Fierel examined the ceiling of the labyrinth. "It's not something we want to deal with."

"Sporathun?"

"Most likely."

"Where are Cursman and Mal?"

"They're alive; I'm sure of it."

My leg really hurts. Krista wanted to complain to Fierel about how she felt. *Darkwing was always there to listen to me, but I really don't have anyone like that in Dreadweave Pass. That could be a good thing, though. Maybe it is time for me to learn how to handle things on my own.*

Fierel stopped in her tracks and remained stiff, eyeing the path ahead.

Krista turned her head, watching the paladin. "What is it?" she whispered.

Around the curved hall, two more demon hands accelerated in a wavy motion toward Fierel and Krista.

"Please, no," Krista whispered.

Fierel gracefully slid Krista off her shoulders, allowing her to fall to the ground. The paladin bent her knees, holding her sword with both hands, her eyes watching the hands zoom closer.

The left hand—nearest of the two—clamped its fingers down, forming a single point with its claws.

Fierel let out a yell and swung her sword forward. The blade and claws of the hand collided with resistance. The metal peeled into the bone of the index finger until the pressure forced the fingers apart, the blade hacking into the flesh, chopping the hand in two.

The right hand arched upward and spread its fingers far apart, aiming for Krista.

The paladin pulled her sword free from the split hand and ran toward the right hand. It dove downward while Fierel leaped up, her blade aimed high.

The hand shifted to the side, avoiding her initial strike. It continued toward Krista, its long arm following the path of the hand like a snake slithering. Fierel struck down at the moving arm and her sword sliced through the flesh of the demon, cutting it in two.

The decapitated hand fell with a heavy thud to the ground, scattering dirt into Krista's face.

Fierel landed on her knees, blade pointing backward.

Krista let out a sigh of relief. "I would so be dead without you."

Fierel rose to her feet, smirking. "It's what I was born to do." She strolled over and reached out for Krista's hand. "Let's keep moving."

The paladin helped her up from the ground. Krista used all her strength to avoid standing on her wounded leg. *All this action is making it a bit easier to tolerate the pain.*

While they walked, the leg began to flare in agony again, the movement causing the drying blood to break and new blood to seep out.

I'm a warrior. Krista pressed her lips together. *I can handle pain.*

"I think we're nearing the centre," Fierel said.

"Then we can leave?"

"I'm not sure if that is the end of the labyrinth. I never knew the nature of this game."

Krista nodded. "It's where Mal and Cursman will be?"

"Yes."

The demon is there, though. There's probably going to be more hands. The image of her leg tearing open flashed in her mind again. "I'm scared."

"You need to understand that life isn't a flower, Krista. There will be times you will have to take part in events you're not fond of; we all have done so. This may be one of them, and it may be frightening, but I promise you that you will not die here."

"What about my leg? What if it's infected? I don't want to cut it off! There's still a chance it could happen."

"You'll be fine!" Fierel shouted. Her voice bounced off the walls. "Sorry."

"I'll stay focused," Krista said apologetically.

The long hallway came to an end with a sharp turn to the right.

Fierel stopped before reaching the end. She slipped Krista from her shoulder, leaning her against the wall. "I think we're here."

Krista felt her heart pound and her eyes widened. "The demon is around the corner? How do you know?"

"By reading the signs. Stay here." Fierel pointed at a wall.

Krista rested against it, feeling the cold surface through her jacket. It sent shivers down her scales. *Be careful, Fierel.*

Fierel kept her blade lowered while she crept up to the turn in the hallway. Her back was pressed against the wall, breathing steady. She stopped inches away from the edge and leaned over, peeking around the corner. She waited for a couple of moments then brought her head back.

"What?" Krista asked.

"It's there."

"The centre beast?"

Fierel brought a finger to her lips. "Hush. It's sleeping."

"How is he sleeping if his hands were attacking us?"

"I suppose the hands have minds of their own—like patrol units in the labyrinth."

"Do the hands ever wake him up?"

"I don't know, Krista."

"What do we do?" Krista asked.

"We need to kill the centre beast."

"But why? What did he do?"

Fierel shook her head. "It's a minion of Dega'Mostikas and that makes it a threat. Besides, by the looks of it, the demon is attached to the floor and ceiling of this labyrinth, like it's supporting the weight."

"Like he's a column?"

"Yes."

Suddenly, a group of four hands came darting from around the corner toward them.

Krista pointed just as they were about to reach the paladin.

Fierel clutched her blade with both hands and swung upward. The blade sliced two hands clean from the arms, blood splattering at her face like squished fruit. Fierel dodged the third hand and the fourth grazed by her head, the claws ripping into her cheek and earlobe.

One hand rotated back and darted for Fierel again while the other hand kept accelerating toward Krista.

Krista gasped and pushed herself from the wall, giving herself a head start to run. She took her first several steps forward, putting pressure on her wounded leg. Her balance shook but fear of the hand kept her moving, ignoring the pain.

"Help!" Krista cried. She glanced back to see Fierel had slain the third hand, the arm wriggling on the ground like a headless snake. The fourth hand was a split second away from grabbing Krista.

"Keep running!" Fierel shouted while she sprinted toward the arm, raising her sword.

The hand clamped onto Krista's ankle just as the sound of slicing flesh resounded through the hall. The pressure from the hand softened immediately and it let go of Krista. She slumped against the opposite wall, shaking and panting for air.

"We did it!" Krista called out.

A new hand sprung from around the corner, aiming for Fierel.

"Look out!" Krista shouted.

The paladin spun around while the hand clamped down, ready to strike like a spear. Fierel swung her blade at it, but was too slow. The hand rushed over her upper arm and pierced into her shoulder blade. Fierel dropped the sword from the force and was thrown into the wall, a foot off the ground, held up by the clamped claw impaled into her flesh.

"No!" Krista grunted while lifting herself and she ran toward Fierel. *What am I thinking?* She was useless to Fierel, but maybe she could get the sword and cut the hand off. *I have to try. No more running.*

A second hand glided from the corner, passing Fierel and aiming for Krista.

"Shit!"

The hand was only paces away from Krista. She held her breath while it closed in. *I can dodge it.*

The hand extended its fingers, aiming for Krista's knees.

Krista used her good leg to jump aside. Her foe sprung upward immediately, grabbing the ankle of her wounded leg.

"Krista!" a male voice shouted.

The hand yanked Krista back to the ground, knocking her face-first into the dirt. It tugged on her leg, pulling the skin of the open wound.

She cried out and rolled onto her back, wiping the mud from her eyes.

"Krista!" the male's voice shouted again, closer. The gritty tone was familiar.

Cursman!

The hand yanked on her leg, dragging her body through the dirt. "Cursman! Save us!" She turned her head up, seeing the other side of the hallway. Cursman's hair swayed with each step he took, sword held to one side with both hands.

Krista was dragged past Fierel, who had a dagger in her hand. Fierel stabbed the hand that impaled her relentlessly, making several puncture wounds. The hand pulled the paladin free from the wall and both Krista and Fierel were dragged around the corner into the centre of the labyrinth.

The centre room was circular with a floor littered in skeletons. Mounds of bones spread up against the walls, and the room reeked of rotting eggs and animal corpses. The hands dragged Krista and Fierel to the middle, where a cylindrical being as tall as the ceiling had its skin stretched along the ground and upper surface, disappearing underneath the rock as if it were fused to the labyrinth. The skin was a mustard colour and was covered in scars, giant pores, and dozens of swollen bumps. The boils on the skin were semi-transparent, with liquid filling about two-thirds of each bubble.

Dozens of tubes ran from all over the cylindrical body and disappeared into the maze.

The hands, Krista thought.

The two hands lifted Krista and Fierel up from the ground, at least 30 feet in the air, where the middle of the cylindrical body was.

Directly across from Krista were two closed eyes, flaring nostrils, and a wide mouth with thick lips of the same yellowish skin tone.

The centre beast's eyelids peeled back suddenly; translucent residue tore between the lids. The eyeballs had no pupils—just a glassy white. The creature opened its mouth and the entire room began to rumble as it inhaled.

"Mortals!" The beast's deep voice dragged out the vowels, the sound reverberating through the labyrinth. "Why dare you disturb my slumber?" It clenched his jaws, showing the yellow-stained teeth and black gums inside its mouth.

Krista screamed and tried to lift herself up to pull on the hand that clutched her ankle. The motion caused her leg to spark with pain and she fell back down, swaying upside-down.

Off to the side of the centre beast's face, a lump burst open with a pop and a new hand stretched from the open hole, white liquid pouring from the bubble as the skin deflated. The slimy new hand swooped toward Fierel, snatching her by the neck.

The centre beast shook its head slowly. "Messy." It exhaled deeply, the air creating a devastating wind that blew past Krista and Fierel. The breath was warm with an amplified stench of the room.

Krista gagged and felt vomit heave into her mouth. She spat a mouthful of bile to the ground and shook her head. *Stay strong. Gotta be strong. I'm a warrior.*

Fierel held the wrist of the arm with both hands while she gasped for air. "The gods will smite you!" she shouted. "Lord, please surround me with favour as with a shield today. Please strengthen your wall of protection around me, keeping me safe from tricks of the adversary, and from all harm. Lord, fill my thoughts with your thoughts and let my words be your words. You are my strength, my shield, and my defense."

The beast laughed; its entire body rippled with each bellow. "You have no shield here, paladin." The hand brought Fierel closer to the beast. "You believe the gods will smite me? As they smite the tainted souls that scatter their Heavenly Kingdoms? The Truce of Passing has set us all free."

Krista turned her head around, scanning the room. *Nothing but bones. Where is Cursman? What can I do?*

Fierel closed her eyes and began to mutter more words.

I hope Fierel has a plan.

The beast continued to laugh. "A banished paladin trying to perform an exorcism on me?"

"Let us go!" Krista cried.

The centre beast turned its attention to Krista. "What for?"

"We're running from a vampyre. Please."

"Fallen angels are a fine meal. It's been about a thousand years since my last angel."

Krista squinted, gathering her courage. "Your last one? Was she named Glamorous?"

The beast frowned. "The name sounds familiar. Yes. Yes, she was lovely; I swallowed her whole as she fell from above. A gift from the gods indeed."

"Are her bones on the floor?"

"Enough questions, mortal! Why should I spare your life? I have not seen mortals in centuries—not since the labyrinth descended to Dreadweave Pass."

Fierel's chanting grew louder. "My Heavenly Father, sanctify me. The body of your son, save me. Water from the side of your holiness, wash me of the evil that surrounds me. Passion of the holy spirit, strengthen me in my time of need."

Krista looked at the entrance to the centre again, but still no Cursman. *Where is he?* Her eyes trailed along the outer edge of the room, hoping to spot him hiding in the bones. *There!* Between two bone piles, Cursman kept himself hidden underneath a skeleton, staring up at Krista and Fierel. *What is he waiting for?*

The beast brought Krista closer to Fierel. "Yes, it's been some time since I tasted a mortal. I'll enjoy digesting you two for the next dozen centuries!"

Fierel continued to chant. "Oh, Lord, sanctify us!"

The beast's mouth opened wide, the rubbery, grey inner walls of its mouth stretching as it stuck out its slimy black tongue.

I can't take this. Krista closed her eyes. *Maybe my wounded leg will kill me first.*

A high-pitched shrill came from the labyrinth. The sound of bones breaking bounced off the room's rounded walls.

The centre beast quickly snapped its mouth closed and brought Fierel and Krista away from its face. "More souls wandering my labyrinth? I have not had this much action since the demi-gods perished."

Krista opened her eyes, looking down at Cursman. The man had moved further to the side of the centre beast. He kept the skeleton on his back while he crept toward the beast, his sword held low.

But that is not where the sound came from. Krista looked over to the opposite side of the room, where she spotted a glowing blue lump with black smoke around it.

Mal! Krista smiled.

A second figure leaped from behind the labyrinth walls and on top of the stone. Sporathun shrieked again and unbuckled the two blades from his belt, breathing rapidly. "Release the girl!" he shouted.

"Ah—the awaited vampyre! You know, I don't take orders from the likes of you." The beast opened its mouth and, in a single motion, launched Fierel onto its tongue. She flailed wildly, trying to grab on to the bumpy surface of its flesh, but the saliva was too slippery. The beast lifted its tongue and Fierel slid downward while bringing her hands together, continuing to pray to herself.

"Fierel!" Krista cried.

"Don't toy with me, demon." Sporathun leaped off the wall and rolled down a bone mound. "Let the girl go!" He held his two blades ready while he charged at the centre beast.

The beast sprouted three new hands from boils higher up its body, the liquid spraying in the air. Several of the warm, slimy droplets fell onto Krista's face. She tried to shake it off, but it dripped down her cheeks leaving oily trails.

Krista glanced at Cursman to see the man had reached the base of the centre beast's stretched skin. He had pierced his sword into the skin and was beginning to carve along the rim, slicing the flesh from the base.

One of the fresh, oily hands absently moved down to where Cursman had cut and scratched the area. As the fingers touched the wound, the centre beast grunted and looked downward, gasping at the sight of its sliced skin. "Who else is here?" Cursman had disappeared from Krista's and the centre beast's lines of sight, but the trail of carved skin was visible.

Krista was alarmed. *Is he freeing the beast?*

The three hands, including the one the beast had scratched with, spiralled down at Sporathun, clamping their fingers together to make sharp points.

Sporathun leaped into the air, far higher than the walls. He spun his two blades as the hands closed in on him.

The hands attempted to evade the attack, but the blade sliced them open first and they collapsed to the ground, blood spurting from the wounds.

Sporathun landed with a roll and rose again, maintaining his momentum.

The centre beast growled and its body began to rumble. Six hands exploded from the boils on its back, aiming for the fallen angel.

The sudden movements caused the beast to wobble side to side like a tree about to topple.

Sporathun somersaulted several times and, on the last acrobatic movement, swiveled himself in a whirlwind motion from the heel of his foot, blades violently spinning around.

Four of the hands got too close and were chopped into more pieces than Krista could count, dropping to the floor like slabs of meat.

The beast closed its eyes and began to rumble again, making the entire cylindrical body ripple. Its eyes flung open and its mouth gaped wide while every boil on the body burst at once, sprouting more long-armed hands that dove in unison at Sporathun.

A rain of white liquid sprinkled over Krista from the newly spawned hands. Several drops fell into her open wound and she cringed. The liquid bubbled up at contact with her blood and her flesh began to sizzle.

Sporathun skidded to a halt, lunging his blades upward, sideways, and every direction to push away the swarm. With each swing, he sliced more hands into chunks, drenching himself in their blood.

The hands buzzed around Sporathun, moving together like a school of fish, trying to find openings to strike at the fallen angel. His speed built with each volley of hands until they barely reached closer than the tips of his blades.

Krista looked around for Malpherities, who remained motionless in the skeleton mound. *I need to get out of here.* She stretched upward again, trying to reach for the hand that clamped around her ankle. Her leg's pain escalated from her movement and she cried out, falling back from the shock and dangling upside down again. "I can't—" she muttered.

One hand dodged Sporathun's weapon and impaled him in the back, piercing through his stomach in a mess of dripping blood and organs.

Sporathun grunted and dropped his one blade. With his free hand, he clutched the wrist of the demon hand. It tried to wiggle free while the vampyre squeezed harder, the sound of squishing flesh amplifying until the hand popped free, exploding in a bloody burst from Sporathun's grip. The arm wiggled and pulled out through the wound, returning to the centre beast with its hand little more than pulp.

The fallen angel's open wound began to shrink, the organs mending themselves back inside, followed by the muscle tissue and skin sealing over.

The centre beast squealed like a dying pig. "Vampyre of wrath!" It began to wriggle in its stationary position. The excessive movement caused the skin fused to the ceiling to tear and the body swayed widely.

"He's going to topple. Help me! I need down from here!" Krista cried out.

The demon let out a howling whimper as a sudden bright glow came from its stomach, lighting up the thousands of tightly compacted blood vessels and thick layers of fat around the beast's innards.

The light began to die down and, from above, Krista could see the silhouettes of two figures in its stomach.

Fierel? Krista's eyes widened.

The beast continued to sway, each swing lasting longer and growing more violent. The skin from the beast's top and bottom peeled further back.

The army of hands that swarmed Sporathun diminished with each strike he made. A ring of mutilated hands surrounded him, lying on the stone in a pool of blood; his entire chest was soaked in it, and his kilt shined with wetness.

The beast waved to the right, putting more tension on what little of the fused skin remained. The swaying began to slow and the body tilted harshly, forcing all its weight on the last shred of skin.

Krista looked to the ground. If they crashed, they would hit one of the piles of bones, crushing Sporathun in the process. *I can't wait for help.* She made another attempt to pull herself upward, reaching for the hand that clutched her. Krista bent one-third of the way but it was of no use; even ignoring the pain, she couldn't reach high enough and she fell back down.

Another light sparked from the core of the centre beast. This one caused its entire body to thunder. The light got brighter and seemed to concentrate on the front of the beast.

The centre beast let out a scream of pain as the exterior of its skin began to burn and smoke, catching fire and shriveling from the centre point of the bright light. The outer rim of the burning hole ignited with white flame.

The movement pushed the beast's body sideways. The skin began to peel excessively and its body collapsed.

"Help me!" Krista shouted.

Sporathun looked up at the falling demon and darted to the side toward the front of the beast. What few hands remained followed behind him, snapping at his feet.

The centre beast groaned. Semi-transparent blood poured from the torn upper seal, down over its body, and onto the bone mounds below, washing the skeletons aside.

The hand that held Krista reached upward as the demon's mass collided with the ground, crushing the bones beneath. The impact forced the hand to fly sideways, losing its grip and throwing Krista toward a wall.

She screamed at the top of her lungs as she sailed straight toward the top corner of one of the surrounding walls. "Help!" she cried. *I'm going to die.*

A pair of firm hands grabbed her, stopping her in mid-air. They felt like the centre beast's hands for a moment, but she looked up into the fused eyelids of Sporathun.

"Let me go!" she squealed. Krista squirmed in the fallen angel's arms but his tight grip on her body wrapped around her waist and shoulders, locking her in place.

The vampyre landed on a bone mound, cracking a number of remains in the process. He glanced over toward the centre beast as the fire from the hole in its body began to consume its face. The beast was now motionless, mouth open and eyes rolled back. Its body had torn away entirely from the floor and the ceiling, the corpse lying lifeless on its side. The labyrinth walls behind the beast began to collapse backward, each wall colliding into the next and falling behind it like dominoes, splashing into the pools of the centre beast's blood. The noise of crashing stone echoed through the maze, each collision fading into the distance. The ceiling where the centre beast had been attached started to crack and rocks fell from the midpoint, exposing the surface above.

"Let her go, Sporathun!" Malpherities's voice boomed through the chaos. He hovered atop the wall directly above Krista and the fallen angel. His tentacle hair appeared electrically charged, his eyes shone bright white, and the black smoke around his body was twice his usual spread.

"The girl is mine!" Sporathun's tongue flickered. "I have won; be gone, ghoul."

"Don't make me hurt you." Malpherities extended his arms, his claws stretched wide.

Sporathun chuckled. "Do you honestly think you stand a chance?"

"You know what I keep locked in here." Malpherities tapped his chest, pointing at the bright blue core of his body. "Don't think that I wouldn't. You taking her to the Weaver will set everything back that I've worked toward; everything that you, too, have been a part of."

For a moment, Sporathun looked uncertain. "You wouldn't. You'd kill us all."

Cursman ran out from behind the corpse of the centre beast, his sword in hand, eyes on Sporathun. Several cuts had appeared on his body and sweat dripped from his face—that, or droplets of the beast's blood. He watched the collapsing ceiling from the corner of his eye to avoid falling rocks as they splashed into the pools on the floor.

The white fire inside the centre beast's corpse faded, leaving behind a dark tunnel.

"Sporathun!" Fierel's voice echoed from the darkness.

Krista squirmed in the fallen angel's arms. "Fierel!" she screamed.

The vampyre laughed with a wide smile. "You are all fools! I have won."

From the dark core of the demon's stomach, two beings emerged. One was Fierel. She held the other, a girl who appeared limp and unconscious, dangling around her arm. The girl was barefoot, with skin as white as a sheet of paper. Her slim figure was wrapped in a tattered sky-blue dress.

"Turn and face me!" Fierel shouted as she stepped out of the demon's corpse. Both Fierel and the girl were covered in slimy stomach fluid. The acid dripped from the paladin's chin and she panted, staring at Sporathun. The cuts on her cheek and ear had been washed clean.

Sporathun sniffed the air and his jaw dropped, loosening his grip on Krista. "It cannot be," he muttered while taking a second sniff. "My . . . Glamorous?"

Fierel stood tall, holding the unconscious girl whose smooth face was covered by her long blonde hair. Broken bones and ragged flesh sprouted from her back with soggy remnants of feathers left behind.

Sporathun dropped Krista to the ground and his arms dangled while he stood in awe.

Krista scurried to her feet, placing her hands on a skull to help push herself up from the bones and regain her balance. She tried to stand on her wounded leg and immediately collapsed back down. She grunted and rolled onto her back. *No use.*

Sporathun shook his head and began to walk toward Fierel. "They lied to me." He clenched his jaws. "General Dievourse," he muttered through closed teeth. "That lying warmonger."

Cursman ran along the outer perimeter of the room toward Krista, avoiding the distracted Sporathun. "Krista!" he called out.

She made a second attempt to get up, this time avoiding putting pressure on her leg. Krista made her first step with ease and limped down the bone mound, dragging her wounded leg.

Cursman sheathed his sword and grabbed Krista with both hands. She fell into his arms, wrapping herself around his torso. "I'm so happy to see you."

He placed his hand on her head. "We're not out of here yet."

Sporathun stomped the ground with one foot. "They lied!" he shouted again.

Malpherities's dreadlocked hair relaxed and laid flat, and he hovered down from the wall. "Cursman, assist the paladin. Our best chance is for Fierel to perform an exorcism on Sporathun." He rushed over to Cursman. "I'll take Krista."

Krista leaned over and fell into the ghoul's arms.

Cursman unsheathed his sword and walked carefully along the edge of the room toward Fierel. Malpherities followed behind him, but shifted his direction toward the collapsed walls where a bright light could be seen at the far end.

"The exit has been revealed with the centre beast's death," the ghoul said.

"They lied! My Glamorous is here!" Sporathun dropped to his knees. "They lied!" He slammed his closed fist into the ground, spraying muddy blood droplets over his skin.

Cursman extended his arm to Fierel, taking Glamorous into his arms. He held his sword in the other hand, keeping it pointed toward Sporathun. "Let's get moving! Krista is wounded," he said while examining the torn flesh on Glamorous's back. "By the looks of it, so is she."

"Let me finish this." Fierel cracked her knuckles and stormed toward Sporathun. "His reign of terror ends here."

Krista shook her head. "Fierel is wounded. One of the demon's hands pierced her shoulder."

Malpherities took a deep breath, pressing his lips together tightly.

"Can she do the exorcism?" Krista asked.

"Fierel, we can leave!" Cursman took a step toward her.

"Back off, Cursman," Malpherities said.

"We can dump Glamorous and be done with this," Cursman argued.

"You think that would be enough to get Sporathun off our tail? The Weaver needs Krista's blood so he can begin his war on the Heavenly Kingdoms. Sporathun's sin needs to feed his vengeance."

Cursman wiped his face and watched Fierel close in on the vampyre. "Damn it."

The paladin pressed her hands together, mere paces away from Sporathun. "From anxiety, sadness, and obsessions, we beg you. Free thee, oh Lord, from hatred, fornication, envy, we beg you. Free thee . . ." She stopped a foot away from the vampyre, took a deep breath, and continued. "Oh Lord, free thee from thoughts of jealousy, rage, and death," she muttered.

Cursman shook his head. "She sounds so weak."

"Stay clear," Malpherities called out. "Sporathun is entering another blackout. We've got seconds before he will tear us to shreds. Fierel's holy prayer is the only thing that can prevent it. Physical contact will only stimulate him."

"We beg you, free thee, oh Lord, from every form of sinful sexuality. We beg you, free thee, oh Lord, from every division in our family, and every harmful friendship. We beg you, free thee, oh Lord, from every sort of spell, malefice, witchcraft, and every form that Dega'Mostikas presents. We beg you, free thee, oh Lord." Her hands spread apart and her pendant lit bright white, channeling through her necklace and into her skin. The light moved through her bloodstream and out from her palms, forming a ball of white, smokeless fire between her hands.

"They lied! She lives!" Sporathun raised his head at the bright light. "Don't you understand that General Dievourse lied?"

Fierel lifted her right arm high, the fireball hovering above it. "Oh Lord, we beg you to free thee, upon the name of the Father, the son, and the Holy Spirit. I, Fierel Flamesworth, expel this unrighteous soul from these lands, Crasoe the fallen! May God have merc—"

Sporathun crouched then sprung upward, his sharp horns puncturing through Fierel's breastplate. Blood squirted from the wounds and oozed down onto the vampyre's skull. He continued to charge forward with the paladin impaled on his head.

Fierel spat blood from her mouth and the fireball in her hands flickered. "Have mercy on your soul!" She slammed her right hand down toward his neck, only to have her hand caught by Sporathun's.

He squealed as the white flame crossed over onto his hand, burning his skin. The fallen angel stumbled to the ground, skidding in the mud. Fierel landed first, with the vampyre's horns pushing deeper into her chest.

Fierel cried out in pain. "Father, give me strength!" Her right hand shook, trying to gain dominance over Sporathun's.

"We need to go now!" Malpherities shouted. "He's losing his conscious state—blacking out."

Cursman muttered a curse under his breath. "What of Fierel?"

"Be my guest to save her." The ghoul turned and rushed toward the series of collapsed walls.

"Fierel!" Krista shouted. "We can't leave her!" She looked over the ghoul's shoulder.

Sporathun lifted Fierel's body off the ground several times, pushing her back into the dirt, blood spraying from her wounds.

"We can. She failed to perform the exorcism," Malpherities hissed.

"But she's our only hope of killing Sporathun, right?" Krista clutched the ghoul's arm. *Is Fierel going to die for my sake?*

"Fierel's good as dead," said Cursman, a few feet behind and carrying Glamorous over his shoulder. "This gal is now our only hope of dealing with Sporathun."

Krista shook her head. "It's not right. Is there nothing we can do for her?"

"Lord, free thee from sin!" Fierel shouted.

Sporathun snorted, nostrils flaring, and ground his teeth.

What would Fierel do in my position? Leaving her behind was not in Krista's character. She had been left behind by Darkwing in the City of Renascence too many times and knew what it was like to be abandoned. *I'm helpless, though. I can't walk; how could I fight a fallen angel?* She looked over Malpherities's shoulder again.

The white fire was beyond Sporathun's arm and consuming half of his head and torso, burning his flesh down to the bone. His body generated new muscle tissue by the second.

Fierel gained the upper hand and forced the vampyre to the dirt, pulling herself free from his horns. The two clutched each other by the wrists, arms shaking and muscles tensing to gain dominance of the white fire.

Sporathun headbutted the paladin's nose sharply; her head swayed side to side and the fireball began to wither away. He threw Fierel to the side, knocking her into the mud.

The fireball faded and the white light from the pendant diminished, leaving Fierel limp on the ground.

Sporathun stood up and let out an ear-shattering roar. He slammed back down onto his knees, shaking his head and slamming his fists against his skull. Each time he pounded his face he let out a puff, exhaling heavily.

The further Malpherities carried Krista, the brighter their surroundings were. A red-tinted light came further up ahead. Sporathun and Fierel looked like small figures in the distance; it was almost impossible to tell who was who now.

"This will lead us back to the surface of Dreadweave Pass," Malpherities said.

Behind him, Cursman nodded.

Krista sighed. *She is alive.* But for how long? She was still with Sporathun. Fierel was a strong being and Krista could only hope that Fierel could escape Sporathun before he decided to kill her.

The group travelled in silence for several minutes, walking over the collapsed walls to the far end of the labyrinth where the outer wall had been broken by the impact of another wall, exposing a long mud path that ramped upward to the brighter surface.

Sporathun's shouts of frustration echoed in the depths of the labyrinth, slowly fading away once the group reached the surface. They emerged on the opposite side of the ruins from where they'd entered; the large hill was on the other end.

Malpherities pointed to the incline. "We'll return to the path we came from. Anything further out here is just desert. We will aim for the forest—it will make it harder for Sporathun to find us."

"What was Sporathun doing? Why didn't he come for Glamorous?" Krista asked, glancing at the limp blonde in Cursman's arms. *I must keep my mind off Fierel.*

"He blacked out," Cursman replied.

Krista nodded. "So, seeing Glamorous made him go crazy?"

"Yes, his anger over what happened to her is intense. Vampyre of wrath."

Malpherities nodded. "Not to mention what he said about General Dievourse."

"Aye, sounds like General Dievourse had told him they had Glamorous, which would partly explain why he was after us from the start."

"He can't harm Fierel like this, can he?"

Malpherities shook his head. "He is essentially throwing a temper tantrum. Anything that moves, he will attack like a mad bull. Yet if she doesn't get up soon, he'll return from the blackout and there is no telling what he will do with her."

Krista frowned. "If he won't harm Fierel, we could have saved her!"

Malpherities let out a long, drawn-out sigh. "What don't you understand about the blackout? Anything that moves, he'll attack. He's like a rampaging animal."

The group moved in silence around the edge of the Ruins of the Mortals Run, back toward the hill.

Safe in Malpherities's arms, Krista replayed everything that had just happened: the centre beast snatching her leg, Fierel being devoured, Sporathun's skillful fighting, and him relentlessly beating Fierel. *I can only hope she is okay. What would she do if she were in my place?* Pray—it was the only thought that came to her. *I don't even know who I would be praying to. What type of god would allow any of this?*

Cursman panted as they reached the hill. He took a moment at the bottom to catch his breath before travelling upward. Malpherities had few issues hovering to the top. Cursman, carrying the unconscious Glamorous, took a little longer but did not fall far behind.

Once they reached the summit of the hill, Cursman stopped. He gracefully slipped Glamorous from his shoulder. "All right." He kept the fallen angel wrapped in his arms, studying her face. "She's not as ugly as Sporathun." He smirked.

The vampyre's head jerked forward, mouth wide open. Her right arm lifted upward, hand reaching for the sky. The torn wings on her back blackened and crumbled into ash beneath her, leaving her back with two large scars. She brought her hand to her throat and attempted to scream but no sound came out and she thrashed in Cursman's arms.

Cursman grunted. "Damn it! I can't keep hold of her."

Malpherities shrugged. "She'll calm down. Her wings have just burnt. It seems that she was preserved inside of the centre beast's stomach and her transformation to a vampyre was incomplete until now."

"So she thinks she just fell from the Heavenly Kingdoms?" Cursman asked.

"Basically, yes. Her body's state is the same as the day the gods banished her." The ghoul pointed at the ashes of her wings. "They must have been burning off while she crashed into Dreadweave Pass—until she was consumed by the centre beast."

Glamorous tried to scream again. Her neon blue eyes darted back and forth between Cursman and Malpherities.

"She's mute." Cursman sheathed his sword and gently brushed her hair aside.

The vampyre flinched but relaxed her face and let Cursman touch her.

Krista felt her leg wound flare up again and she grunted. *Be strong.* "She cannot talk?"

Cursman shook his head. "From what I read in Smelg's library, she had the most beautiful voice in the Heavenly Kingdoms. The gods were so cruel that they stripped her of her talent."

"Mal . . ." Krista spoke in a soft tone, pointing at her still-bleeding leg.

The ghoul eyed the wound. "That's a problem. Cursman, we need to find Krista a doctor. That wound cannot stay unattended."

Krista shook her head. "I'll be fine, really." *I need to keep strong; a warrior would withstand a wound.* "I want to know what we're going to do with Glamorous. Without Fierel, how can we kill Sporathun?"

Malpherities shrugged. "Perhaps we don't have to kill him."

"Why?"

The ghoul shook his head. "Well, I am guessing his interest doesn't lie just with you. He wants Glamorous."

"Then why does he need me at all?"

Malpherities shook his head. "Weren't you listening earlier?"

Cursman nodded. "Think of it this way: The gods banished Glamorous and Sporathun to Dreadweave Pass. They've suffered a lot. His obsession with vengeance won't be fulfilled just by getting Glamorous back. He will need to feed his sin—whether he realizes it now or not. And what is the next thing he can use to feed his wrath?"

Krista shook her head. "The gods?"

"Exactly." Malpherities spoke. "They're the ones who banished him and Glamorous. Won't Sporathun wish to help the Weaver get into the Heavenly Kingdoms? It would let him unleash all his anger—his wrath—onto the gods for banishing him and Glamorous in the first place."

Cursman sighed. "Possibly. I don't know any more than you do. All I know is we have his lover."

Krista looked to the ground. "Great."

Glamorous began to squirm in Cursman's arms again. He grabbed hold of her around the waist and her arm. "Think she heard anything we said?"

Malpherities continued to travel down the gravel road. "She's still in shock, so chances are, no. We'll deal with the details of Sporathun when we find a doctor. The important thing now is to save Krista's leg."

The shackles on Malpherities's arm began to vibrate for a few moments. A moment later, the metal dissolved into the air and the silvery particles were picked up by a breeze, lingering a moment before blowing into the desert.

Krista squinted. "Mal, you're free?"

"It would appear so," he replied grimly.

"Did Fierel set you free?"

Cursman frowned. "Lead the way." He pushed Glamorous, forcing her to take her first step.

Krista felt her heart sink. "Mal, does that mean Fierel set you free?"

"In a way, yes." The ghoul replied.

"In a way? Is she dead?" Her mind buzzed with questions. *Fierel was supposed to help me find Danil so I could get out of Dreadweave Pass. Am I going to have Mental Damnation forever?* The thought of trying to survive in hell made her sick. *I want my old life, with Darkwing. Where are you?*

Malpherities raised his arm and displayed his wrists, which now had white crosses burned into them. "Fierel's legacy will live on, and her sacrifice won't be in vain."

A tear fell from Krista's eye. She took a steady breath and exhaled heavily. *Don't cry. You're a warrior.*

CHAPTER XXIII: PAINFUL BEAUTY

CHAPTER XXVI

We're Alone in Our Perspective

PATIENT: KRISTALANTICE SCALEBANE

DAY: FOUR
ENTRY: FOUR

Tonight, Paladin and I have made the decision not to constrain Kristalantice to the frame of her bed. With or without the restraints during previous nights, she has bled and received numerous bruises. I have seen this mysterious circumstance before in several cases, yet it still puzzles me that her body is inflicted with wounds when all possible movement is repressed. Children who have highly active imaginations—the ones Mental Damnation favours—have more aberrant scenarios with the disease. But the situations cause more strain on their system, lessening their lifespan.

The thought is troublesome. I would like all my patients to survive the disease and Krista would be a substantial step toward understanding how to cure it.

Mental Damnation is very much a mind game; the victims must convince themselves that the illusions are not real. Unfortunately, anyone who attempts to help the diseased can only offer moral support, which makes it exceptionally challenging for me, from a doctor's perspective.

There are a number of herbs and medicines that can be used to slow the effects, but sometimes when I prescribe my patients with them, I ask myself: why bother?

It sickens me to think such thoughts, but it can be challenging to keep an optimistic outlook after failing dozens of times in the past to cure this disease.

Yet I cannot concede so easily. Like I have mentioned before, I have had the highest success with patients that keep an open mind, expressing how they feel and what they see. Unfortunately, Krista keeps herself closed off from me. She is open-minded toward Paladin, though, which helps as he shares her experiences of Mental Damnation with me. I'd like to understand why she prefers to talk with Paladin. Krista doesn't have any spiritual beliefs, yet she voluntarily spends time with Paladin and Father Isaac. I fear she may have bought into the illusions that Mental Damnation plays, which are based on the victim's surroundings. In the High Barracks of Zingalg, we are very much encompassed by our faith. To Krista, this is all new to her, and is possibly the most prominent experience she has had in the barracks—that, and being the first of her people on the surface world since their banishment.

Her closed-off behaviour toward me could be in direct relation to the religious portion of her time spent here, thus Mental Damnation would reflect this and project it as a fear in her dreams. This would explain why she is interested in God, angels, and all lore accompanying it. She is a curious child and wants to understand.

r. Alsroc rested his crossed ankles on the edge of his desk, his polished, brown leather shoes pointing upward while he held his thin suede journal containing his notes on Krista. He started a new diary for each new patient diagnosed with Mental Damnation, letting him record their interactions and behaviour during the time of infection. From these journals, he duplicated the important information into his textbook, *Disease Analysis*. The book—a work in progress—contained the most valuable information Dr. Alsroc had collected about Mental Damnation to date.

Regardless of the outcome of Krista's experience with the disease, I can see myself transcribing most of her experiences with Mental Damnation into the Disease Analysis. It wasn't every day that Dr. Alsroc got to see another race infected with Mental Damnation. *Why does it favour humans? Yet another mystery of the disease.*

He closed the journal of Krista and placed it on his desk, next to the rough sketches he had collected of the dream characters Mental Damnation projected. His eyes trailed over the drawings, something he had done countless times before, trying to imagine what the characters must really look like to the eyes of a patient.

Dr. Alsroc picked the sketches up and bit his lip, examining the blue drawing of the ghastly character, Malpherities. He fixated on the face, the horns, and emotionless expression across the crude sketch.

Not the most common of the characters to be projected by the disease, but Malpherities has appeared occasionally in the past. Unlike the other characters, this one was continuously seen by the victim, even during the day. *Malpherities is a friendly character if the victim listens to him.*

I hypothesize the disease uses him as reinforcement, in cases where the diagnosed isn't convinced that the other nightmarish visions are real. It's like the disease's first line of defense upon initial infection.

Dr. Alsroc's mind drifted back to when he'd shown the drawing to Krista, to the way her eyes widened and jaw dropped open. *She sees him.* Any victim who had seen Malpherities had been more difficult for Dr. Alsroc to work with. They were unpredictable and more likely to die within a short period of time, typically no more than a week.

Even the way she acted with Marilyn when she was washing clothes. Her mind broke down and the schizophrenic effects of the disease were in full force. She actually believed that this Malpherities character was attacking her, even though she dove at the tub on her own, and choked herself with her own hand.

Dr. Alsroc tapped the drawing and muttered, "Is he the real reason you are so closed off from me? A figment of your imagination implying that I am not to be trusted?" It was hard to say, and Dr. Alsroc would have to put faith in Paladin to persuade Krista into talking with him.

I would prefer her to start expressing her thoughts with me before she meets any of the other characters the disease introduces. Dr. Alsroc put the drawing of Malpherities on the table, revealing the sketch previously underneath it in his hand. This drawing was of a bony, pale man with long, thin hair wearing a deep-red suit of armour. His eye sockets were wide and black, with white eyeballs that seemed to float in the centres.

Dr. Alsroc knew this character as General Dievourse, the first character the victims met if they did not see Malpherities first. *He is quite iconic for death, with his ghostly skin and devilish armour. The suit he wears is tailored to represent the hellish landscape that the victims claim to be in. I am grateful that Krista hasn't conjured him yet, as any victim who has tended to have no more than a day or two left before they die.* General Dievourse had been guaranteed to show up in every case of Mental Damnation; the question was when.

Dr. Alsroc put the paper aside and looked at the next drawing, two squiggly lines used to represent arms that ended in six-fingered hands, the extra finger being a second thumb. *Then there is the Weaver, the last character the victim sees.* It never failed; every case had ended at the Weaver. *He is supposedly the one who makes the final judgment on the victim, which always causes their death. Yet it's strange—none of the victims have ever reported seeing more than his hands. The description of snake-like arms and long fingers does remind me of an abstract representation of the true physical appearance of the disease.*

Alsroc had dissected deceased victims to examine the disease's internal bodily effects. He discovered that victims' brains were wrapped in a threadlike web of black-and-mud-green slime. The brain itself had been compressed from the entanglement, about two-thirds the size of a healthy brain.

His patients had told him before their death that the Weaver was the ruler of the hellish world known as Dreadweave Pass. This projected character was responsible for the symptoms of psychosis the victims experienced during the night. *I've held my patients before their final minutes of life, when they claim to be face to face with the Weaver's hands. Their lives end in one of two ways: In the first, they mutter that the Weaver announces they are pure and the victim convulses violently, bleeding out of every orifice until they have no more blood left to spew.* Dr. Alsroc swallowed heavily and put the drawing of the Weaver down on the table. *In the second scenario, the victim mutters 'impure' and claims that General Dievourse has been ordered by the Weaver to execute them. Shortly after, they drown in their own blood from internal bleeding. This death is less violent and is often seen in older patients. Still a gruesome death, but less tragic for their loved ones to watch.*

Dr. Alsroc tapped his fingers together. "It always ends in one of two ways. Why is it so consistent with the characters, symptoms, and death?" The ludicrous idea of the victims really crossing into another world in their dreams had entered his mind before. What if Mental Damnation was a spiritual portal into hell, and they really were seeing horrors of the afterlife?

The doctor swung his feet back onto the ground and sighed. "Unlikely." *If they were, why would they share so many traits with schizophrenia? Why would their bodies experience so much physical pain here if they are no longer of this world?* Besides, anything that was not yet understood could, and eventually would, be explained with logical reasoning and solid facts. *Until then, the unexplained is always explained thus by the simple-minded: it is the work of God.* Dr. Alsroc was a faithful man, but he knew that worldly situations were created by those in it, not by supernatural powers.

A knock was heard at the door, breaking Dr. Alsroc's thoughts.

"Come in."

The doorknob twisted and Paladin pushed the door open. His eyes were open, yet they sagged slightly, like he needed a good night's rest.

"Dr. Alsroc, it's Krista."

Alsroc raised an eyebrow. *Perhaps restraining her would have been the better option.*

Paladin put his hands behind his back. "She wounded her leg and was lashing around violently before several of my men and I pinned her down." He took a deep breath. "We figured she would stop after we restrained her but she hasn't tired and her strength is exhausting ours."

"You need something to neutralize her, then?" Dr. Alsroc stood from his desk and hastened to the opposite side of his office where he stored his herbal remedies and chemical solutions.

"Preferably, yes; we've tied her down to the bed with leather straps on her tail, ankles, wrists, and mouth. Anything to stop her from inflicting pain to herself or us."

"Has she hurt any of your men?"

"Just a few scratches; her claws are sharp and her strength, unnatural."

Alsroc opened the cupboards above the counter. To the left was where he kept his natural choices and to the right were his chemically produced options. He had hand-picked and created most of his medicine, but occasionally, he had things made when he did not have the resources available.

"Considering our circumstances, we'll use one of my more potent solutions." Dr. Alsroc took a thin black vial from the left side of the cupboard. There was a label around it reading 'Dwale'. It was an anaesthetic potion created through a mixture of bile, opium, lettuce, bryony, and hemlock.

Dr. Alsroc snatched a cloth from the counter and turned to face Paladin. "Normally I'd prefer using psychoactive solutions for Mental Damnation, but for the time being, we've got to treat her as a wounded patient in shock."

"Whatever you see fit, doctor. As long as we can put her to rest for tonight. We can look at other options tomorrow."

The doctor nodded and the two exited the office, rushing through the halls. They hadn't shut the door behind them, as time was of the essence. It wasn't often that Dr. Alsroc ran; only when he was required to, which, more often than not, involved a patient with Mental Damnation.

"I'm getting too old for this rushing around, Paladin," Dr. Alsroc panted.

Paladin smirked. "Perhaps if you spent less time in your studies and more time implementing the health advice you give your patients, you wouldn't be having this problem."

Dr. Alsroc knew that Paladin was right, but to him it was a worthy sacrifice. *I'm willing to pay the price of my health for those in greater need. If I cure Mental Damnation, I will save dozens of lives and help the families that it currently destroys.*

Paladin led Dr. Alsroc up to the second level where Krista was being kept. Her muffled screams echoed off the walls as the two rushed to the top of the staircase toward her room. Several High Barracks residents lingered in the halls, whispering to one another and staring at Krista's door. Fear was obvious in their eyes as they listened to her groans and cries.

Paladin reached the door first, twisting the knob and pushing it open. "After you," he gestured.

Dr. Alsroc burst into the room to see Krista lashing uncontrollably on the bed. There were worn leather straps around her ankles and wrists that were beginning to tear from her constant tugging. Her tail was strapped to her right leg. The bedframe bent inward slightly from the vigorous force of her arms.

Three of the night guard attempted to hold her down; two of them each held one of her legs and the third held her arms. Her eyes were closed and hidden behind her tattered feathers while she screamed through the straps in her mouth, biting down on the leather. Her legs thrust up unpredictably, causing the men to jerk with her movements. Her scalp-feathers vibrated violently with each movement she made.

The doctor pulled the cork off the vial. Tipping the glass over, he dabbed a cloth over the opening to soak some of the potion. He ran toward Krista's bedside, placing the cork on the vial and slipping it into his pocket with a single hand.

"Kristalantice! Snap out of it. You're dreaming." He lightly tapped her cheek.

She mumbled through the leather straps, but it was impossible to make out what she said.

"Untie her mouth!" Dr. Alsroc demanded while placing the damp cloth against her nostrils, then he gently rubbed it against her skin. He had to have her drink the potion for the full effect, but a subtle hint of it for her to inhale would hopefully ease her aggression. Thankfully, the effects kicked in quickly.

Paladin came to Dr. Alsroc's aid and carefully took the strap out of Krista's mouth, saliva and traces of black blood dripping from where she was biting down.

Internal bleeding: a side effect of these nightmares.

"Please, no . . . The hands!" she cried.

Hands? Dr. Alsroc squinted, and his heart skipped a beat. Even though Krista hadn't mentioned General Dievourse yet, hearing her say "hands" could only mean the disease was projecting the Weaver.

"Grab her mouth and hold it open; we'll pour the dwale into her." Dr. Alsroc tucked the cloth into his pocket and pulled out the vial. *I can't give up hope yet.*

"The hands got me!" Krista began to squirm violently and her limbs jerked, knocking the three night guards away.

Paladin grabbed her head with a firm grip, one hand holding her jaw open and the other clamping her forehead, forcing her mouth open. "Now!" he shouted.

Alsroc pulled the cork off the vial and poured the potion into her mouth. She gargled and sputtered while Paladin closed her jaw, forcing her to swallow the dwale.

Paladin let her go once she took a heavy gulp and hissed. "Let us go!" she yelled and thrust forward, causing the strap on her right arm to break. Her hand lunged toward Dr. Alsroc, whacking his face and throwing him to the floor.

The night guard near Paladin attempted to grab her free arm but she elbowed him in the face, accompanied by the sound of breaking cartilage.

"Nothing but bones," she groaned through her teeth, while Paladin tried to restrain her right arm.

Dr. Alsroc rubbed his right eye and cheek, which took most of the blow. *That'll bruise.* He got up from the ground and rushed to assist Paladin.

"Help!" Krista shouted. "I'm going to die."

"Calm down, Kristalantice!" the doctor said between heavy breaths. He and Paladin managed to pin her free arm down against the bedframe's headboard. Her left arm—still strapped—jerked aggressively, trying to reach for Paladin or Dr. Alsroc.

"Let me go! Sporathun has me," she squealed.

Sporathun? "You're dreaming, Kristalantice! It is only a dream. You're here with us." Dr. Alsroc spoke soothingly. Her tone had become less aggressive; it was either the dwale taking effect, or the Weaver had her and her life was going to end in one of the two scenarios.

Krista's body began to slow down and her breathing returned to a steady pace. "No use," she mumbled.

The three night guards, Paladin, and Dr. Alsroc all panted heavily while holding their positions, hoping she wouldn't have another spasm.

"Don't cry . . ." Krista shook her head. "A warrior mustn't feel remorse." Instantaneously her limbs relaxed and the men let her go with one last breath of relief.

Paladin stood up and examined the night guard with the bloody nose. "We'll have to mend this."

Dr. Alsroc pressed his lips together and sat beside Krista, examining her breathing patterns, which were bizarrely normal. He stroked his jawline, watching and waiting to hear anything about the Weaver.

"Where are you, Kristalantice?"

"We left her." Krista's lips trembled and she breathed heavily.

"Do you know where you are?"

Krista's breathing was steady and her head turned to the side while she mumbled something else, but it was impossible to hear. She was in a steady sleep now, which made it clear that there was no Weaver in her dreams. *Who is Sporathun?* It was not a name Dr. Alsroc had heard before.

"Go mend this man," Paladin said to the other night guards. "Alsroc, is she stable for the night?"

"Yes, she is. You might want to use that other leather strap for her right arm, though. Just in case."

Paladin nodded. "Of course. You seem deep in thought. Is this not a typical scenario for you?"

Dr. Alsroc had forgotten that Paladin had never dealt with a case of Mental Damnation firsthand before. "No, it's not. She mentioned hands, and I presumed she was referring to a projection known as the Weaver—the last character the disease shows before it claims a life."

"What was it?"

"I don't know. She spoke of a Sporathun."

"Not something you're familiar with?"

"No, I am not."

Paladin exhaled heavily. "Sporathun is a name I have heard of. He is one of the fallen angels in hell. How would she know about him?"

Dr. Alsroc shrugged. "She had been talking to Father Isaac. Tomorrow, can you ask her about the events of tonight?"

"I will."

"Be easy on her. She's showing serious signs of stage two of Mental Damnation, the stage of Dreadweave Pass. Her body is covered in wounds, muscles are growing rapidly all over her body, and she is bleeding from her mouth. Krista is going to be exceptionally tired when she wakes, physically exhausted from the struggles she had tonight and mentally drained from the nightmares."

"Understood. Are there other stages?"

"Yes, she hasn't shown any suicidal intentions yet or loss of time that I know of, which are also symptoms of stage two. But I'm sure they will start to appear. There is one final stage—stage three: Mental Combustion. This is the stage where the victims gain sporadic knowledge of complex skills, experience apophenia, and then inevitably, their death."

"Sporadic knowledge? Why?"

"Hard to say how they get it. Possibly the disease heightens their subconscious observational capabilities while they are awake, then blasts the knowledge into their conscious state when they are asleep. The sudden increase in information makes the brain rapidly active which helps feed the disease. That, with the addition of nightmares and the characters projected, creates too much strain on the mind and body, eventually draining the last bit of energy they have and killing them."

Paladin folded his arms. "She does have unusually good swordsmanship."

Dr. Alsroc's eyes widened and he turned to face Paladin. "How so?"

"One of the boys told me she had a duel with them, and she won. She claimed she learned it back home in the underworld, but I highly doubt it; she's too naive to know how to fight. Could it be a direct result of Mental Damnation?"

"Most likely."

"So, is she in stage three?"

Alsroc rubbed his forehead. "Sometimes the symptoms blend in stages, but she very well could be."

"How much time do you think she has left?"

"If she is in stage three, less than a week."

ENCYCLOPEDIA

Characters

Abesun (abe-son) – Half human and half vazelead, his name translates to 'obscene' in Draconic. Abesun wanders both the underworld and surface world, able to move between the two undetected by the holy shackles created by the Paladins of Zeal. He is unaccepted by both humans and vazeleads due to their racial dispute toward each other. He is a known survivor of Mental Damnation, bearing the mark on his hand.

Alistind – A red scalp-feathered vazelead who used to be a missionary for the Eyes of Eternal Life before they were mercilessly slaughtered by the Renascence Guard. She now follows Darkwing on his quest to find out what happened to Krista in the temple.

Alsroc Lithius, Doctor – Physician at the High Barracks who often journeys throughout Zingalg to investigate the mysterious disease known as Mental Damnation. He has a long-running history with Paladin and the two remain in disagreement over the disease. Doctor Alsroc is certain that it is a worldly issue and not spiritual. Paladin has agreed to let Alsroc handle their latest case, Krista, to the best of his own abilities.

Ast'Bala – One of the Five Guardians of the vazelead, Ast'Bala is the only of his kind with red skin. He is the second of the guardians to become corrupt with Mental Damnation and to be chosen as a gatekeeper by the Weaver. He hand-picked Krista to be reaped by a gatekeeper of their world, which ends up being Danil.

Cae Norphyl (say nor-fill) – The youngest of the Five Guardians, he is easily identifiable from his smoky-grey skin and blue-flamed eyes. Ast'Bala said Cae was the first to become infected with Mental Damnation and he was forced to kill him.

Crasoe – An angel from the Heavenly Kingdoms who was the most powerful warrior the gods had to offer. His sister Rahiie was also of great importance during the War in Heaven.

Creator, the – Known as God among the humans. The being who created the Heavenly Kingdoms, the mortal realm, and Dega'Mostikas's Triangle.

Cursman (curse-man) – Known as 'the betrayer' according to General Dievourse, Cursman was a puppet in the Weaver's army who escaped the fallen god's grasp.

Danil – One of the Five Guardians, and the older brother of Demontochai. He becomes consumed by Mental Damnation, becoming a gatekeeper, from Ast'Bala's touch during a battle in the marketplace in the City of Renascence. He mysteriously uses Krista in a ritual that brings them both to the surface world and shatters the shackles created by the Paladins of Zeal.

Das – A well-profited vazelead in the High District who is known for lavish parties. Krista had gone to his party in hopes of obtaining food, only to be discovered and ultimately banned from the High District.

Darkwing Lashback – Krista's closest friend who has known her since before their people's banishment to the underworld. His intentions are good-natured but his actions are no proof of it. He once had interest in the Blood Hounds before Krista mysteriously vanished from the Eyes of Eternal Life's temple. Now he searches for a way to the surface world to find what happened to Krista after Danil captured her.

Dega'Mostikas (deh-gah-moss-ti-cas) – The root of all evil.

Demontochai (dee-mon-toe-kai) – One of the Five Guardians, Demontochai is the younger brother of Danil. He shrouds his identity under a steel mask, keeping a cloak and plated armour on at all times. He remains the only guardian to maintain order in the City of Renascence after Ast'Bala's corruption.

Dievourse, General (die-vorsse) – The Weaver's primary general in his army. He answers directly to his master and is tormented by his own thoughts and desires. He is one of the few puppets of the Weaver to be blessed with free will. With the new gatekeepers Ast'Bala and Danil, he has formed his own allegiance to gain freedom from the Weaver's grasp.

Draegust Bronzefeather (dray-gust) – The leader of the former gang known as the Blood Hounds. His plucked feathers create a shaved undercut hairstyle that makes him easily identifiable among his people. He wishes to redeem himself from his ruthless and selfish behaviour by working with Darkwing on his quest to find Krista.

Douul Longtooth (do-all long-tooth) – The first

Lieutenant of the Renascence Guard.

Doyel – Chef at the High Barracks, he makes most of the food for the boys and soldiers in the barracks, aided by several assistants.

El Aguro (el-a-gooro) – One of the Weaver's gatekeepers who guards an unknown world. He was the one who initially found the vazelead people and the Five Guardians. The Weaver has also tasked him with governing over the City of Blood.

Father Isaac – Priest of the High Barracks church.

Fanlos – One of the original Blood Hound members, presumed dead after their attempt to assault Demontochai.

Fierel Flamesworth – A paladin in Dreadweave Pass who allies with Krista and Malpherities after she rescues them from the Weaver's puppets in the Blood Swamp.

Fleerew – A half-Corrupt found on the far side of Magma Falls. She is known for her shamanistic practices, giving her supernatural powers. Darkwing and his crew meet her in hopes of finding a way to the surface world.

Fongoxent (fong-oh-zent) – Draconem of gold. He discovered that the vazelead people and the draconem shared a common ancestry during the Drac Age.

Forrlash (for-lash) – A Renascence Guard who patrols the Lower District in search of gangs and scum. He captured Krista and Darkwing in one of his purges, losing his partner in the process before the prisoners were set free.

Franch – One of the paladins on Mount Kuzuchi, close friend of Zalphium. He perished during the ice storm caused by Drac Lord Karazickle.

Fythem (fi-them) – The citadel prison's head torturer. He decides where prisoners go and when they should be interrogated for information.

Glamorous – An angel in the Heavenly Kingdoms who is known for her beauty and mesmerizing voice.

God Ha – A god in the Heavenly Kingdoms responsible for the security of the heavens. He works closely with Crasoe to ensure the Truce of Passing is intact.

God Lo – A god who leads the Ring of Judgment.

Hazuel (has-you'll) – One of the Weaver's previous gatekeepers. His key was torn from his rib cage by Abesun, killing him in the process so the half-breed could escape from Dreadweave Pass.

Jeuth – A redheaded boy who is training at the High Barracks of Zingalg. He is friends with William.

John, Captain – Serves directly under Paladin at the High Barracks, carrying out his commands. He is also responsible for the soldiers at the barracks, sending them on tasks and maintaining order within the barracks walls.

Lewin – A boy training in the High Barracks of Zingalg.

Karazickle (cara-zic-el) – Also known as Drac Lord

of the Night. The last of the drac lords and the most dangerous of his kind. A paladin named Zalphium accuses Saule, the leader of the Paladins of Zeal, of being the Drac Lord in disguise through a formula of transmogrification. His current location remains unknown.

Kristalantice Scalebane (Krista) – A young vazelead who struggles with her own identity after her family is killed during their people's banishment. She has a habit of latching onto those stronger than her for protection opposed to growing as her own being. After reaching the surface world and being infected with Mental Damnation, she now struggles with her own mental wellbeing. Currently she is torn between the mortal realm and the dreamworld of Dreadweave Pass as a result of the disease. Krista has found herself of great interest to the humans, the Weaver, and her new friend Malpherities.

Lieutenant, the – General Dievourse's loyal servant. He executes any command given to him by Dievourse without question. Built from various flesh parts—like all the Weaver's puppets—he remains silent awaiting a command.

Loathsan, King – The king of Zingalg.

Malpherities – A ghoul who resides in Dreadweave Pass. He takes an interest in saving Krista and her case of Mental Damnation. The two have a lot of friction in their relationship because only Krista can see him in the real world. Eventually the two of them learn to work together.

Marilyn – Maid at the High Barracks of Zingalg. She is one of the few maids there, which causes her a lot of work. She is standoffish and does not warm up to people easily. Paladin rescued her from her mother and father at a young age and now he tries to teach her the ways of God.

Muluve Scalebane (muh-love) – Krista's mother who was murdered by the Knight's Union during the vazelead banishment.

Necktelantelx (neck-tah-lan-tell-ex) – One of the drac lords of the drac age. Current status remains unknown.

Paladin – The last of the Paladins. He assumed the name 'Paladin' so the world would remember what they once were. He is first in command of the High Barracks where his responsibilities include training the boys and managing the soldiers and staff. He is lost in his past and longs for the days of crusades.

Quilech Swifttongue (quill-etch) – Fleerew's sister. She is a high-ranking officer in the Renascence Guard.

Rahiie (ra-hee) – An angel in the Heavenly Kingdoms, she is the sister of Crasoe. During the War in Heaven she was badly wounded by Dega'Mostikas himself. His touch mutated her being and infected her mind. She has since recovered and now serves in the Ring of Judgment.

Risen One, the – The mysterious being who the Eyes of Eternal Life worships. They believe he is in a state of limbo and needs his followers to awaken him. After Danil's involvement with the cult, it is whispered that they had relations to the Weaver.

Salanth Scalebane (sall-an-th) – Krista's ill-fated little brother who was killed during the vazelead banishment.

Saulaph (sah-ool-af) – An albino vazelead who could only find shelter through the Eyes of Eternal Life. He worked as a missionary to recruit more members into the temple. Danil managed to control his mind with his dark powers as a gatekeeper and sacrificed the albino's life to complete a necromantic ritual of blood.

Saule (sa-ool) – Founder and leader of the Paladins of Zeal. Responsible for the order of banishing the vazelead people to the underworld. He is accused of being Karazickle, Drac Lord of the Night, by a young paladin named Zalphium during the banishment of the vazelead people.

Scalius Scalebane (scale-yes) – Krista's father, a carpenter who taught Krista about self-defense and morals. He perished by the Knight's Union during the banishment of the vazelead people.

Shoth – Co-founder of the Blood Hounds. He left the gang finding himself unable to commit fully. Still working as a for-hire killer for the Blood Hounds, he was eventually caught by the Renascence Guard. He escaped during the prisoner release caused by Ast'Bala.

Smelg – A bird-like humanoid in Dreadweave Pass who acts as a chronicler. He had worked closely with Cursman in the past.

Smyth – At equal place in the High Barracks with Captain John, answering directly to Paladin.

Snog – Blood Hound member who followed Draegust closely. He is presumed dead after their attempt to attack guardian Demontochai.

Sporathun (spore-ath-son) – A fallen angel who was banished to Dreadweave Pass. He caused immense destruction in anger of his expulsion before General Dievourse could intervene.

Talif – A black-haired boy training at the High Barracks of Zingalg. Friends with William.

Weaver, The – Ruler of Dreadweave Pass. Victims of Mental Damnation see him just before they perish. He is said to be a fallen god banished from the heavens for his unholy practices of fusing souls against their will. His knowledge is said to have come from the Book of Consulo which has the power to revert all creation. He demands for his gatekeepers to find children so he can use them in a necromantic ritual of blood that will set him free.

William – One of the boys training at the High Barracks. Krista is charmed by his blonde hair, blue eyes, and warm personality. The two of them continue to try to spend time together which causes him to lose focus on his training.

Wrinkle Scale – The elder vazelead who runs a potion shop that Krista and Darkwing broke into. He had informed Krista that he is the uncle of Abesun. Wrinkle Scale and his pet shade join Darkwing on his quest to find Krista. He leads them to the shaman Fleerew who knows of where Abesun would be.

Zalphium (zal-fee-um) – A young paladin who had discovered the truth about the Paladins of Zeal leader, Saule. Exposed Saule to his brethren during the banishment of the vazeleads. He is presumed dead after Karazickle summoned an ice storm.

Zeveal – One of the Five Guardians of the vazelead people. Battled Ast'Bala just after he corrupted Danil. His current status remains unknown.

Factions/Groups

Blood Hounds – One of many gangs found in the City of Renascence, led by Draegust. Also, the gang Darkwing was infatuated with and ultimately joined. They strongly believed in anarchy, attempting to bring the downfall of the Renascence Guard and the Five Guardians. The group was massacred by Demontochai when they attempted to overthrow him and claim the City of Renascence for themselves.

Corrupt, the – A group of vazeleads whose bodies reacted poorly to the metamorphosis fumes of the underworld. Their physical forms and minds degenerated, making them behave like rabid animals, craving anarchy. They stray from civilization and resort to cannibalism for food.

Council of Just – The overruling group of the brave and bold heroes who led humanity out of the dark times of the Drac Age. They have been entrusted with making critical decisions for the best of all humanity.

Drac Lords – The leaders of the draconem. They hold higher intelligence and otherworldly powers than their lesser kin; this gives them the rightful place as rulers of their kind. All except for Karazickle are believed to have died during the Drac Age, defeated by the humans.

Eyes of Eternal Life – A vazelead cult that resided in the underworld desert not far from Magma Falls. They worshipped the being known as the Risen One who promised them freedom from the humans' banishment if awakened. They believed they offered the vazelead people an alternative to living under the Five Guardians and Renascence Guard. Danil had lead Demontochai and the Renascence Guard to the hidden temple, which resulted in their execution of the temple's inhabitants.

Five Guardians, the – The leaders of the vazelead people who united their race under a single civilization. They were able to achieve this because their bodies reacted uniquely to the metamorphosis fumes from most of their kind, giving them super strength, size, and draconic wings. They had recently fallen apart after Ast'Bala and Cae had come into contact with Mental Damnation.

Gatekeepers, the – Privileged beings chosen by the Weaver to guard the rifts to various worlds in the mortal realm. They personally hunt souls for the Weaver to complete the harvest. There had always been two gatekeepers until El Aguro discovered the vazelead people. This convinced the Weaver to maximize his efforts in reaping souls. He converted three of the Five Guardians into gatekeepers: Cae, Ast'Bala, and Danil.

High Council – The high council of the Eyes of Eternal Life oversaw the temple members' efforts in freeing the Risen One. They spoke with him directly to free him from his slumber. They had assigned tasks to the temple followers to find a way to free the Risen One before they were all murdered by the Renascence Guard.

Knight's Union – Brave men from around the world who spent their entire lives training in battle. They allied with the Paladins of Zeal to end the Drac Age and to banish the vazelead people from the surface world.

Paladins of Zeal – Holy men who devoted their existence to the church of God and mystical rites. They allied with the Knight's Union to end the Drac Age and to banish the vazelead people.

Renascence Guard – The military of the vazelead people created by the Five Guardians to lead their people back to a righteous path. They are committed to ridding their people of gangs and those who follow false faiths. Their sole purpose is to unify their people as a single entity with the Five Guardians. The Renascence Guard captains wear bronze armour compared to their brethren. The gate guards wear less armour than those sent on execution missions.

Ring of Judgment – A group of angels and gods within the Heavenly Kingdoms whose purpose is to judge souls on their virtue and determine if they are worthy to live in the heavens or if they will descend into one of the three hells of Dega'Mostikas's Triangle.

Savage Claw – One of the gangs that reside in the Lower District. The second largest gang next to the Blood Hounds.

Places

Blood Hound Hideout – Located near the southern outskirts of the City of Renascence.

Blood Swamp – A swamp filled with blood pools located in Dreadweave Pass. The trees in the forest breathe and feed off the blood that rains from the sky. Krista finds herself here when she first crosses into Dreadweave Pass.

Chamber of the Dishonoured – Located in Dreadweave Pass, used by the Weaver and his army for detaining beings too powerful to convert into puppets. They are kept here in hopes they can eventually be turned to the Weaver's side.

City of Courage – Capital city in the Kingdom of Zingalg.

City of Renascence – The unified efforts of the banished vazeleads to bring their people together. The city was built against a mountainside and sectioned into three areas: The Lower District, the Commoner's District, and the High District.

City of Blood – The largest city in Dreadweave Pass. It is where mortals have learned to build a new life in hell. The city is governed by Gatekeeper El Aguro.

Citadel – The large castle that resides in the High District. It functions as the home of the Five Guardians and training grounds of the Renascence Guard. The far-right wing extends into the Commoner's District, functioning as the city's prisons where they keep convicts and gang members of the city.

Citadel Bell – The only indicator of time in the City of Renascence. Its workings remain a mystery to the common vazelead people. They only know that one ring indicates midday, two rings means midnight, and three rings means morning.

Commoner's District, the – One of the three districts in the City of Renascence, it is home to middle-class vazeleads. Situated between the other two districts, it is also home of the marketplace—where commoners trade their goods among one another.

Dega'Mostikas's Triangle (deh-gah-moss-ti-cas) – The triangular shape that forms the three hells of the afterlife.

God's Tears – the only river of water in Dreadweave Pass. Legend says that the water pours from the Creator's tears themselves for he cries at the chaos that his creations have become.

Dreadweave Pass – The nightmarish hell victims of Mental Damnation find themselves in. It is said to be one of the three hells in Dega'Mostikas's Triangle. Ruled by the Weaver and his army of puppets. The Heavenly Kingdoms use it as a state of purgatory where souls can redeem themselves from their mortal lives of sin.

Eyes of Eternal Life Temple – Located near Magma Falls, it is home for the cult Eyes of Eternal Life. It now remains a dark, empty underground chamber littered with corpses. All the scrolls, books, and knowledge belonging to the cult have been destroyed by the

Renascence Guard.

Evergut – A small town in Dreadweave Pass.

Heavenly Kingdoms – The ideal place a soul resides in the afterlife. The gods, angels, and souls deemed worthy live eternally in the kingdoms. It is divided into seven sectors, each one based on the Seven Heavenly Virtues.

High Barracks of Zingalg – The barracks designated to train the mightiest warriors in the kingdom. It is run by Paladin, the sole remaining member of the Paladins of Zeal. The barracks often takes boys at a young age to start their training early, so they can be resilient and ready to serve their king as soon as they become men.

High District, the – One of the three districts of the City of Renascence. It is the smallest of the three and only home to the upper class of vazeleads. The streets are scattered with art installations, sculptures, and unique architectural designs.

Jawless Cavern – A cavern located in Dreadweave Pass. Its name was given for the cave's stalactites that look like sharp upper teeth.

Kingdom of Zingalg (zin-gal-g) – A country comprising the continent of Zingalg in the South Atlantic. It is home to the largest mountain in the world, Mount Kuzuchi. Currently ruled by King Loathsan.

Kuzuchi Forest (cu-zu-chi) – The forest area at the base of Mount Kuzuchi. Krista's home village was not far from the mountain; her and her father used to pick berries from the shrubs located in the forest.

Lower District, the – The largest of the three districts in the City of Renascence, it is where the gangs and scum reside. Most of the buildings are built from clay, blackwood trees, and stone. The upper half is where the Savage Claw reside while the lower half is the Blood Hounds' territory.

Magma Falls – The only water source in the underworld comes from this large mountain—or presumed pillar—with a pathway leading to the surface world, as directed by Abesun. The water runs down the mountainside and into a large lava pool creating immense amounts of steam. Vazelead farmers harvest water to bring to the City of Renascence on the near side of the mountain, whereas the far side is littered with Corrupt.

Mortal realm – The realm of the living as defined by the Heavenly Kingdoms. There are numerous worlds found in this realm; the exact number remains unknown.

Mount Kuzuchi (cu-zu-chi) – The tallest mountain in the world. Its height extends beyond the clouds—high enough that if you reached the peak, you could hear angels sing. It is also the only known gateway into the underworld.

Slum Tower – Located in the South Lower District. It has become one of the primary locations for the city's homeless population. It provides shelter from the harsh winds, gangs, and Renascence Guard.

Talon, The – El Aguro's tower in the City of Blood. His gate is at the top of the tower, just below his nest where he keeps his crows.

Temple of Solitude – Located in the Heavenly Kingdoms, the temple offers a quiet place for beings to pray to the Creator.

Temple of Zeal – The Paladins of Zeal's primary headquarters, reserved for serving God and training. Its current state remains unknown since the paladins were destroyed by the Drac Lord Karazickle.

Tier of Diligence – One of the seven tiers in the Heavenly Kingdoms.

Tier of Temperance – The lowest tier in the Heavenly Kingdoms, where God Ha's chamber resides.

Twisted Hermit, the – A large tree in the centre of the High Barracks of Zingalg. It is often used as a gathering spot for the boys due to the shelter it provides.

Underworld, the – An incredibly dark place beneath the surface, lit only by the molten lava that surrounds the landscape. Most of the land remains uncharted and uninhabitable from the darkness, harsh winds, and heat, except for by beings who mutated adaptations from the metamorphosis fumes. The underworld is also native to the giant beasts and bugs who roam the vast sand dunes.

Zingalg – A continent in the South Atlantic. Ruled by a single kingdom.

Items

Aldrif cheese (al-drif) – A dairy product made by vazelead farmers from their aldrif cattle.

Dwale – An anaesthetic potion created through a

mixture of bile, opium, lettuce, bryony, and hemlock.

Disease Analysis – An ongoing journal written by Dr. Alsroc discussing his discoveries with Mental Damnation.

Book of Consulo – A legendary book that is rumored to hold enough power to revert creation. The Weaver is believed to have used the book to initiate his necromantic arts.

Blood Coins – The primary currency used in Dreadweave Pass.

Dracoins (drah-coins) – The currency used by vazelead people in the City of Renascence.

Fallen Angel Encyclopedia, the – A book written by Smelg, among other historians, detailing each angel to fall to Dreadweave Pass.

Races

Angels – Servants of the gods in the Heavenly Kingdoms. Their chanting can be heard by mortals atop Mount Kuzuchi.

Demon – The children of Dega'Mostikas.

Draconem (drah-co-nem) – A large flying reptilian kind with several subspecies. The older, wiser draconem such as the Drac Lords rule over their lesser kin. A notable Drac Lord is Karazickle, Drac Lord of the Night.

Ghouls – Spectral beings that are quite like shades with the exception of mobility. A notable ghoul is

Malpherities, who takes an interest in Krista.

Gods – Powerful beings who reside in the Heavenly Kingdoms. They dictate what happens in the mortal realm and in the afterlife.

Humans – The most dominant race throughout the known world. They have been able to advance their technologies and reproduce their kind quicker than any of the other sentient races. Two of their factions, the Paladins of Zeal and the Knight's Union, are responsible for ending the Drac Age through allegiances with the nymphs.

Nymphs – Supernatural beings that have knowledge of words of power that can manipulate simple minds. The nymphs and humans formed a union to end the Drac Age, utilizing their respective strengths.

Puppets – Beings created by the Weaver through means of necromancy. They are his sentient servants constructed from body parts of various souls while maintaining each body's consciousness. There are three primary types of puppets: gatekeepers, drone puppets and free-willed puppets.

Shimen – An ancient race found in the Kingdom of Zingalg. They live within the forests and mountains. Shimen are tall, slim, and agile creatures with hooves for feet and two coil-shaped horns on their foreheads. Humans believe them to be of demonic descent due to their witchcraft, this is yet to be proven true.

Troll – A tribal race with the ability to manipulate the weather.

Vazelead (vayse-lead) – Meaning 'Drac Men' in Draconic, they are a reptilian race originating in the South Atlantic and the Kingdom of Zingalg. Naturally their lifespans last for hundreds of years, bodies and minds maturing slowly.

They were banished from the surface by humans to live in the underworld because the humans believed they served the Drac Lord Karazickle. This has yet to be proven true or false.

In the underworld, the harsh living conditions mutated their appearance to have dark, smooth skin and scales running down their backs. Their eyes glow with fire, believed to be caused by their desire for vengeance upon mankind.

Vampire – Bloodsuckers. People who have been infected by the xephile bat.

Vampyre / Fallen Angel – Angels who are consumed by one of the Seven Deadly Sins and are often mutated in physical appearance. They rely on the sin that consumes them to sustain their life force. If they fail to satisfy their urges, they will begin to dissolve.

Creatures

Aldrifs – Cattle of the vazelead farmers, they are used to produce dairy products.

Dahk – A type of demon that resides in Dreadweave Pass. They are commonly eaten by the souls who reside there.

Desert Crawlers - Creatures that live throughout the deserts of the underworld, they feast on any flesh they can find. When found young, they can be tamed and used as watch dogs. They are commonly used by farmers to guard their fungus fields.

Dune Diggers - Large, bulky creatures used by the vazelead people as cavalry and as a source of meat. Their faces are often covered with a muzzle to protect civilians from their sharp teeth.

Dune Worms - Large worms that live in the desert of the underworld. They are hunted by the vazelead people for their meat.

Lifeless Ones - Bodies without a soul found within Dreadweave Pass.

Shades - Difficult to tame, shades are mysterious reptilian creatures of the underworld that have many rumours surrounding their ethereal form. Their appearance remains as mysterious as their telepathic abilities, able to send complete sentences into people's thoughts.

Xephile - A type of bat that turns people into bloodsuckers.

Eras

Drac Age - A time when powerful drac lords ruled the world. It was eventually brought to an end when the humans learned words of power from the nymphs.

Vazelead Banishment - After the Drac Age, humans

became the dominant race throughout the globe. They grew paranoid of other races gaining power and were willing to punish any being that posed a threat. Saule, the leader of the Paladins of Zeal, accused the vazelead people of being loyal servants to the Drac Lords. Because of this, they were banished to the underworld where they could no longer be a threat.

War in Heaven – The war between the Heavenly Kingdoms and Dega'Mostikas's Triangle. Ended by the Truce of Passing.

Languages

Draconic (drah-con-ick) – Language of the draconem. Vazeleads also spoke a weak version of it when they were initially discovered by humans.

English – The common tongue among the humans, in Europe and the Kingdom of Zingalg. They forced the vazelead people to learn the language when they enslaved them.

Disorders

Mental Damnation – A brain disease that causes horrific hallucinations, hostile dreams, psychosis, and paranoia. The afflicted believe that they cross into hell during their sleep. The physical effects include self-inflicted trauma, barbaric behavior, sporadic muscle growth, and decaying of flesh.

Plants

Blackwood Trees – Whether a root or an actual tree, it is a type of plant that grows rapidly in the underworld. It is commonly used to build structures in the City of Renascence and by farmers for their water harvests.

Alron Mushrooms – Commonly found in the underworld, this fungus is cultivated and eaten by the vazelead people.

Misc

Day Cycle – Eyes of Eternal Life designation for days dedicated to attempting to free the Risen One.

Law of Unity – Created by the Five Guardians, the basic law includes modest concepts such as outlawing murder and theft. A further 'unity law' under development would trump all other laws: when in public, vazeleads are to conceal all skin, including their faces, under clothing.

Metamorphosis Fumes – A natural element in the air of the underworld. Anyone who inhales the fumes will have their body's evolutionary process drastically increased, quickly mutating them to adapt to the underworld's harsh environment.

Necromantic Ritual of Blood – A powerful blood ritual that requires a sacrifice of the innocent. Their blood is used to trick the holy power of the subject's imprisoner into thinking they detained an innocent being. The shackles then break, freeing the ritual performer.

Prayer Pods – Designated areas in the Heavenly Kingdoms where beings can pray to the Creator.

Prayer of Power – An ability performed by paladins, capable of many different feats depending on what they desired to achieve.

Realm Crossing – An ability activated using your sixth sense which allows you to cross from the mortal realm into the afterlife. Victims of Mental Damnation believe they have realm-crossing abilities against their will.

Stage One: Initial Takeover – The first stage of Mental Damnation, consists of symptoms that are seen in the common cold (headaches, lack of energy, and physical discomfort). Near the end of the first stage, their condition will cause a drastic change in behavior, and the disease will start distressing the mind and its better judgment.

Stage Two: Dreadweave Pass – In the beginning of the second stage of Mental Damnation, the victim's dreams become exceedingly aggressive. The tormented will talk about the world of Dreadweave Pass in their dreams and claim to be there for days on end, tortured by the demons that inhabit that world.

Seven Deadly Sins – Everything evil falls under one of the Seven Deadly Sins. These are the behaviors that deny souls into the Heavenly Kingdoms. They are also the effects that cause angels to convert into vampyres. The seven sins are lust, gluttony, greed, sloth, wrath, envy, and pride.

Seven Heavenly Virtues – As defined by the gods, all beings should strive to focus on these virtues. The seven are chastity, temperance, charity, diligence, patience, kindness, and humility.

Scum/Street Runner – Homeless in the City of Renascence. Name given by commoners and the Renascence Guard to identify those who are not contributing to their civilization.

Silent Day – Eyes of Eternal Life designation for resting days where the temple members are free to do as they please.

Truce of Passing – An agreement between the Heavenly Kingdoms and Dega'Mostikas's Triangle to allow peace between the angels and demons.

Poem References

Chapter 1 - Paradise
Chapter 2 - Play Nice
Chapter 4 - Locked Memories
Chapter 5 - Big Time Hunting
Chapter 11 - Second Dose
Chapter 14 - Wrath
Chapter 19 - Denial
Chapter 20 - Rats In A Maze
Chapter 21 - Reunited

Thank you for reading Purity, would you consider giving it a review?

Reviewing an author's book on primary book sites such as Amazon, Kobo and Goodreads drastically help authors promote their novels and it becomes a case study for them when pursuing new endeavors. A review can be as short as a couple of sentences or up to several paragraphs, it's up to you. You can find review options on Goodreads or your preferred online distributor such as Amazon or Kobo.

Additional Work by Konn Lavery

Mental Damnation Series | Seed Me Horror Novel | YEGman Thriller Novel

S.O.S. - YEGman Novel Soundtrack | World Mother: Seed Me Novel Score.

Find *Seed Me, YEGman, S.O.S - YEGman Novel Soundtrack* and the *World Mother: Seed Me Novel Score* at:
www.konnlavery.com

About the Author

Konn Lavery is a Canadian horror, thriller and fantasy writer who is known for his Mental Damnation series. The second book, Dream, reached the Edmonton Journal's top five selling fictional books list. He started writing fantasy stories at a very young age while being home schooled. It wasn't until graduating college that he began professionally pursuing his work with his first release, Reality. Since then he has continued to write works of fiction, expanding his

interest in the horror, thriller and fantasy genres.

His literary work is done in the long hours of the night. By day, Konn runs his own graphic design and website development business under the title Reveal Design (www.revealdesign.ca). These skills have been transcribed into the formatting and artwork found within his publications supporting his fascination of transmedia storytelling.

www.ingramcontent.com/pod-product-compliance
Lightning Source LLC
Chambersburg PA
CBHW051205120726
47905CB00004B/992

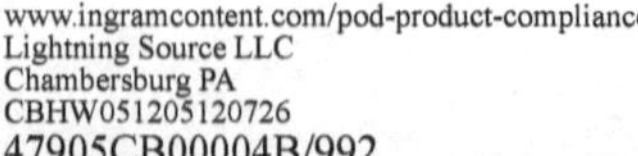